WHITE

A NOVEL

Book Three of The Firebrand Trilogy

David Kettlehake

BROTHER MOCKINGBIRD

Books in The Firebrand Trilogy

GRAY: BOOK ONE
Scout and her small group of friends are some of the few left alive after a storm of epic proportions flooded the world. Together, they have learned how to survive–until people start to change. As they search for a cure for whatever is turning normal people into mindless, murderous creatures, they quickly learn that the biggest threat isn't from the devastation outside, but from each other.

BLACK: BOOK TWO
The storm that wiped out civilization killed billions across the globe, leaving only a handful of people alive. Scout is one of those few. Desperate to find a cure for going Gray, she decides to strike out on her own. But old enemies sometimes return, and when they do, they don't come alone. Scout will have to fight to survive–not just the monsters facing her now, but those of her past as well.

Other Books by David Kettlehake

Strawman (2012)
Fever (2016)

Library of Congress Control Number:

Cover Design by: Purple Penguin Designs

For information please contact:
Brother Mockingbird, LLC
www.brothermockingbird.org
ISBN: 978-1-960226-10-5 Paperback
ISBN: 978-1-960226-12-9 Ebook

For the real Scout.
I hope you found your way.

I don't know how, but I'm back in the furnace room.

The thick stench of fuel oil hits me before I can even open my eyes. The refined chemical reek of it turns my stomach, filling the back of my mouth with thick saliva. I gag, sort of a cross between a burp and a cough, then slap a hand to my mouth to hold back the vomit that is dangerously close to erupting between my fingers. It's not only the smell of the stuff that's getting to me. No, it's what the stench signifies, the way it's force-feeding me memories of my time locked down here with Eve while we waited to die.

Screwing up my courage, I force my eyes open. From the tiny windows overhead, dim light slants down at crazy angles, just like I remember from before. Dust motes, lazy in the heavy air, drift in and out of the rectangular beams. I'm sprawled across the concrete floor with my cheek against the cold, gritty surface. When I push myself up on one arm and get my legs under me, there's an awkward weight holding me down. Panic stabs at my already reeling mind as I tug at the heavy chain locked tight around my waist. Terrified and confused, I trace the links back to the steel bracket, a chunk of metal so massive it could be anchored to the foundation of the church itself. I slowly reach for the wall and run my quivering fingertips over the cold steel. This doesn't make sense. When Singer and I escaped, I yanked the damn thing out and ripped away a chunk of concrete in the process. But now it's perfect again, like it never happened. How can that be?

"Hi, Scout," says a voice to my side. I jerk in shock, and my jaw flops open like the mouth of a ventriloquist dummy. My breath catches in my chest.

It's Eve.

I swear she wasn't there a second ago, but she's sure as hell here now. The green of her robe is so bright and vibrant it could be brand new. Her brown hair is tied back in a neat ponytail, and a big, genuine smile fills her pretty face. The purplish birthmark covering most of her left cheek is the same, but she doesn't seem nearly as concerned with hiding it as she used to. There's no chain around her waist, which, honestly, seems a little unfair.

"Eve? What…how?"

She smoothly kneels down and touches a hand to my cheek. The thick fabric of the robe makes a soft rustling sound as she moves. "My sweet Scout. I've missed you."

"But, Eve, how are you here? Jacob said… He said…" I can't bring myself to say it out loud, not to her face. *Jacob said you were dead. They killed you when you went Gray. That's what they do here in the furnace room.*

Our noses are so close we're both cross-eyed trying to stay focused on each other, and I almost laugh at how silly we must look. Eve tenderly places the tip of her index finger on my lips. Her skin is warm, and I notice for the first time I'm shivering. It wasn't this cold down here before. I also realize there's no white in her hair at all, which hits me harder than it probably should.

"Scout, dear, you need to do something for me," she says, and her stern tone and the set of her eyes reminds me how determined she can be. I always admired that in her.

I sit up straighter. I reach out for her, and she takes my shaking hand in her very warm ones. I feel my eyes misting up and her image blurs until I blink her back into focus. I can't believe how happy I am to see her again, to have her here next to me once more. I never got to say goodbye before, back when Singer and I escaped. She tried to attack him and I knocked her out, before I really understood how strong I was. By the time she woke up, if she ever did, we were long gone. My tears feel unnaturally hot on my frigid skin.

"Eve, I'm so sorry. We left you down here. We left and I never got to say goodbye!"

She places her palm against my face again, and

it dawns on me that the touch of her skin is soothing and warm, but not scalding, not like a Gray. She dabs at my wet cheeks with the hem of her robe.

"I understand," she says, gifting me a small smile of forgiveness. "There wasn't time. You had to leave. Singer was right, if you'd stayed longer, you would've been trapped down here with me until, well, you know. But we don't have time for that now. Look at your hands."

It takes me a second to catch up with her abrupt change of subject, but I hold my hands up in front of me. To my surprise, they're tinted an unhealthy bluish-white all the way past my wrists, almost to my elbows. My fingernails are the pale purple of the inside of a seashell. That can't be good.

"What's happening to me?" I whisper, turning my hands back and forth in front of my face.

"You're freezing to death," she replies matter-of-factly. "Your feet are in the same shape. Scout, what's the last thing you remember before waking up here?"

"Freezing to death? Um, I was in my kayak, out on the open water. I was, uh, looking for another source of supplies, since that warehouse across the channel from Church Island was pretty much flattened in the tornado. We aren't running low yet, but we will sooner or later if we don't find another source."

"And then what happened?"

I close my eyes tight, as if doing so will somehow

sharpen my focus. It doesn't. I shake my head, frustration mounting over my inability to recall any meaningful events before waking up in this horrible place. Despite my joy at seeing her, I'm slightly annoyed; if she wants something from me, why doesn't she just come right out and ask?

"Think back," she urges, compressing her lips. "You were in the kayak, and you looked behind you, to the north, and you saw something. What was it?"

I open my eyes and stare at her. Then my gaze drifts behind her to the uniform gray of the concrete wall over her shoulder. There's something about that solid, blank expanse that tickles the threads of a memory, eventually weaving those threads into a complete tapestry. I sit up with a jerk.

"I remember! There was a storm coming. But this time it wasn't a tornado or a thunderstorm. No, this time it was a blizzard." I think back, the vision suddenly sharp in my mind. There was a bright white wall flying toward me, a massive thing that extended from one end of the earth to the other, unbroken and towering into the heavens. As the winds and snow smashed into me, I remember the temperature plummeting, falling far below freezing in a matter of seconds. The winds were so fierce they nearly swamped my kayak. One minute the sun and blue sky were there, and the next there was nothing but a blinding, uniform white.

"The blizzard was on me before I could do anything," I continue in a softer voice, my gaze still locked on the wall over her shoulder. "I mean, we've had crazy weather ever since that thunderstorm at the Mound, but nothing like this before. The temperature fell so fast the water around me turned to slush and started to freeze right away. Before I knew it, the kayak was locked in ice and I couldn't move. I was trapped."

"Then what?" Eve asks.

It's rushing back now. The confusion and uncertainty. The terror. I'm not scared of facing a menace like a Gray. Well, not usually. For the most part, I can handle that. But an elemental and soulless threat like this, something I can't outthink, outrun, or outfight? That horrifies me.

"Um, eventually I knew I had to move or I was going to freeze to death in the kayak. It was a nice day earlier when I left, so I was only dressed in shorts and a T-shirt. I was afraid the ice around me wouldn't hold my weight, but it was so cold it had to be inches thick already. I picked a direction, and started to walk. But the wind! The wind was so strong, I was blinded and couldn't see anything."

"And then?" she urges, cradling my bluish hands again in her warm ones.

"Any normal person would have died in minutes. That's how cold it was. My strength and healing powers were keeping me alive, at least in the beginning. But there are limits to everything, and this blizzard was more than I could handle. I remember…falling down. On the ice. I was so tired all of a sudden." My vision snaps back to her face that's still so close to mine. Her breath smells like minty toothpaste, which almost makes me smile. My voice drops to a whisper. "I fell down. That's the last thing I remember, before waking up here."

She nods at me. "Yes, and you're still down. But here's what I need you to do. I need you to shout these two words as loud as you can. 'Help me.' Got it?"

I shake my head, confused. I'm suddenly so exhausted it's hard to make sense of what she's saying. "I don't understand. What's that going to do? There's no one else out there. Nobody could live through that."

"You need to trust me, Scout. There's no time for debate here. You need to shout 'help me' as loud and as many times as you can. Now!"

I'm struggling to keep my eyes open, my lids obscenely heavy all of a sudden. Eve grabs my shoulders and gives me a few hard shakes, so vigorously that the back of my head cracks against the wall.

"Ow, that hurt," I mumble at her, my words slurred.

"Good. You need to stay awake. Now do what I told you."

My head droops down until my chin is resting on my chest. "Hmm. How 'bout later? I just need a little nap first."

Eve shakes me again, then grabs my hair and pulls my head back. "No. No napping. If you fall asleep now, you'll die."

Her voice is faint and far away, and some of the words are missing or blurry. It reminds me of the times my dad used to listen to baseball on the radio in the car and the AM station would fade in and out. Thinking of my dad is nice. I realize I haven't thought of either of my parents in a while. I try to justify that by reminding myself how hectic life has been since I got back to Church Island, but that's a crappy excuse and I know it. Thoughts are fast, easy, and don't require any effort. Time has been stealing their memories from me, simple as that.

"Scout!" Eve screams at me. "Come back!"

I blink a few times, and see she's still in front of me. "Oh, hi, Eve," I mumble, my tongue and lips no longer operating as a team. "It's nice to see you again. We're not going to drink wine again, are we? That made my head hurt so bad…"

"Focus, Scout. Stay focused. You need to scream 'help me' as loud and as many times as you can. Now!"

"But I'm so tired…"

"Sleep when you're dead, Scout. But do what I say first. Yell it. 'Help me!'"

She isn't going to give up on this, is she? If I know Eve, and I think I do, she's going to keep hounding me until I do what she says. That's what made her such a good leader before she went Gray. She knew what she wanted and went for it. I'd love to grab a quick nap, but she's not going to let me unless I cooperate.

"Fine," I mumble through lips that have no more sensation than a garden hose. "But you do it with me, okay?"

She smiles. "Okay. Ready?"

"Yeah."

Eve takes a deep breath and yells, "Help me!" In this small space her voice is incredibly loud, inhumanly loud, louder than physics should allow. It's almost as if some celestial being cupped godlike hands around a world-sized mouth and broadcasted an SOS across the cosmos. She inhales to go again, and I remember I promised to do it with her.

"Help me!" we both shout, and while my own voice is little more than a squeaking mouse next to her roaring lion, the combination of the two is greater than hers alone. The walls vibrate with the strength of our cries.

"Again!" Eve orders.

We do it again, and again. I'm more awake now, but my hands and arms are going numb and I can't stop shivering. If anything, the trembling is getting worse. It's progressed to a full-body convulsion so violent I'm afraid I'll pull a muscle. Eve puts her hand on my cheek again. Her eyes are shiny wet, but she's smiling.

"Good job, Scout. That should do it."

I'm shaking so hard I can barely form words. My teeth are chattering. "Do what?"

Instead of answering me, she leans close and kisses me on the mouth. My lips almost seem to thaw at her touch, at least for a few moments. This isn't the first time she's kissed me, and I'm okay with it. We linger like that for several seconds, and in my mind, I hear her one last time.

"Goodbye, dear Scout."

I find that my eyes are shut, or the room has gone black, I don't know which. Eve is gone, although I can still sense her lips against mine. I try to reach for her, but my hand grasps at nothing but the past.

"Eve? No, come back! I never got to say goodbye!"

She's no longer here. The furnace room has vanished, too. The reek of the fuel oil, if it was ever there at all, is shredded by winds so strong it's like hot needles against my exposed skin. I try to open my eyes, but my eyelashes are frozen together. I weakly scrape at the frost until I can see again, and discover I'm back where I fell earlier, too exhausted and cold to go any farther. I can't understand what Eve was trying to do. There's no one out here to help me, and I'm going to die by myself on this vast wasteland of ice. I close my eyes and feel the wind as it batters me, too cold to do much but whisper a numb goodbye to both Eve and Singer. Any tears that fall from my eyes are blown to crystalline dust.

Then I feel something, a bump in the back, like someone just nudged me with a toe. I flap an arm toward whoever or whatever it is, but even that small movement depletes my scant energy reserves. I can do nothing when I feel two arms slide underneath me and pick me up. Whoever it is lifts me with ease and holds me close to their chest. I feel blessed heat radiate from them to me, and I can't help but snuggle towards it.

I finally regain enough strength to open my eyes again. At first all I can see is blowing snow, but then I catch a glimpse of white hair whipping around a familiar angular face. My head falls back against her chest.

It's Google's Gray, the one that ran off when I blew up the car.

She's back, and she's saving my life.

I have zero recollection of what happened after that. The next thing I know I'm pressed close to the Gray in a dark space. The heat radiating from her is enough to take the edge off the bitter cold, and I can feel my fingers and toes coming back to life in painful tingles. I'll never know how close I came to dying out on the ice, but without Eve and this Gray, I'm sure I'd be dead right now. I've had a lot of close calls since all this began, but never anything like that. I shiver, a long hard one that starts at my head and works its way down to my toes. It's not from the cold this time, but from the reminder of my own tenuous mortality.

I struggle to sit up, pulling away from the Gray. I guess I should call her Susan, the name Google gave her, since she did just save my life. I don't like making these things more human than I have to, but I owe her that much. I scoot away from her a little more, but we're still close enough that the heat coming off of her is a tangible thing. It reminds me of those times when mom and I would bake cookies and we'd crack open the oven door to check if they were done. The cramped space we're in, whatever it is, does a nice job of retaining her warmth. It's so dark I can't see her or anything else, but I'm in no hurry to do anything about it.

"I don't know if you can understand me," I finally say, "but thank you. You saved my life."

There's no reaction from her, not that I thought there would be. Of course, since I can't see a thing in here, she could be playing rock, paper, scissors, for all I know. I blindly feel around wherever we are, and determine we're in a tight space a few feet square, or just big enough for the two of us sitting up. There's a small line of dim light on the ground to one side that must be the gap at the bottom of a door. Groping around in the dark, my hand brushes against an icy cold object. A doorknob. I give it a twist and push. Light and freezing air flood our space, and I realize we're in a small closet. Susan doesn't move or react when I stand and step out.

The remains of a house are all around me. The walls of the place are still intact, but the windows are broken and the roof above our heads is open to the elements. Snow is piled up in corners of the room in little drifts, and a thin layer of it dusts the ruined furniture like glittering ash. The air is still brutally cold, and while it might not be as bad as before, it's still frigid enough to form snot-cicles inside my nose every time I inhale. I don't know how the Gray figured out to bring us here, or even that the closet was one of the few places where we could survive. How did she know what to do? And more importantly, how the hell did she know where I was or that I was in trouble? I've underestimated these creatures' intelligence before, and it looks like I have again. I really need to stop doing that.

Then I remember Eve, and what we did in the furnace room. We called for help. We called for help, and somehow this Gray knew it and did something about it. I lock eyes with her as she sits unmoving on the floor of the closet. She stares vacantly back at me, her ashen face as expressionless as the Sphinx.

"You knew. You heard me and you knew. How?"

Then it comes to me. I remember when Simon, Google, and I were in the boats, after we left Rumpke Mountain and were headed to Church Island. I'm not sure why I did it, but I recall staring at Susan. I didn't know what I was doing at the time, but I stared at her hard. I was focusing on nothing but her, filling my mind with her image, when she suddenly lifted her head and looked at me. It was like she was waiting for me to tell her something. I dismissed it then as a fluke, as nothing more than a weird coincidence. But what if it wasn't? What if she really heard me, even though I didn't *say* anything? I catch myself staring at her again.

"Can you hear what I'm thinking?" I ask. "Is that

what happened? You heard me calling for help? Do we have some sort of telepathic link or something?"

My first reaction to my own question is a hard no, let's get real here. That sort of thing isn't possible. Telepathy isn't legit. Thoughts exist in only your head. They aren't solid, material things. You can't just toss them back and forth like two people playing catch with a Frisbee. They don't work that way.

Just then her head moves. It's a small movement, just a tilt, like a dog hearing barking in the distance. I almost jump back in surprise.

Well, okay, that just happened. Another coincidence?

If she really can hear my thoughts, that would explain so much of what has happened. Like how Hunter controlled his minions, including those murderous fast Grays, the deadly duo he called Thing One and Thing Two. Or how my brother was able to command his group of Grays back at that farmhouse. If they really can communicate with these things using their minds, that would explain so much. Even though, to be fair, of all the strange things I've seen since the Storm first hit, telepathy might not even break into my top ten list of weird crap.

"One way to find out," I say to myself, my breath puffing in front of me in the frigid air. I vigorously rub my bare arms with my hands. "Let's do a little test, okay?"

Susan is still squatting in the closet, doing nothing except tracking me with her dead eyes as I move around the room. Her arms are wrapped around her knees to help protect her from the cold, but she doesn't look as chilled and uncomfortable as I am. That makes sense, I guess, considering how hot Grays are all the time.

"Um, okay, something easy but not too easy. Let's try this." In my best commanding voice, I say, "Susan, get up."

Nothing. She continues looking blankly up at me, not twitching a muscle. She doesn't even acknowledge that I said anything. Okay, Round One was a bust.

"Hmm. Let's try something less complex for Round Two. Susan, um, raise your arm."

I lean forward in anticipation, but again, she gives me nothing. Damn. I thought for sure that would work. Now I don't know what to do. Plus, even though it's warmer outside than it was, it's still cold as hell and the shivers have started again. The air on my bare skin is so cold it actually hurts. I'll work on Round Three of this telepathy thing with her later, but right now I need to find some clothes. This crazy blizzard got the best of me once, and I have no intention of letting it do so again. An image of my favorite winter coat pops in my mind, a bright magenta one a family friend gave us when their own daughter outgrew it. It was puffy and toasty warm and had a hood ringed with fake white fur, and was a lot more expensive than anything my mom or dad would normally get me. I could really use one like that right now, but at this point I'd settle for anything. I glance down at Susan and, with the image of the coat clear in my mind, I form the words 'let's go' in my head, and give her a 'follow me' motion with my hand.

She stands up and steps out of the closet, walking up next to me.

I'm shocked. For one thing, I keep forgetting how damn big and imposing she is. I'm no giant, far from it, but she's at least a full head taller than me. Her shoulders are broad and muscled, a swimmer's physique. She hasn't wasted away like most Grays her age have by now. She must be eating a lot of something, but I don't want to dwell on what that could be.

Besides all that, the fact she just followed my order is what's really got my attention. She wouldn't or couldn't do the other stuff I asked the first time around. Maybe it was too complicated? Or perhaps what I was asking wasn't clear enough? Either way, she got the message just now when I made a simple non-verbal command and coupled it with an unmistakable gesture. I don't know if it takes both for her to understand, but this is certainly progress. Well, progress might be a little strong, but it's a start, anyways.

This has to be what happened when Eve and I called for help in that dream, or delusion, or whatever the hell it was. Susan somehow heard me and did what I asked. She could've been miles away for all I know, but she still heard me calling for help. The more

I think about it, the more unbelievable it seems. But here she is, standing next to me, and that should be proof enough.

With one eye on her as she shadows me, I start foraging for something to help keep me warm. Wherever she steps, the snow is melted by the heat of her bare feet, before refreezing into ice almost immediately. Looking around, there's nothing here in the small living room that will help. I head through a doorway into what was the kitchen, but it's a bust here, too. I retrace my steps through the living room and into a bedroom. The roof over this part of the house is intact. There's one window letting in a sliver of light. Once my eyes adjust, I spy an old bed, still made up as neatly as the day the occupants left.

"Jackpot," I say.

I pull the bedspread off. It's a white and black checkerboard quilt, like a tablecloth at an Italian restaurant. But the real treasure is the thick wool blanket underneath it. I put both of them to my nose and take a whiff, expecting to smell either death or mold. Both smell cold, if that's a real thing, but I can't detect anything else. I pull out Chuck and make a long slice in the middle of each one. I tug the wool one over my head like a poncho. Or is it a serape? Either way, the wool is scratchy against the bare skin of my neck and arms, but it has such an immediate warming effect on me that I can live with that minor discomfort. I lift the checkerboard quilt up and slowly slide it over

Susan's head with all the care of someone reaching out to pet a strange dog. I don't care if she just saved my life, the primal section of my brain hell-bent on survival is still leery of all Grays. To my surprise and relief, she doesn't flinch or react at all when her head pops through the slice in the bedspread. If anything, it humanizes her a little, making her appear less of a threat. Her ashen skin is several shades darker than the white squares.

"There," I tell her, tugging the bedspread around and settling it on her shoulders. "That should keep you warm. If that was even a problem. Now let's get out of here. I know someone who will be happy to see you."

I think back to the time I scared Susan off by accident, when Google, Simon, and I were trying to find Church Island. Hunter's two murderous minions were tailing us. To frighten them off, I blew up an old Mustang we found on the side of the road. Sure, my little stunt got those two creatures out of our hair for a while, but Susan disappeared, too. Google was supremely angry with me for that. In fact, I thought he'd never forgive me.

Reliving that makes me think I haven't seen much of our resident genius lately. He's been holed up in one of the classrooms downstairs for the last few weeks, working on some project. I've seen a lot of people coming and going from that room, but I have no idea what he's up to. To be honest, for the most part I've given up trying to keep track of him. I've got enough to worry about.

We pass through the living room and out the front door. Around us I see nothing but dead fields and the remains of some broken fencing that stretches off into the distance. The foundation of what I assume was a barn is off to our left. Besides the solitary house, there's nothing else around. Thankfully, the blizzard has moved on, and the sun is back out in a clear blue sky that stretches from one horizon to the other, reminding me of a perfect winter morning before the Storm. The air outside smells clean and cold, the stench of this rotting, flooded world at least temporarily locked in ice. It's an awesome, exhilarating change, and I take a few moments to breathe in the pure air. And while it's still bitterly cold, it seems a little warmer than it did in the house. The sunshine is awesome on my face. I turn to Susan.

"Let's go find my kayak," I tell her, with an image of my trusty boat in my mind. I make an exaggerated "follow me" gesture with my hand again, and start off.

After a few steps I look back, and she's following several paces behind me. Her original tracks leading to the house are easy to spot, just like they were on the floor inside, icy gray etched into the otherwise snowy white ground. They lead in what I'm pretty sure is to the east. I track her old footsteps through the dead fields, and after fifteen or twenty minutes we come to where the frozen flood water meets the land. The brown toxic stuff I've lived through since the Storm is solid ice and extends as far as I can see into the distance. I grew up in Cleveland, with Lake Erie only a few blocks away. Each winter Mom would scare us with tales of kids who ventured out on the ice when they shouldn't. Her stories invariably ended horribly, with some poor guy falling through and dying, with nothing left of him but an orphaned glove on the ice. And while her warnings didn't stop me and my friends from our own ice capades, I've always been a little leery of the stuff.

This vista in front of me conjures up memories of a newly-frozen Lake Erie, but a pristine one, before the force of the ice farther out smashed huge, jagged slabs against the shore in geometric jumbles. With Mom's warnings blaring in my head, I take a cautious step onto the surface. There's some muted cracking as my weight settles on it, but it's thick enough to hold me. I carefully shuffle a few more paces away from shore. When nothing happens, I take a deep breath and venture farther out. Susan is apparently even less trusting of the stuff than I am, because she pauses with her toes just inches from the edge and makes no move to follow me. I don't know if she comprehends there's water under this frozen brown stuff, or she just doesn't like or trust walking on it. Whatever the reason, she's glued to that spot.

"Come on, Susan, let's go," I tell her, and I have to stop myself from following that up with a dog whistle.

A breeze hits me in the face, and it's so bitterly cold the tears in the corner of my eyes freeze. I can't remember that ever happening before. I'm really starting to wonder how low the temperature got. I'm sure Susan feels the cold, but I'm convinced that's got nothing to do with her being frozen in place.

She shuffles her feet a little on the hard ground, but makes no other move to follow me. I'm cold, tired, and upset that I didn't get to say goodbye to Eve again, even though I'm sure it was just a crazy dream of some kind, and it wouldn't make up for not doing it the first time. Plus, I'm worried about Singer and Carly and everyone at Church Island, since I'm sure this blizzard hit them, too. All my frustrations, worry, and exhaustion ignite at once in a white flare, and in my mind, I scream at her to *JUST COME ON!*

She leaps forward onto the brown ice like she's been zapped in the ass with a cattle prod. Once she sees she's not underwater and drowning, her dim mind must realize it's okay and she starts to walk toward me, but cautiously, like a blind man edging toward a cliff. She puts one foot down carefully before taking the next step, her hesitancy clear. I notice her tracks are even easier to see here than on land, a clear and discernable melted outline of bare feet on the muddy ice.

We don't have to go far before I spot a shape in the distance. As we get closer, I see it's my kayak. I let out a sigh of relief. When we arrive, I try to yank it free of the ice, but it's stuck. Using Chuck, I start hacking away at the ice the color of watery manure, shards of the disgusting brown stuff flying in all directions. When I'm confident I've done enough, I give it another hearty tug, and it breaks free with a crunch.

"Okay," I tell Susan, who has been standing dutifully by while I did all the work. "Let's get back to Church Island before this stuff melts under our feet. I have a feeling a certain someone is going to be very happy to see you."

I grab the rope tied to the prow and start pulling. The kayak easily slides behind me, bouncing along with hollow plastic thuds over the rough ice. Susan follows quietly, looking like some sort of bizarre superhero as her poncho billows and snaps behind her like a cape.

CHAPTER
THREE

It's difficult to judge time when you're trudging on a featureless frozen lake with only the sun overhead and your shadow to keep you true, but I'd have to say an hour or more passes before I spot a faint smear of smoke on the horizon. I silently congratulate myself on my reliable sense of direction. If that's Church Island, and I sure hope it is, then I was aimed in almost the exact right spot. A gold star on my forehead for me.

"Come on," I tell Susan over my shoulder. "We're almost there."

There's no change in her demeanor or actions. As company goes, she's not much to write home about. She's as silent as Tiny, and always keeps a few respectful steps behind me, like I'm the queen in a royal procession. If I didn't hear the snow crunching as she walked, she could be a black and white checked ninja for all the noise she makes. It's impressive, although I wouldn't mind a little conversation.

A few more thousand steps go by, and I can begin to make out the outline of the church itself, the red door just beginning to take shape. Smoke drifts up from an unseen chimney in the back. Probably Harold bustling away in the kitchen, if I had to guess. Beyond the church is the low, long line of Cedar Ridge, but it's too far away to make out any features, not that there's much left there to see since the tornadoes leveled the majority of it. What was once a quaint little burg is now just rubble and flattened buildings. Except for the theater, that is. It's battered and bruised, but it's still standing, like the last true Hollywood hero.

Soon we're close enough that details dial into focus. Same as with the theater across the channel, the church was sturdy enough to withstand the worst of the storms. Okay, a section of roof over what used to be the sanctuary has had shingles ripped off, and some of the stained-glass windows were blown out, now replaced with tan sheets of plywood. But the rest of the building came away unscathed, including the bell tower. You might say God was watching out for the place, if you believe in that sort of stuff. Me? I just thank whoever built it for making it as sturdy as a bomb shelter.

When we're within shouting distance, one of the plywood windows creaks open a few inches. I'm too far away to tell who it is, but someone's there, watching us. The inhabitants of Church Island are nothing if not diligent.

"Hey!" I yell as loud as I can. "It's me. Scout! I'm coming in!

Nothing happens for a few seconds, then the plywood swings open all the way and a face appears in the window, a pale round circle against the darkness. I'm not blessed with my friend Simon's amazing eyesight, so I can't tell who it is from here.

"Who's that with you?" comes the reply, faint with distance.

I turn back to Susan, her black and white poncho fluttering about her. Even as far away as we are, I'm sure they can pick out her tell-tale white hair.

"A friend" I finally shout back. "She's with me."

The face in the window disappears. After a minute, while I dance a little from one foot to the other trying to stay warm, it's back.

"Come to the door and wait. Do not enter."

I wave at them, and glance back at Susan. "Just follow me. Slow and easy, understand?"

The Gray doesn't give any indication that she does, but by now I shouldn't expect anything else. We start walking again, aiming at the red doors. After a hundred or so feet, we step off the ice and onto the asphalt parking lot. The flooding has receded a lot since the rains stopped, to the point where the entire parking lot is free of the ice and water. In fact, looking beyond the church, the tops of playground equipment that have been completely submerged since the Storm are visible now. If this keeps up, like Singer once said, the water-filled barrier between Church Island and the town will vanish. If that happens, Grays will have free access to the place. A shudder runs through me under my heavy green blanket when that cheery thought hits me.

I climb the ice-covered steps and wait in front of the red doors as instructed. I glance over my shoulder to make sure Susan is still behind me. She is.

"Remember, let me do the talking," I tell her, chuckling softly at my little joke.

I hear the huge door being unlocked, and it creaks open a few inches. One of Jacob's bright blue eyes is peering at me through the narrow crack. His stare lingers on my face for a moment, then jumps over my shoulder to the Gray standing behind me and goes wide.

"Jesus, Scout, what the hell are you doing? What is that thing doing here? And why haven't you killed it already?"

I open my mouth to tell him, then snap it shut. How in the world am I going to explain all of this? *Well, you see, Jacob, it's like this, see, I was dying on the ice because of that freak blizzard, and Eve — your predecessor, remember her? — she came to me in what I guess was a dream and told me I was dying and together we screamed and* voilà, *this Gray showed up and she was smart enough to carry me back to a house where we sheltered in a closet until I was safe, and then we walked for a few hours, and here we are. Cool? I'll take Q & A now.*

Yeah, there's no way he's going to go for any of that. Even though he's young and can be a bit of a jerk once in a while, he's a pretty solid leader. Not as good as Eve, of course, but not too bad. He suffers from a chronic lack of imagination, and is way too black and white to believe a story that weird, even with all the crazy crap we've seen in our short lives. Hell, even running it through in my mind, I barely believe it myself. I decide to go for the short and sweet, putting a hold on the embellishments.

"That blizzard came up on me fast, and she helped get me to shelter. I wouldn't be alive without her."

The small slice of Jacob's pale face I can see through the partially open door scrunches up in distaste, like he's eating scrambled eggs and just crunched into a big hunk of shell. He shakes his head.

"No way, that's not possible. Grays don't do that."

I give him a tight grin and shrug, hands out at my sides. As calmly and as matter-of-factly as I can, I say, "Don't know what to tell you, but this one does. She's also the one who saved Google *and* your brother back at Rumpke Mountain, too. Go get one of them and ask. I'll wait."

I guess he's taking my advice, because the door slams shut with a solid thud that vibrates up through the soles of my shoes. With a sigh, I turn back to my companion. Susan stares down at me, but otherwise is still as a statue. Jacob's words echo through my head: *"What is that thing doing here? And why haven't you killed it already?"* I find myself wondering the same thing. Yes, she saved me, and yes, she saved Google and Simon back on Rumpke Mountain when Hunter attacked. But she's a damn Gray. What do they know of friendship, loyalty, or humanity? Nothing, that's what. They're killers, and that's all they've ever been. They're ravenous, brainless creatures who will do whatever they have to in order to survive. How many innocent people has this one slaughtered before? Why in the world am I letting her live? What is wrong with me?

Then the red door bangs open and Google is standing there, panting, his eyes wide behind those thick glasses of his. Jacob and some of the others are behind him, each one aiming a pistol over my shoulder at Susan's head. Google's jaw drops open comically, then he rushes past me like I'm invisible and grabs Susan around her waist. He's so small and slight compared to her that he could be a lost child hugging a parent. He's got his face buried in her checkered poncho. She makes no move to return the embrace.

"Oh my god, Scout," he says, his voice muffled. "You found her. You really found her."

I find myself smiling at the two of them, realizing this is the reason she's still alive. A warm sensation that the cold can't blunt spreads out from my chest. Thinking back, I never grasped how horrible I felt for accidentally running her off in the first place. The crazy little genius is more important to me than

I thought, and I guess I could never get over having him blame me for her loss. Bringing the two of them together again was always in the back of my mind, although I never thought it would happen. Especially not like this.

"Actually, she found me. In fact, she saved my life."

Google's shoulders shake a little as he sobs into her poncho, but eventually he stops and pulls away. His face and eyes are red as he looks up at me. As he considers all this, I swear I can see the neurons firing away behind that curious stare.

"She saved you? How?"

Like before, I really don't want to get into details now with Jacob and his guys here. "Why don't I tell you all about it later, over dinner or something. I haven't eaten all day, and I'm starving."

After a second, he nods. Grasping Susan's poncho, he starts to lead her inside. Jacob steps forwards with a hand up, trying hard to show he's still in charge here. "Wait! Where do you think you're going with that thing?"

Google stares back at him. He's regained his composure, and is once again the serious kid I've grown accustomed to, one way too mature for his age.

"Inside, of course."

Jacob shakes his head. "Nope. No way in hell. That thing is not coming in here."

Jacob is half a head smaller than him, but when the little kid straightens up, he almost seems to tower over the entire group. When he speaks, his voice is resolute and unyielding. "She's coming inside with me, or we're both leaving. Do you understand? And all the help I've been giving you will go with me. Do you really want that?"

I almost whistle out loud at the threat. Since he got here, Google's done some miraculous stuff, like repairing a few of the solar panels so we have more juice, and setting up and running the shortwave radio. I won't learn about this until later, but he also tied the solar panel batteries into the huge furnace downstairs to warm up the lower level during the blizzard. Gasoline may have gone bad years ago, but I guess the fuel oil in the tanks is still good. Not only is he blindingly smart, he's also pretty damn handy with a wrench.

The two of them squint, gunfighters staring down one another across a dusty street. Jacob understands the threat but hates having his authority questioned, especially in front of his guys. "Google, you can't be serious. I can't have a damn Gray inside. She'll scare the crap out of everybody. She's dangerous!"

Google tilts his head and shrugs. "Either we both come in, or we both go. Your choice."

Jacob glances behind him at the other guys, but no one wants to offer an opinion. To a man, they understand how vital the little genius has become, but no one is willing to admit it out loud to their leader. Jacob stares at each of them one at a time, but they all find somewhere else to look.

"Come on. I don't think she's a threat," I add, trying to help. "She's traveled with us before, and we've never had a problem. And, like I said, she's already saved this guy here and your brother at least once."

Jacob tilts his blond head back, staring at the blue sky and swearing vigorously under his breath, before he comes to a decision. The poor kid has aged a lot since taking charge here, and now sports a webbing of thin lines tucked in the corners of his eyes. He's almost growling when he snaps, "Fine. She can come in. But she has to stay locked in the furnace room. I can't have her wandering around scaring the crap out of everyone."

Google considers this option for a moment, then nods back. "Agreed. But no chain. And I'll stay with her. And we need to feed her, too. Have someone bring food."

Jacob exhales noisily and shakes his blond head, still muttering to himself, but we can all tell he's going to give in to Google's demands. He steps aside, as do the rest of his guys.

"Come on," Google says, grabbing a handful of her checkerboard poncho and leading her inside like he owns Church Island, which he very well might by now. I'm reminded of his time at Rumpke Mountain and how he lorded over the place. "Let's get you something to eat."

As we move by Jacob, he makes eye contact with me. His eyebrows are drawn together in an angry snarl of white hair and wrinkles. He's clenching and unclenching his hands. He is not happy with me, but I'm okay with that. I smile and pat him on the shoulder as I pass by. To his credit, he doesn't flinch.

"Good choice," I assure him.

CHAPTER
FOUR

It's bitterly cold inside the sanctuary, and the air is so still my frozen breath hangs in front of me in a cloud of ghostly smoke. The guards up at the windows are bundled up in so many coats and scarves I'm surprised they can move at all. Their eyes, the only part of them I can see, track me as I walk past. I probably know a few of them, but I can't tell who's who covered up like that. Google and Susan must have gone down the steps by the entrance already. I'm not too worried about them now. I'm more concerned with making sure the rest of my friends are okay and letting them know I'm still alive.

I quickly jog up the steps at the end of the sanctuary to the open room by the library where we live. I poke my head inside, but no one's there. I head out the other way and down the steps two at a time to the gym and the classrooms. It's much warmer down here so close to the kitchen, and I feel myself gradually thawing out a little. Some people are hanging out playing and talking, especially the younger ones. After a closer look I spotted little Carly at a table over in the corner, her head bent low over a project of some kind.

"Carly!" I shout, cupping my hands to my mouth.

She jumps up with a squeal and scurries over to me, arms flailing around, somehow expertly dodging tables and chairs. She's gotten so much taller lately, to the point where I really need to drop the prefix "little." Her long black hair flops in front of her face. She tucks it behind her ear just before she grabs me around the waist. We keep asking her if we can cut it, but she won't let us. Words flow from her mouth in a continuous stream, without a breath.

"Scout, I was so worried! Where have you been? You were gone all night! Oh my gosh I'm so glad you're back!"

I hold her close, giving her a little back and forth shake, overjoyed she's still safe and sound. "I got caught out in that blizzard. But I'm fine. I'm just glad you're okay."

Her words continue to pour out in a torrent, almost without punctuation. "I know! I've never seen snow before. And it got so cold! Jacob and Google made us all go down here where it was warm. Google did something with the furnace so it was warmer. He's so smart, even though I haven't seen much of him. He's been so busy talking to people. And we were worried sick about you. Singer was going to go look for you, but Jacob wouldn't let him. Boy was he mad.

I've never seen him so mad! He even punched a wall!"

"Where is he? I need to talk to him right away."

She tucks another stray strand of hair behind her ear. "Um, I think he's helping Harold in the kitchen. That's where he was a little bit ago."

I exhale in relief, happy he's safe, and uttering thanks under my breath that Jacob locked him down for his own good. "And Tiny's okay, too? Where is he?"

She thinks for a second, scrunching up her round face. "Oh, yeah, he's fine. I think he's playing with Annie in the classrooms. That's the last place I saw him."

"Okay, thanks. I'll be back in a little bit. I need to let Singer know I'm all right."

She gives me another squeeze, then skips back to the table and whatever she was working on before. I suspect it's another drawing or art project of some sort. I leave her there and round the corner into the heat of the kitchen. On the far wall I can see the fireplace roaring, and the smell of food instantly reminds me how hungry I am. But I hold off, since I'm dying to see Singer and let him know I'm still among the living.

I spot Harold first, sweating buckets as he preps the next meal. His brown hair is slicked back and his cheeks are red from working down here in the heat all day long. As long as I've been on Church Island, I've probably spent the least amount of time with Harold. He works non-stop, never taking a break except to pee and sleep. Looking at him now, it strikes me he's mildly cuter than I originally thought. Honestly, if these were normal times, I could see him as the once-geeky but now good-looking older brother of one of my friends. Completely out-of-bounds, but still nice to look at. I'm about to ask if he knows where Singer is when a pair of long, strong arms envelop me from behind, and any stray thoughts of Harold's attributes are quickly banished. I would know those arms anywhere. I turn in his embrace and stare up into his liquid brown eyes.

"My god, Scout, thank heavens you're okay," Singer sighs, pulling me in tight. He's so strong I'm actually having a hard time taking a breath, but what a way to go. "We were so damn worried. What the hell happened? Where have you been?"

His long hair is back in a tight ponytail that accentuates his thin face. That hair, once jet black, is peppered with white, a telltale sign of our partial change. Sweat rolls down his cheeks and has soaked an irregular V down the middle of his shirt. Like Carly, he's taller and thinner than when we first met, and I have to tilt my head back to look him in the eyes. I return his hug, burying my head in his damp chest and savoring his musky aroma. I can feel the sweat through his shirt. It's as hot as a kiln in here and I can barely stand it, but I wouldn't trade this moment for anything in the world.

Finally, although I really don't want to, we break our embrace. "I got caught out in that blizzard," I explain, and then tell him everything else that happened after that. Unlike with Jacob and the rest, I don't spare any details, even the part with Eve and the furnace room. He doesn't laugh, or look at me like I'm crazy, which I love him for. His facial expressions cover the full spectrum of surprise and shock as he listens, and he tilts his head sideways a few times, but not once does he doubt my story. I never expected he would.

"Wow, do I have a lot of questions," he finally says.

I smile up at him. "Yeah, so do I."

He looks down and to the side as he gathers his thoughts, chewing on his lower lip. "Okay, this Gray, Susan. She's here now?"

I nod. "Yeah, she's in the furnace room with Google."

He scratches his head. "What the hell are we going to do with her?"

I shrug. "I don't know. Nothing for now, I guess. As far as I can tell, she's harmless. To us, at least. We just need to keep her fed and she should be fine. That's what we did before."

"And this telepathic thing you've got with her. How's that work?"

"Beats the hell out of me. It's freaking me out. But it has to be the same kind of link my brother had with those Grays at the farmhouse where those people were buried, and what Hunter had with his minions. It's the only explanation."

"And the Eve dream? That's new."

I shrug. "I don't know. I mean, that's what it had

to be, right? Even though I've never had a dream like that before. It was so damn real."

We talk for a while longer, mainly asking each other for answers to questions neither of us have. Eventually we get tired of saying "I don't know" over and over. He takes my hand in his and tugs gently, and we exit the heat of the kitchen. It's quieter out in the hallway, and about twenty degrees cooler, thankfully. I was starting to sweat pretty heavily myself in there, and I haven't had a chance to clean up lately. I really hope I don't stink, and it takes all my willpower not to give each armpit a quick sniff-check just to be sure. That would be embarrassing.

Singer motions with his head towards the furnace room down the hall. "Mind if I go check her out? I've never seen a Gray that I wasn't trying to kill, or that wasn't trying to kill me."

Stepping foot in that room is the last thing I want to do. In fact, if I never see that place again it will be too soon. But, if I'm being honest, I'm very curious how she and Google are hitting it off. He always had a special kind of rapport with her, to the point where he could lead her around on a leash like a pet. I'm curious if he's ever noticed the kind of telepathic link that she and I seem to have now, or if it's something else entirely. But still, the furnace room?

"Sure," I reply, trying my best to conceal the anxiety that's wrapped icy tentacles around me. To be honest, I'm pretty proud that my voice hasn't gotten all squeaky. Good job, me. "I, uh, don't think that would be a problem."

He stops, picking up on my concern. "Are you sure? You don't have to come with me. I know what that place means to you."

I wave my fears away with a lot more swagger than I feel. "No, no. I'm fine. Really. Let's go."

Singer leads the way, and I follow a few paces behind him. I can see the outline of his harmonica tucked into the back pocket of his jeans. Honestly, I'm pretty pleased at how well I'm keeping up appearances through all this, even though I feel a river of nervous sweat rolling between my shoulder blades and down my back. When we get there, Jacob's got two guys stationed outside, which I should have expected. But I'm surprised when they step aside and let us pass without any problems. Okay, apparently, they're here to make sure Susan stays in, not to keep us out. The pulley and weight system that ensures the door stays tightly closed creaks and moans as Singer muscles it open. I steel myself to walk in, then stop like I hit a brick wall. It's not that I don't want to go back in there. I don't. In fact, I'd rather dive naked in the toxic water outside with a hundred papercuts than set foot in that horrible place again. No, that's not what made me stop. It's that Google and Susan aren't the only ones in there. Annie and Tiny are, too. Even more shocking is that Tiny is on the floor next to Susan, staring at the Gray silently.

"Hey, Scout," Annie says, sparing me a quick sideways glance before focusing protectively back on Tiny.

"Annie, what the hell are you two doing in here?" I snap, all fear of the place suddenly expelled.

Contrary to the rest of us, Annie has filled out even more lately. Regular meals and caring for the kids have been good to her. Her thick red hair is a lion's mane imbued with the deep amber of a summer sunset. What I wouldn't do to have hair like that instead of mine, this boring brown stuff speckled with white.

"Tiny and I were in the classrooms, playing," she explains, almost in a daze, like she's not at all sure what's happening. "And a little bit ago he just got up and ran out. I chased after him, and we ended up here, outside the door. He was banging on it, trying to get inside. I had no idea there was one of these *things* in here," she adds, motioning toward Susan with outright disgust. Her encounters with Grays mirror ours, so I get it. "I grabbed him and tried to run out, but Google promised me it was okay, and it looked that way since he was sitting right next to it. After I caught my breath, we went the rest of the way in and he just sat down and started staring at it, like this. Why is he doing this? What does it mean?"

I shake my head. "I have no idea. How did he know she was here? Who told him?"

"No one," Annie assures me. "It was just the two of us in the room at the time, playing. We didn't talk to anyone and haven't seen anybody all morning."

Singer and I exchange a look with each other, and, ironically, I know we're both thinking the same thing at each other: is it the telepathy thing again? He raises an eyebrow and shrugs, as confused about this as I am. What else would make Tiny come down here? And how did he know Susan was here in the first place? I rub my forehead with my hand. All these questions and no answers are making me crazy.

Just then Tiny stands and starts making motions with his hands at Annie. He's never been able to speak, not verbally, but lately he's been using some sort of sign language to communicate, something he must have made up on his own. To my knowledge no one here knows American Sign Language, including me, so that can't be it. When we first found him in an abandoned house, he couldn't have been much more than eight or nine months old. At least, that's what we thought at the time. Now, looking at him, we may have underestimated his age. These days he looks closer to two and half or three. Annie watches him for a moment before shaking her head.

"What's he saying?" I ask.

Annie purses her lips. "I'm not sure. He's been do-ing this lately, but I only know a little bit. I think he's talking about that thing."

"It doesn't mean anything to me, either," Google chimes in. "But it's some sort of language. The ges-tures aren't random. And he keeps repeating them."

Singer kneels down so he's closer to eye level with him. Tiny doesn't stop motioning with his hands. His wispy brown hair is tussled, like he just woke up from a nap. His big round eyes are wide and his lips are compressed into fine lines. If I had to guess, I'd say he's getting irritated.

"I don't either," Singer admits, his voice low and soothing. He's always been good with the kids, too. "Who understands him?"

Annie doesn't have to think about it. "Carly. Carly does. I don't know how, but the two of them have been practicing this. If anyone can translate for us, it's her. I'm sure of it."

Singer doesn't wait for me to ask but trots out of the room. In no time he's back with Carly in his wake, gripping her small hand in his. She stares at Susan with eyes so huge she could be an anime character. I squat next to her and put my arm around her small shoulders. She's shivering.

"It's okay, honey," I assure her. "There's nothing to worry about. She won't hurt you. Are you okay?"

It takes a moment for her to answer. I swear, she's actually stunned to silence for the first time in her young life. "What's that doing here?" she finally asks quietly, her voice quivering as she points at the Gray.

"It's okay," I repeat. "It won't hurt you. In fact, that's the same Gray that saved Google and Simon before. She's helped me a couple of times. She's a…a friend. Her name's Susan."

"A friend?"

"Yes, she's a friend." Wow. I can't believe I just said that.

"She really is friendly," Google assures her. "I'm right next to her, and I'm fine. See?"

Carly tilts her head to the side and stares at Susan. Slowly, she slides a foot forward. The Gray is watching her without any expression, just the same dull gaze she always has. Carly eventually reaches out a trembling finger and touches her on the knee. Susan doesn't react, and after a second Carly pulls her hand back, clutching it with the other.

"She's so hot."

"Yes, she is. They all are," I tell her. "But, honey, right now I need your help. Tiny is trying to tell us something, but none of us understand him. Can you tell me what he's saying?"

Carly shakes once, as if breaking out of a trance. "What? Oh, sure, Scout. That's easy. We've been working on this. You know, making it a game. He's getting pretty good. He's really a smart little guy."

She focuses on Tiny, who hasn't stopped gesturing angrily with his hands, complicated movements that involve a lot of pointing. After watching him for a few seconds, she begins to sign at him. They go back and forth for a bit, Tiny's hands moving faster than Carly's. My head is bouncing side to side so fast I could be watching a ping-pong match. Then there's a period when he goes solo, and she just watches. Finally, Carly

makes a fist and thumps it against her chest. She turns
to me.

"Well?" I ask.

"He doesn't have all the words," she starts. "And
that makes him…um." She trails off.

"Mad? Frustrated?" I suggest.

"Yes, that's it. That makes him frustrated. But he
wants to know where she came from, and what she's
doing here. He says he can…hear her."

"Hear her?" Singer asks softly. "What's that
mean?"

Carly signs at him again, and we all wait as Tiny
replies to her. "He doesn't know. He doesn't have the
words to figure it out. He just keeps saying she's different."

"Is that it?" Singer asks.

"Oh, there's one more thing," she adds.

"What's that?"

"You've been calling her the wrong name. He says
her name's not Susan."

CHAPTER
FIVE

It's evening, long after dinner, and all the residents of Church Island are gathered in the gym for the night. The upstairs rooms are still too cold to sleep in, so as a group we're sprawled all over the hardwood floor on blankets, cots, or whatever else we can find. We're packed elbow to elbow, with barely any room to roll over. The furnace is running, and the air is tainted with that awful smell of fuel oil. Thinking back to the rainy nights in the boat, it's not the worst place I've bunked down before, although I'm really missing my bed with Singer up in the library. The chatter of the younger kids has trickled down to an occasional murmur or discrete whisper. Someone close by farts loud and long, and half a dozen kids giggle. Someone else responds with a realistic retching sound, which breaks even more of them up. I moan. It's going to take forever to get everyone asleep.

Singer is next to me, his thin frame snuggled up next to mine. It's warm enough in here we don't need a blanket, but I still like to have one on. His hand searches around for mine, and he clasps it tightly when our fingers finally discover each other's. I find this so soothing I nearly sigh out loud.

"I missed you last night," he whispers, his mouth close to my ear. "I was worried sick. Please don't ever do that again,"

I press my head into the crook of his neck, content to just lay there and be with him. My time on the ice and in the abandoned house with Susan seems so long ago, almost as if it happened to someone else instead of me. I've lost a lot of memories of my life before the Storm, but that's one I'll be happy to forget. I inch closer to him, the natural heat from his body almost too much under the blanket.

"I missed you, too," I mumble, halfway to sleep already.

He shifts around a little, pulling his head away. "How did Tiny know that Gray was here?"

"Mm. I don't know," I murmur softly into my pillow.

"And the name thing? How did he know you guys have been calling it by the wrong name? Or is he just guessing?"

Okay, apparently, he's not ready for sleep yet. I pull back and try to look at him, but it's too dark in here to make out more than the outline of his face. It's a nice face.

"I don't know that either," I answer with a yawn,

trying to be attentive, even though my mind and body are sending me all kinds of signals that I need to crash.

"I've never seen one of those things so docile," he says, more to himself than to me.

Yep, he's definitely not ready to call it a night. I sigh and lift my head, propping it up with my hand. "I haven't either. Well, except her, of course. She's been that way ever since Google kind of adopted her on Rumpke Mountain, not long after I captured her. She's been different ever since. I can't explain it."

"What are we going to do with her?"

I shrug, even though the movement is lost in the dark. "I can't answer that, either. She'll probably stay here with us, don't you think? Beyond her bizarre relationship with Google, now there's some kind of weird connection between her and Tiny, that's for sure."

He moves around, eventually laying on his back. I can just make out the outline of his nose and chin, his skin a few shades darker than the darkness in the room. I gently place my arm over his chest, feeling his heart beating slowly.

"Did you know there's an old Chinese curse that goes something like 'May you live in interesting times,' or something like that?" he says.

No, I didn't know that, but it certainly sounds about right. "Interesting times? We're definitely living through those, perhaps now more than ever. Things have been weird since the Storm hit, but even more so now."

"Right?" he continues. "I mean, we're just getting used to it being one way, and then everything changes. I don't know what to expect. Now we've got this crazy weather, Grays that aren't like anything we're used to, and some kind of telepathy? I mean, what the hell?"

I don't answer him. I just grunt groggily, hoping he'll take the hint.

"Google thinks the weather is going to stay all freaky like this for a while. He thinks it's Mother Nature trying to find a new equilibrium, or something like that. He went on and on about it while you were gone. I really didn't understand much of what he was saying, but that was the gist of it, I think."

My head slips off my hand, and I jerk awake for a second. "Uh, okay."

Singer takes my response as a cue to continue, much to my drowsy dismay. He shuffles around a little more, getting comfortable. "I don't know how he knows all this stuff, but I think we should be prepared for more storms like yesterday's blizzard."

Instead of answering, I snuggle my head back into the crook of his neck. He finally figures out I'm calling it a night and doesn't say anything else, but as I drift off, I'm pretty sure he's still wide awake. His mind may be going a mile a minute, but mine stalls completely. I'm out in seconds.

The next morning after breakfast, Singer and I head up to the sanctuary. A good night's rest has done wonders for me, and I'm feeling as happy and content as I have in days. The temperature in that huge room is noticeably warmer than yesterday, to the point where I can't see my breath anymore. I spot Jacob and Simon talking to each other at the other end of the room, their heads close. I take Singer's hand and we make our way towards them. With their blond hair and similar features, it's so easy to see they're brothers. In fact, Simon could be a younger carbon copy of his older brother. I still can't believe I never noticed it before they were reunited. They see me and Singer coming and stop talking, then wave us over.

"Hey, guys, what's up?" I ask.

"Hi, Scout," Simon replies with a quick smile. "Glad to see you made it back safe and sound."

"Glad to be here."

Simon glances at his brother, then back to me. "Heard you brought back a guest, too. I bet Google was happy."

I nod at him, aware of Jacob's icy stare in my direction, his coolness having nothing to do with the temperature. "As a matter of fact, I did. And yes, he sure seemed to be, although you know it's always hard to tell with Google."

"And now we've got a damn Gray in the furnace room," Jacob chimes in. "I told my guys to spread the word that she's here, so everyone doesn't freak out. But that's not our immediate problem now. We've got bigger issues."

The way he said that makes the hair on the back

of my neck stand up. My mom always used to say that a sudden reaction like that meant someone just walked over your grave, which does nothing to improve the situation. I stand up straight and exchange a worried glance with Singer. My previous good mood has vanished. "What do you mean?"

Jacob motions to the scaffolding with his chin. "Follow me. It's easier to show you."

Intrigued and anxious, we follow him as he climbs up the scaffolding next to us. It's not a challenging climb at all. With our enhanced strength, Singer and I are up there in seconds, easily beating the two of them. Once we're all in place, Jacob swings open the plywood barrier protecting the window. A surprisingly warm breeze brushes across my face. He points toward the town of Cedar Ridge, far across the frozen channel.

"What am I looking at?" I ask, puzzled, staring at the ruined city. From here it looks the same to me. Destroyed and depressing. A jumble of leveled buildings and houses with only a few crumbling walls still standing.

"You can't see them?" Simon asks.

I squint, but I'm still drawing a blank. "No. See who?"

Jacob passes me a pair of binoculars. I lift them to my eyes and spin the little wheel to bring everything into focus. What I see causes my heart to drop so hard I'm surprised the rest of them can't hear it hit

the floor. Right across from us, where the frozen channel meets the shore in Cedar Ridge, a large group of
Grays has congregated. I try to count bodies, but I
lose track around thirty. Stunned, I fumble with the
binoculars as I pass them to Singer. He peers through
them and gasps.

"Holy crap," he mutters. "What are they doing
over there?"

Simon squints out the window. He's been blessed with incredible eyesight, so much better than mine
or anyone else's. He can see what the rest of us can't
without assistance.

"They're not doing anything," he replies quietly,
as if by talking too loudly he might attract their attention. "They showed up there this morning. And more
keep coming. They're just standing there, staring at
us."

"I don't understand," Singer says, his gaze still
locked on the Grays. "I've never seen so many before,
not in one place. Not unless…"

"Unless what?" I ask, my voice pinched.

"Not unless they're being, you know, guided by
someone. Like Hunter."

Jacob retrieves the binoculars from Singer's loose
grip. "We thought the same thing, but we haven't been
able to spot him. As far as we can tell, they're doing
this on their own."

"Why?" I ask. "What are they up to?"

Both brothers shrug in perfect unison, which

would be kind of funny if I weren't so scared. "We don't know," Jacob replies, worry coloring his young voice. "But we all know Grays don't like water, and so far, that fear seems to carry over to ice, too. None of them have made a move yet."

I nod. "You're right. They don't like ice. Susan, the Gray from yesterday, was terrified of walking on it with me, until I made her."

Jacob narrows his eyes at me. "I was going to ask you about that. She was with you on the ice yesterday. The fact that she did that is concerning now, to say the least. You say you made her do it. How?"

I recall then that I never gave him any details of what happened to me before I got back to Church Island. I don't know if he'll believe me now, but I can't see I've got any choice but to tell him.

"You're not going to believe me."

"Really?" he asks, dramatically waving his hand at the deadly group gathering across the ice. "After what we've all lived through? I might. Try me."

I sigh, then go into more detail about how Susan saved me. I don't want to tell them about my dream about Eve, but I have to. Nothing I say will make any sense if I don't. When I'm done, I fully expect them to call me everything but a liar, but to my surprise, they don't. Like me, they've seen and experienced enough weirdness that the unbelievable has become believable.

"In this dream, you say you and Eve shouted for

help, and the Gray found you?"

"Yes," I reply.

"Which means," Jacob continues, thinking out loud, "that she had to come on the ice not once, but twice. Once to save you, and once when you both walked back here. Is that right?"

Damn, I hadn't thought of that. She did come out there by herself. Sure, when we left the farmhouse, I had to give her a swift mental kick in the ass to follow me, but not the first time. Could my mental cries for help have been that strong while I was dying on the ice? Or was she already out there for some other reason? Suddenly, I'm even more concerned with the massing Grays across the channel than I was before.

"Yes, I guess that's right," I admit, a finger to my lips. "I hadn't thought of that."

Simon glances back and forth between his brother and me, trying to keep up. "What are you talking about? Are you saying those things might cross over here whenever they want to? Is that what you're saying? We're not really safe here at all?"

As one, we turn and stare out of the window. I can't see the clustered Grays from here, but I can almost sense their menace as they gather in the distance. Finally, after a few tense moments, Jacob turns to all of us. He's got the same expression on his face that Eve had when she meant business. The resolute set of his jaw, the tight bunching of his blond eyebrows. The way the tendons in his thin neck flex. He's feeling the responsibility for all the lives on Church Island even more than usual. I don't envy him one bit.

"Yeah, I think that sums it up. Simon, go tell everyone we need reinforcements up here. Make sure everyone else is armed and ready. We could be facing an attack at any time. It could be in an hour, a day, or never. But we need to get ready."

His brother's already pale face somehow goes a shade whiter. He scrambles down the scaffolding and takes off at a run, leaving the three of us to consider what might happen soon.

I nudge Singer. "That means us, too. We'd better get ready."

"Damn. I was just getting used to the peace and quiet," he says, sighing.

CHAPTER
SIX

Several hours have passed, and the Grays haven't made a move. This waiting and not knowing what may or may not happen is killing me. I'm a doer, not a waiter. We've all suffered through stressful times before, but this is different. I remember a world history class when we talked about the trench warfare during World War I, where the German and Allied forces fought for months at a time, sometimes only separated by a few dozen yards of no-man's land. I don't know if it's possible to rank one horror over another, and I eventually conclude they all suck.

Singer and I are in the library. I'm sitting on our bed while he straps on a pair of boots. He must see something in my face, because he stops what he's doing and reaches out a hand, resting it on my arm. He likes physical contact like this, and I have to admit I'm pretty fond of it, too. It's one of the zillion things about him I like.

"You okay?" he asks.

I nod. "Yeah, I guess. This whole thing with the Grays is getting to me."

He nods at me, going back to lacing up a boot. "I would hope so, because it's weird as hell and it's getting to me, too. But Jacob has everyone ready just in case. The doors are locked and barricaded, and anyone who can hold a gun or bow is ready for it. I'm pretty sure we'll be safe. This place is like a fortress."

Whether he's just humoring me or not, I don't know, but I appreciate his outward show of confidence. I manage a smile that's probably a lot grimmer than I intended.

"Really? That's the best you can do?" he asks with a playful smirk. "You look like your dog just died. Anyway, we do what we always do and prepare for the worst, and hope for the best. Besides, we've got something the Grays don't."

"And what's that?"

"Our not-so-secret weapon. We've got us. The two of us are more than a match for a dozen of those things."

I smile at him again, and this one is less strained. He's right, of course. The two of us in slo-mo can make up for a lot, even against the growing number of creatures massing across the channel. But even so, simply knowing that something awful could happen at any moment and there's nothing I can do to stop it is enough to chip big chunks off my block of confidence. I wish I shared his conviction – forced or not.

"What do we do now? Just wait?" I ask quietly.

"Well, sort of. First, we prepare, which everyone is doing. Then, we go about our lives as best as we can. And then we wait."

I fall back on the bed, my unseeing gaze aimed straight up. "Oh, God, that sounds horrible."

Singer laughs softly at my exaggerated distress. "Trust me, Scout. I'm not going to let anything happen to you."

He sits on the bed, then lays down beside me. Neither of us says a word, and that's just fine with me. I'm hyper aware of him next to me. His bare arm is against mine, and it's more comforting than he can ever know. I sigh long and loud, snuggle my head next to his, and try my best to believe him. He says he'll never let anything happen to me, and whether he knows it or not, I'll never let anything happen to him, either. I would die before I'd let him get hurt.

"Play me a song," I say.

He rolls sideways a little and retrieves his harmonica from his back pocket. He plays a few soft notes, testing it.

"What would you like to hear?"

"I don't know. Surprise me."

He thinks for a moment, his eyes unfocused, then starts to play something. The first few notes are held long and soft, so long I can't for the life of me figure out how he can do that in a single breath. I wait for the song to increase in tempo, but it doesn't. It starts off mournful and stays that way. It has a bluesy feel, sad, but not so depressing I want to walk into traffic or anything. His mouth is sliding up and down the silver harmonica like it's an extension of his hands. I close my eyes and listen, content, until the last note drifts to nothingness.

"That was beautiful. What was it?"

"'Sophisticated Lady.' I first heard it played by a guy named Toots Thielemans."

I roll over and laugh, my fears and anxiety temporarily vanquished. "His name was 'Toots'? And he played the harmonica? You're kidding, right?"

"Nope. His real first name was Jean-Baptiste, but he went by Toots. He was considered one of the masters of the harmonica."

"Never heard of him," I say, still laughing, the name Toots for some reason striking me as maybe funnier than it should. It's probably got something to do with my heightened stress levels.

"I don't doubt it. But he was a fascinating guy. Born in Belgium, came to the US when he was older. He was supposed to be an engineer or something, but he loved the harmonica. Said he took it up because it was so small and the sound was so close to his mouth. He played with all kinds of famous people. Ever heard of Benny Goodman?"

"I've at least heard of him. Sure his name wasn't Toots Goodman?"

"Uh, no. Nice try. How about the theme for Sesame Street?"

"Uh, yeah. Big Bird. Elmo. That whole bunch. Who hasn't?"

"He played on that, too."

I shake my head in wonder. "You really know a lot about this stuff."

"Yeah, I guess. But it's not all that relevant now, is it? I wish I'd had a dad who taught me useful stuff. Like wilderness or survival skills. Or hunting. That would be a whole lot more helpful these days than all this music stuff."

I give him a little nudge with my elbow. "Hey, don't ever say that. Don't ever apologize for this wonderful skill and knowledge. These days we need something beautiful, like your music."

He grunts what I think is a yes, then twists his head and kisses me on the cheek. He really is a special person, and not just to me. If we ever get over this, if the world ever gets back to something we can call normal, we're going to need thoughtful, intelligent people like him. I mean, we're always going to have jerks like Hunter around, so we need to balance everything out, right? I've told him that before, and I hope he believes me.

"What were you like in school?" I ask him, my voice a little sing-song with fatigue. "You know, before all this happened."

"What do you mean? Like grades?"

"Yeah, sure. Grades. Sports. All that stuff."

"Well, it was only middle school, you know. I did okay, I guess."

I prop my head up my hand, awake now. "What do you mean, you did 'okay?' You're going to have to do better than that."

He laughs, but the sound he makes is more sad than funny. "Okay, fine. Yeah, I got good grades and played all the sports. Football, baseball, basketball. All of them."

"I bet you were the quarterback of the football team."

"Ha! You're wrong there. I was a wide receiver."

"And I bet you were great at it, too. Probably great at all that stuff."

He turns to me and smiles, his face just inches away from mine. I notice for the first time that his nose is the slightest bit crooked, like it was broken at some time before we met. I can't believe I never saw that before. I thought I knew his features inside and out.

"Okay, yeah, I was pretty good at all that. But none of that matters now, does it?"

We don't speak for a little while, each of us momentarily stuck in our respective pasts. I think back to my own time in school, which was, shall we say, significantly less successful than his. I wasn't a great student, and I certainly wasn't an athlete of any kind. I was more invisible than that, the type who would be hanging inconspicuously by their locker while the Singers of the world strolled past with their group of loud friends, yelling and joking. Singer and my brother would have been kindred spirits, I'm pretty sure.

"I don't think we would have been friends in school," I whisper sadly.

He rolls over. I'm pretty sure he's about to object, but he stops and his eyebrows knot in thought. He stares at me, but his gaze is distracted and turned inward. My heart skips a beat, and for a second, I'm afraid he's judging me with what is versus what might have been. Or what should have been. Then his focus sharpens and he rolls onto his back.

"Yeah, well that would've been pretty stupid of me then, right?"

I smile warmly at him. "You don't miss your past? What might have been?"

"Oh, sure. That stuff was fun, don't get me wrong. But I'd give it all up in a second for what we have now."

I've said it many times before, but this world is awful. The death and destruction we're living through are beyond anything anyone could have imagined. I hate all of it. But even the worst circumstances can have positives attached to them. My positives are here next to me, and the people around me. Before Singer I wasn't just a glass half-empty kind of person. No, I was the type of person who dumped the contents out, then shattered the glass on the floor and ground the shards into dust. But not now. Now I'm learning to take what I've got and enjoy it to the best of my ability.

Is that personal growth? Maybe so.

We lay quietly for a long time, comfortable, feeling the warmth of each other on the bed. I'm content enough with my life as it is that I'm almost dozing again. Then the dinner bell rings and Singer sits up.

"Time to eat," he says, helping me to my feet.

"I think you should play something after dinner. We could all use it. But not 'Sophisticated Lady.' Keep that one for me. How about something upbeat? I think that would be fun."

He smiles. "Okay, sure. I know just the thing."

"Perfect."

After dinner and a rousing version of "American Pie" that gets everyone in the gym on their feet, Singer and I decide to help out Harold in the kitchen. We didn't do much but hang out in the library all afternoon, and we both feel a little guilty for not pulling our weight today. As usual it's beastly hot in there, but not as bad as usual since Harold lets the fire burn down a little every evening. Our full-time cook welcomes the extra sets of hands, even if he doesn't come right out and say so. He stays true to character and goes about his business in relative silence, only talking if he sees one of us doing something wrong. I've always wondered about him, and why he works so hard here all the time. He never socializes with anyone that I know of, not even sitting down with us at meals.

We scrape the last of the plates clean and wipe

down all the silverware. Without the promise of constant rain, we have to be more careful to ration our water. We've still got a lot in the cisterns on the roof, but that won't last forever. As we're stacking the last of the plates and I realize it's just me and Singer, I ease close to him and tilt my head his way, giving him a sideways, conspiratorial look.

"What?" he asks, glancing around and keeping his voice low.

"I'm curious. What's the deal with Harold?" I ask, keeping an eye out in case he comes back.

Singer purses his lips. "What do you mean?"

"I mean, what's his deal? He's always in here working like a dog. He never does anything fun or even talks to people outside the kitchen. What's up with that?"

"Beats the heck out of me. Maybe he likes it in here."

Hmm. Maybe. But I'm not sure if I buy it. This place is terrible, and he works day and night. It's grueling. I've always thought I had a good work ethic, but this guy makes me look like a bum. Also, he's one of the oldest people on Church Island. Way over 240 months, if I had to guess. I'm sure he would have gone Gray by now if that hadn't stopped happening here. On top of all that, I would have expected someone his age to have a girlfriend or a boyfriend or something, but he doesn't seem interested in anyone or anything outside of the kitchen.

"Why does it matter, anyway?" he asks. "He seems happy enough. Or at least not unhappy, considering everything."

"I don't know. Just curious, I guess."

We finish stacking plates and do what we can to prep for the morning. We're both sweaty messes, our shirts sticking to us in very unflattering ways. I pick at mine and try to pull it away, but the damp cotton snaps right back to being clingy and gross.

"Ugh. I feel disgusting," I tell him. "I'm going to go get cleaned up. Meet you back at the gym in a little while? We can hang out with Carly. I haven't seen much of her lately."

He agrees, and I make my way back upstairs. It's noticeably chillier up here, but nothing like it was the other day. Once in the library I shut the door, strip down, and grab a small towel from a bucket by the window. Like I said, we've got cisterns on the roof that catch and collect rainwater, but it hasn't rained in a long time. We've had to shift into a conservation mode lately, which means our entire room has to share a single bucket of water. The stuff is freezing cold, which is just as much fun as it sounds, and I hurriedly wipe myself down with a damp cloth. When I've gotten at least the top layers of grime off, I put on some clean clothes and consider it a win. Some deodorant would be nice, but we don't have any. My speckled brown and white hair is longer than it's been in years, down below my shoulders, and I use the rest of the water to clean it the best I can. Satisfied that I probably won't knock anyone over from overpowering body odor, I carefully use Annie's coveted brush and finish up.

"Human once again," I sigh, smoothing my fresh T-shirt.

For my last bit of grooming, I brush my teeth with a dry toothbrush. No way I'm going to use the bucket water for that now. I run my tongue around my mouth and, as usual, sigh and wish I had some toothpaste.

Done, I make a judgment call and dump the water out the window, just like people did in the old days with the contents of their chamber pots. Except here the water runs down the roof, into the gutters, and out the downspout somewhere below. The window in the library looks out over the frozen muddy water, not in the direction of Cedar Ridge. The brown ice that extends in the direction Susan and I came from looks like frozen, foamy coffee. I can spot darker colored patches where it's starting to thaw. This is what Lake Erie looked like in the spring, when it was getting warm outside, but the thick ice hadn't had a chance to completely melt yet. I open the window a crack, and a light breeze lets in cool, fresh air, devoid of any of the stench we've gotten so used to over the years. I don't like the ice and what it might mean to our security, but I am a big fan of the clean air. I close the window and head downstairs.

I enter the gym, and Singer sees me. With a nod in my direction, he trots upstairs to get cleaned up, although now I feel a little guilty because he'll have to get fresh water in the bucket. I wander around to see what everyone is up to. Quite a few people are missing, I realize, and figure they must be on guard duty around the church. Remorse at not lending a hand bugs me, and I leave the gym for the sanctuary. It's still chilly as hell in there, especially in my T-shirt, but it's not so bad I can't stand it. Looking up, there are more people than usual on the scaffolding around the large room and standing guard. I clamber up the same one as before. I don't know the two young boys up there this time, but they know who I am. Each one gives me a nod.

"Any change?" I ask, squinting out the window. The evening sky is darkening toward Cedar Ridge, but it's still bright enough to see the remains of the city.

"No. Well, I don't think so," the first one says. I think his name is Barry. He's got a square face that always looks like he's about to ask a question. I motion to the binoculars, and he hands them over. The other guy, a redhead with so many freckles splashed across his nose he almost looks tan, doesn't say anything. He just nods at what his companion said.

"Thanks," I tell Barry. Or is it Gary? Now I'm doubting both choices. I put the binoculars to my eyes and peer across the channel. My gut does a little flip-flop at what I see.

"There are more," I say, my voice hushed. "I can't

tell how many, but the group looks bigger than it did before. That can't be good."

The Grays are all bunched together so it's hard to get an accurate headcount, but it certainly looks to me like their numbers have increased. And what's creeping me out even more is that they aren't actually doing anything. They're just standing there staring at the church. A few are milling around, but the rest aren't moving at all. What in the hell are they up to?

I lower the binoculars. "Where's Jacob? Is he around?"

The redhead points back into the belly of the church. "He said he was going to get some rest. He's probably crashed in his room."

"Okay. If anything changes at all, you be sure to come and find me," I tell them. "Well, find Jacob first, then come and get me or Singer. Okay? Right away."

Singer and I have enough cult status that even though we're not in charge, we can usually get people to listen to us. The two of them nod vigorously in unison, and I swing back down to the floor, sticking the landing like a pro.

Back in the gym, I look around the noisy room and spot Singer. He's so tall it's easy to pick him out from the others. He sees me and motions me to his side. Like me, he's clean and in dry clothes. His long hair is still a little damp and shiny, and is pulled back in a tight ponytail, just the way I like it. It's a good look, and I can't help but smile warmly at him from across the room. I find myself thinking not so pure thoughts about him as I move through the crowd. I try to tone down the silly grin that's plastered across my face as I get closer. Am I blushing? I hope I'm not blushing.

"What's up?" I ask loudly over the echoing din of voices.

He nods over his shoulder, his eyes almost sparkling. "It's Google. He wants to talk to us."

"What about?"

"He says he's got something. It may be the cure."

My pulse rockets into triple digits, and for a moment I'm frozen and don't know what to say or do. The words THE CURE bounce around the inside of my skull like a scream echoing around the Grand Canyon. I mean, I've been searching for some sort of antidote for this plague ever since I left Church Island, and all this time, with the hundreds of Grays I've killed, the dangers we've survived, and the sacrifices we've made, it's remained my one goal and purpose. To me it's as important as Frodo destroying the One Ring in *Lord of the Rings*. Or Harry's search for the meaning of the Deathly Hallows. Or Indiana Jones and his quest to find the Ark of the Covenant, before the Nazis, you know, got their faces melted.

I'm doing a really lousy job of containing my excitement as I finally break out of my trance. I grab Singer's hand and the two of us practically sprint through the clumps of people playing games, talking, reading, or whatever else they're doing to pass the time. Honestly, except for going on raids or guard duty or tidying up, there's really not that much here to keep people busy. We have occasional classes that the older ones like me put on, but those have been sporadic at best. I would think everyone would be worried about the Grays gathering at Cedar Ridge, but if they are, they're not showing it. I don't know if I envy them their ignorance, or wish I could be more like them.

I'm practically dragging Singer with me into the room where Hunter got patched up when we first arrived. For the most part it's still the first aid room, but it also doubles as a classroom and a bedroom. Several cots line the walls. The place is lit by a bunch of candles, and the smell of melting beeswax tickles my nose in a very pleasant way. The warm, thick aroma reminds me of spending time with my family at church, on the rare occasion we went.

Jacob and Google are both in there already. Our leader is sitting on a cot out of the way, and Google is standing next to a large whiteboard filled with so many arrows, boxes, and writing it reminds me of a graphic I once saw of the London tube stations. The lighting is poor, and I can't read much of what's on it, but I pick out my name in several places.

"What's all this? Tell me you figured it out! Does all this show the cure? Is this what you've been working on the last few weeks?" I blurt out to the room in general, the multiple sentences blurring into one.

Google nods, as composed as ever. "Indeed. Well, I'm fairly certain I have. But it's really impossible to know for sure, as I'll explain later."

I blink several times, my heart racing at a sprinter's pace. In sharp contrast, Google is as at ease and composed as I've ever seen him, leaning with his butt against a table like he's waiting on a burger and fries from McDonald's. How can he be so calm? Come to think of it, since it's Google, maybe it's just smug cockiness. That would make more sense in his case. Of course, if he's actually figured this out, I can forgive him for pretty much anything. I'm almost vibrating when I take a few steps toward his huge whiteboard. I reach out my finger to trace some of the lines and notes.

"No, no," Google orders, stepping in front of me with his hands raised. "Don't touch the board. No one touches my board."

I try not to roll my eyes at him. "Oh my god, I wasn't going to touch your precious board. Fine. Tell me what it all means."

He lowers his arms. "Let's talk about your condition first."

"My condition? What do you mean?"

"This odd yet very helpful incomplete Gray state you're in. You're not completely normal or fully Gray. I know you've wondered why you, your brother, Singer, and Hunter all have this, and no one else does. Right?"

It takes me a moment to react. Hell, yeah, I've wondered. Besides the cure, it's something I've thought about a lot. Like, all the time. Why me? Why us? Why are we the only ones? If I was sitting, I'd be on the edge of my seat right now. I realize my mouth is hanging open, and I close it with a click of my teeth.

"You figured that out, too?" I ask in something of a monotone, more a statement than a question.

Google nods. He points to the left section of the whiteboard. My name is written in the middle of a bunch of arrows and other names, including my brother, Singer, and Hunter.

"This is a timeline of events prior to and after you began your change," he continues. He points to a square in the upper left-hand corner. "I already know your story and feel comfortable with the facts. But I've also spent time interviewing others, like Annie and Carly. Using that information and filling in some gaps on my own, I've pieced this together." He points to a block with a big number six in it. "Here is the Motel 6 you all stayed in prior to your companion Dog be-ing attacked." His finger traces an arrow to another square with "Dog Attacked" written in it.

"Okay," I say. "What does that have to do with it?"

"Nothing yet. Just establishing the timeline. After the attack, you stayed a number of days in the office building. That's when your brother first started going Gray, and you followed your group's protocol and made him leave. To "take a hike," am I right?"

My face locks up while my breath freezes in my chest. My heart almost seems to turn to stone, like it's gazed into Medusa's eyes. Guilt, anger, frustration, and sadness all grapple for domination in my mind at what we used to do. The logical section of my brain insists we had no choice, but the emotional side beats the logical side into a bloody pulp. My vision blurs as my eyes swim with involuntary tears.

"Yes," I finally answer, my voice cracking. "But I don't want to talk about that."

Google, amazingly, senses how my emotional state just fell off a cliff. I mean, the guy is brutally smart, but he's always sucked at decoding human emotions. He pauses for a moment, and when he continues, his voice is almost sympathetic. Not quite, but almost.

"I'm sorry, but bear with me. All of this is important. After your brother left, and when your supplies ran low, you were forced to leave the office building where you were staying. You eventually ended up having to leave the safety of the boats and cross at the highway. That's where the Grays attacked you, right?"

I shudder at the memory of Lord taking a hike supplanted by the equally unwelcome vision of Dog's body rolled up in a blanket and left in the trunk of a car. He was a quirky, odd little guy, but I liked him. He was always trying to be helpful and was kind to a fault. But then the Gray tore him apart, and none of us could stop it. A horrible way to die, especially after all he'd been through. I nod blankly and he continues.

"But just prior to that attack, what happened to you? You were away with Hunter for a little bit, right? Looking for a way across. Annie says you were acting weird after that. Was it something that happened when you and Hunter were alone?"

Suddenly this is too much. I haven't thought about Hunter and what he did to me for a long time. It's not like I've forgotten it, because I can't. I never will. But I've been able to shove that awful memory deep into the back of my mind where horrible thoughts live out their dark and miserable lives, only periodically clawing their way into the light of my consciousness.

"I don't want to talk about that either," I say, with a sideways glance at Singer. His eyes in the dark room have narrowed to slits in an expression I've never seen on his face before. I never told him what Hunter did. I couldn't.

"So, I was right," Google says. "Something did happen. What was it?"

"I said I don't want to talk about it!" I snap.

"I'm sorry, Scout," Jacob says, speaking up. "But this really is important."

Singer tries to come to my emotional aid and rests his hand on my arm. His touch, usually so warm and comforting, is alien and unwelcome. It's not his touch, exactly, but the thought of Hunter right there in front of me, staring down at me with his wild eyes, his hand locked on my wrist. A touch from anyone right now would scorch like acid.

I sigh, my chest quivering. I know how vital this is, but it's so damn hard.

"Fine," I say into the silent room. "Before we were ambushed, he…he attacked me. And then he sucker punched me in the face. He said I was his, and I had to do what he said. Like he was my master, or something. He…groped me from behind."

"What else?" Google asks, his voice so flat he could be reciting the periodic table.

"He forced himself on me. He…kissed me. Hard. So hard it hurt." It's almost embarrassing to talk about this, as if it were my fault and I should feel guilty. Which makes no sense, since I didn't do anything wrong. I look at Singer out of the corner of my eye. He's staring right at me with that strange expression I can't read. For a second, I barely recognize him.

"I thought so. I was never sure, but I figured that was the case. It makes sense." He turns and scribbles a few notes on the whiteboard, in a square that was previously blank. "And then when you encountered your brother later on, he bit you on the arm hard enough to draw blood, right?"

"Yes. I still don't know why he did that." I rub my arm where the teeth marks were, although there's no scar or any indication that it ever happened. Not physically, at least.

"And soon after that did you notice a change in your condition?"

"Just a little while later. When I slammed shut the

trunk where we…where we put Dog's body. I slammed it so hard something in the car broke. I think a tire blew. That's the first time."

Google makes a check mark next to another box. "Interesting," he says, more to himself than to us. "Now let's back up a little bit. When did your group first find Tiny?"

His abrupt change of subject catches me off guard, and it takes a second for me to get my bearings. "Uh, I don't know. Right before we got to the Motel 6, I guess. We found him in an abandoned house and took him with us. He wouldn't have lasted another day by himself. He was just a baby. Why?"

"And since you found him, no one in your group has gone, shall we say, conventionally Gray?"

I cock my head at him, my interest piquing despite the painful subject matter. "Yeah, I guess. Not conventionally, if that's how you want to put it. My brother had his weird partial change, and so have I, although mine's not as extreme. His was a lot closer to being a true Gray, but not all the way, if that makes sense. But Annie is at least as old as I am, maybe older, and she should have changed long ago. And like me, Hunter or Singer only changed part way. And Carly and Tiny are way too young."

Google nods and makes some positive noises with his mouth. He scribbles a few more notes on his board. The entire thing is filling up with his tight little script. He takes a step back, the marker to his mouth as he thinks. He taps it against his teeth a few times, the clicking loud and jarring in the otherwise hushed room.

"It all makes sense now," he murmurs, staring at his board.

"What makes sense?" I ask, glancing at Singer and Jacob, but they seem to be in the dark, too.

Jacob stands and moves next to Google. He's not tall, but he dwarfs the little genius. I watch his blond head move side to side and up and down as he tries to follow the crazy arrows and boxes filling the white-board.

"I'm with Scout," he finally admits, hands on his hips. "I don't get it either."

Google sighs, one of those sighs that's meant to be an indirect dig at our intelligence levels. It's very annoying. I'm used to him doing it, but it's still very annoying.

"I'll summarize for you," he says. "All of this is tied together. You and your partial transformation. Singer, Hunter, and your brother and their incomplete change. Why no one is going Gray anymore here at Church Island. It's all very clear." He points to a small box in red ink with a single "T" written inside.

"It's Tiny," he continues. "I'm fairly sure Tiny is the cure against going Gray."

CHAPTER
SEVEN

"Wait a second. What do you mean 'it's Tiny?' I don't understand," I say, shaking my head like I'm clearing out a month's worth of cobwebs. "How could a person be the cure? That doesn't make any sense." I shoot a quick glance at Singer and Jacob, who are just as stunned and in disbelief as I am. That makes me feel a little better.

"Follow along with me," Google replies, not at all bothered by our dubious reactions. Come to think of it, he's probably enjoying them. "You guys find Tiny in that house. Up until that time people in your group went Gray just like normal. Correct?"

It takes me a heartbeat to react, but then I think back to members of our group and how many of them we've lost. I remember Tommy and Misumi and Flash, just three of the kids who changed and we forced to take a hike. There were others, but I'm afraid their names have been diluted by time and my faulty memory. We've all lost so many friends and family to this horrible fate. I'm sorry to say I've kind of lost track.

"Yeah, I guess," I finally say, my voice catching.

"And since you found him, no one has changed."

"That's not true," Jacob jumps in dramatically, as if he were scoring a point in a debate. "Eve changed. She went Gray right after they all got here."

"That's correct," Google admits, pointing to him with the marker. "But I'm guessing she was never in close contact with Tiny, was she? And her change happened shortly after you all arrived, I believe. His proximity effect never had a chance to work on her. It was already too late."

Jacob starts to argue but stops. "Proximity effect?"

"Yes, that's what I'm calling it for now. But let's keep going. You find Tiny, and not long after that Lord starts to go Gray. You couldn't know it at the time, but his change would not be like any other. He only partially transformed. And you, Scout, you did the same. My theory is that something in your family genetics gives you a kind of limited immunity, or going Gray somehow impacts you differently. There's no way I can know which. But whatever it is, your brother figured this out after the fact, which is why he bit you. He was hoping to transfer this incomplete immunity to you, in case you didn't possess it already. My guess is he didn't need to, but he couldn't know that. My grasp of genetics is basic at best, but I'd say whatever gift he wanted to share with you, you already had it."

This is all coming so fast I can barely keep up. Proximity effect? Partial immunity? How would that even happen? I mean, sure, some people have a much hardier immune system than others, but would that carry over to something like going Gray? Two people in a family get a cold, and while one might only suffer sniffles for a few days, the other one feels like death warmed over for weeks. Or one might get horribly sick, and the other never does at all, even though they live together. It used to happen to my parents all the time.

Jacob steps forward again. "Hold on. That doesn't explain Hunter. And Singer. Why wouldn't they go completely Gray? Are you saying they have this genetic immunity, too? Sorry, but that's too far-fetched to me. Three of these people, all just happening to find each other like this? And all with this immunity?"

"Good point," Google replies, tapping his temple, perhaps as a sign of respect. "But you would be wrong. Hunter and Singer don't naturally possess that immunity. Or they didn't. My guess is Scout passed hers on to each of them."

I shake my head. "Wait. What? Passed it on? How?"

"Hunter kissed you, right? Which means you, shall we say, exchanged bodily fluids with him. Saliva. The transfer, for lack of a better term, must have happened then. And you and Singer have been in a relationship for some time now. I have to assume you've done the same to him. My theory is that whatever level of immunity you possess, you unknowingly passed it to them."

Singer and I exchange knowing glances. Of course we've kissed. Dozens of times. Perhaps hundreds. And Hunter and I certainly did, even though it was totally against my will. I even recall the taste of blood when he forced his mouth on mine. I don't know if the blood was mine or not, but now I'm grossed out that it could have been his.

"I thought so," he continues, our silence confirming his assumption. "And you may wonder why your brother's change was so much more complete than yours. My sense is that either your immunity is stronger, or your prolonged exposure to Tiny helped moderate your symptoms. In fact, if you had found him days or weeks earlier, you may not have changed at all. His proximity effect again. Tiny's natural immunity and ability to pass it on has not only kept everyone else here on the island from going Gray, but may have tempered your change, too. I think the longer people stay near him, and the more contact they have with him, the more it stops or hinders the process from taking place at all."

"Like Annie," I mumble out loud, but to myself. "She's with him constantly, and she's still completely normal. She should have changed by now. She's one of the oldest ones here. Way over 240 months."

"Exactly. My guess is everyone here at Church Island is basically immune now, and will never go Gray."

None of us say anything after Google delivers that bombshell. Jacob stumbles back and almost falls on his cot in shock. Singer gropes for my hand, and this time I gladly accept his touch. This is amazing. Is this it? Do we really have a cure?

Singer says, "Tiny is like some kind of living vaccine? Something in him somehow stops the process from happening, and because of him everyone at Church Island is cured?"

Google pauses to think. "I can't say for sure, but the facts and the timeline don't lie. And no, before you ask, I don't have any way of knowing if his presence is required forever, or if you just have to have prolonged contact with him for a while. Also, will his abilities increase as he gets older? Will they diminish? I have no idea. We'd have to set up several control groups before we could be sure, and I don't know how we'd do that here. Plus, who would want to risk something so potentially dangerous and deadly by being in a placebo group?"

I think back to when we first found Tiny. I didn't want to take him with us. Back then, before Church Island, I was convinced little ones were nothing but a burden in this awful world. In fact, at one point I didn't even want to bring Carly with us. Kids are too hard to take care of, and they slow you down and consume limited resources. For a second, a sickening dizzy sensation rolls over me and my knees feel weak.

What would have happened if I had successfully lobbied against them? What if we had left Tiny to die? My god, we would have lost our only chance at survival. At salvation.

"In other words," Jacob says, staring at something a million miles away, "we have to do whatever we can to keep him safe. And I mean whatever it takes."

Google nods. "Oh, yes. He's vitally important. And not just to the people here, but perhaps for the entire world. We can't know if he's the only person or not with this ability. He could honestly be the only way humankind survives all this."

I suddenly sit up straight, my eyes alight. For the first time in a long while, I allow hope to establish a foothold in my heart. Google just said it. Tiny could be the savior of humanity. He could save hundreds. Thousands. Maybe even more!

"We need to take him out into the world," I proclaim to the room. My voice is strong and resolute, so determined that Google takes a step back. "We've been wrong all along. I'm not the Firebrand. Tiny is! Tiny is the true Firebrand. We need to share him with the rest of the world. Expose him to as many people as we can. If he's the cure, we need to do this. This is what we're meant to do!"

I see the realization light up Singer's face. Google, usually numb to overt displays of emotions, lets himself smile, his wise eyes crinkling behind those huge lenses. I'm happy he's reacting like this, because it means I'm on the right track.

Reaching for Singer, I draw him into a massive hug. Anyone else I squeezed that hard would suffer several fractures, but he can take it. I carefully pull Google into the embrace, and start laughing in relief. I may be crying and laughing at the same time, but they're tears of joy. There's finally something we can do, some way of putting a stop to all this senseless death! It's what I've been dreaming of for so long!

"Hold on. Not so fast," Jacob says, and something in his tone threatens to extinguish all traces of our optimism. Slowly, I turn to him. He's standing with his arms crossed, and even here in this small room his strained expression looks miles away from us.

"You heard what Google said. We don't know what this 'proximity effect' Tiny has might really do," he continues. 'What if you take him and our immunity wears off? What if you leave with him and we all start going Gray?"

Singer takes a sudden step toward him, but Jacob doesn't back down. He makes eye contact with each of us in turn.

"No, as leader of Home, I can't allow that."

I shake my head, desperately hoping I heard him wrong. "What are you saying?"

"I'm saying," he states flatly, leaving no room for misinterpretation. "That Tiny stays here. With us. And that's final."

CHAPTER
EIGHT

The devastation I felt when Lord took a hike wounded my spirit so deep, I was sure I'd never recover. Those first days of denial are a black blur to me, a period of depression beyond anything I thought possible. Only with the help of Carly and Singer was I able to navigate my way out of those depths and back to the light. And even now, if I think too hard about it, I can fall back into that morass of hopelessness.

But this…this is even worse.

To know that we may have finally found some way to prevent the deaths of so many people, and be blocked from using it? To possess a way of halting the possible destruction of humankind, just to be stopped by the decision of a single person? I feel a tremendous flush of rage boil up inside me, and simultaneously sense the familiar cluster of bees buzzing at the base of my skull. Despite myself and not even willing it to happen, I suddenly snap into slo-mo.

The world around me stops, like always. The

sound of people talking is cut off. The flickering of the candle flames becomes oddly hypnotic, as if they are performing a gentle, underwater dance. Google is standing there with a slightly bemused expression locked on his face. Singer is frozen where he stands, his eyes just flaring up in anger at Jacob's proclamation. Except for the rare one-off, I've always been under attack or physically threatened for slo-mo to kick in. Google once told me he thought getting mad would do it, but I've never been able to control it to that extent before.

The problem is I don't have an outlet for it. My rage is directed at Jacob and his refusal to let us share Tiny. I could push myself through the wet concrete in this slo-mo world and take him out with no effort at all. A simple punch, or a light push into the wall, is all it would take. I could snuff out his life with no more effort than it takes to squash a spider. We could take Tiny, and no one could stop us. But that's not how I'm wired, damnit.

My fury starts to abate, and just like that the bees cease their buzzing and I feel myself return to normal. The slo-mo came and went so quickly that Jacob and the rest didn't even realize it happened. Singer continues staring daggers at Jacob, who is resolutely holding his ground against our combined anger. I kind of hate him right now, even though I admire his determination.

"I'm sorry," he continues, unaware of how close

he just came to personal harm. "I'm in charge here, and I have to look out for my people. Until we figure out how Tiny's immunity is spread, and if it sticks around or not, I can't let him go anywhere."

I take a step toward him. "And how the hell are we going to do that?" I snap, my voice cracking. "You heard Google. There's no way of doing that without a control group, which we can't do. If we don't take him out of here and share him, you might save everyone on Church Island, but you'll be committing the rest of the world to death."

Jacob's face crumples, but his resolve doesn't. He puts one trembling hand to his forehead in despair. "Don't you think I know that?" he cries out. His tortured expression is of a man staring at his desolate existence in a shattered mirror. "But Eve put me in charge. She told me to take care of everyone, and it's my job to make sure they're safe. That's what I'm doing."

"So that's it?" Singer asks, his own rage churning just below his usually sedate surface. I've never seen him like this, and it's a little scary, to be honest. He takes another step toward Jacob, but I reach out and take hold of his arm. He could easily shake it off, but he doesn't.

Jacob exhales a long breath through trembling lips. "Yes, I'm afraid it is. My decision is final. Tiny stays here. I'm sorry."

With that, he pushes himself off the cot and hurries past us and out of the room, anxious to get away from so much combined rage. We all turn to watch him go, then look back at each other in stunned silence. After a few strained moments, Google gently places his marker in the tray at the base of the whiteboard.

"Well," he says with a grunt of amazement, "I considered quite a few outcomes from all of this, but I never saw that coming."

Back in the library, we light a few candles to help chase away the dark, although they do nothing to ease our black moods. Outside, daylight has almost retreated completely and I can't see much of anything, but that's fine with me. I'm not really focusing on the outside world. My thoughts are all internal, fury mixing with sadness and despair in a combination of emotions too complicated for me to describe.

"We could just take him, you know," Singer says from behind me. "They couldn't stop us."

I don't answer immediately. I've already considered that, of course. We could take him and there's nothing they could do about it. Singer and I are more than a match for anything these muggles could muster against us.

"Yeah, I know," I sigh. "But they'd try to stop us, you know they would. They'd be following orders, like they're supposed to do. And what are we going to do? Hurt them? Kill them? It would happen, you know.

It's inevitable. I can't do that. These people are our friends."

He sighs in reluctant agreement, and joins me at the window. We both know there's no version where that wouldn't end badly for a lot of innocent people. And what if Tiny got hurt? The little guy doesn't have any special powers. He could easily be injured or even killed if things went sideways.

"I know," he sighs. He puts both hands on the windowsill and stares blankly outside. Between us we have two perfectly good sets of eyes, but at this moment they see nothing but a murky path leading to humanity's end.

"I don't know if I can stay here any longer," I tell him, putting into words what I've been considering since Jacob's decision. "Not now. Not knowing the cure is here and we can't do anything about it."

He doesn't appear shocked at my statement. "Yeah, I get it. I don't think I can, either. Where would we go?"

I sweep my hand across the darkened ice in front of us. "Out there. Somewhere. I don't know. Maybe we could find someone else like Tiny. There have to be others like him, right? I can't sit here doing nothing while so many people out in the world are going to change and die. It would be too painful."

Singer nods. "Okay. I go where you go, Scout. It's you and me."

I feel a lump forming in the back of my throat,

and I lean my head against his arm. He has an uncanny way of saying the right thing at just the right time, and for that I'll always be grateful. Yeah, this world is just a few degrees short of total crap, but a part of me is happy things have gone this way. I mean, I wouldn't have met Singer otherwise.

"Thanks," I tell him. "Just you and me, against the world."

We stay there for a while longer, until the darkness outside is complete and all we can see are our own distorted reflections in the glass. Eventually we blow out the candles and crawl into bed, not even bothering to get undressed. I'm almost asleep when I feel Singer cover us both with a blanket. I think he says something to me then, but I'm already out.

Eve is here with me again. It's as real as before, but this time there's no panic or pending emergency to freak me out. My head is in her lap and she's stroking my hair, her fingers working through the knots and snags. The fabric of her green robe is coarse against my cheek. She's murmuring something to me, words or phrases I can't hear or understand. But whatever she's saying is working because I feel the tension flowing away from my soul like released water easing pressure from a dam. I want to talk to her, but she puts a finger to my lips and smiles. Her mouth moves and I swear she says something about me and Tiny. I snuggle deeper into her lap, happy, but I'm not quite as content as I should be. I have the nagging feeling I should be doing something. Or going somewhere.

When I open my eyes, it's still nighttime. Eve is gone, but that urge to do something hasn't faded. There aren't any clocks so I don't know what time it is. It feels like the middle of the night. There are no sounds coming from outside of the library. I lay there for a long time, Singer's head close to mine. I listen to his steady breathing, long and slow, in and out. He snores once in a while, a little snorting noise that makes me giggle under my breath. Annie still shares the library with us, but I don't think she ever came to bed last night. I assume she's staying with Tiny down in the lower rooms where it's warmer.

After what has to be an hour or so, the first rays of the sun throw a thin sliver of light against the far wall. After six years of rain and gloomy skies, seeing the sun come up each day is still a wonderful sight, almost a miracle. I ease out of bed and pad silently over to the window. A tiny slice of the sun is visible on the distant horizon. The sky above it is a thousand different shades of pink and orange, a watercolor vista growing clearer and brighter as it washes out the colors a little more with each passing second. The ground below is still too dark to make anything out, but the walls of the church I can see are changing from neutral shades of black and gray to their true colors. It's so pretty that for a few moments I forget about all our problems, which is a blessing. I sigh out loud and try to remind myself that, despite everything, I'm still alive and with Singer.

A movement down in the parking lot catches my eye. At first, I figure it must be one of the guards on rounds and don't give it too much thought. Then I spot someone else, then another. I stand on my tip-toes and peer down, trying to pierce the gloom, but the angle isn't great and I can't make anything out for sure from up here. In fact, a few moments pass and I don't see anything at all. I figure the darkness is simply playing tricks on my eyes. Then I catch more move-ment and I jerk upright, my system suddenly flush with adrenaline. I rush over and shake Singer so hard I nearly throw him out of bed.

"Wake up!" I shout at him. "Singer, wake up!"

He shoots up in bed, his head twisting back and forth in alarm. "What? What is it?"

Just then the church bell starts ringing. Not the slow and easy ring of a Sunday morning calling peo-ple to worship, but a long, constant peal that splits the air like an ax. Over the din of the clanging bell, voices can be heard shouting. Footsteps are pounding up and down the hallways.

I pick up Chuck and slam him into the sheath on my thigh as Singer leaps out of bed, unsure what's happening. I grab his shoulders. Our noses are only inches apart.

"Grays are on the island!" I scream at him.

CHAPTER
NINE

We fly out of the library and into pandemonium. People are scrambling everywhere, sprinting towards the steps at either end of the room, banging into each other, some even getting knocked down. Half a dozen younger kids are crouched against the walls, sobbing in fear, not knowing what to do or where to go. Singer spots them too, and together we round them up and herd them into the library.

"Lock the door behind you, and don't open it for anyone but us!" I shout at them. Heads nod in teary unison as they pull the door shut. Once I'm sure it's locked, we dash down the steps and into the sanctuary. The second we run in, multiple gunshots as loud as thunder fill the room, the muzzle flashes imprinting on my eyes. Blue and red blobs cloud my vision. Guards high on the scaffolding are firing out the windows, screaming at each other in panic. Others are launching arrows, but those muted twangs are lost in the overwhelming roar of the guns.

"We've got to make sure Tiny is safe!" I scream above the noise, my hands cupped to my mouth. "And Carly, too!"

Singer nods. "Want to split up? You head back and go to the gym, and I'll take the steps to the basement."

More people are scrambling up the scaffolding to lend a hand. I quickly glance around for Jacob, Simon, or the little kids, but they're not here. I'm so scared I'm shaking, but I can't let that stop me.

"Okay," I yell at him. "Meet you at the furnace room. Stay safe!"

He doesn't wait but takes off at a dead run for the basement door at the far end of the room. I sprint back the way we came, up the small flight of steps to the fellowship room, and then down the stairs towards the gym, taking them three at a time. I burst into the gym, and spot a dozen kids huddled against the back wall. I catch a glimpse of a black-haired head in the crowd, and scream out Carly's name so loud it tears at my throat. Her head pops up, and when she sees me, she runs and crashes into my legs.

"Oh, Scout, what's happening?"

I hug her and rub her back, feeling her trembling. "I don't know, honey, but I need you to stay with me."

I don't give her a chance to respond, but latch onto her wrist and drag her with me to the classrooms, the other kids following close behind. There are other children already in there, but Tiny isn't one of them.

"Where's Tiny? Has anyone seen Tiny?" Several heads shake no. "Okay. Just stay in here. Lock the door and stay here. Got it?"

An older girl steps up and slams the door, and I hear it lock. Carly and I check the other rooms, but they're empty. We run to the kitchen where we nearly crash headlong into Harold. He's got a butcher knife in each hand, holding them like he knows how to handle himself in a fight. Unlike everyone else, his face is calm, almost serene.

"What's going on?" he asks, his head unmoving, but his eyes darting around behind us.

"I don't know. I think Grays are on the island. I'm trying to find Tiny. Have you seen him?"

"No. I haven't been out of the kitchen."

"Damn! Okay, I'm going to check the furnace room."

He dips his head in a nod. "Cool. I'm coming with you."

We take off at a run down the hall, and I nearly crash headlong into Singer. When he sees Carly, the relief on his face is clear.

"Come on," I tell him. He flings open the heavy door so hard it crashes into the brick wall behind it. I nearly collapse in delight when I spot Tiny and Annie pressed up against the far wall under the windows. Susan is standing guard over them, or at least that's what I think she's doing. She's all twitchy, her hands fluttering at her side like a pair of wounded birds. She senses the nearby Grays, I'm sure of it. She's still sporting the black and white poncho. The way it billows out around her makes her look even larger and more imposing than usual.

"What's happening?" Annie screams, her arms wrapped protectively around Tiny.

"I think Grays are on the island."

"Oh, no! How? What are we going to do?"

Now that I'm here, I realize what a great question that is. To be honest, I don't know. But, if I've learned nothing else throughout all this, I know when you're being attacked it's always best to take the high ground. This furnace room may be as sturdy as a bunker, but there's just the one exit, and being trapped in this horrible place terrifies me. We need to get out of here and head up, perhaps back to the library. It's the safest place I can think of.

"Follow me," I order everyone. "We gotta go. It's not safe here."

Annie starts to protest, but I yank Tiny from her arms. We're about to step into the hallway when Singer pats at his side. He smacks a palm to his forehead.

"Damnit, I forgot my knife. I left it upstairs."

Harold doesn't offer one of his, so I pull Chuck out and thrust it toward him handle first. It feels weird to voluntarily pass him along to someone else, even if that someone else is Singer.

"Here. Take Chuck. I'm carrying Tiny and we may need you to have both hands free."

He takes the knife from me, and hefts it once. He's

smart and follows my logic without another word. We take off out the door and back towards the gym. I chance a look over my shoulder and see Susan bringing up the rear, which even in my terrified state I find interesting since I never explicitly ordered her to do it. I hope no one freaks out that she's with us and tries to kill her, but Jacob said he already spread the word about her, and with the black and white blanket on she looks less threatening. We sprint through the open space and run up the steps, passing panicked guards as we go. There are more shots echoing from the sanctuary, and some sustained yelling, high-pitched screams of fear that barely resemble human voices. When we get to the library, I see the door is standing wide open and the room is empty. Cursing loudly, we pile in and I slam and lock the thick wooden door behind us. Susan faces the doorway stoically, as if this is just another day at the office for her.

"The kids! What happened to the kids we left here?" Singer shouts, spinning around, as if they could be hiding behind the furniture or drapes.

I shake my head. "Damn it! I don't know. Someone must have come for them."

He growls under his breath in frustration, the tendons in his neck throbbing. Tiny is clutching onto me with all his might, trembling. Carly's had an almost normal life lately, with time and new experiences painting over the canvas of her terrifying past. But now she's clutching at Annie's legs and whimpering softly, her face white beneath her jet-black hair. I feel terrible for both of them, but all I can do now is protect them with my life. Which is what I'm willing to do.

Outside the window, the sun is up and we can see the parking lot and areas beyond. The ice that covers nearly everything as far as we can see has subtly changed again. There are lighter and darker patches scattered randomly around, reminding me of black and white pictures of the moon's surface. In a few spots it looks like it's melted completely, icy water showing through. Below us, close to the building, I see a handful of bodies strewn about. Grays, now dead and locked in those awkward poses that can only take place through violent death. The bell in the tower sputters and stops ringing. I reach out a hand and grab Singer's arm.

"The bell. What does that mean?" I ask, my voice a low hiss that still sounds loud in this sudden silence.

Instead of answering, Singer quickly steps around Susan to the door. He puts his ear to the dark wood and listens. With an anxious glance my way, he slowly reaches down and unlocks it. I take a half-step toward him, ready to protect the kids, but he waves me back. Chuck in one hand, he opens it a crack, and peers out. After a second, he exhales and throws it open all the way. Jacob, sweating and breathing hard, is standing there with a pistol in his hand. People are milling around behind him, but they're no longer freaking out and panicking like something from a mob scene.

"Oh, good, it's you. It's okay," he pants, wiping sweat from his forehead with a hand that trembles from adrenaline, nerves, and fear. "We got 'em all. It's okay now. Thank god you've got Tiny with you and he's safe."

I puff air through pursed lips and stare at the ceiling in relief. It's amazing how a shared threat like this can temporarily diminish my earlier anger and frustration with Jacob. To be fair, I'm just glad he and everyone else seem to be okay. Now that the threat has passed, Annie slumps to the bed and starts to cry, her sobs coming in staccato snatches. Carly plops to the floor with a thud, not even bothering to brush the hair out of her eyes. I think she's too stunned to cry.

"What the hell just happened?" Singer asks Jacob.

He shakes his head. "We don't know. Eight Grays somehow got enough balls to cross the ice. They were over here before we knew it. They were trying to get in the church but couldn't. We were able to take them out. A few came really close."

Annie looks up. Sniffing away tears, she asks, "How close?"

"Let's just say I'm glad the front doors are really solid."

She gasps and reaches out a hand to Carly. The rest of us look at each other with wide eyes. I think it dawns on all of us that the once-invulnerable Church Island may not be so invulnerable after all.

Jacob scratches his head. "Funny thing, though. I had sentries outside the church, but the Grays didn't go after them. They just wanted inside."

That strikes me as odd, but I don't have time to wonder about it right now. Singer sighs and rubs a hand over his face. "How many does that leave over at Cedar Ridge?"

"I don't know," he replies. "Dozens. Maybe more. Maybe fifty."

"Christ. How are we going to stop all of them if they decide to cross at the same time?" Singer demands, leaning closer to Jacob to get his point across. "I mean, eight was almost more than you guys could handle. If they all come at once, we're screwed. Scout and I can do a lot, but that's too many even for us!"

Jacob doesn't answer right away. He's staring at us like I used to stare at math problems on the board in school, praying an answer would come to me if I stood there long enough. Like me back then, he doesn't have a clue, and either doesn't want to admit it, or is scared to. Even though he's pissed me off lately, situations like this make me feel sorry for him. Thankfully he's in charge here, not me.

The three of us take turns looking at each other in a three-way staring contest, as if we're waiting for a cartoon light bulb to pop into life over someone's head. Seconds pass, and no light bulb, real or otherwise, manifests itself. I let my gaze slip to the sun shining in the window, then I spot the bucket there on the floor. I remember pouring the contents out the window and into the downspouts. Something comes to me.

"Jacob, do we have a long hose anywhere?"

He lifts an eyebrow at me. "A hose? You mean, like a firehose? "

"No, not a firehose. A garden hose. Or better yet, hoses. Plural. Do we?"

"I don't know. Maybe. Why?"

"Yes or no."

While Jacob scratches his head and thinks, Harold speaks up. He's been so quiet I almost forgot he was here. "Yeah, sure. In the maintenance shed out back. There's a bunch of garden hoses and other stuff there. Why?"

I smile, which feels weird and out of place after what we just went through. Carly must sense something positive in the conversation, because her big eyes have regained their focus and she's staring hopefully at me. I give her a nod and a little smile.

"Go find Google," I tell Jacob. "I've got something I need to run by him."

Several hours later, Google and I are standing outside in the parking lot, sweating in the hot sun. We've been working hard out here, along with as many people as Jacob could spare. Our resident genius nods his head and glances sideways at me, his thick glasses reflecting the bright sunlight.

"Actually, Scout, I'm impressed. This is a good idea."

Wow. Google just gave me a compliment? The way he said it wasn't very complimentary, however, like he was congratulating a dog for sitting on command, but I'll take what I can get. I'm telling myself I don't really care what he thinks of me, but earning some praise from him is a rare event indeed.

Gone is the cold snap that accompanied the blizzard. It's really warm out now, at least in the 70s. The sun shining brightly overhead makes my scalp itch. The "pale as a vampire" look most of us have lived with for the last five or six years is gone. In fact, with so much time in the sun since the rains stopped, I'm quite a few shades darker than I have been, my arms and face tanning nicely. Others, like poor Simon, haven't been faring as well, with any exposed skin now a bright red that will hurt like hell tonight. The heat coming off the asphalt parking lot is so intense I can feel it seeping through the soles of my shoes.

Besides the people that have been helping us, there are a ton of guards outside the church, in the parking lot, and in full view of Cedar Ridge. Every one of them, whether boy or girl, is armed to the teeth, a few of them loaded down with so many weapons I'm curious how they plan to walk, much less fight. I've also noticed they've calmed down a lot since the attack. Some of the boys are being boys, joking around, elbowing their friends, and giving each other crap about their aim, or how they screamed like a girl during the attack. Typical boy stuff. *Bloodied.* Yeah, they've been bloodied by that earlier assault, which should help them maintain their cool next time. Simon, pink neck and all, stands a little distant from the rest. He's here to keep an eye on the Grays still grouped together across the channel, ready to warn us if they make a move.

We've been working nonstop at my Google-approved defensive measure for hours, but now we're done. I step back and admire our handywork. To be fair, it doesn't look like much. Okay, it pretty much doesn't look like anything at all, just a long string of garden hoses linked together, starting out of sight on the roof of the church and ending in a garden-variety spray nozzle down here. Singer steps up between me and Google, sweat glistening on his skin and dripping from the ends of his black hair. A drop dangles from the tip of his nose.

"Think this will work?" he asks, wiping at his forehead with the back of his hand.

I've sweated through my T-shirt. It's all clingy and uncomfortable again, and I pluck at it to pull it away from my skin. "I don't know. Maybe. Google seems to think it will. Right?"

"Oh, yes, it's basic physics," Google chimes in. "You can't argue with gravity."

Singer grunts quietly. "Let's hope so."

"I wouldn't worry too much," Google adds. "As warm as it is, the rest of the ice in the channel will melt in the next few days. Grays won't be able to cross after that. They have shown they may come over ice, but they can't swim. That's a fact. Again, like gravity."

I've never wanted the sun to keep beating on us as much as I do then. On the other hand, this relentless heatwave and lack of rain will continue to dry up the channel, which will eventually give them easy passage across. I don't want to mention this, but I do anyway.

"Yes, but that's a problem for another day," Google says. "We need to survive this first."

Eerily pragmatic of him. But while that's disheartening and a problem for future Scout, here and now Scout is pretty relieved. As my Dad used to say, "Do what you can, with what you have, where you are." Sage advice, Dad. I can almost hear him reciting that in my head, and it makes me smile a little, small crinkles forming at the corners of my mouth. Thinking of my Dad reminds me of something.

"Hey, has anyone talked to Ted lately?"

Google and Singer exchange a look between them. Both shake their heads.

I stab a thumb over my shoulder at the church. "Let's go see how he's doing while we've got a break. I'm wondering if he's seen anything weird lately. Come on. You too, Google. We'll need you."

Ted is, for lack of a better term, an anomaly. When I found him, I was the first person he'd seen up close for five years. It was quite a shock to him. It was also a shock to me, since Ted is over 50 years old and hasn't gone Gray yet. We originally thought it was because he was locked in the Mound, an old nuclear facility that was shielded and hermetically sealed from the outside world. The Mound has its own air and water. We figured that somehow kept him from changing.

But later, when he knew we were in trouble, he courageously left the protection of the Mound and came out to help us. I was sure he'd start to change after that, but he never did. He's still himself, looking every bit like an aging hippy, and the oldest man I've seen in half a decade. Somehow, and we may never know how, he's never gone Gray.

The three of us leave the parking lot behind and head toward the church entrance. Once inside, we open a door heading up a rickety stairway that's got all the ambiance of a haunted house. The interior walls are rough and unfinished with clumps of dried plaster oozing between wooden slats. Spiderwebs and dust lay thick and almost undisturbed. Whoever built this church must not have thought much of the guy charged with ringing the bell, because they sure didn't feel the need to pretty this part up. There's a rope as thick as my wrist dangling down, knotted at the end, and vanishing into the darkness above us. I lead the way up the steps to a landing, then continue up a half a dozen more until we're on a narrow platform that rings the small space at the top. The church bell itself is next to us, a massive thing of unbelievably thick, dark metal. Its matte black surface is covered in dust and a ton of unbecoming bird crap. Tucked in a corner is Google's shortwave radio on a small desk. It's covered with some plastic sheeting to protect it from the elements.

Google pulls off the plastic, folding it up neatly and setting it on the floor next to him. He scoots out a small stool and sits, wiggling his butt to get comfortable. He fiddles with some wires and connects them to the battery, then flicks a switch. Lights across the radio pop to life and he adjusts a few dials. I'm glad he knows what he's doing, because I certainly don't.

"Anyone know how to work this thing except you?" I ask, watching his hands move.

He doesn't answer for a moment, still concentrating. "Simon has been up here a few times with me. He's getting the hang of it. It's really not that hard, as long as no idiot changes the settings."

We lugged the equipment up here after we arrived. We don't have an antenna except the small one we brought with us, and Google insisted the equipment needed to be as high as possible. From what little I know, being up high isn't crucial since shortwave signals bounce off the atmosphere, or something like that, but he insists the higher we are the better it works. This hunk of electronic wizardry is his baby, and I've learned to never mess with anyone's baby.

He clicks the microphone button. "Ted, are you there? Come in, Ted."

We wait, hearing only hissing static. He repeats himself several more times, but the only response is the same white noise.

"Maybe he doesn't have it on," Singer says.

"Maybe," Google replies. "Let's hope that's all it is."

Great, now I'm starting to be concerned, and it's not like we didn't have enough to worry about already. After the tornado and Hunter's attack at Cedar Ridge, a few of us took some boats filled with supplies to the Mound. We spent a few days with Ted, relaxing, eating enough candy to make us twitchy, and taking showers. Yeah, real ones, with hot water and everything. Those were glorious days. In the end, we asked him to join us here at Church Island, but he declined. He thought it would be weird. Not that there was anyone around who would give a damn, but he thought an old guy living with a bunch of kids on an island sounded a little too "pedophilish," if that's even a word. Plus, he wanted to keep an eye out down south. It all made sense, even though I hated leaving him alone in that huge network of caves and rooms under the mountain. Now, standing here and not getting any response from the shortwave, I'm starting to worry my gut was right and letting him stay there was a bad decision.

Suddenly there's a crackle from the little speaker and I jump. "Hey, guys, this is Ted," he says, his voice electronic and flat.

I snatch the mic from Google's hand, ignoring his disapproving glare. "Hey, Ted. We were getting worried about you. How's it going?"

"Oh, hi, Scout. It's fine, besides the normal crushing boredom, of course. That freaky blizzard a few days ago broke up the monotony. I'm assuming you got that, too?"

I click the mic and bypass any more pleasantries, filling him in on the last few days. The storm, the attack, Susan, and anything else I can think of. Except for my dreams with Eve. I keep those to myself, more and more convinced they were nothing but weird hallucinations brought on by the cold, stress, and my near-death experience. That's a thing, right?

"I'm just glad you're all okay," he says when I finally finish.

"Thanks. Do me a favor and take Curly out and check around, will you? Just to be sure."

Besides the boring but civilized surroundings Ted has at his disposal in the Mound, he used to have three drones he could control and use to scout out the area. He called them Larry, Curly, and Mo, three names Simon found highly amusing for some reason. Unfortunately, Mo and Larry ran out of juice and plunged to their deaths earlier, but Curly is still operational. It's Ted's last window to the world outside of his caves, and he guards it jealously. Can't say I blame him.

"Yeah, okay, I can do that. It's a nice day and he's all charged up. Anything in particular you're looking for?"

I glance at the other two with me for direction. Neither offers anything. "I don't know for sure, but does it make sense to say you'll know it when you see it? Any Grays gathered together. Weird activity. Stuff like that. Anything out of the ordinary."

Ted's on board with that. He asks for an hour, and

we sign off. While we wait, Google spins through different settings on the dial in search of other signals. A few times we hear a sound or two, a strange garbled bit of static or an alien off-key guitar chord, but that's it. He swore he once heard a syllable or two, but this lack of results is what we've come to expect.

When about an hour has ticked away, Google returns the dial to its original setting, and we wait. I brush away cobwebs from the low rafters and peek through the slats on each side of the bell tower, paying particular attention to the improved view across the channel. I'm not sure if it's a good thing or not, but nothing over there seems to have changed. We're all getting a little antsy when we hear a click.

"You guys still there?" he says, and there's a wobble in his voice that makes me stand up straight. Singer hears it too.

"Yeah, we're here," I respond, the microphone suddenly slick and sweaty in my hands.

"You know, since the rains have stopped, I can see a lot more. Curly's camera is amazing, to be honest. I don't have to take him out as far as I used to. I can go higher instead and zoom in."

"And?" I ask, anxious to hear where he's going with all this.

"And I can see a lot more exposed land than I used to. A bunch more each time I take him out, as a matter of fact. The water is receding from places faster and faster. I can clearly make out the old waterline, since there's all kinds of muck and trash up to where it used to be. There's a ton more land, old roads, and the remains of buildings visible, too. But that's not all. I spotted Grays. A lot of them. It looks like they're all heading roughly south. I've never seen anything like it. If I didn't know better, it looks like a mass migration or something."

I gulp. "Why? Any idea what they're up to? This isn't how they usually act."

"No kidding," he replies. "Before, I've only seen them in small packs. Two or three at the most. But there are hundreds of them. I wish I could take Curly farther and see where they're going, but I can't risk him. He's getting old and his stamina isn't what it used to be." He chuckles at something, an inside joke I don't get.

"Did you see any, you know, normal people with them?" I ask, thinking of Hunter. I'm also thinking of my brother, but I keep that to myself.

We can't see him shake his head, but we can hear it in his voice. "I couldn't tell from this high. I'll try again later, after Curly's had a chance to recharge."

Ted and I talk a little more, but he's got nothing else to share besides reiterating his extreme boredom. The highlight of his day is that he's about to whip up some mac and cheese that we left him. He was living off a Willy Wonka diet of candy bars and Coke before I found him. He thanks us for the food, like he does every time we talk. Google tells him he'll be back on-line later, then powers down the equipment.

"What the hell do you think is going on?" Singer asks the two of us.

Google shakes his head. "I don't know. A mass migration? We've never seen anything like that before. But if the actions of the Grays here on Cedar Ridge are any indication, I'd say they're headed somewhere for an attack of some kind. I can't imagine what else they could be up to."

I shudder, then peek through the slats across the channel again, where the fifty or so Grays are still milling around. I don't know where those hundreds of Grays are headed, but I'd sure hate to be there when they arrive.

CHAPTER
TEN

Later on, we meet up with Harold in the kitchen and give him a hand with dinner. Watching him move around the place, I can't help but remember how I saw him during the attack, not at all afraid and with those two big knives at the ready. It reminds me of how the real Scout, my namesake, saw her dad in *To Kill a Mockingbird* when he shot that rabid dog. She witnessed a side of him then that she never knew existed, an unexpected ability that both impressed and startled her. From that point on, he was more to her than just her father, the small-town lawyer. That's how I'm looking at Harold now. He catches me checking him out, and a small grin crosses his face. I swear he wiggles his eyebrows at me, like he's laughing at a shared joke he's making at my expense. Embarrassed that he busted me, I quickly return my focus to stirring the big pot of au gratin potatoes warming in front of me.

After dinner, Singer and I help clean up again. It's tough to do a good job without being able to use much water, but we do our best. Even with all my scrubbing, whatever Harold fixes in that pot tomorrow is going to have a slight hint of cheesy potato in it. I don't think anyone will complain.

Night comes, and Singer, Carly and I are back in the library. It's warm enough now that sleeping with a few additional blankets is just fine for her, and besides, I think she likes being close to us. To be fair, I like her close to me, too. At Jacob's order, Tiny and Annie are still downstairs with him.

Carly's already asleep, her hair an untidy black mop around her face. Singer and I move quietly around the room as we get ready for bed. He blows out the candles and crawls into bed next to me.

"We never really got to finish our conversation," he says quietly, his head next to mind. "We talked about leaving. You still up for that?"

The ceiling above me is one big expanse of black. Eyes opened or closed, it looks the same. I'm sure this is some sort of metaphor for our situation now, that no matter what we do, we have no idea what lies in front of us. I still think we need to move on, to look for others like Tiny who might be able to help, but Church Island is the closest thing to a home most of us have ever had. Plus, there's Carly. Can we really tear her away from here? She was so upset when we left the Motel 6 and the office building. She gets attached to places. If Singer and I leave, can I honestly pull her away? Or worse yet, can I bring myself to leave her behind?

"I don't know if we should," I finally answer, the darkness above pressing down on me. I tell him what I've been thinking about Carly.

He shrugs. "I don't know. I'd hate leaving her here, too, but would she be any safer with us? I think that's what we have to figure out before we make a decision. We have to choose what's best for her, you know?"

I roll against him, my face snuggled against his chest. That is the question, isn't it? Is she safer here, with all the defenses Church Island can muster, or with us out on the water? I think I know the answer, it's just one I don't want to accept.

"I think we need to go and see if we can find another Tiny," I finally tell him. "And we should leave them both here. They'll be better off staying, and at least have a chance at a normal life. Or what passes for one. I think the two of us should go. Soon. Maybe tomorrow, before I change my mind."

He doesn't reply but kisses me on the cheek. If he notices the salty taste there, he doesn't bring it up.

The next morning, after a breakfast of powdered scrambled eggs that really did have a hint of au gratin potatoes to them, the two of us start to pack up our few possessions. Carly is downstairs with the rest of the kids. She told me she planned on putting together a show with some of the others, and she'd be ready for us in a little while. She's been performing these lately, ad libbed skits with a few other kids she could convince to play along. Like any good parent, or substitute parent in our case, outwardly we've been very enthusiastic on her behalf, while inside we playfully groan at the thought of sitting through another one of their stage productions. Did my parents have to suffer through these things? Yeah, I'm sure they did. I guess I have to put in my time, too.

My backpack is bulging with everything I own, including some books, my thin blanket, and a supply of small rocks we've been hoarding. We also have beef jerky we've been holding onto, along with some water bottles. Chuck is secure in his sheath on my thigh. Singer is already done packing. I wanted to take the wool poncho with me I found with Susan, but it's so big and bulky I can't fit it anywhere. It's amazing how many things I've accumulated since I've been here that I'll have to leave behind. I used to travel so light. It's time to do that again.

"So how are we going to do this?" he asks. "Pull a Houdini and vanish without saying goodbye? A big farewell? A party? Break out the communion wine again?"

"God no, not the wine. No, as much as I hate goodbyes, we need to do it right. Besides Carly, I need to see Simon and Google before we go. They're our friends, and we owe them that much."

Singer chuckles once. "Google, a friend? He's more android than human, isn't he?"

"Yeah, I guess so, but we've been through a lot. I can't just duck out."

I check a few more pockets in my pack, making sure the little red lighter is there, the one Google found in that old farmhouse. I've kept close track of it ever since. Google may have figured out Tiny is the true Firebrand, but old habits regarding my days tending the fire die hard, and it's comforting to know I've got it. Next to Chuck, it's probably my most valuable possession. Even more so than my books, which is odd for me to say, but I guess I've grown more practical lately. My brother would be proud.

"Works for me," he says, patting his pockets one more time. He removes his pack and adjusts the straps. His is more complex than mine, and comes with an additional strap around his waist to help keep everything stable. He slings it back on and clicks the middle strap together, tugging it tight. It makes him look even thinner, if that's possible.

"As much as I'd like to take my kayak, it only fits one person," I say, adjusting my own shoulder straps. "Guess we'll have to take one of the Jon boats. Ugh. I don't know what else Jacob will let us have as far as supplies go, but one of those annoying things can hold a lot. We may need it."

"And we can also sleep in it if we have to," he adds with a playful twinkle in his eye.

I close my eyes and groan. "Oh please. I swore I would never do that again." But that gets me thinking, and I change my mind and grab the thick wool poncho. The thing is likely impervious to rain, will make a great pillow, and it's already shown it can keep me warm in the worst possible weather. It's so thick and dense I'm guessing it might be bullet-proof, too. I roll it up tight and decide to carry it for now. There'll be plenty of room for it in the boat with just the two of us.

I glance around the library one more time. All the books lining the walls are familiar and welcoming, even the old leather-bound ones with subjects and titles that sound terribly boring. The lending library shelves are where I've spent the bulk of my time. I run my fingers across their frayed paper bindings, savoring the sense of wonder each brings out in me. I don't know when I'll ever see this many books in good condition again. As much as I hate leaving the people here, walking away from such a treasure trove of imagination might be hitting me harder. I sigh and turn away.

"I guess I'm all set. You?"

He's leaning against the doorframe, patiently watching my farewell. He doesn't quite share my love of the printed word, but he understands it. He'd probably feel the same if he had to leave his harmonica behind. He nods at me.

"Yep. I'm ready. Let's roll."

He pats me warmly on the shoulder and we start to walk out. At the last second, I duck back to the shelves and grab a paperback at random, not even looking at the title. I spin him around and cram it into a zippered pocket on his backpack. I don't know what it is, but it's thin and the pages are yellowed.

"What's that?" he asks, twisting his head around in his best owl imitation to see what I stuffed in there.

"I don't know. One for the road, you know?"

He gives me a warm, tolerant grin. "Okay. Now are you ready?"

After one more quick look around, I nod. "Yep. Let's go."

We leave the library. I have a strange feeling I'll never see this place again, and that makes it every bit as sad as I thought it would.

The gym is so thick with bodies it reminds me of my house at Christmas when the relatives would invade. The big room is shoulder to shoulder packed, made even worse since some of the kids have cleared out tables at one end of the basketball court and are playing a game of HORSE to pass the time. Each player in turn takes a shot, and if he makes it then the next kid has to make the same shot from the exact same place. If he misses the shot, he gets a letter starting with H. The first one with HORSE is the loser. The dribbling of the ball on the concrete bangs louder than a string of firecrackers.

We thread our way through the players and the tables where Carly is holding her own type of court with her friends, five or six kids she's been hanging around with. She's the type who makes friends wherever she goes, and Church Island is no exception. When she sees us, her eyes light up and she claps her little hands together.

"Oh, good, you're here. We're just about ready."

I blink. "Ready? For what?"

She rolls her big brown eyes. "For the show, silly. As soon as those annoying boys are done with their game, we're going to put on a show. Remember?"

Ah, yes, her show. I really had forgotten. That, or it was a case of selective amnesia. "Of course. We didn't forget." I deliver a subtle elbow to Singer, who nods along with a grin.

She peers at the packs on our backs. "Where are you going? You're not going out on the ice again, are you? Already? I don't like it when you go."

I thought I could tell her we're leaving, but suddenly I realize I'm not able to. Not yet, at least. Instead, I kneel to her level and take each of her shoulders in my hands. "Let me get those boys out of your way, so you can do your show, okay? How's that?" The non-answer serves its purpose and she smiles wide.

"Okay, thanks!"

She scurries back to her friends while I start clearing out the game of HORSE. Luckily, they were down to two players, and when one of them sinks an impressive hook shot and the other misses, the game is over and a new champion is crowned. I shoo the rest of the players away over their groans and complaints in order to make room for Carly and her theater troupe. There's a set of concrete steps behind them with a small raised platform at the bottom. It's not much of a stage, but it gets them off the floor and slightly above the rest of us. Behind me Singer is rounding up every-one in the room.

"Come on, people," he's telling them in a loud voice. "Let's go. The show's about to start."

As I would expect, not everyone is thrilled to sit through a production put on by a bunch of six-year-olds, but some are bored enough that even this looks interesting. Everyone pulls up a piece of floor and takes a seat, until there are about thirty of us scattered around facing the stage. While the last of them are getting comfortable, Singer moves up front with Carly and her group. Together, they dig through a bag at their feet and start putting on costumes, homemade ones from paper, blankets, and whatever else they've been able to round up. Several of them carefully set cardboard crowns on their heads.

Annie sits down next to me with a grunt. "What's the play?"

"I honestly have no idea. And what's Singer doing up there? Did he help them with this?"

She shrugs, just as confused as I am. "Beats me. Sure looks like it."

When all the kids have their costumes on, Singer turns to us, smiling. He spreads his arms out wide and the audience quiets down.

"Ladies and gentlemen, thank you for coming. Please sit back and relax, and enjoy this production of Shakespeare's classic play, *Hamlet*, as performed by the League of Little Lutherans."

My hand finds my mouth as memories wash over me. *Hamlet* was the book I found back at the Motel 6, before Singer and I became an item. It was the old, crusty lump I could read but not understand, the one Singer read and interpreted for me when we were in the office building. I've carried it with me ever since, protected by a Ziplock bag and my force of will. That time we spent together is when I began to fall for him, and I've been falling for him ever since. He sits down next to me, his smile so big it lights up his entire face.

"*Hamlet?*" I ask, laughing. "You're really going to have these kids perform *Hamlet?* Isn't that a little dark?"

"Oh, absolutely," he replies, laughing right along with me. "They barely have a clue what they're doing. This should be fun."

I drape an arm over his shoulder and rest my head against him as the play begins. A boy slightly older than Carly faces us. He's wearing a paper crown that's too big for his head. It keeps slipping down over his eyes. He lifts a cardboard sword, the point aimed at the ceiling.

"I'm King Hamlet," he proclaims in a high voice that is still dozens of months away from puberty. "But I'm a ghost. I rule these lands."

Carly steps up, also with a crown on her head. "Go away, ghost. I'm the real Hamlet, and I'm a prince!"

"No, you're not," insists the first boy. "You're a girl. If anything, that makes you a princess."

Another boy steps between them, brandishing his sword and looking as menacing as a little kid with a paper crown can. "You're both wrong. I am Lord Chamberpot, and I rule this land!"

Hardly anyone in the crowd would know what a chamber pot is, or that he's actually supposed to be Lord Chamberlain, but his acting is so over the top they all burst out laughing. The plot deteriorates from there pretty fast, until the three boys are dueling with their cardboard swords and Carly is behind them, hopping up and down and trying to get a word in edgewise. After five minutes of this mayhem, Singer gets up and separates the combatants. He tries to line them up to take a bow, but he'd have more luck herding cats.

"And that, ladies and gentlemen," he yells above the laughter, "is *Hamlet*. Let's give them all a hand!"

Nearly as one, we all jump to our feet and applaud. A few people whistle. In hindsight, we all appreciate the entertainment and a break from that strange combination of boredom and tension. Finally, the entire troupe faces the crowd and takes a long bow. Both Hamlets lose their crowns, which causes even more peals of laughter. Carly runs over to me.

"Did you like it?"

"I loved it," I tell her warmly, and she can see in my eyes I'm being sincere. "You'll always be a princess to me."

Her smile is so big and happy I can barely stand

it. She claps a few times in joy, and bounces up and down on her toes.

"I knew you would. Well, Singer knew you would!"

She scampers back to the stage and helps the others stuff their costumes in the bag, chattering with her friends the entire time. Watching her here, seeing how she's grown so much and how happy she is, I'm now convinced I can't take her away. I could tell myself she'd be better off with me and Singer on the water, but that would be a lie. She's safer and happier here than she ever would be with the two of us outside of Church Island. I glance at Singer, and it's as if he knows what I'm thinking. He smiles, but it's tinged with enough sadness that it might as well be a frown.

I reach out to him, but as I do, the church bell explodes into life. The jarring noise is loud even down here, the clanging bouncing off the hard walls. The tender touch I meant for him becomes a panicked grab as I snatch at his arm.

"Oh, no, not again!" I yell.

Singer's about to say something when Simon flies into the room, bent over and gulping for air. His words, when he finally catches his breath, are thick with panic.

"The Grays are coming across the ice. All of them! Let's go!"

He turns and sprints back up the stairs. Most of the people in the gym stare at each other in fear, frozen where they stand, as the lingering echo of Simon's warning fades away. Before I have a chance to react, Singer turns and faces the stunned crowd.

"You heard him, let's go!" he screams, pointing upstairs. "Anyone that can fight, come with us. The rest of you lock yourselves in rooms and don't come out until we tell you it's safe. Now go!"

The force of his command instantly uproots them. Older kids grab younger ones and run for the rooms. Others sprint for the steps, strapping on weapons as they go. I see Carly herding little ones into the classrooms outside the gym, and as much as I hate to leave her, I know we have to. Singer pulls me behind him and I almost trip because I'm too busy making sure she's safe and I'm not watching where I'm putting my feet.

"Come on!" he yells at me. "We've gotta go! If all the Grays are coming, they're going to need all the help they can get."

I'm not used to him being so forceful, but I sort of like this take-charge side of him. The two of us fly up the steps and crash through the side door. The morning sun is bright and hot, temporarily blinding me. When my eyes adjust, I see the sky overhead is a deep blue, like an ocean has been suspended above our heads. It would qualify as a beautiful day pretty much any other time. The two of us take off around the building, passing everyone else as we go. The smacks of our footfalls are loud on the hot asphalt of the parking lot, only partially drowned out by the church bell's frantic ringing.

Ahead of us a dozen or so of Jacob's fighters are setting up in a tattered line, facing the channel. Even though they've been bloodied by the earlier battle, they're fumbling with their weapons and are so jittery I'm surprised they haven't peed their pants *en masse.* Singer and I skid to stop. He snatches a bag from his pack and jams it in my hand. Inside are a hundred or so small rocks, weapons only the two of us can use. I do the same for him. He hefts the bag as if measuring its potential for destruction. Chuck is in my other hand, his blade as shiny as armor.

"You ready?" he asks between tight lips. His deep brown eyes have a hard, flinty edge to them I never figured he'd be able to pull off.

I try to speak, but I'm so nervous my voice has decided to go on strike. All that comes out of my mouth is a weird croak I quickly mask by clearing my throat. Instead, I give him a thumbs up, and together we move to the line of fighters. Jacob is there, baking in the scalding sun. His blond hair is so fine and sweaty he looks bald from ten feet away. He's not nearly as anxious as I expected.

"What are they doing?" Singer asks.

"Not much." Jacob points with the barrel of his pistol, a black revolver with a white handle like something out of a Western. Towards the channel, I see a group of Grays moving toward us. There's a lot of them, but there doesn't seem to be as many as I thought. They're coming directly at us at a pace faster than a walk, but slower than a run, as they pick their way over the ice as if navigating through a minefield.

"Watch," he says, never taking his eyes from the encroaching threat.

I don't understand what he's talking about, and why he isn't more concerned than he is. I stare at the mob coming toward us, and two Grays near the front suddenly vanish through a dark spot at their feet. A magician couldn't have made them disappear any faster.

"They're falling through the ice," I say, my voice working once again. "They're falling in and drowning. Why are they doing that? Why are they so desperate to get over here?"

"That's what I've been wondering," Jacob says.

A word comes to me I've probably never used in conversation before. *Lemmings.* These Grays are like lemmings blindly following each other off a cliff. But as I continue watching, I realize these monsters may be a few IQ points smarter than those rodents. When one or more disappear in front of them, they give that spot a clear berth and keep coming. Their numbers continue to thin, but I'm still afraid a lot will eventually make it here.

"Good riddance," Jacob states. "Let every single one of them fall through. I hope the stupid things all drown."

Another one vanishes through the ice. The remaining mob sees their comrade disappear, and they detour wide. I tug at Jacob's sleeve. "I don't know. A lot could make it. See? They're figuring this out."

A group of twenty or more bypass a huge open area of slushy brown water. Another dozen follows behind them, safely navigating the danger. As close as I can determine, they've already made it more than halfway across. Even worse, the remaining ice between us and them seems to be less hazardous. They pick up speed.

Jacob takes note of this, too. He mutters a curse under his breath and barks some orders, commanding his fighters to shore up the line. Muted whispers come from the armed kids all up and down the row as they watch the Grays advancing. Someone far down the row starts to cry softly. The *click clack* of weapons being loaded is jarring, the metallic sound cutting through the non-stop ringing of the church bell and the pounding of my heart in my ears.

Stepping in front of his fighters, Jacob points at the Grays, now less than a hundred yards away. "Remember," he yells, "always aim for the head. That's the only way. Nothing else will stop them!"

Someone out of sight far down the line jumps the gun and shoots early, a single shot that makes me nearly leap out of my skin. Before Jacob can command them to hold their fire, a dozen more ring out. Thirty or so Grays charge at us and stumble, but keep coming, nearly impervious to injury from this distance.

The advancing creatures continue closing the gap.

They're less than fifty yards from shore, close enough that I can begin to make out specific characteristics here and there, like old scraps of clothing, a sport coat, or a pair of cargo shorts. A shiny belt buckle flashes in the sunlight. One is still wearing a necklace that glitters around its neck. I desperately pray none of them were people that I once knew, kids that we ordered to take a hike in the past. Not that it matters now. No, now they're just Grays, intent on slaughtering us.

When the first one is just a few dozen yards from shore, Jacob's fighters open up in earnest. The gunshots meld into one long roar, like the sound of a hundred bowling balls striking a thousand pins. Smoke rises from around the fighters, and the stench of gunpowder burns the inside of my nose. My eyes begin to sting. The lead Gray twitches and jerks as bullets riddle its body, but it refuses to go down. No one here can shoot well enough to kill it. I hate to say it, but none of them are as good as Hunter.

"Jacob, wait!" Singer yells at him, his hands out. "This isn't working. Let us do what we can. Tell your men to stop shooting. We can help, but we can't dodge bullets."

Kudos to Jacob that he's listening to anyone during all this. He dashes out in front of his fighters, waving his arms and commanding them to hold their fire. It takes a few seconds for them to listen and obey, but finally the shooting stops. Jacob turns to Singer, panting.

"Go. They're all yours. But be ready to get out of

there if things get hairy."

Singer nods at him and takes a deep breath. He's staring at the rushing mob with his knife in one hand and a handful of stones in the other. I see his body shake, vibrating like a plucked piano wire sounding out a note no one can hear. Then he blurs and goes into slo-mo. He's moving almost faster than any of us can follow. He's little more than a smear of indistinct colors as he advances on the charging Grays.

The lead attacker is headed at Jacob. But before it can take another step toward him, a Singer-sized blur passes in front of it and a red line appears below its chin, opening like a grisly second mouth. Slowly, its head tumbles away from its body. Singer, like me, knows how to stop these creatures in their tracks.

Only a second or two later, the five Grays behind the now dead leader spasm and begin to topple over as dime-sized holes appear across their bodies and heads; Singer just launched a fusillade of stones at them. I can't see the full extent of the damage from here, but from experience I know those exit wounds are each the size of a fist. Limbs are blasted off before my eyes, and several of their heads explode like water-melons smacked by a baseball bat. With Singer's tre-mendous strength and speed, each of those stones is deadlier than a missile. Cheers erupt from the fighters as they witness the decimation of the first wave.

But their euphoria is short-lived. The rest of the advancing Grays spread out across the ice and continue charging at us. A few vanish as the ice gives way, but the rest are undeterred and keep coming. I try to count how many are left, but they're moving so fast I can't. There are still dozens, maybe more. But it doesn't matter; there are too many for Singer to handle alone. He's about to be overwhelmed!

And then, finally, I feel the tingle in the back of my neck. My first thought is *it's about damn time!* My second one is, *how does Singer turn his on so easily?* I really need to figure out how to do that before it's too late.

But now is not the time for that. Around me, all sound stops. Well, that's not exactly right. I can't hear the yelling and the ringing church bell any longer, but in their place is the deep rumbling of a distant wave undergoing one long crash as it pounds the shore. The massed Grays spread out in front of me are no longer advancing, but I can finally see Singer clearly again. He's moving forward slowly, his bloody knife held in front of him, his face knotted in a grimace as he forces his way through the wet cement of slo-mo. I'm behind him. He can't tell I'm here, so I try to shout his name to get his attention. My mouth opens but nothing comes out, and I realize for the first time you can't talk in slo-mo. I struggle my way toward him, but each step takes all my strength. Since he's moving forward, too, there's no way I'll ever catch him.

Frustrated, I decide to take the fight to the Grays instead. There are several to his left that are too far away for him to get to, so I head there. The bag of rocks is in my hand, so I grab a handful and fling them at the three. My toss is a low, flat plane, like a pitcher throwing a sidearm fastball. The stones spread out as they leave my fingers, and half a dozen strike the frozen Grays. Just like when Singer did it, bloody holes blossom all over them, and all three will soon be dead. They just don't know it yet.

I fling another handful at a group behind those three, and without waiting to see what happens I grab a third handful and do it again. And again, until the bag is empty. I swivel my eyes toward Singer and see he's doing the same, but it looks like he's almost out of ammo, too. Unfortunately, there are probably twenty of the creatures still standing, and they're so spread out that neither one of us will be able to get to them all. My stomach drops as I realize we're about to be overrun.

I catch movement to my right and see Singer has finally noticed me. Without a pause, he slowly points behind us and up, towards the roof of the church. It takes me a few heartbeats to understand what he's saying, but then it comes to me. *My Google-approved defensive measure.* I give him a glacial nod and turn away, heading back towards the church. I swear, it feels like it takes agonizing hours to get there as I fight through the thickness. I'm almost in tears from the strain of struggling to move, along with worry I've just left Singer alone, but at this moment I realize it might be the only thing that saves us. I finally get to the hose and grab the spray nozzle, uttering a silent prayer my crazy plan might actually work.

Nozzle in hand, I fight my way back toward the Grays. In the time I've been gone, they've advanced another few yards, and out of the corner of my eye I notice Jacob's men are all lifting their guns to fire. Panicking now, because I can tell these idiots are going to start shooting even though the man I love is still out there, I redouble my efforts and push harder than I ever have before. Muscles straining, my eyes watering, I move between them, dragging the hose. When I get to where the ice meets the parking lot, I squeeze the trigger.

And nothing happens.

If I could scream, I would. A long, agonizing one full of frustration and denial. Then I remember everything outside of my slo-mo world still obeys the normal laws of physics, or motion, or whatever. I squeeze the trigger again. And hold it. And pray.

A few dozen of my seconds later, I'm rewarded with a stream of thick reddish-brown liquid oozing slowly out of the nozzle, like Silly Putty being squeezed out of one of those toy hand-presses. My internal scream of agony turns to one of joy, and I aim the liquid down at the ground where it hits the asphalt, splatters, and puddles. I move from one side of the parking lot to the other, always keeping one eye out for Singer, the Grays, and Jacob's men with their itchy trigger fingers. It seems to take all day, but I finally make it to the other end of the parking lot just as the stream from the hose slows, then trickles to a stop. Behind me the thirty-foot-long puddle has spread out to a few feet wide in most places. I drop the hose, and hardly notice when it tumbles gently to the ground.

All this has taken more time than I hoped, and most of the Grays are coming dangerously close to the edge of the ice. Bodies of dead ones are scattered everywhere, most of them courtesy of Singer, but there are still too many for us. Singer sees me and starts to move toward Jacob and his fighters, swimming through the thickening cement in a much more efficient manner than I've ever been able to master. I grab the pack from my back and dig through the pockets, finally locating the small red lighter. I flick the little Bic, but nothing happens, and with a mental curse I realize it probably won't work unless I'm operating in normal time.

Not only do I have problems turning slo-mo on when I want to, I've never been very good at shutting it down, either. It's got an infuriating mind of its own, and usually stops whenever the danger has passed or when I've been injured. I honestly don't know if I can do it on my own. I glance up and I'm shocked to see how close the Grays are, and I try to tamp my panic down. I sit on the hot asphalt of the parking lot, and do my best to calm my nerves. How the hell do people in a crisis relax? I don't know what else to do, so I take a few deep breaths, and close my eyes. I breathe in through my nose, and out my mouth, over and over, and feel my pulse begin to slow. I realize I'm out when, all of a sudden, the deafening sounds of people yelling and gunshots going off crashes into my ears. With a hand that's much steadier than it has a right to be, I flick the little wheel on the lighter. As soon as I'm blessed with a tiny flame, I almost shout with joy and touch it to the puddle in front of me.

Yellow and blue fire leaps up as the fuel oil catches. The flames leap upward several feet high and roar down the long puddle with a mad *whoosh* of displaced air. Where a second ago there was nothing, now there's a thirty-foot-long wall of fire between us and the attacking Grays. Jacob and his men all stumble back in shock, falling over each other, confused and mystified that there's suddenly an inferno in front of them where there was nothing a moment ago. Shouts of surprise ring out as they back away from the intense heat.

As shocked as Jacob and his fighters are, the reaction of the Grays is even more extreme and satisfying. I found out at the Mound they can be temporarily incapacitated by loud noises like the klaxons in the parking lot, and we've always known they have a healthy respect for water and the danger of drowning. But those threats pale against their absolute, primal fear of fire. For whatever reason, this seems baked into their DNA, impacting them in an almost primitive, animalistic way. I'll never forget how Susan took off

when she saw the burning car. She wasn't seen for
months. Even something as small as the lighter's flame
in the basement farmhouse was enough to terrify her.

But that was nothing compared to this.

As one, they scatter faster than roaches under a
kitchen light. A few sprint back the way they came,
heedless of the ice and what it might mean. But as
many as twenty don't retreat. Instead, they take off in
both directions, almost parallel to the intense flames
that are starting to melt the parking lot itself. I can't
tell if this is intentional, or if they're too stupid to
know any better. Either way, as fast as they are, they'll
reach the ends of the flames and will be able to come
at us from both directions.

Dammit to hell. Sorry, Google, but this may not
have been such a great idea after all. I've bought us a
little time, but that's it.

CHAPTER
TWELVE

I don't know where he came from, but all of a sudden Singer is right beside me, blood spatters covering his face and shirt. He yanks me to my feet and we sprint to Jacob's side. People all around us are shouting and panic-firing into the flames as the Grays circle around. Singer and I have our knives out and are ready to fight, but Jacob grabs my arm and pulls me so close the tips of our noses are almost touching.

"Go! Find Tiny and get out of here!" he screams at me.

"What? No! We're not going to leave you here. You'll die," I yell back.

He swiftly levels his revolver over my shoulder and squeezes off three shots. The gun is so close to my ear he may have just deafened me on that side. Behind me I see a Gray that somehow got around the fire already. Jacob's shot blew half its face off, and the creature is on the ground flopping around as if it's being electrocuted. There's an insane quantity of blood already around it on the hot pavement.

"We'll hold them off as long as we can," he barks. "But nothing matters now except Tiny. You've got to save him. For everyone!"

I'm about to shake my head no, but I feel a vice nearly crush my forearm and an irresistible force starts dragging me away. It's Singer, pulling me from the fight. I struggle against him, but I'd have more luck resisting a tow truck. I scream and rant at him to let me go, and try to smack his hand away, but he's not listening to me. My vision is blurring with tears, but even so I can make out more Grays looping around the defensive fire on either end. Jacob's men are hitting them with everything they've got, but it's not going to be enough.

"Let me go!" I cry, still being dragged backwards. "They're all going to die!"

Singer doesn't answer me. Unblinking, he keeps his eyes locked straight ahead of him. His face is a mess, covered with dirt, blood, and tears. His normally tranquil eyes are red and swollen, but we're not stopping.

"Scout, don't fight me. You heard him. We've got to save Tiny."

"But they'll all be killed!"

"And if we stay, we'll die, too. And so will Tiny. And Carly. We've got to get him out of here. It's up to us."

I scream at the heavens in rage and frustration, but inside I know he's right. The rest of us don't matter now, just Tiny. He's the true Firebrand, the possible salvation for all of humanity. With him, maybe we can save the world. Without him, nothing else matters.

I stop struggling and start running with him, wiping tears from my face. We round the corner of the church and fly through the doors to the gym, down the steps, and nearly crash into Harold. He's got his two knives out.

"What's going on?" he asks me, as oddly calm as ever.

"Grays have breached the line. We've got to get Tiny out of here. And Carly. Where are they?"

He points upstairs. "In the library with some of the others."

All three of us sprint up the steps. We run through the fellowship hall to the library. I try the door, but it's locked. With a growl, I slam my palm against it and the wood splinters as the door crashes open. Inside is Tiny, cradled in Annie's arms. Carly is there, too. Google and Simon are huddled together on the other side of the bed. Susan is standing guard over all of them, her hands fluttering. Everyone but her jumps in shock at our noisy entrance, then they breathe a collective sigh of relief when they realize it's us.

"Come on!" I order them. "We've gotta go. Now!"

It must be something in my voice, because all of them leap up and follow us out the door without question, even Susan. We hurry toward the church sanctuary. Singer has Carly in his arms. They're in the lead with me bringing up the rear. Annie is still holding Tiny. She's not really built for speed on a good day, but carrying him is slowing her down even more.

"Here. Give him to me," I say, snatching the little guy out of her hands. "He's slowing you down. I'll take care of him."

She starts to protest, but clamps her mouth shut and nods. Above all else, she's been the one to take care of the kids, and I think she realizes I'm better suited for keeping him safe. Her hands linger on him for a split second, but thankfully she doesn't argue. We bolt through the empty sanctuary towards the red front doors. Simon glances over his shoulder at me, panic etched into his young face.

"Where's my brother? What's happening?"

Panting, I yell, "Grays made it across. There's too many of them."

He slows down, but I push him forward, urging him on. Singer slams through the big doors and we clear the few steps onto the ground. Ahead of us, maybe thirty yards away, there are six or seven boats pulled up onto the parking lot near the ice. We angle toward those, but at the last minute, Simon peels off.

"Simon!" I scream, reaching for him, but he's already too far away from me. "Get back here!"

He turns once and looks right at me, breathing hard. His hands are clenched into tiny fists at his sides. His voice is almost pleading when he screams, "I'm going to help Jacob. I already lost him once. I'm not going to do it again!"

I yell for him to stop, but he isn't listening. Little legs pumping hard, he rounds the corner of the church and is gone. Singer grabs my shoulder and spins me around.

"I'm sorry, Scout. He's gone!"

It's like my soul is made of parchment paper, and I'm watching as it's shredded before my eyes. I almost double over in despair when I realize what just happened. *No, not Simon!* Not the sweet little kid who loves old TV shows and quoting movies. The boy I accidentally reunited with his long-lost brother. We've all suffered through more lifetimes of despair and sadness than anyone our age should ever have to. I don't know how much more I can handle. I stare at the spot where I last saw his small frame and blond head. Singer gives me a single second to grieve, then pulls me towards the boats. I know he's right and don't fight him.

The rest of the group is already there. Harold is urging everyone to get in one of the boats, a larger one that should be able to hold all of us. Google is bouncing around from foot to foot impatiently and grabbing at Susan's arm.

"Come on, come on," he yells, his voice high and pinched.

Annie stumbles into the boat. When Singer and I get there, he nearly tosses Carly in the front. Harold points at the ice.

"So how are we going to do this? Boats work best

on wet water, you know?"

Singer grabs a rope that's tied to the bow. "Everyone, get in! Scout and I will pull us across until we get to open water."

Harold nods agreement, although his raised eyebrow says he has his doubts. Everyone but me, Singer, and Susan clamber in. I toss Tiny back to Annie, who eagerly bundles him tight to her chest. She snatches at Carly and hugs her close. Singer starts to pull, and the bottom of the boat screeches as it slides across the asphalt. Just then Google pipes up again, and his panicked voice sounds so similar to the shrieking coming from the boat that, under any other circumstances, I'd be laughing.

"They're coming!"

Behind us, a pack of Grays has made it past Jacob's fighters. They've rounded the church and are pounding over the parking lot right at us. A quick head count tells me there's at least ten of them. Several have blood streaming from bullet holes riddling their bodies, but to them the wounds are superficial and barely slow them down. I hear Singer gasp behind me.

"Hold on tight!"

Everyone on board screams as Singer takes off. Annie is nearly thrown completely out, but Harold grabs her by the hair and steadies her until she can latch onto the side. Google hangs on with both hands, his face the color of milk gone bad, and with way too much white around his irises. In seconds the boat bumps off the parking lot and slides onto the ice and picks up speed as Singer puts his back and legs into it. Susan and I are right behind them. She's way more surefooted on this stuff than I am. Her loping, assured stride makes it look easy.

The boat bangs side to side as Singer navigates the uneven, treacherous surface. He changes direction suddenly to avoid slushy water ahead, and everyone cries out as the boat whips sideways. I nearly fall several times on the slick surface, mainly because I keep looking back to see what might be coming after us.

The Grays have reached the edge of the parking lot and pull up short, staring at us and milling around. If they were normal people, I'd say they were debating what to do next, and for a moment I think we're in the clear. But the creatures have something different in mind, and as a group they step off the parking lot and onto the ice.

"Holy shit!" Harold says. "Here they come. Row harder, Singer!"

"Why are they doing this?" Annie cries out in anguish, hands to her red face in despair. "What do they want?"

I honestly didn't think Singer could go any faster, but suddenly the boat surges ahead like a turbo kicked in. Susan and I have to sprint to keep up, and I nearly wipe out again when I hit a slick spot. It's been warm for days, and the once-thick ice is thawing all around us, bouncing ominously under our feet like the squishy, synthetic flooring of an outdoor playground. Directly in our path I spot what looks like an irregular dark brown patch about ten feet in diameter. It undulates a little, almost as if it's alive. It has to be slush.

"Singer, look ahead!" I call out, pointing.

He veers to the right, angling away from it. Unfortunately, the Grays benefit from the basic geometric law that the shortest distance between two points is a straight line, and they gain precious feet as they angle toward us. Singer has his back to them and can't see they're closing in on us, but they are. He stumbles a few times, and I wonder how much longer he can do this.

The Grays are in a full sprint and continue closing the gap. Singer has to dodge around a few more patches of brown slush, and each time he does our attackers close on us. Meanwhile, in the boat, Annie is barely holding it together. She's clutching Tiny and Carly to her chest so hard I'm afraid she might accidentally hurt them. Harold is facing backwards in the boat and keeping a watchful eye on what's happening with the Grays. Unlike Annie, he's showing no signs of panic. How can he be so damn calm?

"I'm going to need a break soon, Scout," Singer yells at me over his shoulder, gasping between each word. "I can't do this much longer."

I hate to break it to him, but I don't know how much help I'll be. What with all the running and the fighting in the parking lot, I'm already wearing out. Singer navigates the boat onto a solid patch of ice between two huge areas of slush, almost like a bridge between a pair of large ponds. I'm about to tell him I'll take over when, without warning, Harold bails out over the side of the boat. He rolls a few times, then springs to his feet with both knives out and ready.

The two of us nearly collide, and I slide to a stop a few feet past him, pinwheeling my arms for balance. Susan stops, too, although she manages to do so much more gracefully than me. I dash back to his side, snatching at his shirt.

"What are you doing?" I scream, my voice cracking as I tug at him. "Come on!"

He shakes off my hand. "No. I'm done running. I'm going to end this."

I get the feeling there's more to his running comment than what's happening now, but a therapy session will have to wait for later. Before I have a chance to do anything, he leaps up in the air and slams both feet down on the solid channel of ice we're standing on. A thick crack appears below us, accompanied by a groan like a door closing on rusty hinges. He does it again, and the crack spreads, spiderwebs bursting outward in all directions. A large chunk of brown ice to my right breaks away and bobs in the slush. More moans and snaps ripple throughout the ice bridge beneath our feet.

The Grays can't be more than twenty feet away.

Not that there's always a rhyme or reason to it, but this is usually the time during an attack when my slo-mo would kick in. While I'm desperately wondering where the hell it is, I see Harold jump high in the air and slam his feet down a third time. Loud pops like gunshots crackle away from us, and the entire slab of ice shifts dangerously under our feet. I throw my arms out to help keep my balance.

It's too late to do anything else now, I realize, and a strange sense of serenity comes over me as I finally understand what he's trying to do; no bridge means Singer and the others have a better chance to get away. Harold and I exchange a knowing glance, like soldiers volunteering for a suicide mission behind enemy lines. With a nod at me, in tandem we leap into the air. I'm much stronger than him, and when our feet slam onto the ice this time, a thousand fractures explode beneath us. I'm waiting for it to disintegrate under us, but somehow the ice bridge holds. A second later, the first of the Grays arrive.

I'm just pulling Chuck out as Susan charges in front of us. She grabs the lead attacker and lifts it over her head, then snaps her arm and slams the creature down like she's cracking a whip. The impact is so ferocious I feel the concussion vibrate up through my legs, reminding me of the sickening sensation I felt when my dad hit a deer with his car. A second one is right behind the first and reaches for Harold. Faster than my eyes can follow, his knives flash and half a dozen deep gashes blossom across the Gray's chest and face. The damage isn't enough to kill it, but the wounds are so sudden and severe it stumbles backwards, staring at itself, as if its dull brain can't comprehend the severity of what just happened.

"Get to the boat!" Harold roars over his shoulder. His two knives flash again, and more gashes bloom rosy red across the Gray's neck and chest. "I'll hold them off!"

Damnit, I can't wait on my stupid slo-mo any longer. I'm about to weigh into the fight when Susan grabs two creatures and bangs them together like some schoolkid pounding chalk dust from erasers. Then in one effortless motion, she lifts them above her head and smashes them onto the ice. A huge hole appears beneath them and they all start to tumble into the water. I scream, sure she's a goner, when the tingle finally starts at the back of my neck and the rest of the world puts the brakes on.

It's about damn time, I yell to myself.

The pair of Grays Susan smashed to the ice are almost completely underwater, the brown slush splashing up and around them like carnivorous flowers engulfing prey. Susan is in mid-fall with water already up to her knees. Her poncho is expanding outward at the bottom like a parachute catching air. As fast as slo-mo will allow, I rush towards her. She's nearly waist-deep by the time I get to the edge, and a crazy idea comes to me. Well, my only idea, if I'm being completely honest. She's too far from the edge for me to reach her, and I've got nothing to toss her that she could grab. Instead of slowing down, I clench my teeth and push harder. As I get to the jagged edge of the hole, I dive directly at her, flattening my body as I go. If I could, I would laugh out loud right then, knowing I must look like Supergirl soaring through the air. I open my arms, and when I impact her around the chest it feels like I've just smashed into a truck loaded with bricks. My momentum is diminished but still carries us forward, and she's slowly pulled from the water as I hold on tight. It seems like we're in the air forever as we fly to the other side. When we crash-land on solid ice, my slo-mo predictably clicks off. We tumble over one another until we come to rest in a tangle of arms and legs about ten feet beyond the hole. The two Grays that were at her feet disappear beneath the surface without a sound.

I lay on the ice and gather my wits, patting myself to make sure I'm not injured. I'm okay, but I'm afraid an impact like that might have been too much even for Susan. However, after a second or two, she sits up and shakes her head, then looks at me with that neutral expression she's mastered so well. She wobbles a little as she stands, but otherwise doesn't seem to have suffered any side-effects from my flying tackle. I get to my feet as well, smiling at her. She doesn't smile back, of course, but I swear her head dips in a nod. Just a small one, but dammit it was there, I'm sure of it. I'm so shocked that for a second I almost forget about what's going on around us.

I spin around and locate Harold. He's got his hands full in the middle of the remains of the ice bridge, somehow holding his own against the remaining attackers. He's sliced up three more and they're piled at his feet, which slows the rest down. Sweating like he's back in the kitchen, he glances up and sees the two of them are safe. Without so much as a nod or a wave, he crashes his feet down once more with what has to be the last of his strength. With the sustained roar of a tree being felled, the ice bridge completely disintegrates. One second it's there, and the next it's not, shattering beneath him like a sheet of glass dropped on concrete. He goes under without a sound.

"Harold!" I yell, rushing to the edge. I slide forward on my stomach and reach for him just as his two knives vanish below the dark surface. The rest of the Grays, every last one of them, fall into the abyss. A few claw at pieces of ice too small to support their weight, and then the freezing, slushy water swallows them up. They leave no trace except a scattering of bubbles on the surface that temporarily marks their final resting place.

I hear screaming and figure it must be me as I thrust a hand toward Harold. His head pops clear of the surface for a second, arms flailing. The panic etched into his face tells me he can't swim. He flails around as he tries to stay up, but he doesn't know how. He thrashes some more, but despite his efforts he goes under again, just out of my reach. I'm sobbing and fishing around in the icy water where I think he should be, dead certain he's gone forever. I thrust my other hand into the numbing slush, refusing to give up, when Susan tosses me to the side. She flops down on the edge and sticks her head and both long arms into the frigid darkness. The ice underneath her begins to crack and crumble, and I grab hold of her ankles and dig my heels in. I'm not going to lose her, too!

Seconds pass as she gropes around, and with each passing moment my head drops farther in despair. I'm almost ready to give up when she lifts her arm clear of the icy water, and she's got Harold's wrist locked in her grasp. I tug at her ankles with everything I've got, and I wildly overcompensate and heave both of them behind me, well clear of the edge. Harold rolls and slides like he wiped out on a skateboard. He's gasping and spitting, but at least he's breathing. In his one hand he's still clutching a knife, but his other blade is gone. I drag both of them back a few more feet until I'm sure we're on a stable section of ice, and then I fall down on my ass, panting with my head between my knees. Susan stands and calmly brushes off her black and white poncho. She's not even winded. After a couple of tense moments, Harold struggles to his knees and pukes up a few mouthfuls of liquid the color of burnt coffee. He shakes his head and coughs, then blows more brown stuff out of his nose, one nostril at a time. He looks up at me and we lock eyes. I can't believe it, but the crazy fool is smiling. My relief is so intense I grin back at him before a wave of manic laughter hits me. He pushes wet hair out of his face and laughs right along with me.

"Well, I'll be damned," he eventually says. "That actually worked."

CHAPTER
THIRTEEN

I help Harold up, then guide his limp arm over my shoulder as we do the slowest three-legged race ever towards the boat, Susan following behind. She's calm again, which I'm pretty sure means there aren't any more Grays around. Behind us Church Island is nothing more than a bump on the horizon, so distant it could be a low cloud or trick of the eye. I don't know how far we ran during all that, but it has to be close to a mile. Maybe more.

Singer is sprinting toward us, the boat and its occupants in the distance behind him. He has to dodge around slushy spots, but he can really move fast when he wants to. Before he gets to us, I turn to Harold.

"Thank you for saving us. But don't ever do anything that stupid again," I caution him, although there's no anger in my voice. I sound more like my mom gently chiding me for burping at the dinner table. He doesn't answer me, or even make eye contact. "And what was that 'I'm done running' stuff? What's that all about?"

Harold does a great job ignoring me. He's shivering, his clothes soaking wet and cold. He's got his free arm wrapped around him to conserve warmth. His brown hair is plastered flat to his head and his lips are tinged that awful color of freezer-burnt hamburger. I wish I could help him, but I don't have anything dry he can change into. I consider loaning him Susan's poncho, but it's just as wet as everything he's wearing. His best bet now is to let the sun do its job and warm him up.

I'm considering how to prod an answer out of him when Singer reaches us and throws his arms around me, squeezing me so hard I gasp. I return the embrace, but I'm too tired to do much more than that.

"What the hell happened back there?" he asks, now holding me at arm's length and checking the three of us out one at a time. He notices Harold dripping wet and shivering, and his eyebrows form a question. "I mean, what the hell, I was running with the boat, and I didn't hear you anymore. I turned around and you guys were taking on, like, a dozen of those things."

"Harold happened," I reply, tilting my head in his direction. "It was his idea. All I did was follow along. Right, Harold?"

He stares at me, his face neutral, but I get the feeling he's less than happy being the focus of this praise. I have no idea what he was thinking when he jumped out of the boat, but I get the impression he didn't care if he lived through the attack or not. I'm not comfortable calling what he did suicidal, but I don't know what else it could have been.

Singer, unaware of any of this, beams at him with the full force of his smile. He gives the cook's shoulder a hearty slap. "Way to go, man. That was a bold move. Crazy as hell, but it paid off."

Harold's mouth twitches into a thin grin. He pats Singer's shoulder in return, then starts trudging toward the boat with his back bowed. Susan follows him a few paces behind him, leaving melted footprints in the ice as she goes.

"What's the matter with him?" Singer asks, staring at Harold's back.

"I'm sure he's exhausted," I reply. Whatever is going on with our cook, I decide to keep it between the two of us for now. "He almost drowned, and would have if Susan hadn't saved him. And he doesn't have the benefit of our strength and stamina. Come on. Let's get back to the others."

Singer accepts my explanation, and we start towards the boat. We're about halfway there when he touches my arm. "Before we get back to the others, got any idea what we do now? Do we go back? You guys took out a lot of Grays back there. I'm not sure how many could be left at Church Island. It might be safe now."

We walk in silence as I mull this over. He's right.

We could go back. Between us and Jacob's fighters back there, I have to imagine we killed most or all of the attackers. Even if a few are still alive, Singer and I could easily handle them. But I think back to the conversation he and I had right before all this happened, that Tiny and Carly would be safer there than with us on the water. Or ice, in this case. Has that changed? What would be better for them? I remind him of our talk.

"Agreed. We did say they'd be better off with the others," he admits. "But I'm not so sure now. Grays managed to get on the island once. Even though they might not be able to do it again in the short term, we could have another freak blizzard and the channel might freeze over. Or, even if that doesn't happen, it's just a matter of time before all this dries up and they can just walk across. I used to think it was safer for them there, but now…? His voice trails off, gesturing with his eyes toward the fighting we left behind, leaving the uncertainty hanging in the air between us.

I nod, not just because he's making good points, because he is, but because I'm thinking along the same lines. After that attack, I'm confident nobody else can keep Tiny and Carly as safe as we can.

"I'm with you," I finally admit when we're almost up to the others. "What just happened back there showed us Tiny is too valuable to leave with someone else. His proximity effect, as Google calls it, is way too important. We can't rely on anyone else for that. Not anymore. I vote they stay with us."

Singer raises his hand. "I second that, or whatever we're supposed to say."

Despite what we just went through, I laugh once. "I almost feel like I should bang a gavel or something. So, we're in agreement. They stay with us. All of them."

He smiles down at me, one hand raised to the blue sky. "The ayes have it. Now the million-dollar question: where do we go?"

"I don't know. I really don't. Let's get back to the others, and we'll try to figure that out."

When we're only a dozen feet from the boat, Carly leaps over the side and dashes into my arms, ignoring Annie's frantic howls to come back. I lift up her small frame and carry her back, nuzzling into her dark hair. I want to hold her forever, to keep her safe from the dangers of this world. Each day I'm with her she becomes more important to me. More important, I realize, than just about anything. I kiss her cheek and plop her gently onto the seat next to Annie. Tiny signs something to her, and she gestures back at him. Her little face, framed by her black hair, is serious as they go back and forth a few times.

"What did he say?" I ask her.

"He wants to know if the Grays are all gone and it's safe," she says, brushing a few dark strands out of her face. "I told him it was. That's right, right?"

I smile at both of them. "Yes, tell him it's fine, and he's safe. You're going to stay with us now, and we'll take care of you. All of you."

"You mean I'm not going back to Church Island? What about my friends?"

The way her little face crumples wrenches at my heart, and it's all I can do to keep it together in front of her. But I have to, for her sake. "I'm sorry, honey, but we can't go back. It's safer if you stay with us now."

Tears glisten the corners of her eyes. "But what about my friends? Are they okay?"

I kneel down close to her, holding onto the edge of the boat. "I'm sure they are," I say, almost certain it's a lie and forcing what I hope is a convincing smile. "I'm sure Jacob and everyone kept them safe and sound. But you're better off with us now. Just like before, when we were on the boats all the time. It'll be fun."

I'm not sure she believes me, and it kills me to deceive her like that, but this is what parents have to do once in a while, right? They do and say what they need to in order to keep their kids safe and sound and out of danger. I never thought I'd admit this, especially the way I thought of kids in general when we first found her, but I've come to see both of them as part of my family now. She sits back on her seat and leans against Annie, thinking, and finally nods at me. My heart melts a little as I tussle her hair and stand up. Harold, Annie, and Singer are all looking at me, and I get the sinking feeling they're all waiting for me to decide what we're going to do next. Crap. I don't like being a leader, and never have. I felt sorry for Eve and

Jacob when they had to make tough choices, and the same goes for me. I hate to tell them I have no clue, so I stall.

"Let's keep going until we find open water," I recommend, trying not to make it sound like I just made it up. "I'll feel a lot better when we're off this ice for good."

To my relief, they're all on board with that. Harold gets out of the boat to lighten the load, then Singer and I both grab the rope and start pulling. The ride is smooth and slow now, with none of the manic crashing around they suffered through earlier. Not too much later, the ice all around us is nearly gone, with nothing ahead of us but slush and brown water. Everyone piles in the boat except Singer, and we hold on as he pushes the boat off the ice. At the last second, he hops in gracefully and grabs an oar. With so many of us aboard, the aluminum craft is sitting low on the water, but it's sturdy, and as long as we're careful there's no danger of sinking or capsizing. As we begin to paddle, I take a look at the horizon behind us. I can't see Church Island at all anymore. There's just a flat white line of horizon. We're all alone out here now. I'm okay with that.

Above is nothing but sun and the endless sky, while surrounding us is the now familiar sight of brown water strewn with trash and chunks of floating ice. We paddle quietly along. There's very little conversation in the boat since we're all deep in our own thoughts and too exhausted to spend energy on needless chatter. As one we let the solitude and sunshine ease some of the horrors of the recent past. On a side note, the melted ice has released the stench of our drowned and decaying world again, which is something I'd almost forgotten about. I know my nose will get used to it again, but right now the reek of roadkill baking in the hot sun is enough to turn my stomach. Google and Carly look a little green. I get it completely.

We continue our slow and easy progress to nowhere. Our only objective now is to get as far away from Church Island as possible. With nothing actively trying to kill us, my mind takes the opportunity to wander to other pressing subjects, such as the fact we have very little food and water, no shelter, and nightfall isn't far off. I vowed I would never sleep in one of these awful boats again, but it looks like I may have to break that pledge. Instead of dwelling on what I can't control, I grab my backpack and start rummaging through it.

"Who's hungry?" I ask with forced enthusiasm.

Carly's hand shoots up, as does Google's. I dole out some of my meager supplies, and together we munch on beef jerky in silence. Annie rips up small pieces of the tough stuff and doles them out to Tiny one at a time, his jaw working overtime. Carly pulls and tugs at a piece between her teeth, finally tearing off a hunk and munching it vigorously. I pass around my bottle of water, cautioning everyone to take it easy since we don't have much left. As far as a meal goes it pretty much sucks, but it is what it is. When we're all done, I clear my throat to get their attention.

"Well, we're back to the question of where we should go. Like I said before, we don't think it's safe at Church Island, not after that last attack. Anyone have any ideas?"

Singer waits politely for a second, then says, "How about north?"

"Why north?" I ask.

He shrugs. "No real reason, I guess. Except you told me Ted saw all those Grays heading south. Staying as far away from them sounds like a great plan to me."

"That makes sense," I reply, although a tiny sliver in the back of my mind for some reason disagrees with that. "Anyone else? Speak now."

Harold and Annie glance at each other, but both shrug in near unison. I honestly don't know a thing about Harold's past before his days as a cook. For all I know he's been there since the Storm, which means he really doesn't have much of a clue what it's like out here. Annie spent time with us before, but she's been on land for well over a year now. I take their silence as agreement with Singer.

"As far as I'm concerned that sounds okay," I continue, sounding more positive than I feel. "We've got Tiny, and we can start looking for others we might be

able to help. I've got no idea how much time someone has to spend with him to get vaccinated, or whatever we're calling this proximity effect thing, but we
need to start somewhere. It's what we wanted to do all
along, right?"

I check out the rest of the group. Susan is sitting
at the back of the boat. She has nothing to add, of
course. Google is huddled next to her, so close he's
nearly on her lap. He isn't talking, but looks deep in
thought, which is pretty standard for him. Harold is
staring into the distance, apparently somewhere else
at the moment. It doesn't appear anyone else has an
opinion.

"Okay then. Unless anyone objects, it looks like
we're heading north." I hesitantly reach for an oar,
but stop when Google's hand goes up.

"Yes?" I ask him.

"I'm not so sure that's the best decision. I think we
should consider going south."

Singer massages his brow and shakes his head, as
if he were expecting some sort of challenge from the
little genius. I look at Google with a raised eyebrow.
"Okay, I'll bite. Why the hell would we do that?"

"Think about it," he answers. "You had to notice
how strange the Grays have been acting lately. None
of them have been behaving rationally since they
started gathering across the channel. Well, as rational
as we've known them to act."

"That's true," I concede, unsure where he's going
with this.

"We've never known them to congregate like they were before that attack, right? And going onto the ice is something they would ordinarily only do under extreme circumstances. And they did it not once, but twice! Once to cross the channel, and again to come after us."

Singer's minor annoyance has vanished, and now he's just as intrigued as I am. "What's your point?"

"There should have been no reason for them to pursue us like they did. None. Grays attack people because they're hungry and if there isn't anything else to eat. There were plenty of…" he pauses, like he's searching for the best word choice among a lot of awful options. He glances at the kids, who are staring at him. "There were plenty of food sources on Church Island for them once they got there. They never should have come after us in the first place. It's completely out of character for them. Do you follow?"

I don't know why I didn't see any of that before. Singer's wide-eyed expression says he didn't catch that either. Harold sits up straight, drawn into the conversation and interested despite himself.

"Okay, shorty. Let's keep going with this," the cook says. "The ones that crossed the other night. Come to think of it, Jacob said they never actually attacked anyone, did they? They were trying to get into the church. And the ones that came after us? Like you said, there was no reason for them to act like that. They should have stayed on the island since there's no shortage of food. That's how they work."

"They could have been commanded to behave like that," I remind them. "Remember how Hunter ordered those two fast Grays to protect me? Maybe it was something like that."

"Sure, maybe," Google admits. "That could be it. But we've seen no trace of him. And this just didn't have that same feel. No, to me it seemed like they were doing this on their own, as a group."

"On their own? That's impossible," I reply, challenging him.

"Impossible? I don't think so." He points next to him at Susan, and his voice has taken on that firm and unyielding tone he gets when he's certain he's right. "What about her? Did you ever think a Gray could act like she does? In your wildest dreams, did you ever think one of these things would fight for us?"

I look to Susan, who's sitting calmly in the back of the boat. If she has any idea she's suddenly the focus of our discussion, she doesn't show it. I have to shake my head no. Singer and Harold do the same.

"I didn't think so," Google continues with a smug grin in my direction.

Harold opens his mouth several times to ask a question before he actually finds his voice again. "Okay, what are you saying?"

"I'm saying these Grays weren't after us as a food source. I think they were looking for something. Or someone."

Singer looks at each of us in turn. "Who? Or what?"

Google points to Tiny, still cradled in Annie's arms. "I think they're after Tiny. I don't know why and I can't prove it, but I think they wanted him."

Harold shakes his head. "Oh, come on. Why would you say that? How could they even know he exists? And what would they want with him? He's just a little kid."

Can someone be a born lecturer? If so, then it would be Google. Warming to the subject, he leans forward and taps the side of his head. "Think back to when Susan showed up. Tiny knew she was there somehow. No one told him, he just knew. Scout, you talked about this strange telepathic link you share with Susan, and how your brother and Hunter controlled their Grays. I think those Grays back there somehow sensed Tiny was on the island, and felt like they need-ed him. I'm convinced they somehow know he's spe-cial and were drawn to him."

Harold blinks a few times. "Jesus, kid, just how smart are you, anyway?"

"Extremely," Google answers matter-of-factly, something that's easy to admit when it's the truth. "I'm certain they knew he was there, and they were drawn to him for some reason. In fact, I don't think the group that just attacked us were out to kill any-body. Or if they did, it was just because we were in their way. Obstacles to be cleared. Collateral damage.

I think they wanted Tiny."

At this declaration, Annie draws the toddler deeper into her chest, as if she's trying to protect him from all the threats this world has to offer. I stare at our resident genius for a moment before turning to Tiny and Carly.

"Carly, honey, can you ask Tiny…I don't know, ask him if he could tell what the Grays wanted?"

She nods, eager as always to help, and begins gesturing at him with those complicated hand movements. Without a pause, he signs back at her. They go back and forth a few times, then she turns to me.

"Um, he doesn't have the words, exactly," she says. "But he says he could hear them in his head. Just like he could with Susan. He doesn't think they wanted to hurt him. They just wanted him."

We all sit in stunned silence, the boat rocking gently beneath us. A larger piece of ice clunks into the hull and the sharp metallic thud makes us jump. Could this be true? Were they just after Tiny? The thought never occurred to me. I mean, why would it? Grays have been a constant threat to our existence since the Storm began, and that whole time they had the good manners to act consistently. Yes, we've all noticed the gradual changes in their behavior lately, but this is a whole new level of different. I'm having a hard time wrapping my head around it.

"Okay, okay," Singer says, his words laced with doubt. "Say that's true. Say the Grays just wanted

Tiny. Why? What good is he to them?"

Google shrugs. "I don't know. But that's why I think we should be headed south. If this bunch of Grays wanted Tiny, and he's as special as we all think he is, then that huge group going south may be going that way for the same reason."

The genesis of an idea is forming in my head, but Harold beats me to it. "What a minute, short stuff. Are you saying you think there's another Tiny down south somewhere? Someone else with his same sort of miracle healing power? And those other Grays are going after this other version of Tiny?"

"Exactly. That's exactly what I'm saying. Maybe Tiny isn't the only one. Maybe there's someone else down there just like him. I think we owe it to ourselves and the world to find out. Don't you?"

CHAPTER
FOURTEEN

Damn if I didn't have to break my vow, even I couldn't help it. We're all trying to find a way to somehow sleep in a boat barely big enough for us to sit in, and it's just not possible. I've got Carly sprawled on top of me sweating like a marathon runner, while Singer is jammed up against both of us in the prow. Tiny is snoring on Annie's chest while her butt is on the bottom with her head hanging over the side. Her neck is bent at an angle that defies human anatomy. Harold and Susan are sitting up in the back. She's wide awake, and he's trying not to lean against her because she's as hot as an oven. He jerks every time he starts to nod off, like a passenger dozing on a plane. Google is curled up in a tiny ball on a bench seat near her. None of us is remotely comfortable. At least it's not raining.

On the other hand, the night sky is amazing. In a throwback to pre-Edison days, there's no such thing as light pollution now, and the stars are almost bright enough to throw shadows. The Milky Way is a glittering trail of diamond dust pulsing against the velvet background of the night. The moon has apparently been humbled by this celestial magnificence and is absent tonight. My back aches and my underwear is soaking wet from water puddled in the bottom of the boat, but all that pales against the glory arching overhead. I don't think I've ever seen anything more beautiful.

"Wow," Singer whispers, his head so close to mine I can feel his warm breath on my cheek.

"Wow is right. This is amazing."

"Kinda' makes sleeping in a boat not so bad."

I smile. The gesture is lost in the darkness but still clear in my tone. "Well, I wouldn't go that far."

He shifts position a little. It's cool out, but not too bad. I have my blanket, but our combined body heat is keeping us warm, even for those of us who don't have a little person sacked out on top of them. The backpacks are decent makeshift pillows. Carly mumbles a sleepy nothing and her hand comes around and smacks me in the face. I smile and gently slide it away.

"By the way, I forgot to tell you," Singer whispers. "That was a great idea with the fuel oil. It probably saved our asses."

"Yeah, well, it didn't quite work out exactly as planned, did it? It didn't keep them away."

"Maybe not in the end, but it bought precious time when we needed it."

I haven't had a chance to think about that. When

I found out Google had the huge furnaces working and realized the fuel oil in the furnace room was still good, I thought we could use it to our advantage. What do Grays hate more than anything? Fire, of course. Bucket by bucket, we lugged several hundred gallons of the thick red liquid to the roof and filled one of the empty water cisterns with the nasty stuff. We hooked the garden hoses to the tank, and strung the hoses down to the parking lot. Google insisted gravity and the weight of the liquid in the tank would provide enough pressure for me to lay down a barrier. My little red Bic lighter would do the rest. It worked, to a certain degree.

"Thanks," I eventually say.

"No, really, that little trick saved us."

We stare above us for a few minutes, lost in our thoughts. The boat is almost perfectly still, except when someone moves. Then it lists back and forth a few times, the water lapping gently against the hull until the motion stops. The dark water around us is so calm it could be an extension of the night sky.

"What do you think about what Google said?" I ask a little bit later, still mesmerized by the view.

"About going south? Or that there may be another Tiny down there?"

"Both," I reply after a heartbeat's pause. "Seems like they're pretty much one and the same thing."

He grunts deep in his throat, the sound managing to convey both acceptance and doubt in equal measures. "I don't know. He could be right. I hate to admit it, but he usually is. But just because there may be another Tiny down there doesn't mean we have to find him. Or her. We've said our main goal was to see if his power to cure people is real, and if it is, to share it with the rest of the world."

Yeah, about that… I don't answer immediately, but I'm afraid to tell him my priorities have recently changed again. I mean, ever since I got these weird powers, saving the world is what's gotten me out from between the sheets every day. After all, someone who is passionate about making a change is the true definition of a firebrand, right? From Rumpke Mountain to the Mound to Church Island and all points in-between, that's been me this whole time. Seven days a week, no vacations, no sick leave. My entire life since this began has been dedicated to finding a cure and saving humanity. Look at me, I'm the Firebrand. Blah, blah.

That original decision was as sudden and unchangeable as stepping off a cliff. Now? I can't nail down exactly when this changed, but like someone climbing up a staircase one step at a time, my priorities have been evolving. More importantly, my desire to keep Carly and Tiny safe has shifted. I'm not sure if it's a budding parental instinct in me coming out, or if it's something even more basic and tribal than that, but keeping these two kids out of harm's way has become Job One, even over saving the world. Is that selfish? Maybe. Probably. But I would argue that the little guy snoring in Annie's lap and this precious little person laying on top of me with her hair tickling my neck are more important than just about anything. I mean, if we can save the world and keep them safe, that would be the best outcome imaginable. But if that's impossible, if I have to make a choice between those two results, I've decided I'm going to go with the kids.

"On the other hand," he continues, unaware of my change of heart. "Who's to say what's better for them now? I have no idea what might be waiting for us if we head north. It could be worse. Maybe south is better? Who knows?"

"I get it. I always thought the Mound and Church Island would be safe havens. But look where that got us." I shudder against him as the massacre at the Mound is replayed in my mind. The piles of bodies. BamBam's guts scattered across the road like he was tossed in a wood chipper. So much blood and death, so many innocent kids killed. My rage at Hunter for his role in that is a fire that will never be extinguished.

"Are you saying what I think you're saying?" I continue. "Do you think we should do what he says and go south? Toward the Grays?"

He takes his time answering. The whites of his eyes glimmer as he stares at the heavens. Eventually he blinks a few times and shifts position, the movement causing metallic slaps of water against the hull again.

"I don't know. I guess so. We can always check it out, right? And if it's the wrong choice, then we pile back into the boat and take off. What have we lost?"

That's really what it boils down to, isn't it? Having no clear destination makes changing course pretty damn easy. And he's right. There's an old expression my mom used to say when she had to decide between two relatively equal outcomes: six of one, half a dozen of the other. That describes what we've got here. Even so, going south somehow feels right to me, even if I can't explain why.

"Okay," I concede. "South it is. But the welfare of the kids comes first. Even before saving the world. You good with that?"

I don't know if he caught that my priorities have changed or not. Either way, he doesn't mention it. But he's a smart guy, and I'm sure he noticed. Once again, I'm so thankful he's on my side. I just hope the others are, too.

"Yep. I'm good with that."

In the morning, Carly stirs on top of me and lifts her head. With one eye cracked open, I watch as she twitches her little nose a few times.

"Hey, the stink is gone," she announces, grinning at me widely.

We're both a sweaty mess where her skin was pressed against mine, even though the morning air is cool. I take a tentative sniff and discover she's right.

Sort of. "I'm not sure it's gone, honey. I just think our noses have gotten used to it already."

She takes a few more whiffs of the air like a rabbit searching for predators, then makes an almost comical face. "Oh, yeah. Yuck. It's still there."

I sit up and brush my salt and pepper hair away from my face. I move my tongue around in my mouth and try not to think of the many benefits of toothpaste. "Don't worry. You won't even notice it in a little bit. Promise."

Singer stretches, and I have to dodge one of his long arms as it almost clobbers me in the head. He doesn't look too bad considering what a lousy night we just had. Harold, on the other hand, is sporting a pair of eyes so puffy and red they could be bleeding. He twists his torso this way and that as he tries to work out the kinks in his neck and back. It must be a bitch not having our healing powers.

"That was about as much fun as a first night in jail," Harold grumbles, moving his mouth around and making a face like something died in there. There's a faint shadow of stubble across his chin and cheeks, a reminder he's older than the rest of us. "You say you guys have done this before?"

Singer grins at him. "Yeah. Several times."

"Ugh. I almost wish you had let me drown back there."

I know he's joking, but I don't care for the comment. I haven't forgotten his declaration just before the Grays attacked us on the ice when he said, "I'm done running." I want to talk to him about it, but now is not the time, not in front of everyone. I hand some of our remaining jerky around, and once we've all had a few bites and some water, I let them in on our plans.

"Singer and I were talking last night, and we agree with Google. We think we should go south and see what's down there."

I glance around at their faces to gauge their reactions. Harold shows no more concern than if we were on a road trip and we decided to detour to check out the world's largest ball of twine. Google displays his usual "I was right again" look, which is equal parts annoying smugness and acceptance. Carly and Tiny aren't paying attention to us since they're too busy wrestling with their beef jerky. Only Annie has a reaction.

"You can't be serious," she snaps. Her normally impeccably-kept red hair is sticking up at crazy angles. It's not a look I'm used to, and I try to keep a straight face when a vision of Einstein comes to mind.

"I'm very serious," I tell her. "That's what we're doing."

"We can't! You said yourself that's where all those things are. We can't take the kids there! It's not safe!"

I appreciate how much she cares for the little ones, but I'm tired and cranky, and my ass is still soaked from being in the bottom of the boat. I can feel my last nerve jangling, but do my best to keep my voice level. The two of us fighting won't do anything but upset the kids.

"Annie, we don't know what's safe and what isn't." I remind her of what happened at the Mound and more recently back at Church Island. I shouldn't have to, but I do. "I care for these kids more than you know, and I only want what's best for them. And right now, we think that means heading south."

Her wide eyes jerk toward each of us as she searches for an ally but finds none. She's clutching at Carly and Tiny, her face filled with the unreasoning terror of an animal in a leg trap. Her usually rosy cheeks have gone pale and she's breathing fast but having a hard time catching her breath.

"Don't do this, Scout," she pleads. "These things are after Tiny. Don't deliver him to them!"

"Annie," I assure her. "I will protect both of them with my life. We all will."

"She's right," Singer adds, his face a study in sincerity. "All of us will. We won't let anything happen to them."

"You can't know that!" she screams. "None of you can!"

It takes another five minutes filled with promises and reassurance before she calms down. Singer does a much better job of it than I do, explaining again and again how we won't put the kids in harm's way. Even then, she's latched onto each of the little ones like they're lifesavers in a hurricane. Carly gives me a half-playful look that says "help me," and I put a hand to my face to conceal my budding smile at her comically pained expression, thankful for the lighthearted moment.

Singer and I finally manage to talk Annie off the ledge, her panic subsiding to the point where she can breathe normally again. She's scared, and I can't say I blame her. Heading into possible danger has that effect on people. She's not happy, but she's no longer freaking out. I count that as a win.

Singer and I each grab an oar and start rowing, the rising sun warming the left sides of our faces. Annie refuses to make eye contact with either of us, but that's okay. She's swaying back and forth and humming something under her breath. I'm not sure if it's for the benefit of the kids or for her.

FIFTEEN

I'm not sure I can effectively describe how much I hate these awful aluminum boats. How many levels of hell did Dante talk about? Seven, right? If so, then I'd like to add one and make level eight the destination of the damned for whoever designed these clumsy things. Google's told me before that Jon boats are really designed to have a motor push them along, but that tidbit of information is less than useful right now, and just makes me remember how good we had it before the world died.

Even so, we've made a little headway by the end of the day. We're riding low in the water, wallowing along like a harpooned whale. Thankfully I had my compass stashed in a pocket of my backpack, which means we've been holding our course most of the time. But if it weren't for the combined strength and endurance of me and Singer, we'd be screwed. Harold's been able to give each of us a break once in a while, but rowing is hard work, and he can't go too long before he's fried. When the sun begins to dip be-low the horizon on our right, the three of us are ex-hausted, hungry, and horribly thirsty. I wish I could figure out how to get Susan to pull her weight, but unfortunately my ability to control her like that hasn't worked out. How did Hunter teach his minions to row a damn boat?

We bed down like we did the previous evening. My bottle of water is long gone, and Singer only has a few sips left in his. My stomach is growling like an angry jungle cat is trying to devour me from the inside. I can hear everyone else's doing the same. As a group, we're in a crappy mood and well beyond questioning our decision. When we finally manage to get situated and hunker down for the night, Singer touches his head to mine.

"I know I'm stating the obvious, but we can't stay out here much longer. We need supplies. Mainly wa-ter. Like, you know, yesterday."

I stare out over the putrid water all around us. It's not fair there's so much literally at the tips of my fingers, and we can't drink it. "I know. Especially the kids. I'm open to ideas. I'll even take bad ones."

There's that old saying, that two heads are better than one, but that's not helping now. Neither one of us comes up with anything, except to follow the original plan. Singer plays his harmonica, and while the tune is upbeat, it can't dent our foul mood. The harmoni-ca's notes are thin and a little sad, vanishing into the fading light as if the music is chasing away our hopes. Carly and Tiny are so thirsty they're fussing almost nonstop, sometimes bursting into tears for the slightest reason, or no reason at all. My own mouth is as dry as Ohio in August. Harold, meanwhile, has to keep massaging his legs because dehydration is causing sudden and violent Charlie-horses to knot up his calves. He doesn't complain, but he doesn't have to; he can't hide the pain each time he yelps and frantically massages his legs. Susan is the only one who appears okay. She just sits on her bench seat and stares out at the endless mud-colored horizon, as serene as a corpse. I wish I could be as Zen as that.

"What about Rumpke Mountain?" Singer suggests to the group after a while. "From what you've told me, there's a ton of supplies there. And it's practically on the way."

I try not to jerk when he mentions that place, but I can't hold back a shudder that hits me like an electric shock. Without realizing I'm doing it, I wrap my arms around myself in a defensive hug. I lived there for months and had all kinds of experiences, both good and bad, but now the only thing I can remember is a battlefield's worth of blood and death. I don't know how I can possibly set foot in that place again.

Singer hasn't noticed my reaction. He does a quick survey of the boat. "Harold? Annie? What about you guys? What do you think?"

Neither of them has any history with Google's old haunt, and can't see why we're bothering discussing it at all. They agree without a second's hesitation, then look to me for confirmation. I run my fingers through my hair, stalling. I envy them their shared ignorance.

We could keep going and hope we find someplace better, but hope really isn't a strategy, is it? Before I reply, I give a second's thought to the Mound, but it's so far away I don't think we'd make it. I let out a shuddering sigh, and give Singer a silent nod.

He sees my hesitation. "You're sure?"

"Oh god, no. Not in the slightest," I reply, smiling through my terror. Singer laces his fingers into mine, but my panic barely ebbs. He looks at Google.

"How about you? Thumbs up or down on your old stomping ground?"

"Thumbs up, of course," he tells Singer immediately. If he's thinking back to what happened before we fled his mountain kingdom, he's able to hide his torment a hell of a lot better than I can. "At this point it's the only choice."

Singer nods. "Yeah. Okay. I just don't see there are any other options."

I wonder what would have happened if I had said no? Would they have insisted on going anyway? I pray for everyone's sake the storms and vultures have taken care of the remains there, because no one should have to see what I can never unsee.

Two agonizing days later, I think I spot something far to our left. It's little more than a black bump on the horizon, so distant I can't be sure it's even there. My hand up to shield my eyes, I squint across the foul water trying to figure out exactly what I'm looking at. The bright sun throws shimmering flashes across the miles of brown water around us, tossing the shape into and out of shadows. I wish for the hundredth time I had Simon's eyesight.

My mouth opens to get Singer's attention, but my throat is so dry my vocal cords have gone on strike. Once again, the irony that we're surrounded by miles of undrinkable water isn't lost on me. Frustrated, I stop rowing and weakly nudge Singer, pointing where I want him to look. He's paddling with all the emotion of a robot assembling cars in a factory, dipping the oar in, pulling weakly, then repeating the motion over and over. It takes him a few seconds to grasp that I'm trying to get his attention. He slowly lifts the oar out of the water.

"What?" he whispers, his own voice a shadow of its melodic self. I wouldn't even recognize it as his if his mouth weren't moving.

I point again, and with my other hand physically move his head where I want him to look. His chin drops and he runs his tongue over cracked lips, the movement reminding me of an old man vainly searching for a memory. His head dips forward as he stares blankly, squinting.

"What is it?" he finally asks.

I clear my throat, trying to kick-start my voice. "Dayton. Downtown Dayton. I think."

He's never been here before, so he doesn't know. I nudge him once more, and the two of us start paddling in the direction of the shape. What feels like hours later, we're close enough that I can see it's the top of the tower I spotted so long ago. But now there's more of it. There are at least a dozen floors showing above the waterline instead of just a few, more evidence of the receding flood. The tower's dirty windows reflect the sun, winking at us.

"We're getting close," I tell him, my words carrying no more force than a ghost moving through a room.

Yesterday we spread Susan's poncho over the front of the boat to give the kids some shade. There's a small movement and some moaning under there. It could be Google or Carly, I can't tell which. The lack of water has impacted them more than the rest of us, and their physical conditions have deteriorated quickly the last few days. They barely move now, with just a feeble groan or raspy cough the only signs they're still with us. Tiny is no better off. Annie is holding him loosely in her arms and using her body to shield him from the hot sun. She's so out of it she could be dead, but her chest is still moving, proof she's alive. Her exposed skin is so sunburned it nearly matches her hair. We've all seen suffering before, some of it truly horrible, but witnessing this relentless, slow-motion death of people I love is worse than a knife slowly twisting in my chest.

"How long?" Singer croaks.

I shrug, because I don't know. I zipped from here to Rumpke Mountain in no time with my kayak, but we're creeping along at such a snail's pace I have no idea. As close as it is, I'm afraid we may not make it, not the way we're going.

"I don't know. Half a day? Maybe a full day?"

He sighs, a long, slow one that goes on much longer than I thought possible. Then he lumbers up off the bench seat and makes his way to the back of the boat.

"What are you doing?" I ask, although my voice is so faint I'd be surprised if he heard me. He grabs ahold of the rear gunwale and, before I can react, goes feet first into the disgusting water. Despite the current state of my throat, I yell out and reach for him.

"Get out of there!" I yell.

Harold, who had been dozing fitfully by Annie, sits up with a jerk and a snort. Even Susan, who's been as still as a statue this entire time, turns her head towards the commotion, as if she's actually curious. I reach the back and he's still there, his head above the frigid water, both hands gripping the boat. He's already shivering.

I'm so weak and trembling I sigh and have to sit down. For a moment I thought he had gone crazy and was trying to sacrifice himself or something. My hand flutters to my forehead when I see him there. The wave of relief at seeing him okay hits me like I just avoided a car crash. My dad called times like those

"Oh shit" moments. He grins up at me, his eyes alive for the first time in days.

"Okay, this is really cold," he says through teeth that are already chattering loudly.

"Get out of that stuff!" I repeat.

He smiles up at me. "Sorry, no can do. We'll never get there in the shape we're in. We'll make better progress this way. Now, before I regret this, you'd better grab hold of something."

He starts kicking his feet. The boat immediately lurches forwards, to the point I really do have to grab onto something or I'll risk falling overboard. Once I'm settled, I hold out both hands, beseeching him.

"Will you get out of that stuff, please? We'll do this together."

He's holding his head well out of the toxic stuff. Behind him, his kicking is stirring up the water impressively, including some plastic bags and other trash that's been floating beneath the surface. On each side of the boat is an actual wake, expanding then vanishing behind us. We're not moving as quickly as my kayak would, but this is the fastest I've ever seen one of these stupid boats go.

"Sorry," he says through lips pressed together to keep the filthy water out of his mouth. "Actually, I'm not all that sorry. This is the best I've felt in days. Just use the oar to steer and keep us on course."

Shy of reaching down there and yanking him out, I do what he says. Moving from one side of the boat to the other to steer, and keeping the tower more or less on my left, we follow the compass and head generally south. After a few minutes of this, Google's face eases out from under Susan's poncho, like a turtle's head timidly poking out of its shell. He stares at the splashing behind us and rubs at his eyes, blinking.

"Oh, good. Looks like you got your motor after all."

The sun is low on the western horizon when I catch a whiff of something on the breeze, a smell even more rancid than what we've become used to. Google must notice it, too. It draws him out from beneath the poncho at a pace that would make a sloth proud.

"Smell that?" he whispers.

I nod. Susan is the only other one of us who might recognize it, but she hasn't moved a muscle in hours. Both of us peer ahead, and my heart flutters when I spot land rising before us, a small mountain with a distinct plateau, tiny wicks of fire decorating its flanks. I turn back towards Singer. I don't know how he's still going. It's been hours now and he hasn't taken a single break.

"We're almost there," I let him know, my voice upbeat for the first time all day. "You should rest for a minute."

Singer shakes his head from side to side. His eyes are screwed shut, the strain he's under clear in the way the tendons bulge up and down his arms and neck.

He's got his hands locked onto the back of the boat like a man clinging to the edge of a cliff. His knuckles are almost white.

I slump back down, worried he's going to do irreparable damage to himself, but unable to do anything about it. At the sound of my voice, Carly crawls out from under the poncho, too. Her face is pinched and thin, as if she's evaporating before my eyes. I reach out to steady her.

"We're almost there, honey," I assure her. She nods at me, although it might just be the gentle rocking of the boat causing her head to bob up and down. Annie is staring at me through slitted eyes but is otherwise motionless. I've never seen a living person look so dead before. Tiny is an unmoving lump on her chest.

"Good lord, what's that stench?" Harold asks quietly.

"It's Mount Rumpke," I tell him. "It used to be the landfill for the entire Dayton area. It always smells like this."

When we're close enough to clearly see the jets of fire from the methane torches, I steer us to where the road should be. Behind us, Singer's kicks have slowed to a point where they're barely stirring the water behind him. I paddle as well as I can, but a single person rowing this kind of boat is about as effective as one hand clapping. In the end, I just try to keep us on course as we inch forward.

Ahead of us, I can finally make out the road leading up the hill. I'm not sure what I expected, but I'm relieved as hell there's no one hanging out at Bam-Bam's spot, which is now about thirty feet farther away from the edge of the water than it was before. I do my best and direct the boat onto the gravel road. Behind us, Singer keeps kicking.

"Singer, stop!" I yell. "We're here!"

It takes him a few seconds to grasp what's going on, but eventually his legs stop moving and his head drops. I jump out into the knee-deep scummy water, kicking aside the trash and filth that's accumulated near the shoreline. I grab hold of both of his wrists and have to yank hard to break his grip on the lip of the boat. I lift him up and carry him to the shore, where I carefully set his shivering body down.

"The poncho! Give me the damn poncho!" I order.

Harold is the first to react. He snatches the poncho off the bow and limps over to cover Singer, tucking the black and white bedspread around him and gathering up enough to make a thin pillow for his head.

"Is he okay?" the cook asks, his face pinched in concern.

"I don't know." I place a shaking palm against Singer's cheek. His dark skin is colder than a corpse. He's trembling violently. "He's freezing. And dehydrated. We've got to warm him up."

Harold glances around, taking in Rumpke Mountain for the first time. There's nothing much to see this close to the water, except some dirt, gravel, and the rubbish that's been left behind as the water level dropped. It's a very underwhelming sight, at least down here. Then his eyes track to the methane torch burning off the side of the road up ahead.

"What the hell is that thing?" he asks.

That gives me an idea. Well, two ideas, actually. I stand and point to Susan, who's still sitting in the boat.

"You. Get over here and keep him warm," I command, gesturing at Singer. She tilts her head at me but doesn't move. Sudden anger boils up inside of me. The world around her blurs until she's the sole subject of my ire. I can sense every detail of her, the broad shoulders, her long white hair, the flat, emotionless eyes.

"Now!" I scream, my fists clenched at my side.

She leaps from the boat with such force it nearly flips over. Annie and the little kids yell and grab onto anything they can as they're nearly ejected over the side. She quickly splashes through the shallow filth and gets down next to him.

"You did that?" Harold asks as he tucks the blanket around them. "I've never seen one of those things obey a command like that before."

"Yeah, I can, but I'm not very good at it. Keep an eye on everyone while I get some supplies. Google, how do I get in your building up there? You locked it when we left."

He digs through his pockets and holds out a small

device, a black rectangle like a tiny TV remote control. "Just push the center button," he says, handing it to me. "Assuming the batteries aren't dead, that should do it."

I stare at him. "You've had this with you all this time?"

He blinks twice at me. "Of course. Why wouldn't I? I knew we'd return sometime."

I shake my head at the little genius. I'm lucky I can keep track of the shoes I wear every day, and he's been holding onto this little device since we left in a hurry over a year ago? I should be surprised, but then I guess I really shouldn't be.

"Assuming I don't run into any trouble, I won't be gone long. If you see anyone but me come down that road, get back in the boat and paddle like hell out of here. Got it?"

Harold takes out his knife and holds it at the ready. The way he handles that thing so easily is both eerie and comforting. I'm reminded of how he sliced up the Grays on the ice. I've never seen anyone but me and Singer do that before, and he managed it without the benefit of enhanced speed and strength. Even in his current state, I'd say everyone here is in good hands while I'm gone. He nods at me.

"Good. I won't be long."

I turn and start to run up the road, but after a few paces I realize how weak I am from the prolonged lack of food and water. I slow to a jog, and then to a quick walk. I try not to notice what I think are white bone fragments jutting up from the dirt when I pass the spot where BamBam was killed. I hurry past them, eyes trained ahead. My legs are already tired, and a headache is starting to build right above my eyes. I'm sure it's tied to dehydration.

When I reach the top, I'm panting harder than a dog on a hot day, and I have to rest with my hands on my knees to catch my breath. I should be sweating from this much exertion, but I'm not, and that can't be a good sign. I only pause for a minute, then move on.

Most of the tin shacks and tents that once populated this plateau were either torn down or destroyed during Hunter's attack. Those that survived haven't fared well since then. Bits of cloth flutter weakly from tent posts like flags of surrender. Large pieces of plastic and metal sheeting that made up other small structures have been scattered or blown away by storms and time. I pass by several pits where kids used to dig for goods to trade with Google, but most of them have caved in and are partially filled with green, disgusting water. If someone has tried living here in our absence, I can't detect any sign of it. That is perfectly fine with me.

CHAPTER
SIXTEEN

Google's cinder block building is as sturdy and un-yielding as a mausoleum, and just as inviting. It's a featureless one-story, flat-roofed block with a metal door. I don't know what it was designed to be original-ly, but it's the only structure here that hasn't changed for the worse.

I ease close, remembering all too well the scores of bodies we left behind. But as I scour the area, there isn't a trace of them. I don't know if Grays or another group of scavengers did something with them, or if they were simply blown away in one of the power-ful storms. Whatever their fate was, I'm so relieved they're gone I have to stop for a moment and collect myself before I keep going.

As I step up to the door, I push Google's remote and exhale in relief when I hear a muted buzz and a click from inside. Because of the abuse it's suffered, the door is warped out of alignment and I have to put some muscle into it. The hinges shriek in protest until they give enough for me to squeeze through. As I edge inside, the fading sun throws a thin rectangle of light on the floor and against some racks of dusty electrical equipment. It doesn't help much, but it will have to do. I head farther in, towards the back where he kept his food, bumping into shelves and boxes full of electrical junk that will never be worth anything again. A cruel joke from elementary school pops into my head: *How do you drive Helen Keller crazy? Rearrange the furniture.* A dozen or so steps in I run into his white counter, the one that used to hold the shortwave radio. I feel around for his light, and when I find it, I twist the on button, but nothing happens.

"Damn," I mutter softly. The thought of this building as a mausoleum is sticking with me like a bad dream, and even the sound of my own voice in this silent place is more than a little startling.

I feel my way to the end of the counter and enter the storeroom. My hands outstretched and fingers fumbling in the dark, I brush against what feels like canned goods on the first shelf. A little farther on I grab something soft that squishes between my fingers. It has to be rolls of toilet paper. I ease farther in, and I'm finally rewarded when my groping hands hit the jackpot. I squeeze, and the distinct and unforgettable crackling of plastic water bottles fills the room, a sound that always reminded me of bubble wrap popping. After more excited probing, I realize it's an entire case of the stuff, still in its shrink wrap. I grab it and retrace my steps through the dark, until the light from the doorway is in front of me. Squeezing through the tight opening, I recall being chastised by Google for not locking the door in the past, so I pull it shut. When I push the button, the buzz and click tells me it's once again secure. I sling the case of water over my shoulder and hurry back the way I came. But before I head down the road, I detour slightly to one of the flattened tents and pick up a few wooden poles that are half buried in the hard ground. As well as I can in my condition, I jog back down the road.

On my way there, I make one more detour. As I near the methane torch, I have to ease in slowly, the searing heat on my face and bare skin almost more than I bargained for. The roaring it makes is like a jet engine at full throttle, an insane whooshing noise so loud I'm seriously afraid it might damage my eardrums. The thick flame is intense, at least five or six inches in diameter, and more blue than yellow, jetting from a nozzle bigger than my arm. I inch as close as I can, until I can almost feel the ends of my hair curl and singe. I stick the end of a tent pole into the torch. Immediately the dry wood catches, burning a bright orange. I roll the pole around and around, and when I withdraw it I see the end is burning nicely. Satisfied, I hurry on down the road.

Thankfully, everyone is just as I left them, except Google, who is hovering close to Susan. Harold is parked next to Singer. He lumbers to his feet with a muted wince creasing his face when he sees me. When he spies what I'm carrying, his face undergoes half a dozen expressions, beginning with pain and moving all the way to astonishment before finally settling on joy.

"What the hell? Where did you find all that?"

I tear open the shrink wrap and hand out bottles to everyone, two to Annie so she can help Tiny. The rest I dump on the ground. I hand the burning pole to Google, who holds it up with the same sort of reverence a knight of the Round Table would grip Excalibur. He looks quickly at Susan to see how she's reacting, but she hasn't moved. I know we're both afraid she'll take off again, but apparently my command to remain next to Singer trumps her fear of fire. Her normally dull eyes are big and agitated in her face, but she's staying put. With my hands free, I quickly snap the rest of the poles into short sections and build a small pyramid next to Singer. I jam the burning end into the base of the pyramid and get down on my hands and knees, bending low so I'm eye level with it. I slowly and evenly blow, and keep going until the rest of the wood catches. Within minutes we have a nice little fire going, the smoke drifting straight up in the still evening. Snaps and pops fill the night air as the wood burns. With a sigh, I finally allow myself to sit down and relax. I grab some water and chug the contents of the first of many bottles. The stuff is an immediate balm on my throat, and right away I sense the tissues of my whole body absorbing it, from the tips of my toes all the way to my fingernails.

Feeling better already, I twist open another one. I gently lift Singer's head and coax him into taking a couple of sips. He coughs and jerks a few times, then sucks down a few swallows. His skin is warmer already, and his color is returning to normal. His eyes flutter open.

"How you doing?" I ask him softly, his head cradled in my hand.

He nods, and when he speaks his voice is little more than wind through trees. "Better."

"Promise me you won't do anything that stupid again. You could have died."

His mouth twitches into a tiny smile, but then his eyes close and he sags into my arms. He may have passed out, but I'm pretty sure he just fell asleep. Still worried, I tuck the blanket around him and kiss him on the forehead. The skin there is cool against my lips, but warmer than it was. I'm no doctor and I can't say for sure, but my guess is he's through the worst of it.

Once everyone has had plenty to drink, I motion to Google and ask him to return to his lair with me. He's visibly reluctant to leave Susan's side, but at my urging he agrees to join me. He's quiet when we reach the plateau. He's again confronted with the devastation caused by Hunter and made even worse by the storms. His head darts around like an anxious hummingbird as he takes it all in. I keep thinking he's going to take my hand for support like a normal kid would, but he doesn't. Regardless, the fact that he's this silent shows how the current state of the place is impacting him. This was his home for years, and seeing it wiped out would distress anyone, even him. He may be blindingly smart and mature beyond his years, but in the end he's still just a kid. His gaze keeps jerking this way and that, the size of his round eyes exaggerated by his thick glasses.

"Are there any, you know…"

"No, the bodies are all gone," I reassure him. "I don't know what happened to them, but they're gone. It's okay."

He nods, his face ghostly pale, and we keep walking around the pits and the ruins of the flattened tents. The ground under our feet is hard, the disgusting mud we were so used to slogging through now dried up and as solid as concrete. We get to the building and unlock the door. After I force it open again, the two of us step inside.

"Let's just get some food now," I tell him. "Tomorrow, when Singer is better, we'll move up here where it's safer."

"Okay."

I follow him inside, and stick close behind him as he moves unerringly through the shelves of equipment. He knows this place as well as anyone would know their own bedroom, and walks confidently through the dark to the back. He turns left where I found the water, then makes a right. In the darkness, I hear him shuffling stuff around as he searches the shelves.

"Here," he says, and hands me a few items. I can't tell what they are, only that they're plastic containers of some sort, each about the size of a coffee can. He slides some other objects around, muttering to himself, then nudges me back the way we came.

"Let's go. This should do it," he whispers.

When we're back in the light, I realize I'm carrying three Costco-sized jars of Jif peanut butter, their red lids almost pulsating at me in the dim light. He's got four boxes of crackers in his arms. We exit the building, and close and lock the door behind us.

"You've had peanut butter in there?" I ask, my mouth suddenly filled with so much saliva I'm surprised I can talk at all. I shake the jars in his face. "You've had freaking peanut butter in there this whole time?"

"Sure. Among other things. You sound surprised."

I don't know whether to punch him or hug him. I'm clutching the containers close to my chest, as if I'm afraid they might evaporate in my arms. I pick up the pace down the gravel road, Google trailing behind me, his little legs straining to keep up. The thought of crackers smeared with peanut butter is egging me on.

That night on the gravel, with the fire burning comfortably next to us, we all gorge ourselves on out-of-date Ritz and expired Jif until the jars are wiped clean. By the time we're ready for bed, Singer is sitting up and joking with us, the worst of his ordeal over.

"Man, are my legs tired," he says, wincing and laughing at the same time as he works the kinks out of his abused muscles. Water bottles are scattered around us like fallen soldiers after a battle, their clear plastic glittering in the firelight. Even Tiny seems back to his normal self, busy chatting with Carly in their secret language. Before we bed down for the night, Google and I make one more trek up the road. Not only does he have food and water there, but guns as well. I've never been good at handling those awful things, but Singer and Harold assure us they are. We grab a few pistols and a rifle of some sort, along with enough ammunition to sustain us through a small war. We also stuff our pockets with some Hershey bars for dessert that were hidden behind the toilet paper.

Our stomachs full for the first time in days and the wrappers of the candy bars flaring up in the fire, we settle down for the night. Carly's face and hands are smeared brown with chocolate, and I do my best to wipe her clean with my shirt. I let the group know I'll take the first watch while they sleep. I doubt anything or anyone will bother us tonight, but I'm going to make damn sure nothing does.

CHAPTER
SEVENTEEN

"Penny for your thoughts?" Dream Eve asks, sitting next to me on the concrete floor with her legs straight out in front of her. She's not wearing any shoes, and the sides and bottom of her feet are filthy. She wiggles her toes and purses her lips, as if slightly perturbed that dirt has the audacity to stick to her like that.

"Honestly? I'm thinking about how weird it is that we're talking again. I don't know why, but for some reason I thought the last time I saw you would be the last time I saw you."

She chuckles at the wordplay and leans her head on my shoulder, a natural gesture I don't mind at all. I catch a flowery whiff of shampoo from her hair.

The furnace room feels very different from the last time I dreamed of her in here. The stench of fuel oil is barely evident, reminding me more of my grandfather's house in the country when he would turn on the furnace for the first time each fall. The massive door is propped open, which either allows the stench to blow out, or permits fresh air from the hallway to roll in. Either way, it's much more pleasant down here than I remember it ever being. I'm not chained to the wall, either, so that's a plus.

Dream Eve sighs, one of those long, drawn-out ones that says her soul is at peace with the world right now. "This is nice. It's too bad this will all be gone when you wake up."

"Yeah, I know," I tell her. Just like before, this feels so real I'm having a hard time believing it's nothing more than a dream, because dreams are not supposed to be this genuine. Besides the smell of her hair, I can feel the coarseness of her green robe against my bare arm. The unyielding concrete floor is doing its best to numb my butt. My subconscious is really putting in overtime with all the details. I didn't know I had it in me.

Her head still against my shoulder, she says, "What are you going to do? You going to stay here? Google's got enough food and water to last for months, you know. Or are you going to head south and see what's going on down there?"

I shrug. "I don't know. I'm afraid the others will want to stay put as long as possible, and I can't blame them for that. But I can't help thinking there's something happening south of us we need to check out. Plus, I can't stop wondering why the Grays have been acting so strange, and how they came after Tiny. What if it's something important? What then?"

"Sounds like you're worried you're going to miss out on something," she says.

I lean my head against the wall and stare straight ahead. "Really? No, that's too easy. I don't believe it."

"Okay, what about this? Maybe you know something deep down you can't put into words. A gut feeling. An instinct. Stranger things have happened to you lately, you know. Telepathy. Commanding Susan to do things with your mind. Tiny knowing what those Grays were thinking. Talking to a dead girl. You have to admit this is all pretty weird."

I give her a nudge with my elbow. "Stop that," I tell her. "I don't like talking about you like that."

"Sorry, but it's true. Can you be one hundred percent sure you don't know anything? Maybe your instincts are telling you something, but you just don't recognize it yet."

"What would you do?" I ask her. "You know, if you were me?"

"Well, if this is nothing but a dream, then technically I am you. Any opinions I have would really be yours, right?"

She's probably right. How can she be anything else but a beloved character of my past, conjured up by whatever part of my brain is in charge of this department? But that doesn't explain how she helped save me when I was dying on the ice. This is all very confusing.

"Fine. If that's true, then what are *we* thinking I

should do? I mean, if this is no more than me talking to myself, then I already know what my decision is, right?"

Eve yawns, her jaw cracking so loudly I can actually hear it pop. She covers her open mouth with a hand, then snuggles deeper into my shoulder.

"Hm. If I were you, I'd pack up as many supplies as quick as I could and check out what's happening down south. Grab Tiny and Singer and get moving. Something is going on, and it's killing you to find out what it is. Grays are traveling down there by the hundreds. Something they've never done before. I have a feeling it's something very special."

I sit up and turn to look at her. She acts a little put out that I've disturbed her, but right now I don't care. "Why do you say that? How could you possibly know something I don't?"

She smiles at me, the purplish stain on the side of her face in sharp contrast to the rest of her tanned skin. Eve used to work so hard at hiding that, but we're beyond that now. She reaches out a hand and brushes the salt and pepper hair out of my face, a tender gesture reminding me of doing the same thing to Carly. She presses her palm against my cheek, and I feel my eyes close. I'm suddenly very sleepy.

"Dear Scout, I can't help you with that. But trust your instincts. Do what you think is right. Go south and see for yourself."

I wake with a start. I'm on the floor of Google's

lair in the dark, the sounds of the others sleeping all around me. Someone snorts and rolls over. I rest my fingertips on my cheek where her hand was moments ago, and swear it's still warm from her touch. I roll over and try to go back to sleep, but that's not going to happen now. I stare at the dark ceiling overhead, waiting for dawn.

We only spend two more days on Rumpke Mountain, although if I took a poll, I bet most everyone would want to stay there forever. Like I said, of everyone in the group, only Google and I have any history with the place. The rest of them see it for what it is, a haven from Grays and an oasis of comfort in a vast waste-land of death and despair. Not since the early days of our time on Church Island or in the office building have they felt more secure and comfortable. I envy them that, and wish I could share in it, but each time I walk outside the building all I can see are the remains of the kids slaughtered there.

Google spends the bulk of his time rummaging through hundreds of bits of electronic gear. I keep ask-ing him what he hopes to accomplish, but he brushes me aside and continues digging through crates, re-moving a cover from some gizmo here, swapping out batteries there. He hasn't been talking or socializing with the rest of the group, either. I leave him alone, figuring it's his way of coping with his own demons.

Singer, however, is almost back to his old self. Like

the others, he's eating and drinking his fill and doing little else but recuperating. Harold has gone full Harold again, and keeps himself busy all day long preparing food and cleaning up afterwards, hardly interacting with the rest of us. What was that old expression? Idle hands are the devil's workshop? He is certainly not idle. I still want to talk to him about what he said when we were fighting the Grays, but we never seem to be alone, and I'm reluctant to bring it up in front of the others. It's evident even to me that whatever's going on with him is deeply personal, and I'm trying to respect that, although not knowing is killing me.

On the third morning, I finally take a stand and tell them it's time to go. I'm immediately bombarded with groans and complaints from everyone except Singer. Not surprisingly, Annie is the vocal ringleader and protests louder than anybody else, clutching Tiny so close to her chest I'm surprised he doesn't turn blue. Harold and Google chime in as well, asking questions I can't answer; Why do we have to go now? Tell me why we're leaving this safe place? I can't explain my reasoning, except to say it's a gut feeling I've got. I leave Dream Eve and her recommendation out of this, convinced no one would understand. Hell, I don't.

In the end, I simply have to lay down the law. Like it or not, I guess they all see me as the leader of this rag-tag band, and my word still carries weight. It's not like me, but I shut them all down and flatly tell them how it is, leaving them grumbling behind me. I grab Singer, and the two of us start making trips to the water's edge, lugging enough food and water down the boat to last us for weeks. The extra weight isn't going to make maneuvering the stupid craft any easier, but we take our time and stack everything strategically so the weight is evenly distributed. On our final load down with the last of the supplies, I catch Singer staring at me. The expression on his normally calm face is hard to read, but if I had to guess I'd say he's torn. He looks like a guy about to break up with his girlfriend, which I desperately hope isn't the case.

"What is it?" I warily ask him. The gravel under our feet crunches as we walk. It's late morning now, and the sun is high in the sky. Its rays are so intense it feels like an extra weight is trying to buckle my knees, dragging me down almost as much as the decision to leave is. Sweat is coursing down my face and stinging my eyes. Singer starts to say something, then stops and clamps his lips together.

"What's going on? Talk to me," I prod again.

"Are we sure," he begins, then stops to gather his thoughts. "I didn't want to argue in front of the others, but are you sure we should leave? I mean, we've got all the food and water we could hope for. Enough to last us months, maybe longer. Shouldn't we stay here? We're safe. All of us, even the kids. You gotta admit, that's a nice change."

He has to know the same thought has crossed my mind a thousand times. He's not totally wrong, and

I know these concerns aren't just coming from him. He's been talking to the others, certainly Harold and Annie, if I had to guess. I don't answer right away, and we make it all the way down to the boat before he breaks the silence again.

"I mean, our goal is to keep the kids safe, right?" he continues as we settle the supplies in the boat, not making eye contact. "I can't think of anywhere better than this, can you?"

I shuffle some cans of food around while I think how to answer him. "You know this place is just temporary, right? We'll run out of supplies soon enough, then we'll be right back where we started. And what if another blizzard hits? If it's anything like the first one, we'd freeze to death in that building. We need to find someplace more permanent. Someplace where the kids will be safe forever, not just now."

He's quiet while he squeezes a final case of bottled water in the back of the boat. I take that as an invitation to keep going. "The whole point of going south was to find out what all those Grays are doing. What if we're too late? What if whatever is happening is happening without us? Can we take that chance?"

He runs his hand over his face, then flicks some sweat from his fingertips. "I know. But what if what's going on down there is, you know, horrible? What if it's another massacre like what happened here? Or on Church Island? What then? We'll be risking the kids for nothing."

I haven't told him about my latest chat with Eve, either, which is a little out of the ordinary since I tell him pretty much everything. If this were a debate, and I was relying on nothing but a gut feeling or what a figment of my imagination told me, the judges would kick me out of the room and down the hall for sure. But I have to trust my instincts on this, and my instincts are telling me we need to go.

"I don't know, but I get the feeling it's something we have to do. I can't explain it any better than that," I answer him.

Singer sighs, staring across the foul water with a distant look in his eyes. The shoreline around us is filled with trash that bobs and swells gently on the surface of the nasty water, almost like it's a living creature. As a general rule the two of us don't argue much, and even if this is pretty tame as far as disagreements go, this tension between us is something new. He's not Hunter, who loved a good fight almost as much as he loved shooting stuff. I step up to him and rest my hand on his shoulder, turning him so we're facing each other.

"This place may feel safe, but it's not. Staying here is only delaying the inevitable. I can't explain why, but I have a feeling we'll find something down there. Something better. You're going to have to trust me on this."

He puffs his cheeks out and blows air from between his pursed lips. For a second, I'm afraid I've lost him too, but then he nods his head.

"I don't get it, but okay. I've always said I'll follow you to the end, and I will. I just hope this isn't it."

He's a foot taller than me, so when I smile up at him, I have to tilt my head way back. "Thanks. And, just in case, I'm going to ask you to be ready to back me up when I force everyone into the boat. I have a feeling we're right on the edge of a mutiny. I may need your vote."

He grins down at me. "You know you can't have a mutiny on land, right? I'm pretty sure that can only happen on the water, and if you're the captain."

I give his shoulder a playful punch. "You know what I mean. Now come on. Let's get everyone and head out."

He salutes me sharply. "Aye, aye, captain. What-ever you say."

My mood has improved significantly as we head back up. I do my best to ignore BamBam's sad remains by the side of the road, preferring instead to remember him as the huge, thoughtful kid he was. Even with Singer's backing, however, I'm still afraid this could be the wrong decision. I hope to hell it isn't.

Damn, I really hate being the leader.

EIGHTEEN

In the end, getting them on board was hard enough, but making them happy about it was too much to expect. Conversation is at an all-time low, and even the little kids sense the tension and keep to themselves. I've never seen Annie so furious, and even Harold is quieter than usual. I was afraid some of them would insist on staying, but without me and Singer there to provide protection, they realize how vulnerable they'd be.

We row southeast all morning. This part of Ohio south of Dayton is hillier than what we've been used to, which means there's an ever-increasing amount of land in our path. The flat landscape of the Great Swamp in northwestern Ohio is far behind us, and more large mounds of dry land are poking out of the water and barring our way. From their muddy and trash-filled condition, these masses used to be submerged, too. But with no rain for so long, the floodwaters continue to back off at an alarming rate. Our progress has slowed dramatically.

After a late lunch, we have to detour around a long, low shopping center recently revealed by the dropping floodwaters. Like a long-sunken battleship forced to the surface, the concrete walls left standing are covered in thick green slime so dark it's almost black. Most of the huge windows across the front of the stores have been shattered, and what remains are square mouths filled with the jagged teeth of broken glass. We can see the rusting tops of cars and SUVs in the parking lot surrounding it, although a few are upside down with their tires up in the air as if in surrender. The place is massive, and I'm certain it wasn't here the last time I came this way. Changes like this are not only concerning because they'll keep slowing us down, but because so much exposed land makes it easier for Grays to make headway. That's never a good thing.

"I wish we could talk to Ted," I say, staring around us.

Google rummages in his backpack and pulls out a small walkie-talkie, similar to the ones we used before. He twists a knob on the top and a crackle of static hisses from the speaker.

"Wait. Where did you get that?" I ask him. The look of astonishment on my face is so extreme it has to be comical. "Seriously, Google?"

"What did you think I was doing back at Rumpke Mountain that whole time?" he asks. "I told you all that stuff would come in handy one day, and I was right." He peers at the device carefully, and fiddles with some dials.

"And you didn't think to tell me before now?"

"I didn't think it was necessary." He clicks a button on the side of the small black device. "Ted? You there? Come in, Ted."

Honestly, for probably the hundredth time, I'm torn between punching him or hugging him. Come to think of it, I might do both. Singer closes his eyes and shakes his head in disbelief, his shoulders moving up and down as he tries to smother a laugh. It's all Harold can do to keep from joining him.

"Come in, Ted. You there?" he asks again.

There's another crackle of static, then we hear Ted's anxious voice. "Holy crap. Google? Is that you?"

The little smartass smiles at me, his grin oozing smug pride, and now I really do want to rough him up. I should have known he wasn't fooling around with all that electronic gear just to take his mind off of our shared horrors. That's not the way his mind works. Rookie mistake on my part.

"Yes, it's me."

I snatch the walkie talkie from his hands. After letting Ted go on about how happy he is to hear my voice, I fill him in on everything that's happened since we last talked. We go back and forth with more questions and answers, until I steer the conversation to the Grays and what we're doing.

"Really? You're going toward them? Why would you do that?"

I ignore Annie's eyes that I'm sure are boring twin holes into the back of my skull. "Something's going on down there, and I have a feeling we need to be there for it. For all of us. Don't ask me to explain it. What have you seen lately?"

"Yeah, well, more Grays have been headed south," he tells us, his voice thick with worry. "I haven't been able to keep track of how many, but it's a lot. They are all going southeast of the Mound, out of Curly's range."

"Can you tell why?"

"No idea. He can't go that far. All I can tell is there's a lot of them, and with the lower water levels they seem to be making pretty good time."

"Have you had any luck spotting Hunter or my brother?"

"No, but that would be next to impossible, you know? Just Grays. Hundreds of them. But," he goes on, "if you're serious about this and stay on your current course, you should be able to get out in front of them. Even though they're still restricted to land, you're not."

"Thanks, Ted. Please keep an eye on everything as well as you can, and get back with us. We're going to keep going."

"Will do, Scout. And thanks."

"Thanks? For what?"

His sigh over the walkie talkie is overflowing with emotions, despair, fear, and more. "I'm just so damn bored," he finally admits. "Besides playing with Curly, there's nothing else to do. It's driving me crazy. At least you guys give me a purpose, you know?"

I feel for the guy, I do, but I don't have any advice for him. "Sorry about that. I really am. We'll keep you company for a while, if that helps."

"Helps? Hell yeah, it helps. I don't know what I'd do if anything happened to you guys. You're just about the only lifeline I've got to the outside world. Just promise me you'll be careful, okay?"

I do my best to assure him we will, even though I have no right to make that claim. I talk to him a little more, trying to stay upbeat, then pass the walkie-talkie back to Google. The two of them carry on for a while, but I'm not really listening. My heart sinks as I realize now I'm not only responsible for the well-being of our own group, but for Ted as well.

Eventually the two of them run out of things to say. I'm the only one here who has actually met Ted in person, and, besides Google and Simon, he doesn't know the rest of us at all. They're just random voices to him and there's only so much to talk about. Google eventually signs off and powers down the walkie talkie.

"How much juice is left in that thing?" I ask.

"Not a lot," he admits. "But I scavenged some other batteries, so we should be okay for a while. I just can't leave it on all the time. I'm going to check in every few hours. That's the best I can do."

Next to me, Singer clears his throat. "You heard

what Ted said, right? We should stay in front of them if we keep going on our present course. But he has no idea of our speed. I can't imagine we're making very good time."

"What are you proposing?" I ask with an eyebrow raised, wary of his answer.

He glances at the back of the boat. "I think you and I should move us along. But this time we'll take turns so neither one of us wears out."

Ugh. The thought of even dipping a toe into that crap-colored water sounds horrible, but he's got a point. We all witnessed how fast we can go like this compared to rowing. I open my mouth to protest, but then clamp it shut.

"Okay, I agree," I tell him after a few seconds. 'But we take turns. No more than, say, half an hour each."

"Great. I'll go first," he says quickly, not giving me a chance to volunteer. He smiles and takes off his shoes, but keeps his shorts and shirt on. He carefully lowers himself into the muck off the side of the boat, sucking in a breath as the frigid water hits his skin. He starts kicking and the overloaded craft lurches forward. Carly grabs hold of the edge and laughs.

"Go, Singer!" she cries out. "You can do it!"

He gives her a fleeting thumbs up before redoubling his efforts. Like before, we're moving fast enough to produce a small wake behind us. We don't have a watch or any way of gauging how much time has passed, but after a while I call out for him to take a break.

Puffing hard, he climbs back into the boat, dripping. His T-shirt is plastered to him like a second skin, and he's shivering, but it's nothing like the last time. He wraps his arms around himself.

"You ready?" he asks through chattering teeth.

"No, I'm not. Not even close, but a deal's a deal."

I take off my shoes and, with a deep sigh of regret, slide into the icy water. It's so cold it makes me suck in a sharp breath, and I start to shiver almost immediately. Thinking back, I realize I've hardly ever touched the stuff before. The thick liquid almost seems to cling to my skin, more like motor oil than real water. It's disgusting, and makes me want to immediately shower in hand sanitizer. As I'm contemplating how to get it off of me when I'm done, my bare feet brush against something invisible, and I almost yelp in surprise.

"What the hell is down here?" I yell up to Singer, ready to spring back into the boat.

"Oh, yeah. It's just trash and crap floating down there. You'll get used to it."

"No, I won't. I never even liked swimming in Lake Erie if I saw seaweed, much less gross stuff hiding where I can't see it. What the hell is it?"

"I don't know. The trash of an entire world, I guess. Mainly things that don't decompose. You won't even notice it once you get going."

He's wrong. This is the most sickening stuff I've ever touched. Even the stench is enough to make me gag. But if Singer can manage to do this twice before, then I can, too. I'm going to convince myself it's just plastic grocery bags, branches, Solo cups, and nothing else. Not rotting clothing, bits of people, or other gruesome crap like that. I get into position at the back of the boat and start kicking. In no time at all, we're moving along, not as fast as we were when Singer did it, but better than if we were rowing. More than anything, I work at keeping my head and mouth up and out of the nasty stuff.

When I was a little kid, my mom signed me up for swimming lessons at the local pool. To graduate from my Guppy class up to Salmon, we had to swim ten lengths of the pool. It was hard, mainly because I wasn't a strong swimmer. Besides that, I was a skinny little thing, composed of little more than bone, muscle, and skin, which gave me all the buoyancy of a brick. I recall struggling along and starting to panic, until I learned to keep my head down and just concentrate moving my arms and kicking my feet. In the end, I was able to complete the required ten laps, only to fail the next test when I couldn't tread water for fifteen minutes. Anyway, when I got done with the laps and touched the wall for the final time, I remember thinking the whole experience wasn't so bad after all.

That's what I begin doing here. My eyes clamped shut, I clear my mind of anything except the repetitive action of kicking. Each time something brushes against my feet or legs I nearly scream out loud, but I keep going. Later, when Singer calls out my name to take a break, he has to do so two or three times before it registers. I finally stop and gratefully accept his hand as he pulls me out. The warm air and sunshine feel glorious as I shiver in the bottom of the boat.

"That wasn't so bad, was it?" he asks, smiling.

"Oh, no. Great fun. Can't wait to do it again."

Still smiling at me, he steels himself and eases back in to take his shift. I hold on as the boat surges ahead, convinced he's better at this than me.

The mood in the boat has mellowed. I'm not sure if it's the distance we've already put between us and Rumpke Mountain, or the fact we actually have something of a destination in mind. More bits of land are visible here and there, some with the remains of houses, others completely barren. The tops of some sturdy brick homes that were once beautiful peek their roofless heads out of the brown water. Here and there we spot a lone chimney. Near the end of Singer's turn, we have to skirt around another freshly emerged spit of land. This one has a Shell gas station on the corner and a few shops and houses with their rotted roofs barely visible. Nasty, unidentifiable stuff is draped across the Shell sign, gross tatters of trash that dangle like Halloween decorations in the still air. Just nosing above the waterline nearby is a mud-covered green street sign on a metal pole that tells us we're near the intersection of somewhere called Far Hills and Stroop Road. I call a halt, and while Singer catches his breath

Google gets on the walkie talkie with Ted again.

"Hey, sounds like you're making pretty good time," Ted says when we tell him what we saw. "You're already in the southern suburbs of Dayton. Centerville, if I remember my geography."

"I don't suppose you can tell how much farther we have to go?" I ask hopefully.

"No clue, sorry. I don't know your final destination. The Grays I saw were still north of your position. They've made it through Dayton already, from what I can tell. You're miles ahead of them."

"What's up ahead of us? Can Curly see that far?"

"He's charging now. He should be ready to go soon. But even with a full battery he won't be able to go much farther than where you are now. Not if I want him to make it back."

I can't ask him to risk our only source of information, even though I'm dying to know what we might be getting into. Plus, pushing him to potentially sacrifice his only outlet into the outside world would be too much to ask. He did that for us once before. I won't ask him to do that again.

"That's okay," I tell him. "Just do what you can and let us know. We're going to stop pretty soon and rest for the night. We can't be completely exhausted when we get to wherever we're going. That's not safe or smart."

We sign off, and Singer gamely starts kicking again. When his time's up, I grit my teeth and slink back off the boat and into the greasy stuff. In no time at all I feel my legs tiring, but I force myself to keep going until my kicks are so feeble I have to stop. Singer helps me onto the boat a second time, where I collapse in a shivering heap. He's about to take his turn, but I wave him away.

"That's enough for now," I manage between gasps. "Night is going to be here soon. Let's call it a day and rest up for tomorrow."

He pats my arm tenderly. "One more round for me, and then we'll stop."

Without waiting for my response, he hangs on the edge and goes in again. I try to work up enough outrage to stop him, but he's already at the back of the boat and moving us along. The sun is low on the western horizon and isn't warming me up as quickly as I'd like. The bone-deep shivers stay with me for a long time. Fifteen or twenty minutes into his turn, Harold suddenly shifts in his seat and points.

"Land ho!" he shouts loud enough for Singer to hear him.

My head pops up. Singer stops, and it's quiet enough that I can hear his heavy breathing over the water lapping against the metal hull. Everyone else in the boat is struck silent and staring where the cook is pointing.

A dark band of land has appeared in front of us, stretching as far as we can see in either direction. The shoreline is littered with colorful trash and debris like everywhere else. Beyond that the ground rises in a slow grade that keeps inching up. Trees are sprouting leaves here and there, a colorful change none of us have seen in a long time. Grass and weeds are growing deep and lush in the open areas beyond the old flood line. To the left of that, a wide road emerges from the water and meanders up the hill. However, as novel as seeing this much land at one time is, it's nothing compared to what's in the distance. Up on a hill there are buildings, a dozen or so, clustered together like dorms on a college campus. The tan brick one and two-story structures are sharply defined by the low sun, with its red and yellow reflected light winking at us from a hundred different windows. One building, set on a rise behind the rest, dwarfs the others and towers at least a dozen stories with regularly spaced windows running up and down the sides. In-between us and the buildings, phone poles are spread out evenly along the shoreline every fifty yards or so, with more marching off in both directions like soldiers in single-file formation. The poles have big black boxes attached to them, but I can't tell what they are from here. Whatever this place is, it looks almost pristine and new, a throwback to a time before the Storm. It's never been underwater, that's for sure.

"Where the hell are we?" Annie whispers.

"I don't know," Harold replies, slack jawed. "But wherever we've been going, I have a feeling we're here."

CHAPTER
NINETEEN

It's late, and the sun is nearly touching the horizon to the west. Singer's in the back of the boat shivering. As worried as I am at everything that's happening right now, I can't help but fixate on the slimy film that's covering me from head to toe. I've never wanted a shower, some Comet, and steel wool more than I do right now. I'm not proud of the fact I'm more concerned with personal hygiene than at our current situation, but I can't help it. I keep trying to brush the invisible stuff off my skin, but it's like wiping off grease. I spit over the side, convinced and horrified some of it got in my mouth.

"What now?" Harold asks the group, but staring at me. "We can't go any farther in the boat, that's for sure. That land looks like it goes forever both ways."

"I say we head to shore," Google chimes in right away. "I don't know if Grays travel at night, but if they can then we don't have a lot of time before they get here. Assuming this is where they're headed."

The two best fighters here, me and Singer, are exhausted. To be fair, Harold has shown he can handle himself very well, but he's just one guy. Yeah, we've got a few guns, but they wouldn't do much against an army of Grays, as we were reminded on Church Island. Except for Susan, Annie and the rest of them are basically useless if things go sideways. I have no way of knowing if there could be a fight, but we haven't survived this long by assuming there won't be one.

"I'm with Google," Singer says, still shivering from his time overboard. "We've come all this way because you insisted, Scout. I don't think we can stop now. I say we go for it."

If we head in, we can't take a chance on being caught out in the open in case Grays show up. If this is even their final destination. If this is even the right place. There are so many "ifs" right now. I just wish I had some way of knowing for sure! Where's Dream Eve when I need her? I don't care if she's a figment of my imagination or not, I wouldn't mind some of her advice.

"Anyone else?" I ask, delaying while the limited options play out in my head. "Do we stay in the boat or take our chances on shore?"

Tiny starts signing to Carly, who stares at him with the intensity of a little kid engrossed by TV. The two of them go back and forth while the rest of us stare at them, clueless as to what they're saying. When they finish, Carly looks at me. Her little face is a mask of confusion.

"Tiny says we need to go. On land. She's waiting for us at the buildings."

I shake my head. "Waiting for us? Who? How can he know that? Who's she?"

Carly brushes a strand of black hair from her face and holds her hands out, just like a miniature adult admitting they're at a loss. "He doesn't know. He just keeps repeating that she's waiting for us."

Harold's gaze shifts, now fixed on the clustered buildings. "Well, if that's not creepy as shit, I don't know what is."

"I don't understand," I continue. "How can he know something like that?"

She shrugs her shoulders. "I don't know. That's what he says."

We all fall silent and still, except for Tiny. He keeps making the same motions with his hands over and over. As far as I can tell, he doesn't look scared. Just concerned, or maybe upset that we aren't doing what he says right away. He's at that age where a typical child would throw a fit, like any normal kid denied candy in line at the grocery store, but he's not like that. I've never seen him act up at all, come to think of it. What toddler that age doesn't have a meltdown once in a while?

I tear my gaze from him and stare once again at the buildings in the distance. They're too far away to make out any details, and the fading light isn't doing us any favors, either. If there are people there, we can't see them.

"Google, get Ted on the line. I want to talk to him."

He fires up the walkie talkie. Our lonely observer from the Mound connects right away. I'm sure he's been anxiously waiting to hear from us.

"Yeah, Scout, what's going on?"

"Ted, you lived around here before the Storm. We're looking at some sort of compound of buildings on a hill. A bunch of smaller ones that look like dorms or small houses, and a single tall one much bigger than the rest. There's a wide road running past them. Can you tell us what this place is?"

"Um, I'm not sure. If you're looking at Far Hills, I used to drive up and down there once in a while, sure, but I didn't live in Dayton. Can you give me any other landmarks? Anything would help."

All of us crane our necks around like prairie dogs when they hear a noise. There's not much else to see, really. There may be some buildings on the other side of the road, but they're of a completely different style and don't seem to belong to the compound. There are a lot of trees. My eyes travel left, and stop, trying to make sense of something. I click the button on the walkie talkie.

"Ted, on the other side of the road there's something sticking out of the water. From here it looks like a tall, very steep roof. Almost like a pyramid. I can make out shingles. But the rest of the building is under water. Whatever it used to be, it had a very distinctive roof. I'm sure it's something you would have noticed before."

Ted is silent while he thinks. "How far did you say you traveled since we last talked?"

I look at Singer and then at Harold. They both shrug at me, clueless and no help at all.

Google says, "Probably a mile or so."

I click the button again. "Google says we probably went a mile, but there's no way to be sure."

"Okay, that helps," Ted replies slowly, as if he's thinking aloud. "I remember a building like that. I never paid much attention to it, but I remember a church right along there with a roof like that. You're right, Scout, it was very distinctive. And it was right off of Far Hills. You say it's across the road from this compound?"

Another church? Really? What is it with all these churches? "Yes. Very close. Less than a quarter mile, I'd say."

"I can't be sure, but if it's what I think it is, I'm pretty sure there was some sort of retirement home across the street from it. I seem to recall a sign out front and a single tall building along Far Hills. I never noticed the name, not that it matters. If I had to guess, I'd say that's your compound."

I thank Ted, promising him we'll be back in touch soon, and click off the walkie talkie. Once I hand it

back to Google, I rub my face with my hands, thinking.

"It doesn't really matter what it was before, does
it?" Harold asks me, and starts ticking off talking points
on his fingers. "It matters what it is now, right? And
who they are. And why all those Grays are headed
here. And if we want to get there before the Grays do.
And we can't get caught out here if another blizzard
hits, because then nothing will matter. Am I missing
something, or is that it?"

I sigh. "No, I think that about covers it."

We discuss it a little more, but democracy rules
in the end. We agree that if we're going to head into
shore, it has to happen now. As a group we know if
we wait and the Grays beat us there, we may never be
able to make landfall. On top of that, the one thing
Harold neglected to mention was what Tiny said
about someone waiting for us. To be fair, that weirded
me out, but I think we're all intrigued by it, too. Well,
except for Annie, of course. She's still staring daggers
at me, her cheeks flushed as she clutches Tiny to her
chest. However, the rest of the group agrees, and one
by one they look at me for final confirmation. I glance
out at the open water behind us at what is certainly
the short-term, easy way out of this. But in the end,
with a deep breath, I nod at them.

"Okay, let's do this while we still have some light."

Singer grabs the oars and tosses one to me. The
two of us put our backs into it and row hard, moving

us toward land almost as fast as we were going with me as the motor. The boat lumbers ahead, leaving the relative safety of the open water behind us.

"Harold, get the guns ready, just in case," I order him between strokes.

He's a step ahead of me and already has the rifle across his lap, busy checking to make sure it's fully loaded. He fills his pockets with ammunition. When he's done, he takes a pistol and sets it on the seat next to Singer. He holds one out to me, but I shake my head.

"No thanks," I tell him. "Just leave it here in case we need it later."

As we near land, the boat cuts through a mass of floating trash and debris. A lot of it. The wind or currents must have pushed it all here. The boat bumps through thousands of discolored water bottles, chunks of Styrofoam, rotting lumber, and all kinds of other junk covered with brown slime. A heavy clunk impacts the bow as a decaying oil drum bobs past us. Water this nasty makes me think we should see fish floating belly up, but they've been dead and gone so long they've decomposed to nothing.

"Keep your eyes out for Grays," Singer warns as he paddles. "Yell if you see anything at all."

With so much trash around us, it's hard to see where the water ends and the land begins. But suddenly the front of the boat lifts up and we jerk to a halt. We stop rowing, but remain as we are, shocked that we're actually here. Wherever here is.

As I would expect, Harold is the first one to react. He jumps knee-deep into the trash and grabs the rope and begins pulling. Singer joins him, and together they tug hard enough to yank the overloaded craft all the way in. Snapping out of my temporary trance, I retrieve my backpack and toss Singer's to him.

"Let's go, everyone," I order. "We don't have any time to waste."

Everyone clambers onto land. The trash is so deep in spots we have to kick it away just to move around. The ground under our feet is thick and gooey and sticks to our shoes as we walk, just like the slop that used to be everywhere. It also smells, a thick stench of rot and mold so overpowering it's a physical presence inside my nose. The reek is just like the water, but magnified a hundred times. Next to me Annie heaves quietly, and I'm afraid she's going to throw up.

I take the point and aim us at the buildings in the distance. Their windows still reflect the setting sun, making them an easy target even in the fading light. We slog through the mud and debris, trying to be silent but failing spectacularly. Harold and his rifle are directly behind me, and Singer is bringing up the rear with a pistol at the ready. A little farther on the trash field gives way to grass, and we push ahead. Annie is carrying Tiny, and Harold has scooped up Carly and has her on his shoulders. I look down and see Chuck is in my hand, and a familiar sense of comfort lifts my spirits.

The grass and weeds are thick and hard to walk through, snatching and grabbing at my ankles like a million tentacles trying to hold me back. No one is talking, and even Carly is silent, her eyes so huge in her round face it's almost cartoonish. A little bit ahead of us is one of the poles we spotted from the boat. I'd guess it's twenty feet tall. Near the top are three black boxes, all facing in different directions. Each box is about the size of a small suitcase, a little bigger than one of those carry-ons people used to force into the overhead compartments on planes. Not knowing exactly what they are is bugging me, but we don't have time to waste. We push ahead.

We're about a dozen feet away from the pole when we're nearly knocked off our feet by a wall of sound. Like the stench of the mud when we landed, it's almost a physical thing, an invisible force that rattles our skulls and turns our brains to mush. We reflexively slam our hands to our ears and drop to our knees, our eyes squeezed shut. The sound is so deafening I can't hear my own screaming. It's blasting from the black boxes, and I realize now that they're speakers. None of us are used to anything louder than a random gunshot, and the ear-splitting racket is so overwhelming I'm surprised it hasn't loosened our bowels. Not far from me, Susan is writhing on the ground like she's strapped to a hot plate. Her mouth is stretched open and the tendons in her neck and arms are bulging almost to the point of snapping. All of us are being im-pacted by this, but not to the extent she is.

Singer crawls to me. He's mouthing something, but it's impossible to hear him over this inhuman howling. He grabs my arm and drags me backwards, both of us stumbling over each other as we try to escape the inescapable. We move back a few feet, and just as suddenly as it started, the sound stops. Its absence is almost as overwhelming as its presence was. Slowly, we remove our hands from our ears, each of us primed to slam them back on if we have to. Wobbling a little, I get to my feet. The others do the same, except for Susan. She's still on the ground, panting like a wounded animal, her eyes screwed up tightly. I've only seen a Gray immobilized like that once before, in the parking lot of the Mound when the dozens of klaxons went off. But this was a hundred times more intense than that.

I say something, but I can't even hear myself. My ears are ringing and feel stuffed with cotton. I work my jaw a few times, but there's a keening in my head that blankets out all other sounds. Singer takes both of my shoulders in his hands and makes sure I'm looking directly at him.

"Are you okay?" he yells, although his voice is so garbled he could be screaming at me underwater. I'm lip-reading him as much as anything.

I nod, still moving my jaw side to side. "Yeah, I

think so."

"What the hell was that?"

I tilt my head toward Susan. "Something to keep Grays away?"

He nods. "Must be. Pretty damn effective."

I nod back at him since it's easier than trying to talk. The two of us walk around to the other members of our group one at a time, checking on them. Besides being in a state of shock at what just happened, they all seem to be recovering. Carly is crying, but her sobs can't penetrate my damaged ears. I pick her up as she buries her head in my shoulder. Like two astronauts communicating through touched helmets, when our heads make contact, I can hear her muffled whimpering. I rub her back until she begins to relax. I put her down, but keep her close.

Thankfully, the ringing in my ears is fading. I'm starting to hear the others as they yell at each other, trying to make themselves heard over the collective din in our heads. Harold wobbles a little as he makes his way over to me.

"What now?" he shouts, motioning over his shoulder. "To the boat?"

I look back the way we came. The sunlight is nearly gone, and only a streaky orange sky is left painted on the horizon. I can't believe we've come this far, overcome so much, only to be stopped now. I was so damn sure this was the right thing to do! But there's no way we can make it past these sound machines. I take a deep breath and run shaky hands through my hair. We don't have any choice now. We have to retreat to the boat. I don't want to, but at least it'll give us a chance to regroup and figure out our next steps. I'm about to agree with him when he grabs my arm, his eyes alive.

"Look!" he shouts, snapping the rifle up to his shoulder.

I follow his eyes and suck in a lungful of air. Coming at us about a hundred yards away, the buildings at their backs, are three figures pushing through the tall grass. I can't make out many details in the fading light, but I can see rifles slung over their shoulders.

"Singer! Harold! Up here with me," I yell as loud as I can. "The rest of you, get behind us!"

They must be able to hear me well enough because, although we're not drilled in this sort of action, everyone follows my orders remarkably well. Harold is on my left with the rifle raised, and Singer is a step behind me with the pistol up and ready. Susan finally sits up, but she's a trembling mess and needs a hand planted on the ground just to stay upright. The three figures coming at us don't slow, they just keep pushing through the grass. If they're alarmed at our aggressive posture, they're not showing it. I still can't hear much, but ironically my heart is thumping incredibly loud in my ears.

When the three of them are only a dozen feet from the pole, they stop. My jaw flops open in shock. The guy in front is in his thirties or early forties, if I had to guess. He has long blondish brown hair parted on the side. He's handsome, in a rugged, news anchorman kind of way. The two behind him are a little older. The one on the left is tall and skinny with slightly hunched shoulders and a sad face. His companion is shorter and thick through the shoulders and neck, and makes me think of either a wrestler or a lumberjack. Both have rifles, but they're pointed down at the ground. The first guy waves the other two to a halt, then takes a few steps toward us. His eyes flick between me and Annie, which strikes me as kind of weird. When he talks, his voice is deep and forceful enough to penetrate the cotton in our ears.

"Which one of you is Scout?" he asks.

Shaking, I take a step forward, but I don't stray far from Singer and Harold. I'm conscious of the thick grass grabbing at my ankles as I lift each foot, like it's intentionally restraining me for my own safety. Singer puts a hand on my shoulder. I'm thankful for the human contact as I stand out here, exposed.

"Um, I'm Scout," I answer, my voice cracking.

With that confirmation, the two in the back whisper something to each other, hands in front of their faces to shield their mouths. The guy in the lead doesn't pay any attention to them, but a wisp of a smile appears and is gone just as quickly, like maybe he won a bet with himself.

"All of you, you need to come with me. Even that thing," he says, pointing at Susan. He isn't loud, but I can hear him well enough through my bruised eardrums. He motions toward the buildings with a flip of his head. "It's not safe out here. But I'm sure you know that."

Harold steps up next to me. His chin juts out once, like he's saying hey to an acquaintance on the sidewalk. If he's at all nervous, he's hiding it well. "Who are you people? What do you want with us?"

"I'm Red," the man replies, not unkindly, although his tone has taken on an edge of impatience that we're not already following his orders. "These two behind me are Shorty and Stretch. I'll let you figure out which one is which. Now come on. We need to go."

My voice, when I discover it again, still sounds weird and distorted in my head. "How did you know my name?"

"I'll explain everything later. Let's get a move on."

Now it's Singer's turn. He moves in front of me protectively, the left side of his body shifting to partially shield me from the three of them. The pistol is at his side and out of action, but his finger is hovering near the trigger. "Not until you tell us who you are and what you want. We can always get back in the boat and leave if we have to."

Red laughs once, a short exclamation that's half bark, half taunt. "Sure you can, kid. And go where? Back out on the water? What if another blizzard hits, eh? Or a tornado? It's been a while, so we're probably due for one soon. You'd be dead in seconds, that's what. Trust me, we're your best shot at staying alive."

With more bravado than I feel, I pat the air in front of me, stalling. "Just give us a minute, okay? We have no idea who you are or what you want, and your little sound machine here isn't exactly welcoming, you know? This is all happening kind of fast."

Red breathes once through his nose, his arms crossed across his chest. "Fine. Go ahead and talk it over. You've got one minute then we're outta here."

I motion everyone together, and they quickly huddle around me. We lean in until our foreheads are nearly touching. Annie is holding Tiny. His hands are moving frantically. Carly is standing in the middle with her gaze bouncing between us and him.

"How the hell did he know who you were? And why isn't he weirded out that Susan's with us?" Harold hisses between his teeth. He's not loud, but I can hear him now. That's promising, at least.

I shake my head. "No clue. But he didn't, not exactly. He was looking between me and Annie. I think he was searching for a girl and didn't know which one I was. Not until I told him."

"Am I the only one who noticed how old these guys are?" Harold continues. "How come they haven't gone Gray yet? How does that work?"

"I don't have an answer to that, either," I tell him. "Besides us and Ted, these are the first people I've seen that haven't changed. Something important is going on here, I just don't know what it is yet."

Singer says, "I don't trust any of this, and I don't like these guys. I say we get back in the boat and get the hell out of here before that army of Grays shows up."

"I'm with Singer," Annie blurts out, bordering on tears again. "Let's go!"

We go back and forth like this, and I'm painfully aware we've already exceeded Red's time limit. He confirms this when he yells out that our minute is up. All eyes in our group are on me, and I freeze until I feel a tugging at my pant leg.

"Tiny says we should trust them," Carly insists from below us. "He says we need to go up the hill, or something like that."

Shocked at what she just said, I stand up and break the huddle. I pause for a second, then turn and face the three newcomers in the near-dark. They're still waiting, although Red is shuffling his feet and glancing around anxiously. I'm not sure what I'm going to do, but then a question forms in my mind.

"Okay, before we go any farther, tell me this: where exactly do you want us to go?" I ask them.

Red huffs once and jabs a thumb over his shoulder "Up the hill, where it's safe. Someone up there wants to talk to you."

Up the hill. That means nothing to me, but it's the exact phrase Carly just used. That can't be a coincidence, can it? Eve isn't here, but I can almost hear her telling me to trust them. I look around one more time. It's so dark now that I can barely see the boat from here. The faces of my friends are little more than pale circles with dark smudges where their features should be. Carly's little hand is still tugging on my pant leg.

"Okay," I tell everyone. "Gather up your stuff. We're going with them."

Annie nearly collapses, and might have if Harold didn't catch her in time. I grab my backpack and turn away from our group, praying everyone will follow me one more time. Red sees me and holds up a hand, a clear signal to stop. He takes a walkie talkie out of his pocket.

"Turn off section SW6," he says into the small device.

I can't hear anyone on the other end, but a few seconds later he motions us forward. I find I'm holding my breath as I inch ahead a few paces. When another blast of noise doesn't flatten me, I keep going with a sense of relief. I glance over my shoulder and see everyone has picked up their things and are lining up to go. Harold is right behind me again, while Singer has taken up a position at the rear, same as before. Annie is off to the side, and for a moment I'm afraid she's not coming, but in the end she does, Tiny still locked in her arms. I can't tell for sure, but the little guy might be smiling.

"Let's get a move on," Red says. "We're burning daylight."

I've never heard that phrase before, but I'm pretty sure I get what he means. Red and his two buddies start walking, taking the same path they did on their way down to meet us. The tall grass and slight uphill slope are enough to make our progress more difficult than I thought it would be. Harold taps me on the shoulder and leans close to my ear.

"You sure you know what you're doing?" he asks.

I've never been a good liar, and now's not the time to start. "No, not really. But we don't have much of a choice, do we? We can't take a chance and stay out here."

I think he's going to say something else, but in the end he doesn't, and quietly drops back a few paces behind me again. We keep trudging up the hill behind the three men as darkness falls around us. I can hear Annie and Carly breathing a little heavier than normal from the exertion. When the sound machine pole is well behind us, Red says something else into the walkie talkie. My ears have healed enough to hear him tell whoever is at the other end to turn SW6 back on, which I'm assuming is the name of the machine that stopped us before. He starts walking again, and like freight cars behind a train, one by one we all start moving along after him. In front of us, the brick structures are a jumble of darker rectangles and triangles outlined against the still of the night. Some buildings farther up the hill have lights on in the windows, but most are dark. When we're almost to the first cluster, the grasses underfoot stop and we're walking on a hard surface. It's either a parking lot or a driveway. It's so dark out now that Red turns on a flashlight so we don't crash into something.

"Come on. We're almost there," he says.

Only a few dozen steps later, he points the beam on a building in front of us. The structure was only lit for a second and I didn't get a chance to see much, but it looked like a small brick ranch home, one of those single-story jobs that are as common as corn stalks all over the Midwest. The windows are dark, but I can make out white curtains behind the glass. Outside, overgrown bushes line a walkway to the front door. He opens the door and steps inside, fumbles around a moment, then the room unexpectedly glows from within. Shorty and Stretch step aside as Red motions us in.

When we step across the threshold, it's like we've been transported six years in the past to someone's grandmother's house. The light Red turned on is an actual working lamp on a table, which is pretty cool all by itself. But it's what the light shows that's left us all speechless; the place is pristine, clean and, shockingly, normal. The flood that destroyed so much of the world somehow hasn't touched this place. It's an amazing throwback to a time before all this happened.

There are a pair of colorful couches and a recliner positioned in front of a TV, just like nature intended. In the corner is a tall, thin cabinet with a glass front that protects about a zillion little ceramic figurines, each one of them smiling and in a different cheery pose. A braided oval rug is a rainbow splash of color that draws my eyes to the center of the room. White lace tablecloths adorn the tables. My grandmother used to call them doilies, I think. I take a whiff and realize the place has a faint aroma of medicine and something lemony, maybe Pledge furniture polish. Several wooden crosses hang prominently on the walls, along with a picture of a smiling, long-haired guy in the place of honor above the TV. Judging by the robe and the way his face seems to glow, it has to be Jesus. As I stand there and slowly spin in place, I get the feeling I'm gawking, but I can't help myself.

Red doesn't react at all to our communal shock. Instead, he moves around the room and turns on a few more lights, and each time he does I have to suppress a small giggle of delight at this return to normalcy.

"There's some food and water in the fridge," he tells us. "The plumbing works, too, so go ahead and take showers if you want, which might not be a bad idea. You'll stay here tonight, and we'll come get you in the morning."

That catches my attention. "Wait. In the morning? I thought you said someone wants to meet us now?"

"She does. She's been talking nonstop about all of you for weeks. But it's late, and she's asleep by now. Get some rest and we'll do it tomorrow."

Google hasn't spoken a word since we first saw the three of them, but his curiosity has apparently exceeded his ability to keep his mouth shut. He steps out from behind me and stands there with both hands on his hips, looking like a miniature professor lecturing a class.

"Who is this person you keep talking about? We at least deserve to know who she is."

Red walks back to the door, one hand resting on the doorknob. "The Abuela. Don't worry, you'll meet her in the morning. Now get cleaned up and get some rest."

"Wait!" I yell, louder than I meant to. I take a step toward him. "You need to know. There are Grays coming. Hundreds of them. Maybe more. We don't know why, but we think they're headed here."

He stops dead in his tracks. "You are chock full of surprises, aren't you? Yeah, we know all about those things." He pauses and stares at me. "What I'd like to know is how you know they're coming?"

I'm about to tell him about Ted, but Singer bumps into me from behind. "We saw them. On land, moving this way," he says. "We couldn't count how many there were, but it's a lot."

Red's eyes dart back and forth between the two of us. "Yeah, we know. The sound machines will keep them out. Don't worry." His gaze lingers on Susan for a second, as if he doesn't trust her. The fact that he's barely reacting to her is still strange as hell.

Harold steps up next to Singer. "If you don't mind my asking, how'd you know they were coming?"

"Don't worry about it. Now get some rest, and for God's sake get cleaned up. You all reek." With that, he steps out and closes the door behind him. It shuts with a click that's loud in the quiet room.

"What does 'reek' mean?" Carly asks innocently, breaking the silence and looking at each of us for an answer.

Google says, "That was an interesting exchange."

I glance at Singer. "Yeah, it was. Why didn't you tell him about Ted?"

He shrugs. "I don't know. But it's clear he's holding back info from us. I figured I'd do the same. Besides, it may come in handy later. But now, before we do anything else, let's check this place out and see what we've got. Any objections?"

No one has any. All eyes track him as he steps up to the refrigerator first. He opens the door slowly, like something might leap out at him. Nothing does. Instead of a threat, however, the tiny bulb inside reveals jars of food, bottles of water, butter, bread, and a lot more. He carefully shuts the door and opens a tall cupboard next to it. Inside are shelves filled with canned goods of all kinds, plus boxes of dried food and cereal, just for starters. Carly, meanwhile, has already forgotten her vocabulary question and is scurrying around to different rooms, dashing inside each one and flicking on lights.

"Bedrooms! With beds!" she squeals, sticking her head back into the living room. "And a bathroom!" She ducks back out of sight, and seconds later there's a flushing noise, a sound few of us have heard in years. She pokes her head into the living room again, a huge smile splashed across her face. "And the toilet works!"

For the next ten minutes, despite our anxiety over all that's happened since we made landfall, every one of us except Susan darts around the little house and explores. None of us can believe what we're seeing, and we're so busy finding the next treasure that we bounce from one discovery to the next like kids on a new playground. If I had to explain to someone what our emotional state is now, it would be giddy. Honestly, it's the only word I can think of that accurately describes what we're feeling. It's a sensation none of us have enjoyed in so very long.

Eventually, though, we run out of steam and gather back in the living room, collapsing on the couches, the chair, or the floor. Susan never budged from her original spot near the door, although someone thought enough to give her a loaf of bread, which she's devouring by the handful. The rest of us are all munching on something different and amazing and washing it down with cold water from the fridge. I found a red tube of Pringles potato chips in the pantry, and I'm stuffing stacks of them in my mouth and crunching like it's my job, savoring the salty taste. My hearing has returned, and all the lip-smacking and moans of joy make it sound like we haven't eaten in months. I polish off the last of the chips, tip the tube up to pour out the crumbs in my mouth, and wipe my face clean.

"Everyone feel better?" I ask, rolling my tongue around to get at the last fragments stuck in the nooks and crannies of my teeth. I have a vague memory about Pringles, something about them not having any real potatoes in them, a potential bit of trivia that doesn't bother me in the least right now. Everyone pauses in either mid-chew or with a handful of something about to be gobbled down. It's almost comical.

"Good. We need to talk about what's going on and where we are. I know this all looks too good to be true, which means it probably is. But it's hard to argue with a clean house and all the food we can eat. I mean, this place has electricity and running water, for god's sake."

"And toilets that work!" Carly reminds us, smiling wide.

"Yes, and toilets that work. Besides the obvious, did anyone see anything weird or out of the ordinary?"

Google raises his hand. "Did you notice there are no stairs anywhere around here? My grandma used to live in a place like this. There's not even a step to come in from the front door, just like her place, so she wouldn't trip. Didn't Ted say he thought this was a retirement home?"

Damn, he's observant. "Good catch. Yes, he did. Anyone else?"

Singer sits up to get my attention. "Nothing else, really. Except look at the lace doilies everywhere, and the little ceramic people over in that cupboard. Google's right. This looks just like some old person's home. I'd say Ted was right. Not that it matters, but at least we know where we are, basically. I guess that's something."

I nod at him. "Okay, so we know where we are.

What about Red knowing who I was? And what Tiny told Carly about someone, this 'Abuela' person, wanting to talk to me? Any thoughts? And who or what's an abuela, anyway?"

Everyone stares around the room at each other blankly, like when my elementary teacher used to demand the class reveal who was making fart noises behind her back. Harold's got a box of Cheerios in his lap and another handful of the little Os halfway to his mouth. He stops chewing and swallows.

"If I remember right from my first and only Spanish class, an abuelo is a grandfather, and an abuela is a grandmother," he tells us. "That much I got. It's everything else about this that's creepy as hell."

Google says, "Yes! How did they know who you were, Scout? How could they know we were coming? Why didn't they react when they saw Susan with us? How do they know Grays are coming? How did Tiny know what 'up the hill' meant?"

I turn and look at the little guy, but he's sacked out on Annie's chest. His hair is a tousled mess, and there's a little bubble of drool in the corner of his mouth that expands and contracts as he breathes. He's got his thin arms around her neck. Just the sight of him safe and sound warms my heart.

"Looks like Tiny is out for the count. Carly, what about you?" I ask.

"Uh, before he fell asleep, I was asking him about the hill thing, 'cause that sounded weird," she volunteers. "But he didn't know anything else. He just knew, that's all he kept saying." She shrugs with her palms up and out, as if apologizing.

"I don't know if it means anything," Harold adds. "But I checked the front door a little bit ago, and it's unlocked. Guess that means we're not prisoners here."

"Not in this house, at least," I reply. "But we're still basically trapped in the compound by those sound machines. No way we can get past those things, even if we wanted to."

The conversation keeps going that way for a while, but we're all exhausted and winding down fast. When there's a longer than usual lull in the conversation, Harold proclaims he's going to see what the shower is like. A few minutes after he leaves the room, I hear the novel sound of water running and splashing. When he's done and rejoins the group, his hair is wet and there's a healthy glow about him I haven't seen before. After he states it may have been the most wonderful thing he's ever experienced, the rest of us rush to take turns and do the same, one at a time. I volunteer to go last, and by the time my turn rolls around the hot water is pretty much gone, but I stay in there as long as I can with the cooling water beating against my up-turned face. I'm so filthy that what I thought was tan is actually plain old dirt, which I watch swirl around my feet as it gets sucked down the drain.

When I step out, my skin all tingly from so much exuberant scrubbing, and still dripping a little with a towel wrapped around me, I notice something. I come to a stop so fast on the wet tile floor I almost wipe out. On the sink is a fresh tube of Crest toothpaste. My pulse loud in my head, I throw open the cabinet door and find a handful of toothbrushes, still fresh and new in their cellophane wrappers. I grab an orange and black striped one and with a shaky hand squeeze a healthy glob onto the bristles. For the next five minutes I vigorously brush like I've never brushed before, giving each individual tooth a thorough scrubbing. When I finally spit and rinse, my teeth are as clean and minty fresh as they've been in years. My smile in the mirror is so big and bright I feel like an actress in a commercial. I'm so happy I nearly skip out of the bathroom to share the good news.

"Hey, everyone, I just…" I say, before my voice trails off, because they're all sound asleep. Carefully, I tiptoe around the room and find blankets, gently covering everyone up. Once that's done, I grab a pillow from the couch and make myself a bed on the floor right by the door. I'd prefer sleeping next to Singer, but I think I'd better bed down here: if anyone is going to bother us tonight, they'll have to come through me first.

After a final check to make sure my family is all set for the night, I finally allow myself to relax. I lock the door, then drift off with my tongue running across teeth as smooth as glass.

CHAPTER
TWENTY-ONE

I sit up with a start at the sound of knocking on the front door. Daylight is streaming through the windows and throwing distorted shapes on the floor. There's one of those long, thin windows next to the door, and I can see a figure outside, peering in. It's Red. A quick look around shows everyone else still conked out. I get up and quietly open the door.

"Why'd you lock it?" he asks gruffly, squinting at me in annoyance. In the daylight he looks older than we first thought. The rough skin on his cheeks and on the front of his nose tells me he's seen a lot of the outdoors during his life.

"Force of habit, I guess." I rub some crusty stuff from my eyes with a fist. I catch a faint whiff of shampoo from my hair, remembering how glorious last night's shower was. My teeth still feel wondrously smooth and clean, and I have to refrain from smiling.

"Yeah, okay. Makes sense, I guess. You've been living out there with those things this whole time by yourselves, haven't you? What'd you call them? Grays?"

Before I answer, I ease outside and close the door behind me. No sense waking everyone else up just yet. The sun is nearly a third of the way up in the sky already, and I can feel its warmth through my T-shirt. I take a second to look around now that it's light out. There are several more houses like ours along a street that runs either direction in front of me. They look almost identical, and for just a moment a creepy image of the neighborhood from *A Wrinkle in Time*, where all the kids are bouncing the balls in unison, pops into my mind.

"We've always called them that," I say, an edge to my voice. "And yeah, that's exactly what we've been doing. You'll excuse us if we're all a little wary of everything."

If Red is offended at my snippy tone, he doesn't show it. He tilts his head a fraction of an inch, then nods. "Huh. We just call them 'things.' And you'll have to tell me sometime how you managed to stay alive this whole time."

"Yeah, well, trust me. It wasn't easy."

We stare at each other for a while, neither of us wanting to be the next one to talk. I don't know why I'm being so pissy with him. Maybe it's because I just woke up? Perhaps. But it's more likely that he just rubs me the wrong way. I've always been very deferential towards adults, but apparently that's changed since we've been on our own so long. Whatever the reason,

I cross my arms and stare at him, waiting for him to take the next step. The seconds tick away.

"Okay, whatever," he finally says, breaking the thick silence. "Like I said last night, the Abuela is waiting for you. She's awake now. Let's go."

"What, just me? What about everyone else?"

"They'll meet her in time. Right now, she's just asking for you."

"No way. I'm not going to ditch my friends without letting them know what's going on."

Without giving him a chance to object, I slip back inside. Singer is sprawled across the nearest couch. He's so tall his feet are hanging off the end and his head is at a terrible, awkward angle. How in the world does he sleep like that? I shake his shoulder and his eyes flutter open. He blinks a few times, getting his bearings.

"Oh, hey, Scout. Morning. What's up?"

I whisper to him, "Red is here. He wants me to go with him to meet this Abuela person."

He sits up fast. "By yourself? I don't think so."

"Yeah, my thoughts exactly. I don't want to go alone, but I don't want to take everyone, either, especially the kids."

He swings his feet down to the floor. "I'm going with you."

"That was my plan. I'll tell Harold what's going on so the rest don't worry."

After some searching, I find the cook buried under

a dozen blankets on one of the beds. Google is there with him. They're both fast asleep. I give his shoulder a single shake and he snaps awake. Unlike Singer, he's instantly alert. I quietly tell him what's going on.

"Sure you don't want me to go with you guys?" he asks. "Two is more protection than one."

"No, but thanks. I'm sure I'll be fine. Just stay here and keep an eye on everyone. We'll be back as soon as we can."

It takes a second before he nods. "Okay. But be careful, all right?"

I give him a grim smile. As I'm leaving the bedroom, I see him pull his knife out from under the pillow and set it on the nightstand by the bed, within easy reach. I tiptoe out of the room, then Singer and I slink quietly out the front door. I close it gently behind me. Red is waiting with his brow furrowed, pacing up and down the walkway.

"Okay, now we can go," I tell him.

"She just wants to see you."

"Sorry, we're a package deal," Singer says from behind me with an overly innocent smile, slipping his T-shirt on over his head.

Red stands there for a moment, as if he's deciding whether or not this is a battle he wants to bother with. In the end, he doesn't respond to Singer's statement, but turns and starts walking, which I guess is its own kind of response. Taking that as our cue, we both fall into step behind him. He's not a fast walker, so we catch up to him almost immediately, flanking him one to a side. We head down our street until it dead-ends into another, and we turn left. Houses just like the one we're in line the road on either side of us, all looking the same except for perhaps a different colored front door, or some slight variations in the overgrown land-scaping. The road we're on slopes upward, but not so much to make walking difficult.

"Tell me about this place," I ask him, spinning my hand around in the air to encompass the entire com-pound. "I've been all over the top half of the state, and I've never come across anywhere like this. With people like you who haven't, you know, changed. I didn't even think this was possible."

Red takes another ten or fifteen steps. When he answers me, he keeps his gaze straight ahead of him, not looking at me or Singer at all.

"It was a retirement home," he begins, confirming what we suspected. "When the rains started, the ad-ministrator loaded up on enough food and medicine to last years. Truckload after truckload of stuff, stashed in the basement. Plus, raw materials and equipment to make more. Stuff we could make, like bread, and butter. She had connections, or something. I've never figured out how, but she knew shit was about to hit the fan. She took her job seriously and wanted to make sure the residents here didn't suffer."

Singer says, "But that was, like, six years ago. She couldn't have stockpiled enough for that many people.

It wouldn't last this long."

Red doesn't slow down. "Ends up, when all your residents are in their late eighties and nineties, not many live long enough for it to be a problem, you know? We lost so many those first few years. There are only a handful left now. The rest of us still alive either worked here or showed up later. Like you. All these cottages were stocked, too. When the owners died, we buried the people and just left everything the way it was. Nobody had the heart to clean them out."

We walk for a few moments in respectful silence. We understand loss, since we've all experienced it on a massive scale, but maybe it was even worse here. I mean, people in retirement homes have already out-lived most of their friends, and even a lot of their rel-atives, so they're already alone. But to be cut off from everyone else you've ever known and not be able to find out if they're alive or dead? To forever wonder what happened to your children and grandchildren? I can't imagine how depressing that must have been. Now I get why Red seems so, I don't know, melan-choly. Is that the right word?

"But what about the electricity? And the plumb-ing? How do you still have all that?" Singer asks, fo-cusing on the practical.

Red waves his arm out, taking in everything around us. I see now that his hands are calloused and rough with nails that are chipped and broken. Those hands have seen a lot of use and abuse in their time.

"This place was built just a few years before the rains, with the bill footed by some very wealthy people who planned on living here themselves. Very exclusive. The whole campus was specially designed to be pretty much self-sufficient. Solar panels, septic systems, well-water, you name it. It was meant to keep working even if we had a major catastrophe. They demanded it, since they wanted to make sure they'd be taken care of if anything happened." He grunted and gestured around us. "No one figured it'd be anything like this, but there you are."

We're about halfway up the sloping road when it starts curving to the left, toward the tall building that's less than a block away. In the front yard of the house on our right is an older man, probably in his late eighties. He's trim and fit, with a head of thick silver hair, and is methodically cutting shrubs along the walkway with a pair of hand trimmers. He sees us and waves, like this happens every morning. He's got a nice smile filled with white teeth that probably aren't original equipment. I do a double-take at the sight of him.

"Hey, Nelson. Nice morning," Red shouts to him, tossing out a half wave.

"Morning, Red. See you got some visitors," he replies in a voice that's breathy and thin from an abundance of life.

"Yep. Going up to see the Abuela."

Nelson waves again. "Tell her I said hello."

"Will do. Don't work too hard."

The old guy waves again and gets back to work. There's a small pile of trimmings under each bush, and judging by what he's got done, I'd say he's halfway through with his task. Red doesn't stop, but waves a final hand toward Nelson as we pass beyond him.

"He's a good one," Red says, more to himself than to us. "Rich as hell, although you'd never know it. We had four hundred or so residents here in the beginning, but we're down to a few dozen now. Nelson lost his wife just last year. Millie. She was a handful, but good for him. Great bridge player."

"That takes me back to my question from last night," I say. "Why haven't you guys all changed? Everywhere we've gone, everyone goes Gray. Everyone."

He lifts an eyebrow in my direction. "You haven't."

"No, we haven't, and we're not sure why," I answer, intentionally not bringing up Tiny and what Google may have discovered about him. I don't know why I'm keeping that from him, but I'm following Singer's lead and holding a few of our secrets close to my chest. It's funny. I didn't think I was good at lying, but it turns out it's a lot easier to do if you're protecting your family. I glance at Singer and he gives me the slightest of nods.

"You still didn't answer her question," Singer points out.

As we continue toward the tall building, we spot a few more people outside. Most are sitting on those fold out bag chairs, but a few are in wheelchairs. They're all enjoying what's turning out to be a very pleasant morning. A few are cradling cups of something in their hands, and I'm betting it's coffee. One house has a flagpole with a faded red Ohio State flag hanging on it, with the oldest woman I've ever seen vigorously cleaning the front windows. Her poofy white hair is so thin it's nearly invisible, like a dandelion held up to the sun. Red greets each resident by name, and they all say hello and throw a pleasantry or two our way. None of them seem all that surprised to see us, which is also weird as hell. Singer and I sneak a glance at each other and shrug.

Finally, Red says, "I'll let the Abuela fill you in on everything. That's her department. Now come on. We're almost there."

We've arrived at the tall building. We walk under a large concrete canopy at the front door. In front of us is one of those double sliding doors that's supposed to whoosh open when you get close, but it's either bro-ken or turned off. Red pushes it aside and walks in, with me and Singer right behind him. We step into a round lobby, a hushed place with a tile floor partially covered by a circular rug. There are a few couches in a ring around the middle of the room, and magazines are expertly fanned out on a table in the center. Pad-ded chairs with wooden arms and legs are pushed up against the walls. It's how I remember waiting rooms in pretty much any doctor's office I ever visited, all cool and clinical, with sturdy furniture that's easy to clean. Red bypasses all this and heads back down the corridor towards an elevator. I half expect him to push a button and hear a "ding" as the doors slide open, but he walks past them to a blank one marked "Stairway."

"Sorry," he says, "but the elevators are turned off right now. They use too much power. Hope you don't mind steps."

I wave him toward the door, a few butterflies fluttering about in my gut. Honestly, I'm surprised I'm not more nervous than I am. "Nope. Lead on."

We head up. Our footsteps on the concrete steps are loud and echo in the empty stairwell. When we get to a landing with a big number five on it, Red stops to catch his breath. If he notices neither of us are winded, he keeps it to himself. After a few minutes of him hanging onto the railing, he nods and we keep going.

At the tenth and final floor, he opens a steel door and we walk in. The smell of medicine and alcohol are strong here, a flashback to hospital visits from my past. We're in the middle of a long, tiled hallway, with pale wooden doors set evenly apart and heading off in both directions. There's a nurse's station across from us, complete with tall file cabinets and dark computer monitors. There's a woman behind the counter. She's in a white shirt and is sitting at a desk, poring over some papers, a nub of a pencil tapping on the counter. She's got a darker complexion, and her black hair is pulled back in a ponytail so severe I can't believe it doesn't give her a permanent migraine. A thin, glittering gold cross is on a chain around her neck. She's in her early forties, if I had to guess, but the etched lines on her face and her heavily lidded eyes tell a different story, one of prolonged exhaustion, sadness, and loss. She doesn't raise her head when we walk up, but her dark eyes lift towards us.

"Hola, Red," she says with a hint of a Spanish accent. She stops tapping the pencil.

"Juanita. How's our star patient doing today?"

She exhales slowly, her cheeks puffed out. "Tired and crabby, at least to me. Otherwise, pretty much the same. This is the girl, I take it?"

Red nods. "Yep. Scout."

She looks me up and down with clinical efficiency, then her eyes track over to Singer. "And who's this?"

"Hi, I'm Singer. It's very nice to meet you."

She gifts us a smile, a small one that's all lips and no teeth that doesn't linger, like the muscles in her face have forgotten how to form one. "Nice to meet you, too. Your parents taught you manners. Good for them."

Singer doesn't know what to say to that, and stands there with his hands crossed in front of him. I smell coffee, and spot a cup near her hand. I never cared for the bitter stuff, but my parents drank it by the gallon. No one speaks for a second until Red points down the hall.

"If she's awake, we'll head on down."

"Sure. Go ahead. She's waiting. *Buena suerte.*"

"Thanks." Red motions and we fall in behind him again. We pass by a few closed doors, then an open one. Inside is an ancient man on a bed, his eyes closed. He's on his back and has some wires leading from under blankets to a monitor near the wall. I'd swear he was dead if I didn't see his chest moving ever so slightly. A gentle and methodical beeping sound comes from one of the machines. If he knows we're out here, he doesn't give any indication of it.

We near the end of the corridor where a window looks out over the compound. I haven't been this high forever, and the view from up here is momentarily disorienting. We're looking out the back of the building, and for the first time I see a handful of greenhouses down there that somehow survived the storms. A sudden and irrational fear of heights keeps me a wary distance from the window, but Singer gets close enough to press his nose to the glass. Red steps up to the last door on the left. He raps gently on it with a knuckle.

"*Adelante*," a small voice says from inside.

Red pushes open the door and ushers us into a typical hospital room. An incredibly old woman is sitting in a wheelchair by the far window, staring out over the compound. Except for deep lines at the corners of her mouth that travel down each side of her chin, her face and features are rounded and worn down, like a once sharp rock that's been tumbled in the ocean for a hundred years. Her dark hair is streaked with gray, but it's the normal, natural gray of aging and nothing crazy like mine or Singer's. Someone has taken the time to brush it recently, and it's pulled back from her face by an ornate clasp. Her thick robe is purple with delicate gold trim, and then I see it's not a robe at all, but an extremely fancy dress, like something a runway model might wear. Several silver necklaces inlaid with turquoise hang around her thin neck and shimmer as they catch the light from the window. All in all, she could be dressed for a night out on the town.

"Oh, *Dios mío*," she says, smiling wide and clasping her hands in front of her. She's wearing rings on her narrow fingers, bright silver ones that sparkle and click together as she moves. "You're Scout. You're really here. Oh, and you must be Singer."

Any trace of nervousness I've been feeling at this meeting is banished in the presence of this regal woman. I wouldn't say I'm unnaturally drawn to her or anything like that, but being with her is somehow comforting, as if we're old high school friends reunited for the first time in ages. I step closer and notice her perfume. I have no clue what kind it is, but it reminds me of something my grandmother used to wear. Like lilacs, or maybe roses. I'm afraid my voice is going to be all squeaky when I talk, but it's surprisingly strong.

"Yes, I am. Who are you? And how do you know who I am?"

"Oh, *querida*, I know so much about you. I've been waiting for you *por mucho tiempo*. I'm just so glad you're finally here."

I have no idea what "querida" means, but the way

she said it makes it sound like a good thing. She reaches out a delicate hand towards me. Her fingers are no thicker than pencils, but when she grasps my wrist, her grip is surprisingly strong. The skin near the tips of her first and second fingers is stained a deep yellow, dark enough to border on orange. I lean closer and the bouquet of her perfume envelopes me with an essence of early spring.

"But how? How could you have been waiting for me? We've never met before. I don't understand."

The joyful smile that's been painted on her face since we arrived twitches and wanes. The frown that takes its place is accentuated by those deep grooves on either side of her chin. "No, querida, there's no way you could, not yet. But before we go any farther, I just need you to know I never meant to hurt you. If there were any other way, trust me I would have tried it, but we're running out of time and I had no choice. Please accept my apologies."

She's asking me for forgiveness, but for what? My head is spinning so fast I could be on the Tilt-A-Whirl at the county fair. I'm so lost I do the only thing I can think of, and nod at her to continue.

The Abuela gives me a tight grin that's a far cry from her earlier smile. "But I'm getting ahead of myself. If I don't start at the beginning, this will never make sense." She drops my hand and clasps both of hers in her lap and begins toying nervously with the gold hem of her dress. Her ancient voice takes on a distant note and her sight turns inward.

"Everything started back when the rains began, when the world nearly died. I noticed something was happening to me. I was changing somehow. The change was slow and steady, as if something was growing within my mind, like a flower slowly blooming from a tiny seed. I found I was developing an ability to…sense things in people. To hear and see things in their minds. And I know it sounds crazy," she tells us, holding a palm up to quash any objections, "but it's true. I've heard it called telepathy, but I'm not sure that's right. And it doesn't work with everyone, and not all the time.

"Whatever it was, this ability continued to grow. Then about three years ago, I began to sense something, something new, a presence I hadn't felt before. At first it was no more than a distant flicker, just a spark, really, like the dimmest star in the vast night sky. I had no idea what I was looking at, but whatever it was, this one spark was so small and inconsequential I almost ignored it. I couldn't even tell where it was. But even so, I had a nagging feeling I needed to keep my mind's eye on it."

"It was Tiny, wasn't it?" Singer blurts out.

The smile she directs at him is a genuine one this time. "Yes, it was. Very good. And as time went by and he got a little older, his spark grew stronger and brighter, until I sensed we shared the same types of abilities."

"Abilities? Plural? You mean something besides

the telepathy?" I ask, although I'm pretty sure I already know the answer.

She turns to me. "Scout, have you wondered why no one here goes Gray, as you call it? Not Red, or any of the residents?" She places her hand over her heart and leans forward. "It's because of me. We may never know why, but something about me has kept these people safe from the very beginning. Just like Tiny has been doing for you and your friends. He will never go through the change, and he will keep everyone around him from changing, too. But you knew that already, didn't you?"

I nod, no longer concerned with keeping Tiny's secret. "Yeah. We just figured it out a little while ago. Well, Google did. We don't know how it works either, but it does."

She points out into the distance, her index finger trembling slightly. "There are others like me and Tiny, I'm sure of it. I've sensed them out there, but I can't find them. They're still just distant stars in that night sky. But I'm straying again."

"Yes, you are," Red mutters from his place by the wall.

"*Cállate, niño,*" the Abuela scolds him, but there's no heat behind it. "I had no idea where in the world Tiny was, but I knew I had to find him and somehow get him here. But he was just a child, not even able to walk yet. Even so, it would have been hard enough before the rains came, but afterwards? The way civilization fell apart? It seemed impossible, but I was desperate."

"Until?" Singer says, caught up in the story.

"Until one day his parents were slaughtered by those things, but not before they hid Tiny away. Thankfully, later that same day he was saved from death by you and your friends. You took him in and cared for him. That was a wonderful act. Not everyone would have bothered."

I've forgotten a lot since the Storm began, but I'll always remember that day. Tiny was wrapped up in a blanket and tucked in a cabinet under a sink in an abandoned house, covered head to toe with mosquito bites. We'd been scrounging for medicine and bandages, like always. Good thing, because we never would have found him otherwise. We figured his parents stashed him there in a last-ditch effort to save him. If she's right, that's exactly what happened.

"I remember," I tell her.

"And then something equally amazing happened. Through Tiny's eyes I found you, Scout, and I could sense something in you, too. It wasn't the ability he and I share to stop the change, no, but something else. You and I shared a connection of some sort. A link, I guess you'd call it, and I remember being so happy, thinking I could connect with you and convince you to bring Tiny here. But that proved a lot more difficult than I'd bargained for, and I couldn't get through to you. I could watch, but I couldn't speak. So, I had to try something else."

A faint alarm bell starts jangling in the back of my mind, but, like Singer, I'm too invested at this point to stop now. I tilt my head at her, my eyes narrow. My words, when I speak, come slow and low. "What did you do to me?"

She motions me closer, and after a moment's hesitations, I step towards here. She takes my hand in both of hers again. "I think it would be easier to let me show you, if that's all right. But please remember, if there had been any other way, I would have tried it."

I nod again, because, really, at this point I don't know what else to do. She squeezes my hand, then her head falls forward. She relaxes deep in her wheelchair and almost seems to deflate a little, like a balloon that's lost air overnight. I'm about to ask what's going on when my vision goes completely black, bottom of the ocean stuff, someplace where light is nothing more than a concept. I feel my consciousness stagger for a heartbeat at the suddenness of it all, and I think I should be terrified, but I'm not. In this dark place I take a deep breath that's not really a breath, and try to peer into the enveloping nothingness around me. In the distance I spot a tiny glow, a white flicker that could be the flame of a candle a block away, or a lighthouse on a distant ocean. Like any creature not born to the dark, I'm drawn to the light, so I take a few steps towards it. My strides are so enormous I'm there before I know what happened. In front of me stands a nondescript wooden door in the middle of an empty space. The light I saw from so far away comes from an old-fashioned keyhole just below the doorknob. I get the feeling it really isn't a door at all, but something my mind has conjured up to keep me rooted in reality.

I step closer. As I do, the door wobbles in front of my eyes, morphing from its original form to the bright red doors on Church Island. It stays that way for a second, before flipping to the front door of the house in Cleveland where Lord and I grew up, then to the brown steel slab at the entrance to my elementary school. It doesn't stop there, constantly jumping from one version to another, some of which I don't even recognize. But whatever form it takes, the doorknob is a constant, always remaining the same, with the keyhole shining below it. My eyes are fixated on the doorknob, and I have a sudden urge to turn it.

When I reach for it, my hand freezes no more than a hair's breadth away. As I stare at the tarnished brass, it dawns on me what this place really is; these doors are a passageway of some sort, and if I open it, I'll be giving someone else permission to enter my mind, to see and experience all I've ever done or felt. By opening these doors, I'll be sharing every bit of shame, joy, and regret I've ever experienced, every embarrassing thought or dream I've ever had. My hand is hovering near it, trembling, when I hear her.

"It's okay, querida. Trust me."

It's the Abuela. Even here, in this place that's not

a place, I recognize her ancient voice.

"Abuela? Where are you?"

"I'm here," she says from the other side of the door. "Everything will be fine. I've been with you before. You just have to open it yourself this time."

"I can't do that," I protest, talking without using actual words. "How can I let you in? How can I let anyone in?"

"I've been there before," she assures me. "Several times. But you're awake now and I need your permission. You have to let me in."

"What do you mean you've been here already? How? I've never seen this place before."

Instead of answering, an outpouring of affection washes over me, binding us together almost into one being. The connection the two of us suddenly share is pure and simple, and not something either one of us could manufacture. Her feelings for me are sincere. I can't begin to comprehend what's happening, but whatever the Abuela's doing, it's blunting the apprehension I felt moments before. She said she's been in here with me before, and I know she's telling the truth, because neither of us can lie to the other in here. I have to trust her.

I reach for the doorknob and twist it open.

CHAPTER
TWENTY-TWO

The darkness and the door are gone, just like that. Where the Abuela was sitting is Eve, exactly as I remember her. The shimmering green robe, the yellow rope belt, the purplish port stain on the left side of her face. She's sitting in the Abuela's wheelchair and holding onto my wrist. On her face is a small, sheepish grin. I've seen that kind of look on someone before. It takes me back to one of my birthdays where my grandmother got me underwear or socks or something, and was worried I wasn't going to like them. I didn't, but I never let her know that.

"Hello, Scout," Eve says, her voice precisely as it should be. She cocks her head to the side. "Do you understand now?"

My free hand flies up to cover my mouth, and I almost stagger backwards. My eyes blink rapidly of their own accord, and when I can see again the Abuela is back, but not completely. Both of them are here now, Eve and the old lady at the same time, like two images superimposed on top of one another. I snatch my hand away from hers, and I sense the door in my mind slamming shut. My dear friend vanishes, replaced once more by the Abuela sitting by herself. I'm so stunned I have to grab onto the arm of the wheelchair to keep from toppling over. My breath is coming in ragged gasps.

"Oh, my god," I finally stammer, my knees threatening to buckle and send me to the floor. I'm lightheaded and dangerously close to passing out. "It's you. The dreams. I haven't been talking to Eve at all, I've been talking to you. My god, you've been Eve this whole time."

She opens her mouth to reply, but at that moment her eyes roll back in her head and she promptly passes out.

I'm so rocked at what I just learned I can't decide whether I should rush to help or sprint out of the room. In the end my humanity gets the better of me, and I quickly kneel down beside her. I take her limp hand in both of mine. Her skin is warm and as thin as tissue paper.

"Abuela? Abuela, can you hear me?"

Red turns and cups a hand to his mouth. "Juanita! She zonked out again!"

Singer gets down low on one knee next to me. "Does this happen a lot?" he asks Red.

"More than it used to. Give her a few minutes and she'll come around. Probably."

Juanita dashes into the room and squeezes between us, almost bowling Singer over in the process. She checks the old woman's pulse. As she's doing so, the Abuela blinks a few times and struggles to sit up, looking around with uncomprehending eyes. Her mouth works as if it's trying to remember what it's like to form words.

"Qué pasó?" she finally asks.

The nurse directs the beam of a small flashlight into and out of her eyes. "You passed out again. I warned you about exerting yourself like that, didn't I?"

The Abuela straightens up in her wheelchair and brushes the nurse's hands away. "Thank you, but I'm fine now. You don't have to hover over me like that."

Juanita stands, her arms crossed. "*Verdad?* Are you fine, really? You've been fainting a lot lately. I'm no doctor, but even I know passing out all the time is not a good sign."

I get up off the floor and perch my butt on the edge of the bed. My feet are planted firmly on the tile floor, relishing in the solidity of it. I'm still feeling woozy and haven't been able to get my breathing completely under control yet. Singer is staring between me and the Abuela, confused and unsure what to do or say. He heard what I said about Eve, but he has no idea what else happened between us. All he knows is she passed out.

"Thank you, but I'm fine now. *Jesu Cristo*, don't

you have others to take care of? Now go away, please."
She makes a shooing motion with her hands, as if
she's brushing flies away from a picnic lunch.

"Don't use His name like that!" Juanita snaps,
then turns on her heel and strides out in a huff. The
old woman waits until the nurse's footsteps fade away,
still staring at the open door.

"She means well. But I hate being treated like a
child."

Softly, as if he's unsure how involved he's allowed
to get, Singer says, "You did pass out, you know."

The Abuela waves his comment away, and takes
a moment to smooth out her unwrinkled dress. She
seems a little better already, her recovery mirrored in
the sparkle deep in her brown eyes. They give me a
glimpse of how she must have appeared as a younger
woman. As striking as she is now, she would have been
gorgeous in her prime.

"Where were we? Oh, yes." She takes a deep
breath to gather her thoughts. Her hands fidgeting in
her lap, she smiles at me sadly. "Querida, like I said, I
have been aware of you for a long time. Right away I
knew you were special, and I needed you to find me,
and to help me. But I couldn't figure out how. Not
until you were caught out in the blizzard and were so
close to death. You were so weak I was finally able to
sneak into your mind by myself, and when I got there,
I saw your friend Eve. Your memory of her was clear
and strong. That was what I needed. You would never

believe a stranger like me, but I knew I could talk to you through her, and you would listen."

I close my eyes and shake my head side to side. A surge of disappointment washes over me, and a thick lump of despair clogs the back of my throat. In my heart I knew Eve was dead, I really did. But it was so wonderful to have her with me again, to talk to her, to let me be with her once more. Her touch. The kiss. It all seemed so real!

The old woman senses my grief. The lines around her eyes and mouth deepen, growing more profound as regret transforms her ancient face. She slowly rolls her wheelchair closer to me, the rubber wheels silent on the tile floor of the room. Right now, she looks every bit of her age.

"Querida. I'm sorry if I hurt you, but I needed you here. Even more than that, I needed you to bring Tiny to me. You call him the Firebrand, and you're right to do so. He truly is special. Yes, I was able to sneak into your mind a few more times when you were sleeping and your guard was down. But, unlike with you, I can talk to him whenever I want. His mind is young and uncluttered and open to me almost all the time. But he couldn't come here by himself. I needed you to bring him."

Still at a loss, Singer sits next to me on the hospital bed. His leg is barely touching mine, but I appreciate his presence more than he could know. He toys with his hands in his lap as he takes all this in.

"Why Tiny? Why him?" he asks.

She smiles and places a hand on her chest. "There are others like me and Tiny, but I haven't been able to locate them. I've felt them out there, somewhere in the world, but we're out of time. I'm old, and I'm not going to be around much longer. We need Tiny to take my place here after I'm gone. To keep everyone safe. He's so very special, but so is the Hill. You haven't been here long, but you've already seen what this place is. What it can be. We've got everything we need here to keep the human race going, to actually start over. Humanity may have one more shot at survival, and you and Tiny are the only way that happens."

"So that's it?" I finally ask, trying to take this all in. "You just needed me to get Tiny here? Okay, so he's here. But you said you needed me, too. Why?"

The Abuela's face closes down, as if a terrible memory just resurfaced after being buried deep in the well of her consciousness. She slowly spins her wheelchair away from us and looks out the window, staring blankly at her past. "When I first started communicating with you through your friend, I realized something. I don't know how to explain it, but it turns out I wasn't just talking to you and Tiny. No, I was sending out my thoughts everywhere. Once I turned it on, it was on all the time. For anyone else to hear. It's like a beacon that can never be extinguished."

"Okay," I say, not at all clear what she's talking about. "Again, so what? What does that have to do with me?"

She shifts her slight weight around, as if the seat of her wheelchair has gotten too hot for comfort. Her eyes are both hard and sad simultaneously. "It means that every other creature with the same kind of ability also heard me calling for you. You've seen firsthand how Grays will follow your mental commands? You do it with the one you call Susan. Others can, too. Like your brother, and that Hunter person you hate so much."

I sit up straight as shock courses up and down my back and stiffens my spine. Since she's been inside my head before, it makes sense she would know about the two of them.

"Yeah."

"It means that those creatures, the things you call Grays, also heard me reaching out to you. But they think I'm calling for them, and they're answering the only way they know how. They're on their way here."

Singer also sits up straight. "Wait. They *all* heard you? Every single one of them?"

She nods slowly, her ancient face battered by guilt at the terrible thing she's done, even if it was unintentional. "Yes, all of them. I can sense them. They're nearly here, and I can't prevent it. Whatever it is I started, I can't stop it. I don't know how."

Singer clutches at my hand, and we stare at each other, unblinking. From the look of awareness dawning on his narrow face, he finally grasps the enormity of what she's saying.

"If she's right, it all makes sense," I say, ignoring the others and speaking directly to him now. "She's been broadcasting to me this whole time. That means there could be even more Grays on their way than just the ones Ted saw. There could be hundreds, thousands, all converging here."

"Holy shit," he mutters, thinking out loud. "That's gotta be why Tiny was able to sense Susan down in the furnace room back at Church Island. And why the Grays attacked us, even killing themselves by coming over the ice to do it. Like Google thought, they weren't after us. We weren't food to them. They wanted Tiny. He must be broadcasting, too, and they heard him. Now both of them are here together, and the Grays are coming for them."

I turn to her and ask, "That's how Red knew they were on their way, isn't it? You both knew because you've been calling them here all along."

She dips her head in a solemn nod. "Yes, and there's no way we can stop them by ourselves, not with the few of us left. That's why you're so important now. We need you to save us. If you can't, and they destroy us, everything is lost."

CHAPTER
TWENTY-THREE

Singer and I are still perched on the edge of the bed in stunned silence when Juanita storms back into the room. The nurse is framed in the doorway with her arms locked across her chest, glaring around as if daring anyone to cross her. She's not what I'd call a particularly imposing person, but she's projecting a pretty formidable aura right now.

"It's time for all of you to go," she states bluntly. The Abuela starts to mount a protest, but the nurse isn't having any of it. She takes a menacing step into the room. "You all heard me. *Salgan de aquí.*"

Too exhausted to fight the nurse's demands, the Abuela says, "Red, please talk to Scout. Fill her in on anything I've missed." The regal old lady looks as if she could pass out again at any moment. She's propping up her head with her hand, an elbow on the hard plastic arm of the chair for support. She waves her free hand at Red, then lets it tumble into her lap, as if that simple act has sapped the last of her strength.

"We don't have much time left. Maybe only a day or two."

Red unfolds his arms and smiles at her with un-expected warmth. He pushes off from the wall then ushers us out the door. Juanita grunts once in satis-faction and turns to go. As the nurse strides away, he steps towards the Abuela. I think he's going to give her a hug or a kiss or something, but he casually slips an object into the folds of her dress. I'm pretty sure it's a cigarette. She pats his hand once, then the three of us leave. We follow the nurse back to her station, where she plops down and starts tapping the pencil again.

"She's getting worse," she says to Red. "I can tell. She looks so much older than she did just last week. She can't even get out of her wheelchair now on her own."

"How much time does she have left?" he asks her in one of those hushed voices reserved for libraries and cemeteries.

"I have no idea. A day? A week? A year? Who knows? As mean as she is, she could live forever, but my guess is she won't."

Red chuckles once. "She's only mean to you."

"Why? For doing my job?"

"Hey, I'm kidding. Just take care of her, okay?"

Juanita's brow unknots and her eyes soften. "You know I will. How can you even say that?"

He pats her hand and tells her goodbye, then the three of us make our way towards the exit. We walk down the stairs without talking, before passing through the lobby and into the late morning sun. I didn't notice it on our way in, but there's a concrete sign outside by the front door with the words *Trinity House* etched on it. Both the T and the H are an oversized font with lots of swirls, like someone went a little crazy in old English script.

"She called this place the Hill," I say, pointing to the sign. "But that's its real name? Trinity House?"

"What? Oh, yeah. That's the official name. But we all call it the Hill. The top of that tower is the highest point in the Dayton area." He leads us toward a pair of benches near the sidewalk and takes a seat. Singer and I sit across from him. He stares down the hill behind us, back the way we originally came, without really seeing anything. He doesn't blink much. I wait for him to speak, but, contrary to the Abuela, he doesn't seem to be in much of a hurry.

"Why'd you pass her a cigarette as we were leaving?" I finally ask.

"You saw that, eh? Yeah, I slip her one once in a while. She'll go sneak a smoke when Juanita's not around. As old as she is, I figure what's the harm, you know? She likes it."

That explains the yellowing around her fingers. Nicotine stains. "My grandfather was the same way with my grandmother," I tell him. "She loved those Little Debbie snack cakes. The chocolate ones. My mom and dad always wanted her to eat better and stay away from the junk food, but she loved them and he couldn't say no to her. She was in her early nineties when she died, so I guess she did okay."

He turns his gaze from the horizon down to me, as if he's seeing me in a whole new light. "Yeah, you get it. Juanita just can't seem to understand that."

Singer has been raptly listening to our conversation. His wide eyes swing back and forth between us while we talk, as if he can't believe this casual conversation is happening. In the silence that follows Red's last statement, his patience erodes to the point where he can't contain himself any longer. I once saw a poster that said the difference between hot water and steam is a single degree, or something like that. Singer's boiling point has been exceeded.

"What is wrong with you two?" he shouts, as worked up as I've ever seen him. "Didn't you hear what she said? Those Grays are only a day or two away. We've got to get ready. We can't just sit here and do nothing!"

Red runs a hand through his hair. He pulls out a cigarette from his pocket and lights it with a stick match. I never minded the smell of tobacco, and it's been so long I'd almost forgotten what it smelled like. It's nice. He takes a big draw, then blows it out through his nose and mouth.

"Son, you don't understand, do you?"

"Understand what? That we're wasting time sitting here? Yeah, I got that much."

Red sighs and points beyond the small houses below us. "Let me walk you through this. We've got the sound machines set up in a perimeter around the entire compound. They're effective as hell at stopping a pack of those things, but that's it. But if we get a whole herd charging at us, especially the speedy ones, I'm pretty sure they'll overrun those defenses in no time. Once they get past that perimeter, there's nothing between us and them. Sure, we've got a lot of guns and ammo, but just a handful of people left to use them. Those things will be all over us, and there's not a damn thing we can do about it."

"Hold on a second," Singer snaps. "You told us those sound machines would stop them. What happened to that?"

Red lifts his shoulders. "I lied. Didn't want to freak you out."

Singer slaps a hand to his forehead. "You lied? Great, just freaking great. You're just giving up? Is that what you're saying?"

Red's face hardens at the accusation, but a second later his resolve weakens, like a piece of steel that's been bent too many times. "Yeah, that's pretty much what I'm saying. We're basically dead men walking. Some of us just don't know it yet."

I can be a little naïve sometimes, and while I'm not always the quickest when it comes to figuring people out, I had a gut feeling about Red. It was mainly little stuff, but one glaring thing even I noticed right away was his complete lack of urgency. About any-thing. I mean, when someone knows a horrible threat is thundering over the horizon toward them, they tend to be in a hurry to do something about it. In fact, the closer the threat comes, the more frantic they become. It's a basic characteristic of survival. That was missing in him.

"Come on," I urge him, starting to get worked up. "There's got to be something we can do. Singer and I, well, we have special abilities that can even up almost any battle."

"The Abuela told me about what you two can do. That's great and impressive as hell, but can you hold your own against a hundred of those things? A thou-sand?"

Ouch. That knocks me down a peg pretty fast. I don't want to admit we can't, but it was proven at Church Island that if we're way outnumbered there's only so much we can do. Worse yet, there were only a few dozen of those things attacking us that time. Not hundreds. Singer knows this, too. His mouth opens and closes a few times, but no words come out.

"Yeah, I didn't think so."

"Then we have to leave," Singer blurts out. "We gather everyone up and get the hell out of here. We've escaped from them before. We can do it again."

Red takes another drag, and sighs. "You don't think we've thought of that? Son, even if we could leave, they'd just keep coming after us because of her.

Plus, we don't have the boats for anything like that. And even if we did, where would we go? We can't take enough supplies with us for it to matter. Besides, most of the people here are so old they wouldn't last a day out on the open water, especially if another storm hits. No, leaving is not an option."

Singer is so agitated he can't sit any longer. He springs to his feet and starts pacing in front of us like a trapped cat, his arms flailing about. Pointing towards our boat in the distance, he snaps, "Fine. If you can't go, then we will. We'll head back out on the water and take our chances there. I'm sorry, but if that's our only option, then we'll take it. Right, Scout?" He looks to me for confirmation.

A few seconds tick by, and I don't say anything. I crane my neck and peer at the top of the towering building next to us. I can't exactly feel the Abuela, but I know she's up there. I also know she's right. As far as I can tell in the short amount of time we've been here, the Hill might truly be the last place able to foster the next generation of humankind. It's self-sufficient, sturdy enough to withstand the storms, plus the flooding never touched it. Sure, we've seen glimpses of civilization here and there before, like Church Island or Rumpke Mountain, but they all had their flaws and failings. Each one was barely holding on, and we've witnessed firsthand how they were just a hiccup away from disaster. Singer is still waiting for me to agree with him, and the longer I don't, the more uncomfortable the silence between us becomes.

"No," I finally say, "we can't abandon this place or these people. We need to figure out how to save them. And to keep Tiny safe, too. I'm done running."

It strikes me then what I just said, and how it mirrored Harold's words when he attacked those Grays on the ice. I may never know what was in the cook's mind and what caused him to declare that, but I know why I said it. I'm sick and tired of being on the run, of constantly being chased from whatever crappy place we're calling home that day. I'm through being hunted and killed, of losing people I love. There comes a time when you find a special somewhere, a place you know in your heart you need to defend, and people you need to save. At some point, you've had enough, and you need to take a stand.

Singer's jaw drops. "Scout, seriously? What the hell? You're just going to stay here and get slaughtered?"

"No, I'm saying we're going to do everything we can to make sure the Hill and all the people here make it." I sweep my hands in a circle. "Singer, look around you. We've never found anywhere like this. And I can't imagine we ever will again. If we leave, where will we go? Back to Rumpke Mountain? What happens when the supplies run out? Or another blizzard hits?"

"We'll figure it out," he says, enunciating each word carefully, almost biting each one off. "We always do."

"No, don't you see? Anywhere we go is only going to be a temporary solution," I counter, my voice increasing in volume. "Face it. We have nowhere to go that can give us a long-term solution. Not like this. Think about it logically and tell me I'm wrong."

He stares at me with an expression I've never seen on him before, one twisted with so much anger and frustration he's nearly unrecognizable. The mild argument we had back on Church Island pales in comparison to this. His fists clench at his sides, and he's leaning toward me. For a second, I'm afraid he's going to go into slo-mo and do something rash. He breathes through his nose a few times, his chest heaving in and out, then spins on his heel and stalks away from us.

"Your boyfriend doesn't seem too happy," Red comments from the bench, watching Singer storm away. He knocks the ash from his cigarette and pockets the butt.

I put my hands to my face. They're shaking. "He'll come around. He's just worried about everyone. I can't say I blame him."

"Yep. He's got every right to be."

I watch as Singer disappears down the road. I hope what's just happened hasn't spoiled what the two of us have. I pray we're strong enough, but I'm scared we might not be. He's been my rock throughout our time together, and I can't imagine not having him by my side. I don't know if I could live without him. I don't know if I'd want to.

I look back at Red. "I'll talk to him. He'll come around."

He stands up. "If you say so. But I'm telling you, it won't make any difference. If those things get past the sound machines, we're all dead anyway. It's just a matter of time."

Unlike the Abuela, I can't sense where the Grays are, but I trust her when she says they're coming. I also know we don't have much time. Whatever we're going to do, we need to get busy doing it. I take a deep breath to gather my thoughts.

"You said you don't have many people left who can help. Just how many are there?"

He thinks for a moment and starts ticking numbers off on his fingers. "Not counting your group, there's me, Shorty, Stretch, and a few others. Juanita, too. All the rest are residents."

"Any of them up to helping us?"

"Sure, I guess. A couple. Like Nelson. I'd say we'd total a dozen, more or less."

A dozen? That's all? Just as I'm starting to freak out at the commitment I just made with such limited resources, I feel the mass of the tower behind me. I turn and stare up at it, thinking. I've never been accused of being all that bright, but I have figured out a thing or two about giving myself an edge in a fight, even when the odds suck. One thing I've learned for sure, it's always better to defend yourself from a position of height.

"I've got an idea," I tell him.

CHAPTER
TWENTY-FOUR

The mood when I enter the little house is tense, to say the least. I was afraid of a mutiny earlier, and it looks like I've got one on my hands now. The second I step through the door, I'm confronted by Annie and Singer, both of them demanding to know what I'm planning on doing. The little kids and Google are off to the side on a couch. They're watching something on TV, of all things. I'm so stunned it's working that I brush aside the two protesters in mid-rant and point at the images on the screen. I can't believe it, but they're watching *Toy Story*, the first one, I think.

"What the hell? How is that thing even working?"

Google spares a second to answer me. "It's a DVD. We found some in the cabinet. I wasn't sure it would work, but we've got electricity so I figured I'd try it."

"Scout, this is awesome!" Carly squeals with joy, bouncing up and down.

On the screen is Buzz Lightyear. He's talking to Woody and his toy friends in the kid's bedroom. I remember the first time I saw this and how mesmerized I was. Most of my friends liked Woody, but I always had a thing for Buzz. Sure, he came across as something of a doofus, but I loved his never-say-die attitude. The people who lived here must have had them on hand for their grandkids or something. This sudden flashback to normalcy has really rocked me, but in a good way. I'm so enthralled by the movie it's all I can do to tear my gaze away.

"Scout!" Singer yells to get my attention. He grabs my shoulder and waves a hand at the TV. "Focus! What are we going to do? We're running out of time!"

Annie barges between us. She's so furious her complexion is the same color as her hair. "We can't stay here. The kids! Think of the kids!"

I glance around to locate Harold, thinking he might be as worked up as these two are. But he's not. He's over in the kitchen, leaning against the counter with his feet crossed. He found a large kitchen knife somewhere, one that looks a little like the one he lost. He's methodically dragging it back and forth over a silver rod with a wooden handle. I recall seeing one of those in his kitchen at Church Island. He must be using it to sharpen the knife.

"I am thinking of the kids, Annie," I tell her evenly, working hard to sound reassuring. "Taking them out of here is just going to prolong the inevitable. We may save them in the short run, but in the end it's no use. We can't make it out there much longer. We have nowhere to go."

"Singer told me what Red said. He said we're doomed, that the Grays will get past the sound machines. And when that happens…" Her hands drift to her face, and tears begin streaming down her round cheeks. Her gaze flicks over to Carly and Tiny, both of whom are slack-jawed as they watch Buzz proudly soaring through the air.

My heart sinks at the sight of the two of them, so young and innocent, and the foundation of my resolve suffers a few cracks. I can't recall how many times I've thought about my distaste at being a leader. I've never wished that responsibility on anyone. Not Jacob. Not Eve. Certainly not myself. But I know deep down I'm right. If we're ever going to have anything remotely like a normal life, if we want the kids to be able to grow up safe and sound, then I have to do what I believe is right. My stomach hurts thinking about it, but if there was ever a time for me to stand up and take charge, this is it.

"Yes, we're staying," I tell them with as much conviction as I can muster, praying it doesn't sound as forced as it does in my head. "We're going to stay and fight. For us, and for this place. Because if we don't, well, in the end it won't matter, because we'll be dead soon enough anyway."

Annie and Singer are both about to launch into another tirade, but stop short when Harold steps up to us. "Listen, guys, I know this all sucks. It really does.

But you both have to admit Scout has helped keep us alive since she got to Church Island. And long before that, for some of you. You may not like it, but she's been right so far. She's been out in this shit-storm way more than we have, and she's still breathing. I say we listen to her."

I wasn't expecting that, but his support is so welcome I could give him a hug. There's something about Harold I'm starting to notice. Maybe it was a characteristic he possessed before that I didn't see, or maybe he's just grown up recently? He's older than the rest of us, so perhaps that's it? Not older like a father figure, but more like a big brother. This air about him is strong enough to make Annie and Singer take a half a step back and listen.

"Guys," I tell them, talking fast while I've got an opening. "This place is more defensible than Red thinks. They've been holed up here forever, not out there fighting for their lives in the slop like we have. We know more about survival than he does. I explained what I want to do, and he's on board." Well, technically, "on board" might be a stretch, but they don't need to know that.

"On board with what?" Singer asks. He's still furious at me, but at least he's calmed down enough to talk instead of yell. That's progress, right?

"All the older residents will stay locked in their houses and out of the way. The Grays aren't after them, right? They want Tiny and the Abuela. The rest of us will head up to the tower. That place is like a fortress. It's concrete and steel, so tough not even the Grays will be able to damage it. We barricade the hell out of the stairway, the only way up, because the elevators are off. Then we position ourselves on the roof with all the firepower we have, and pick them off one by one as they get closer."

"But there could be hundreds of them. Maybe more," Singer points out, arms crossed in front of him.

"Fine. We'll take them out one at a time, until they're all dead. I don't care if there's a thousand of them. Red insists they've got the ammo for that." I look at each of them in turn, trying to gauge their level of acceptance. "Come on, guys, it's the only way. We can do this. For us, for the kids, for everyone."

Annie collapses next to Carly, almost on top of her, actually. The little girl is still so zoned out by the movie she doesn't even notice. Meanwhile, Tiny's hands are dancing in a complicated circular pattern as he watches TV, in what I'm beginning to understand is his way of laughing. I take a step towards Singer, half expecting him to pull away from me. But he doesn't. He levels his brown eyes so they're locked on mine, and I'm heartened to see his earlier fierce determination has waned. Not much, but a little, and that's okay. I'll take what I can get.

"I still don't like it," he says, his voice so low I can barely hear him over Woody and Buzz chattering away. "I still say we should run."

I rest a hand on his arm. "I know, and I hope to god you're wrong. But I'm right. I've thought this through, and you have to trust me on this. It's the only way."

Annie waves me away, as if she's too exhausted to continue protesting. Singer looks down and to the side, thinking, in that mannerism of his I've come to love. Harold's face lights up a little as he sees the two of them no longer fighting me on this. It's clear to everyone here that the two of them don't agree with me, not exactly, but they're at least with me enough to move ahead. He flips his two knives in the air and catches each by their handles effortlessly, like he's practiced this a thousand times. A broad smile opens up on his face.

"We're good to go?" he asks the group. Singer lifts his eyes to the ceiling and nods. Annie waves him away, just like she did with me. "Excellent. Come on, guys, this should be fun. Besides, you want to live forever?"

We don't waste any time, and the rest of the day is spent fortifying the tower. It turns out Red's been the handyman here at Trinity House for years, and his skills really do come in handy. Before I know it, he's got the windows of the first four floors completely boarded up with thick plywood, braced from behind with steel rebar. I have my doubts the makeshift barricades will hold up, but when they withstand a few powerful punches by Singer, I'm forced to reassess my position.

"Impressive construction," I tell Red, admiring his work.

"Thanks," he says, wiping sweat from his forehead. He clips a battery powered drill to his toolbelt. "It's what we used to protect the place from storms and tornadoes. They'll hold against those things. Trust me."

I do trust him. Next, he turns the elevators on long enough for us to shuttle an army's worth of guns and ammunition up to the top floor. I don't even know what most of the weapons are, but I spot a few that remind me of Hunter's rifle of choice, his trusty .30-30. I don't have to like the nasty thing, but I do admire its precise craftsmanship. The steel boxes of ammunition are deceptively heavy, and everyone wisely leaves those for me to carry.

"Too bad you don't have any grenades," Harold says while we're waiting on the ground floor for the elevator. "Those would come in handy right about now."

"Lot of people had guns here, but this was a retirement home, not an armory," Red tells him, then heads back out to tap the residents for whatever else they might have. The Hill may not have been an actual armory, but you wouldn't know it by what we've collected so far.

Harold pushes the button for the elevator, and I find I'm still delighted when it lights up just like the old days. When it dings and the doors glide open, we lug in more ammo and guns and hit the button for the top floor. The smell of machine oil is thick in the tight space, and I wrinkle my nose. It reminds me of the fuel oil back at Church Island, which makes me wonder what happened to everyone back there after we left. I don't like to think about that, but I can't help myself.

We unload our weapons after we reach the top floor. There's an impressive pile growing close to Juanita's station. The nurse is watching us with steady eyes. I can't tell if she's happy or upset at what we're doing, but I can't worry about it. We're about to head down when I hear a voice calling my name. The Abuela is rolling slowly toward us down the tiled hallway. I give her a thin smile. I can't help but remember she's been inside my head before, and probably knows more about me than I do about myself. Seeing her makes me feel exposed, almost as if I've been plopped down naked in front of a stadium full of people. It's a truly strange sensation, and not at all in a good way.

"Hola, querida," she says. "I'm so glad to see you helping us. And you brought someone else with you."

Just like before, she's dressed to the hilt. She's changed outfits for some reason, and is covered head to toe in a shimmering green dress with gold embroidery up and down the edges. Gold necklaces dangle around her neck. Her hair is down now, and is long enough to drape elegantly over her shoulders. She almost seems to shimmer in the hallway lights. From a distance I'd swear she was much younger than her true age.

I wave a hand at the cook. "This is Harold, although you probably already knew that. Harold, meet the Abuela."

Harold dips his head. "*Con mucho gusto.*"

She laughs and claps her hands together. "Con mucho gusto to you, too, young man. Red told me what you plan to do. Are you sure the residents will be safe staying in their homes?"

"Yes. Well, we hope so. We could bring them up here, but Red said he talked to most of them and they'd rather ride it out where they are. He said they were afraid they'd just be in the way and do more harm than good. The Grays are after you and Tiny, not them."

She taps a painted fingernail on the hard plastic arm of the wheelchair. "I guess it doesn't matter, does it? If this doesn't work, it won't make any difference, will it?"

"No, not really."

No one has anything to add to that. After a few seconds, Harold wishes her well, and gets back in the elevator for another load. I'm about to follow him when she reaches out a hand to me. Like before, her grip is stronger than it should be for someone her age.

"What is it?" I ask.

She draws me closer. Her face is cloaked in sadness, the corners of her eyes drawn down. "I know how much your friend meant to you, and I'm sorry if I tarnished your memory of her. If there was another way, I swear I would have used it."

I kneel down next to her, all thoughts of preparations gone for now. "I know, I really do. I understand, I guess. And I'd say there's no way you could possibly understand the relationship we had, but that wouldn't be true, would it? You know me better than anyone else possibly can." I pause for a moment, thinking how to share this with her. I pat her arm. "But you gave me something special, even if it wasn't exactly true. You gave me a chance to see her again. To be with her one last time, even if it wasn't really her. In reality, I should be thanking you."

The Abuela's eyes glisten at my kind words. She dabs at her face with the hem of her dress and strokes my hand. "You're right. I do know you. You hate the responsibility of leadership, but you're so good at it. Believe in yourself and what you're doing, querida. Even if it turns out badly, trust that you did the right thing."

Now it's my turn to start tearing up. I squeeze her hand. I'm starting to stand up when she pulls me back down. Her face is just inches from mine. I can smell the thick aroma of cigarette smoke mixed with her perfume, and I smile inwardly.

"If you ever need help, call on me. Promise me you'll do that."

I'm not sure what she's talking about, but I shrug and nod at her. "Sure, okay. I promise."

"Don't forget."

I look deep into her eyes. "I won't."

She smiles and releases my hand. Once more she looks her years, and a measure of her regal beauty seems to have faded. Exhaustion at this slight exertion has taken its toll, and her head droops. Juanita is next to her in a flash. With a stern look at me, she pushes the Abuela back to her room. I watch them go, then hit the button for the elevator. When the doors slide open, Harold is standing there with another load, mainly ammunition this time. He looks at me.

"What's wrong?" he asks.

I wipe a few tears away from my cheeks. "Nothing, I'm fine. Let's get all this up there."

He hesitates for a second, then we load up with as much as we can carry and head for the stairway to the roof. It's separate from the main stairwell, and has a single staircase that leads up to a steel door with ROOF ACCESS written across it in red block letters. It's propped open, and sunlight shines through. He bumps it open the rest of the way with a hip. I'm right behind him.

We step onto the flat roof. The floor up here is loose gravel mixed with tar. Solar panels cover the majority of it, but there's a pathway to the edge where we squeeze through. The wall circling the entire area is about three feet high, brick with a limestone cap on top of it. Harold takes his weapons and leans them up against the lip, making sure to put the right ammunition with each gun. I honestly don't know what bullets go with what weapon, so I follow along and give him whatever he asks for. At one point I hear him humming something, and I realize he's actually enjoying himself. I stop and stare at him.

"You're in a really good mood," I tell him.

He keeps matching weapons with ammo, but the humming stops. "Am I? Why do you say that?"

"It's not that hard to tell."

"Oh. Well, maybe I am. Is that a crime?"

I purse my lips. "A crime? No, not at all. Just a little weird. Okay, very weird. The rest of us are scared shitless, and you're up here singing to yourself."

Finished, he brushes his hands off on his pants. He pauses for a moment, then steps to the edge, resting his arms on it. He cocks his head to the side as he stares out across the distant horizon like a judge about to pass sentencing. From up here we can easily make out the tops of all the houses, the streets, and the dry land stretching to the east and north as far as we can see. When the Grays show up, that's the direction they'll come from. Once again, I wish I had Simon's vision. Better yet, I wish we had Simon. God, I hope he's okay, I tell myself.

"Scout," he begins, still staring at nothing. His words are soft, almost as if he's alone and peering into the past. "You know how some days seem to last forever, and others are over before you know it?"

"Yeah, sure," I answer him just as softly, wondering where he's going with this.

"Usually, it's the good ones that go by so fast, you know? I loved working in the kitchen. It was hard, but I knew I was helping everyone, and I needed that. Those days just flew by. I'd wake up, take care of the meals, and before you knew it, I was done and it was time for bed. That may not sound like much to you, but it's exactly what I needed." He sighs and kicks at some rocks at his feet. The seconds tick by, and I don't know if he's done or not. I'm about to break the silence when he turns to me.

"You asked once why I did what I did back there on the ice. Remember?"

I step next to him. He's at least a foot taller than I am, probably about the same height as Singer, but built sturdier. "Yeah, I do."

"When the Storm hit, you were in middle school or something, right?"

"Yeah."

"Not me. I was…somewhere else. Where I grew up, there were only two kinds of people. People who got taken advantage of, or ones who took advantage of them. I saw what happened to the poor bastards who were taken advantage of, so I made damn sure I wasn't one of them. I did some really bad stuff for some awful people. Eventually I got caught. Looking back, I'm glad they got me, really. I didn't see a way

out, and locking me up was the best thing for everyone. I was just a kid, but I was not the kind of kid you
would've liked."

"Oh, come on. You? I don't believe it."

He swivels his head down at me, and I'm so startled at the flash of animal viciousness in his gaze it
forces me back a step. I've never seen a look so feral on
anyone before, not even on Hunter. This alternative
version of Harold is terrifying. A second passes, and
the menacing apparition in front of me changes back
to something more familiar and a lot less menacing.

"Believe it. I've done…things. Things I'm not
proud of. Stuff that makes me wake up at night
screaming into my pillow. I just want that to stop. Do
you know what the word 'redemption' means?"

"Yeah, I do."

"Good. So do I."

I'm dying to ask more, but his face closes down
like the door to his past just slammed shut, and he
wordlessly backtracks to the stairwell for another load.
After several stunned seconds of trying to sift through
what just happened, I follow a few respectful paces behind him. As much as we've all been through, it strikes
me for the first time that, even though everyone had a
life before the Storm, it doesn't mean their life didn't
suck.

CHAPTER
TWENTY-FIVE

When we're done lugging everything to the roof, we hurry back to my group. We can't stay in the house any longer, and we need to move up into the tower where it's safer. Carly and Tiny put up a fight, but it's only because they've discovered what every other kid before them already has, that TV is freaking awesome. On the off chance that there's another one in the tower, we pack some DVDs before we go. Out of habit more than anything else, we're about to grab all the supplies we can carry, but stop when Red puts a hand up.

"Just leave it. There's beaucoup stuff up there already," he tells all of us. "More than enough for everyone. Trust me."

It's not the first time he's insisted we trust him, and I am beginning to. We each gather what few personal belongings we have, and make our way outside and down the street. Susan is bringing up the rear, even though I didn't order her to come along. Maybe she's following Tiny because he's broadcasting like the Abuela. I wish I knew what Google's pet Gray was thinking or why she acts the way she does.

Unlike earlier, there aren't any people outside. Everyone is buttoned up inside their homes, locked down tight with the shades pulled. After witnessing that small slice of humanity outside enjoying themselves, seeing the place vacant like this is sad and a little eerie. I just hope I'm right and the few remaining residents will be safe in their homes. It was ultimately their choice, but I'm still worried. It's just the way I'm wired.

Next to me, Carly unconsciously reaches for my hand. She locks onto a few of my fingers, and together we start up the hill. Tiny is being held by Annie, but he sees Carly walking and squirms around and wants down. Annie looks a little hurt, but she mellows when he snags one of her fingers and holds on tight. We keep going past the hushed houses. No one feels like talking. The vaguely creepy feeling that's come over me must be contagious.

When we get to the tower, we follow Red through the lobby and stop in front of the elevator. Carly is entranced with the place, and I feel her twitch a little when the bell dings and the doors glide open. When we step into the tiny space and the doors close quietly behind us, she tugs at my hand. I lean down to her as Red pushes the button for the tenth floor.

"What are we doing?" she whispers into my ear.

I realize then that she's never been in an elevator

before, and has no clue what's going on. How could she? To her this is just a small room with metal walls and a weird door. I smile at her as the floor lurches gently under our feet. The soft hum of electric motors whir around us.

"This is an elevator. A machine that will take us to the top of the tower so we don't have to walk up the steps. It's nothing to be afraid of."

She watches the little display above the buttons as they tick upwards. "I'm not afraid. This is neat," she says, but her tightened grip on my hand says otherwise.

When we get to the tenth floor, the doors open again. Her little mouth forms an O as she stares at Juanita's station in front of us, right where the lobby used to be. We all pile out, and she stands on the tile hallway in a daze while everyone else moves around her.

"It's magic," she whispers.

I laugh warmly at her dumbfounded expression, and kneel down next to her again, our eyes even with each other. "No, it's not magic, but I get why you'd think that. It's like the TV. Back before the Storm this kind of stuff was everywhere. If you want to be really amazed, remind me to tell you about cars. And airplanes. You'll love all that."

Just then I hear an exclamation from down the hall, and I see the Abuela roll out of her room in the wheelchair. When she spots Tiny, her hand flutters to her face, quivering like leaves in a storm. Tiny sees her at the same moment. His eyes go big and round, then he sprints down the hall towards her, his shoes squeaking on the tile floor as he goes. He pulls up short a few feet from her, like he's unsure what to do next. The Abuela holds out her trembling hands, and he slowly takes them in his own. The two of them stare at each other as if they've been reunited.

"What do you think is going on there?" Singer asks me.

"I don't know, but my guess is they're talking to each other," I reply.

The Abuela smiles and nods once in a while, Tiny doing the same every so often. I could be watching two people on TV having a conversation with the sound off. They carry on like this for a few minutes before she squeezes his hand affectionately, smiling. Finally, Tiny turns around, and the two of them join the rest of us.

"Thank heavens I was right!" the Abuela says proudly, her round face glowing. "Tiny is like me. He has the power. I can sense it in him."

Google steps forward, a slightly puzzled clouding his young face. "Of course he does. We already determined that."

She grins at the little genius, her eyes twinkling. "You must be Google, or should I call you by your real name, Loren?"

Loren? Google's real name is Loren? No wonder

he chose to go by Google. Even so, I'm so used to calling him by his nickname that hearing his real one is a little jarring, like finding out you've been pronouncing a word wrong your entire life.

Google jerks once, caught off guard, but quickly regains his composure. "No. Google is fine."

The Abuela laughs, pleased with herself. We've got a lot to do and I'm itching to get busy, but she insists on meeting everyone else. Annie looks a little dumbstruck by everything that's happened since we got on the elevator. Carly hides behind my legs, and it takes me a second to understand why: she's never seen anyone so ancient before, especially not someone so old they needed a wheelchair.

When the two of them have been introduced, the Abuela takes note of the towering figure of Susan standing at the back wall by herself. Anyone else coming face to face with a Gray like this would be terrified, trust me on that one. But the old lady merely cocks her head thoughtfully, and the two stare at each other in silence. Like she did with Tiny, I imagine she must be having some sort of mental conversation with her. Whatever the pair of them are doing, the Abuela breaks it off a few seconds later.

"What was that all about?" I ask, glancing back and forth between them.

"I was thanking her for saving your life," she replies.

I shake my head. "Did she understand you?"

"Well, yes and no. Words are too much for her, but concepts and images can work. She knows what I was talking about. Compared to the rest of these things, she's actually quite bright. I can communicate with her on a basic level, which I can't do with the rest of them. And she's no danger to any of you. In fact, in her own way she's actually rather fond of all of you. Especially you and Tiny, Scout."

"And you got all that? Just now?"

"Oh yes, and more. In fact, by connecting with her before, I bet you could do the same. Tiny already can. You just have to work at it."

Red is standing off to the side, tapping his foot impatiently. He's got a pair of binoculars strung around his neck, and states he's going to the roof to keep watch. I can't tell if the handyman is feeling better about our chances now, or if he's just playing along to humor the Abuela. Whatever the reason, he's moving and acting with more resolve than in the past, and his earlier fatalistic attitude seems to have disappeared. As he's walking away, he turns to me and says over his shoulder, "You and Romeo there should go downstairs and help the guys out. I'm sure they could use you."

I flap a hand to let Red know I heard him. Before we go, I ask the Abuela if there's a TV and a DVD player available for the kids. She's sure there is, and promises Juanita will help get them situated. Harold is carrying the shopping bag of DVDs and shakes them in my direction.

"I'll keep an eye on the kids and figure something out. I'm pretty good with technology," he assures me.

Peering into his eyes, I don't catch any hint of the terrifying version of Harold I saw on the roof earlier. He's back to being the guy we've known as our cook and friend, which is a good thing, because I wouldn't trust the kids with him otherwise. Singer and I hurry down the stairwell. When we reach the second-floor landing, we almost run into Stretch and Shorty, busy lugging heavy furniture down the steps. Both of them are sweating buckets and muttering curses through gritted teeth. I realize this is the first time we've seen them since our initial night here.

"Red said you could use some help," I say.

Stretch, lower down on the steps, drops the end of the heavy cabinet he's carrying. It looks like an entertainment center we had when I was younger. The thud as it hits echoes around the cinder block stairwell. In unison, their eyes travel up and down both of us, and all they can see are a couple of skinny kids. He snorts once.

"No, we're good. We got this," he says, panting and red-faced with exertion.

Singer smiles at him, his arms crossed. "You sure? Because it looks to me like you're struggling a little."

The tall man wipes sweat away from his forehead with a red handkerchief. He squints and he waves expansively at the load in front of him. "Think you can do better, kid? Have at it."

"Yeah? Okay, sure."

Squeezing past the two of them and their heavy load, Singer grabs either side of the substantial piece of furniture and lifts. The expression on the faces of the two men is priceless as they watch him easily walk it backwards down the steps by himself, all the way to the ground floor. He carefully sets the heavy piece down, and slides it against the door to the lobby. He makes a show of slowly dusting off his hands.

"What's next?" he asks them calmly, not able to hide his amusement.

Stretch and Shorty exchange a comical look, then in unison point back up to the second floor. We follow them upstairs. In the hallway outside the door are more cabinets, along with some oversized metal filing cabinets. Singer and I each grab a file cabinet and carry them back down. In a matter of minutes, the landing outside the doorway to the lobby is so jammed full of bulky furniture it would be physically impossible for anything short of a bulldozer to force the door open. They'd have better luck breaking down the cinderblock wall.

"Okay," I ask the pair. "Now what?"

In short order, we barricade all the doors on floors one through four. Once we're done, Singer and I stack more in the stairway right below us, the one leading to the fifth floor. If a Gray somehow manages to get in down below, it'll find its way upstairs completely blocked by a mass of furniture packed tighter than a professionally loaded U-Haul. From here on out, the only way in and out of the upper floors is through the elevator.

"Aren't you worried they'll be able to come up the shaft? It's got a ladder in it, right?" Singer asks.

After witnessing what we can do, Stretch is seeing us in a new light, more as peers than kids. "Naw. We've got that covered. Red says we're gonna park the car just above the fourth floor. There's a trapdoor on the ceiling of it, but there's nothing on the floor. It'll block the shaft big as hell. Nothing'll get through that way."

I admire his confidence. The two of them give us a grunt and start trudging up the steps, mumbling about grabbing a bite to eat. I let them go ahead of us. Singer is about to follow when I gently touch his arm.

"Got a minute?" I ask.

He blinks and stares down at me. "Sure. What's up?"

This is the difficult part. I've discovered over my brief adulthood I'm pretty good at being in a relationship with someone as kind and caring as Singer, but I'm not so good at talking about it if there's a problem. Blowups like the one we had yesterday cause me a ton of emotional stress, and even if talking about it would help, it's still hard for me. And, now that I've got his attention, I'm not sure how to even start the conversation. I clear my throat.

"Are you and me, you know, okay?"

It takes him a second to reply. "What, you mean about yesterday? Yeah, sure. We had a fight, that's all."

"Yeah, but you were so mad. I've never seen you like that before."

He sighs and takes my shoulders in his strong hands. His mouth moves like he's searching for just the right words. "Yeah, okay, I haven't been that pissed in a long time. Don't get me wrong, I'm still not convinced what we're doing is right, but I've made my peace with it. I mean, you're dead set on staying, and I'm not going to leave without you. I would never do that. We're in this together, right?"

"Right."

He smiles down at me, and all I can see is sincerity and compassion in every curve and plane of his narrow face. I'm so relieved my knees wobble a little, and I'm glad he's holding onto me. I reach around his waist and lock my hands behind him, and I never want to let go.

"But if this all goes sour and we get killed, I'll expect a lavish apology that I was right all along," he whispers softly in my ear.

I pull away and see he's smiling. I give his shoulder a punch that's hard enough to force him backwards. He laughs out loud and rubs his arm.

"Hey, that hurt."

I grin back at him. "Good. It was meant to."

He's still rubbing his arm when he turns serious. He says, "Did your parents ever fight?"

I think for a moment. "No. Well, yeah, not much. Not in front of us."

"Mine did. All the time. It's one of the reasons I got into sports. Practice kept me away from home a lot, so I didn't have to listen to them. I hated it."

"I never knew. That sounds terrible."

"It was. They couldn't seem to turn it off. They'd fight in public, or when we were visiting friends or relatives. All the time. It was embarrassing, for them and me."

I don't know what to say, so for once I say nothing.

"I told myself back then that if I ever found someone I cared about, I wouldn't be like them. I wouldn't fight all the time. To be honest, in the end I don't even know if they loved each other anymore. Hell, I'm not even sure they liked each other."

"People are allowed to have different opinions," I tell him. "But that doesn't mean it has to be full of hate and anger. It's okay for two people who love each other to have a disagreement. It's how they express their differences that matters."

"Wow. That sounded really adult and wise."

"It did, didn't it? But it's true."

The mood has lightened, thankfully. He leans down and places his hand behind my neck. He kisses me then, long and gently. When we finally stop, we remain close, our foreheads touching. Eventually we pull completely away, and I spot a twinkle of amusement in his brown eyes. He lifts a finger as if making a point.

"Let me get this straight. What I'm hearing is, it's okay if I disagree with you as much as I want, as long as I'm civil about it?"

I grin and cross my arms. "No, not at all. I take it all back. I'm your captain, remember, and disagreeing with me is the same thing as mutiny. I won't stand for it."

"That sounds like a double-standard. And didn't we determine that it's only mutiny if we're on water? Doesn't look like we're in a boat here, does it?"

I'm considering if additional physical retaliation is something a captain would employ, when we hear a noise in the distance. At first, I'm afraid it's one of the sound machines, and my gut clenches in fear. Then I realize that's not it at all. Someone is shouting from high above us. Singer and I share a confused look at each other at the same moment we hear a door banging open high overhead.

"Scout! Singer! You down there?" comes Harold's slightly panicked voice from the tenth floor. I've never heard anything like that in his tone before, and frankly that scares me more than I thought possible.

I cup my hands to my mouth. "Yes, we're here," I shout up the stairwell. "What's going on up there?"

"We've got another blizzard heading our way!"

CHAPTER
TWENTY-SIX

Singer and I charge up the steps in such a mad rush we take them four at a time. In a dead heat, we burst through the door. Everyone is clustered at the other end of the corridor, in the opposite direction of the Abuela's room. We sprint to where they're all staring in awe out the big window.

"Damn," Singer says from my side. "Is that what it looked like last time?"

Outside it's a nice day with mild temperatures in the low seventies, and the sky overhead is blue and cloudless, as pretty as they come. If I restrict my view just to that, I can convince myself that another apocalypse wasn't knocking on our door. But it's a different matter completely when I turn my gaze to the horizon.

"Yeah, pretty much," I finally answer, my voice subdued.

From where we stand, the white wall hurtling towards us is as solid as a glacier. Huge, tortured waves churn where the base of the blizzard intersects with the brown water. It's impossible to tell how fast it's moving, but I know firsthand the mindless thing is crashing toward us with the force of a hurricane. We stare in joint wonder as the unnatural white mass towers into the heavens and from one end of the world to the other, looking every bit like an alien force intent on obliterating everything in its path. Carly whimpers and steps near me for protection. I grab both her shoulders and hold her tight.

Footsteps slap on the tile floor behind me, and Harold rushes in from the stairwell leading to the roof. He's breathing hard and sweating.

"What the hell were you doing up there?" I ask him, louder than I meant to. "You shouldn't be out there. Are you insane?"

"I moved all the weapons to a safer place up there. Can't have them blowing away, can we?"

Red is off to the side. He sighs and shakes his head. "Dammit to hell, I really hoped we wouldn't have one of these again. I'm gonna have a crapload of work afterwards."

"But you survived it before, right?" Singer asks. "I mean, obviously you did, but should we be worried?"

"Well, that last one went east of us more. And no, nobody died. But this sucker looks like it might be a direct hit."

For some reason the approaching storm takes me back to Sunday school. What's roaring towards us is right up there with the parting of the Red Sea, rivers filled with blood, or one of those other disasters aimed at Pharaoh by a pissed off Old Testament God. "Should we be doing anything else? Didn't you say you used the plywood to protect the windows last time?"

"We did. But we don't have any left over. We only covered up the windows facing it before. All the plywood is already being used on the windows of the lower four floors. There's nothing left."

Singer steps in front of us, once again the voice of reason. "Come on, everyone. We need to move away from the glass and take cover somewhere safe, like an inner room without windows. I'm not worried about this building making it, but staying out here is a bad idea."

Thankfully, one of us is thinking straight. Everyone quickly hurries after Juanita to a room behind her station, one where there are four solid walls and not a single pane of glass. I sprint down the hall to get the Abuela. Skidding into the old lady's room, I find her in her wheelchair, calmly sitting with a book in her lap. The view out her window is serene, with blue sky arcing above us.

"I heard," she says. "There's another storm coming."

"We need to get you to safety," I tell her.

I scamper behind her and push her out the door

into the hall. The others have all taken refuge already, except for Harold. He's still stationed in front of the far window, watching with his hands pressed against the glass.

"Come on!" I yell at him.

He waves at me. "I'll be right there. I want to see this."

I'm tempted to run down there and grab the suicidal idiot and drag him with me, but I can't do that and care for the Abuela, too. Throttling back a frustrated scream at the stupidity of boys in general, I quickly wheel her into the room with the others. There are several chairs and an examination table already in there, and everyone is hunkered down wherever they can squeeze in. There's some degree of terror reflected in each of their eyes, especially the little ones. I'm sure mine are no different. Susan is the only one who doesn't share that; she found a corner behind the bed and is standing there looking no more concerned than any other day of the week. I check out her hands, but they're quiet at her sides, which I take as a good sign. At least there aren't any Grays around.

Suddenly the floor beneath our feet shakes back and forth as the blizzard smashes into the tower with primal force. The building quivers, and a low moaning escapes from the walls as if the entire structure is wracked with pain. I don't know anything about construction, but I can't imagine something this big and rigid is supposed to move or sound like that. Annie cries out and covers her face with her hands, leaning into the kids protectively. Carly lets out a yelp of fear. Just then the door crashes open and Harold dashes in and slams it shut behind him with both hands, panting.

"Holy crap that's intense!" he exclaims loudly. "I've never seen anything like that before."

I can't believe it, but I swear Harold's not scared. In fact, I'd say the crazy fool is more fascinated than anything.

Red chuckles at him. "Yep, we're not in Kansas anymore, Toto."

Toto? I have a dim memory of a crazy movie about witches and sparkly shoes, and some dog named Toto, but I can't place it. I'm half-tempted to ask when the building rocks and bounces under our feet like a lifeboat cut adrift in a storm. The overhead lights flicker ominously as the fixtures bang back and forth. Everyone yells again and grabs hold of each other to keep from being knocked off their feet. Then a new sound starts, a deep, unnatural roaring that surrounds us, as if something is clawing to get at us through the walls. There's a crash somewhere down the hall, followed by two more. That's enough for Carly, who starts crying in earnest. I envelope her in my arms, knowing full well this is something I can't protect her from, but determined to try. For at least ten minutes the horrible roaring noise goes on, like some angry beast determined to destroy each and every one of us.

Then, as quickly it started, the howling outside abruptly stops. The lights flicker and hum a few more times before coming back on full strength. The building starts behaving like a building should and no longer dances under our feet. We all look at each other, almost afraid to say something, as if we might break some spell if we do. Finally, Harold eases the door open a crack and peeks out.

"Hey, I think that's it," he states. He opens the door the rest of the way, and I half expect a wall of frigid air wash over us, but it doesn't. One by one we step out of our temporary sanctuary and into the hallway. At the end of the hall where we were standing before, the window is blanketed with ice and snow, but it's still in one piece. The frost and snow covering it are thick enough we can barely see out of it any longer, but thankfully it didn't break.

"That was a lot shorter than the last one," Red observes, talking out loud to himself.

"Hey, over here," Google yells, pointing to a door to one of the rooms. There's snow drifting under it and dusting the hallway. He carefully opens it and a blast of arctic air hits him so hard he staggers backwards.

"What happened?" I ask him, still hanging back with the Abuela.

He takes a quick look, then shuts the door fast. "The window in there shattered," he says. "Stuff toppled over. That must be the sound we heard."

The rest of us fan out and inspect the rest of the rooms, but everything else seems to be okay. Red checks out the room Google found, then shuts the door and puts a rolled-up towel on the floor to keep the cold out. He mutters something about his growing to-do list.

"All in all," Singer says, "I'd say we came through that okay. Think the residents are all right? We should check on them."

Red nods, then stops when he hears a chirping noise coming from his belt. He unclips the walkie-talkie and puts it to his ear.

"Yeah?" he asks.

We can all hear Stretch when he says, "We got a problem. The sound machines in a couple of the sectors are down. I don't know what happened. I guess they got blown over."

"Damnit, are you sure?" Red replies.

"Yeah. I got three, no, four, red lights on the board. SW6, 7, 8, and 9. Either they're down, or the board is malfunctioning."

Red shakes his head. "Shit. Okay, get your coat and tools, and meet me in the lobby. We gotta get those back up and working right away."

"Will do," Stretch says.

With a muttering growl, Red clips the walkie talkie back onto his belt and heads towards the elevators. Singer intercepts him by the nurse's station.

"I'm going with you," he states.

The handyman looks him up and down, then nods. "Sure. Whatever. Let's go."

I step forward. "I'm going, too."

"I figured as much. You two seem to be a matched set. There are some coats in the closet behind Juanita's desk. Grab them and let's go. The brown one is mine. Let me grab my tools."

Harold says he'll keep an eye on everyone while we're gone, and I know he will. I squeeze the Abuela's hand, trying not to notice the troubled look written in the creases of her round face. Singer is in the closet before I get there, and he hands me a thick winter coat with a heavy hood. I toss it on and zip it up. There are some leather gloves in the pocket, and I slip them on. They're too big for my hands, but they'll do.

Red is already waiting for us by the elevator. He takes the thick tan coat with a Carhart label on the left side of his chest from Singer. He pulls on a wool hat so low I can barely see his eyes. In his right hand he's carrying a toolbox. In his other hand is a long steel bar with an ax head welded on the end. I've never seen anything like it before. When he sees we're ready, he pushes the elevator button. As the doors slide open, we step inside.

"Let's do this," he says.

We bundle into the small space. I'm already sweating from the thick jacket, but I know I'll be thankful for it soon. When we reach the lobby, the bell dings, but the doors remain closed. Red frowns and lays into the override button. We hear a muted buzzing from deep in the walls, followed by a dull clunk.

"That can't be good," Singer says.

Red steps up and slips his fingertips into the narrow vertical crack. He grunts and the back of his neck turns a light shade of crimson as he strains to force them open. After a few seconds of this, he drops his hands and steps back.

"You wanna give me a hand here?" he asks Singer.

Singer mirrors Red's effort, but this time the stubborn doors start to inch apart with the metallic grinding of a garbage disposal full of forks. He flexes and shoves again, and they slam open, each one a little cockeyed. A frigid blast smashes into my face and the water in the corners of my eyes freezes. The inside of the lobby is a disaster, like a tornado spent a few minutes having a party in here. The heavy furniture is smashed against the walls, and the glass front doors have been shattered, swinging back and forth on their tracks. Magazines lay shredded like confetti on the floor all around us. The rug has been tossed out the front door in a frosty heap.

"Damn," Singer mumbles.

"Yeah," Red says.

We quickly exit the lobby. Outside, the grass and parking lot are covered in ice and debris, mainly branches and trash, most of it probably blown here from the shoreline. We don't stick around and gawk, because Red is already hustling down the street towards our house. Hurrying to catch up with him without wiping out on the slick surface, the three of us almost jog down the hill. We come up to Nelson's house, and see the old man waving from the front window. Red waves back, but doesn't stop.

"These sound machines," Singer says, not slowing. "How'd you come up with those? Are they your doing?"

"One of the residents used to be an electrical engineer, or something," Red replies, his thick breath puffing out in front of him as he talks. "Brilliant guy. Quick as a whip. He died a few years ago, but before he did he set all this up for us. We found out early on that those things didn't like loud noises, so he cobbled the whole system together. It's tied to a board in his house where we control it. That's how we turned that one section off when you got here. We monitor the whole network from there."

We get to our street and keep going until the pavement ends. When we step onto the tall grass, it disintegrates under our feet with a loud, crystalline crunch, as if we're walking on splinters of glass. I notice movement to my right, and see Stretch already out here. He's carrying a toolbox and coils of what looks like thick black wire. Red waves at him, and he angles to meet us.

The four of us continue scurrying down the slope. When we get to the spot where the sound machine was at SW6, we can see the thick wooden pole has been snapped off at the base. The speakers are still attached to it, but one of them has been crushed in the fall.

"That's bad," Stretch notes, saying what we're all thinking.

"No shit, Sherlock," Red mutters. "Get those speakers off the pole and stand them on the ground. We'll splice the wires together. It's not perfect, but it'll do for now."

"What do you want us to do?" Singer asks.

He hands me the steel ax. Not looking up, he simply says, "Stand guard."

The two men don't say a word as they furiously strip wires and start splicing them together. It's so cold the rubber insulation crumbles instead of peeling off in neat sections. They twist red caps onto the exposed copper ends to hold them together while Singer watches intently, like he's taking notes in his head. Stretch tries to use some black tape, but it's so frozen it breaks. At one point Red sticks out a hand, and I instinctively hand him the ax. Using the steel handle as a lever, they ease the pole up off the ground and pull out some more wires. As they finish up, Red grabs the walkie-talkie again.

"Is SW6 back up?"

After a second, Shorty answers. "Yeah, I got a green light again."

"Good. Okay, we're moving to the next one. Give us a minute and turn it back on."

"Will do."

The two men repack their tools, and the four of us crunch through a landscape that feels more like Alaska than Dayton. When we get to the next pole, we find it's still standing, but some fallen branches from a distant tree have sheared the wires high up. They stand there for a moment, breathing hard, trying to figure out how to get up there.

"I don't suppose any of you are hiding a ladder in those toolboxes?" Singer asks.

Red turns to him. His lips are already turning purplish-blue from the cold, and the eyelashes of his left eye are frozen together, giving him a semi-permanent wink. He reminds me of an arctic pirate. "No, we don't."

"I didn't think so. This doesn't look too hard. Give me what I need, and I'll climb up there and see what I can do."

Red is savvy enough to give him a shot. He passes over a handful of tools, and watches as Singer clambers up the wooden pole faster than a squirrel. He wraps his legs around it to hold himself in place and starts reconnecting wires, just like the other two did. In no time, he shimmies back down. Red checks with Shorty.

"Yep. SW7 is back up and running."

Over the walkie talkie, Red repeats his earlier instructions about giving us a minute to get clear, and we hurry on to SW8. When we arrive, we see this pole suffered the same fate as the first, and has toppled over, but with more damage as two of the three speakers are crushed underneath it.

"Only one made it," Stretch observes.

"It'll have to do for now. We can fix the rest later, or replace them if we have to."

They use the steel ax handle to pry up the pole again, and drag the remains of the two smashed speakers out. The only surviving one they prop up on the ground. When they reconnect all the wires and ask Shorty for a status check, he tells them he's still getting a red light.

"Dammit to hell," Red mutters. He fiddles with more wires, but nothing he does has any positive effect. With a deep snarl of frustration, he repacks his tools.

"Want me to go back for a replacement?" Stretch asks.

Red wipes at his eyes with a gloved hand white with ice. "Yeah, you'd better."

"Hold on," Singer says. "I can get there faster than either of you. Where are they? I'll get one and hook it back up. You guys go on to the next one. Just leave me some tools."

Red points back toward the tower. "Go through the lobby. Behind the elevator shaft is a storeroom. Grab the biggest speaker you can carry and get it back here. We'll be working on the next one."

Singer doesn't wait and takes off running. With his

speed and strength, I know he'll be there and back here faster than either of these two ever could. In seconds he's already out of the grass and on the icy street, where his footsteps smack loudly against the concrete. The three of us hurry to the next machine.

When we arrive, the pair of them huffing and puffing from exertion, we see that SW9 seems to be in good shape. The pole is still standing tall and the wires are all connected. Red grabs his walkie.

"Shorty, SW9 looks good. You sure it's not working?"

"No, it still shows a red light," comes the answer. "But it was green a second ago. It comes and goes. There must be a short."

"Shit. Okay, tell me if it goes green. I'm going to try some stuff."

Red grabs at the wires dangling down from the speakers, and gives them a tug, but they don't budge. He traces the thick black wires down until they vanish in the frozen dirt at his feet. He heaves again, and pulls a section up from beneath the surface, dislodging chunks of ground as he goes. He keeps yanking, walking behind as more wires are unearthed. He finally comes to a spot where an irregular piece of metal the size of a Frisbee was slammed into the ground from the force of the wind. He pulls again, and the ragged ends of the wire are in his hand. He sticks his other hand out towards me, and I reflexively pass him the ax. He chops at the hard ground until he finds the other buried end. Stretch hands him a two-foot-long section of wire from the coil around his arm.

"Here, boss," he says.

Wordlessly, the handyman takes the offered piece and splices everything together. When he's done, he tucks the wires back underground as well as he can, stomping them back into place. Shorty's voice crackles through the speaker and says the light is green. Next to me, Red sighs in relief, his breath clouding in front of him. They're just starting to pack up their tools when we hear Shorty's voice again.

"SW8 is back up and running, too. I'm getting a green light."

Red turns to me. "Your boyfriend must have taken care of that already. Impressive."

I smile at him. "Yeah, thanks. Glad he could help."

The mood between the two of them is more upbeat than it's been since before the blizzard hit. They're talking between themselves now, even joking a little, as they put away the rest of their equipment. Red hands me the ax, which I sling over my shoulder. The steel shaft is so cold I can almost feel it burning my skin through my thick gloves. As bitter cold as it is out here, I'm impressed those two are handling it as well as they are. I mean, I'm pretty chilled, even with my abilities.

"If it's all the same to you," Stretch says, pounding his hands together, "I'm going to head back. I'm dying out here."

"Go ahead. The girl and I are going to check out her boyfriend's work, then we'll join you. As soon as it warms up, we'll have to get some new poles out here."

Stretch tucks his head deep into his coat, and starts back towards the houses. Red checks his work one more time, then cocks his chin toward the SW8 sound machine. I motion him forward, and together we start trudging through the frozen undergrowth. Our prior footsteps are easy to follow on the ground in front of us. We've only made it a few dozen steps when an all-to-familiar wall of sound hits us, but it's far enough away that its effect on us is nominal. Even so, I nearly drop the ax as I cover my ears.

"What the hell?" I scream.

Red has already thrown down his toolbox and is reaching for the walkie-talkie. He shouts into it, but I can't hear a thing he says over the roaring noise. He jams it into his hood flush to his ear and strains to listen. After a few seconds, he puts his mouth next to my ear.

"Your boyfriend must have set it off. But I'm not taking any chances. Come on!"

Together, the two of us sprint toward the wailing. It gets measurably louder the closer we get, to the point where it's starting to get very uncomfortable, just like when we first arrived. When we're so close I can see the speaker on the ground, I'm shocked when I spot Singer. He's about fifty feet behind it, standing there with his hands to his ears. When he sees us, he points frantically down the hill, away from the compound. What I see makes me stop dead in my tracks.

There, not far from the speaker, are a mass of Grays, at least a hundred. The ones closest to the speaker are writhing on the ground in agony, but those farther away are still on their feet and milling anxiously around like ants on a piece of candy. But what stuns me most of all is the one in front of those still standing.

It's Hunter, and he's pointing a rifle right at us.

There's something about Hunter that makes me recognize him immediately. I don't know if it's one single characteristic, or a combination of many. It might be as simple as the way he stands with his feet spread apart just so, or how he lovingly cradles his gun like it's a newborn child. Of course, it could also be his long red hair all streaked with white, or that annoying swagger he somehow manages without even taking a step. Whatever it is, seeing him there sucks the air from my lungs like I just stepped naked into outer space.

He's dressed in the same short raincoat he wore before, but the hood is tossed back now and reveals his somewhat ashen face. His cheeks have deeper depressions than the last time I saw him, as if a melon baller has carved out shallow hollows. His eyes, spread unnaturally far apart, seem to have receded into his head. Whatever's been happening since our last meeting near Church Island, it hasn't been kind to him. He's more Gray than before, but the fact he's still able to use his gun means he hasn't changed all the way. I'm not sure if that's better or not, but probably not.

His finger squeezes the trigger, the gun barks, and I jerk reflexively. But instead of hitting one of us, a big plastic chunk of the speaker is blown away. The black box jerks and almost topples over, but in the end stays upright and keeps blaring white noise. His thin lips twist into a frown, then he brings the rifle back up for another shot.

"*Run!*" I scream as loud as I can. "He's going to take out the speaker!"

The three of us take off at a dead sprint for the compound. I hear another gunshot followed by a loud smack, and the blaring noise behind us stutters, hums, then fizzles out. I chance a look over my shoulder, and in that freeze-frame image I spot the ruined speaker, Grays slowly climbing to their feet, and Hunter grinning ear to ear.

"They're going to be coming after us any second!" I yell at the two of them as we charge across the frozen field.

Singer and I are holding back to stay with Red, but he's already winded, huffing and wheezing with thick white clouds of breath shooting from his mouth and nose like a dragon. He's not in the greatest shape, and there's no way he'll make it all the way to the tower at this pace. We're not even out of the grass yet.

"Can you go into slo-mo and carry him out of here?" I yell at Singer.

He does a double-take. "Me? Why don't you do it?"

"I don't know if I can. You're better at it than I am."

"But you'll be out here by yourself!" he shouts.

"I'll be right behind you. Just do it!"

As I watch, Singer's eyes unfocus for a second and then he blurs and is gone. As many times as I've gone into slo-mo myself, I'll never get used to seeing someone else do it. A heartbeat later Red lets out a surprised yelp, and he magically disappears, too. One second he's there, and the next he's not, like a volunteer vanishing in a Vegas illusionist's grand finale. In front of me, I catch smears of colors moving incredibly fast toward the compound as the two of them speed away from me.

Now that Red and Singer are out of immediate danger, I put my head down and take off as fast as I can, putting everything I've got into it. Before I know it, I clear the field and I'm onto the street. The surface is slick with patches of black ice, and I'm forced to throttle down to keep from immediately spinning out. I'm not sure I really want to find out what's on my tail, but I take a look anyway. What I see chills my blood more than the outside air. The Grays are coming now, every single one of them, pounding in my wake like a pack of hungry wolves. Hunter is still in the lead, his gun swinging back and forth in his hand. For some reason, he hasn't gone into slo-mo, meaning he either can't do it at the drop of a hat, like me, or just doesn't want to. I'm going with the first option.

When I get to the end of our street and turn left, I realize too late I'm going way too fast and I wipe out on a patch of ice. I tumble into the opposite yard, coming to rest in some bushes with the ax under me. As I scramble to my feet, I see the pack has closed the gap, and is only a hundred feet or so away. They're almost all the way across the field, and they're not slowing down. When they hit the pavement, a handful of them slip and go crashing across the street and wind up in the nearest yard, all tangled up in a flurry of flailing arms and legs. The others ignore them and keep coming. I choke out a short yelp of fear and take off again at full speed, towards the protection of the tower. I've lost precious seconds.

The sound of the pack closing on me is surreal. Real wolves would at least have the decency to be snarling and growling, but the only noise coming from these creatures is the smacking of hundreds of feet on the frozen street. I can hear their raspy breath as they push the boundaries of their endurance, like a group of marathoners vying for first place at the end of a race. I've got enough adrenaline coursing through me to float a boat, and history says I can keep going like this for a long time, but these things can, too. Even worse, from what I can hear directly behind me, they're gaining on me. I never really considered this before, but I'm just now figuring out two very important facts: one, these damn things are faster than me, even though I'm putting everything I've got into it; and two, I'm never going to make it to the tower in time.

"You can run, but you can't hide, Scout!" I hear Hunter laugh behind me.

I'm about one second away from turning to fight when the tingle starts in the back of my neck. I'm one thousand percent certain I won't be able to take them all on, especially if Hunter can go into slo-mo, too, but I'm out of options. The world begins to pause itself in that familiar way, and I turn around to face my destiny. I lift the ax to swing at whatever creature is closest, while at the same moment I feel something grab me around my waist. Not more than a few seconds later, I'm standing in the lobby of the tower, my hair blown around my face like I stepped out of a wind tunnel. My shirt is all twisted around. Singer is standing next to me, panting and grinning.

"What the hell just happened?" I ask. My head is spinning a little, and I have to grab onto his arm for support. He's holding my metal ax over his shoulder.

"I was still in slo-mo and figured you could use some help."

A wave of relief passes through me. "I thought I was a goner. I really did. They were almost on top of me."

He nods. "Yeah. I saw that. But come on, we can't stay down here. There are too many windows and no way to defend this place. We've gotta get upstairs where it's safe. Those things will be here any second."

We hustle into the elevator where Red and Stretch are already waiting for us. Red's never been one to show much emotion, but even he has a trapped, panicky look about him, with lots of white showing around his eyes. Having been in his shoes so many times before, I understand completely.

"Let's get those doors shut," he orders. "I don't much care for our defensive position in here."

Singer leaps forward and slaps his palms flat on the doors. He strains, and my spirits lift when they start to close. But halfway there, they stop. He grunts again, and the silvery surface on each one begins to buckle and warp under the pressure. Outside, the first of the Grays has made it up the sloping road and is getting uncomfortably close to the lobby.

"Scout, a little help?" he shouts.

I rush up next to him, and each one of us takes a door. I'm pushing with everything I've got, but mine only creeps forward an inch. His doesn't budge at all. The opening is still nearly two feet wide, more than enough for the Grays to join our little party inside. Singer and I stop and stare at each other, and he dips his head towards me in acknowledgement that this elevator car may be where we make our last stand. I pick up the ax and heft it in my hand. It's no Chuck, but I like the way it feels. He pulls out his knife, then looks down at me.

"To the end," he mouths.

I want to say something warm and heartfelt, something about how much he means to me, and I'm so glad we got to have this time together, but everything I'm dying to tell him would take hours and we only have seconds left. Instead, I grab him by the back of the head and pull him down for one last kiss. When I pull away, we turn to face the onrushing hoard.

We're both in a fighting stance, crouched and with weapons ready, when we hear a thud over our heads. Afraid there's a new threat from above, I jerk back and raise the ax. Just then a small trapdoor on the ceiling opens and Harold's face appears.

"You guys look like you could use some help," he says.

"Get us outta here!" Red shouts up at him.

Singer grabs the handyman around his thighs and easily tosses him up through the hole and into Harold's waiting arms. I do the same to Stretch, throwing him so hard he clears the opening and lands with a curse and a loud thud overhead. Singer puts his hands around my waist and heaves, and I fly through the trapdoor. I reach down and latch onto his upraised hand and pull him up with the rest of us. In seconds, all five of us are standing in the dark shaft, the smell of fried electrical equipment and grease thick in the tight space.

Harold shines a flashlight on a narrow ladder next to us. "Here you go. Let's get moving."

He slams the little trapdoor shut just as the first of the Grays arrive below us. The sounds they make as they crash into the car is terrifying, frantic banging mixed with the scraping of clawed fingers on the metal walls of the elevator. The car is shaking and bouncing up and down dangerously as more pile in. I have this random thought we're probably exceeding the posted weight limit on this thing. Stretch lets out a yelp and takes off up the ladder, Red so close behind him I'm afraid they'll knock each other off. As soon as they're high enough, Singer pushes me up. The cold steel of the rungs is slippery with grease and time, but I hold on tightly and start climbing.

"Harold, get going!" Singer yells, just as the trapdoor at their feet bangs open and several sets of arms thrust through the opening. A hand grabs the small door and rips it off its hinges. Harold has his knives out and slices at them so fast I can barely see the movement. Two hands are lopped off at the wrist, blood splashing everywhere.

"Go!" Harold screams at Singer. "I've got this."

Singer pauses for a second, and I think he's about to go into slo-mo again, but before he can, Harold grabs him and pushes him up the ladder.

"I'll be right behind you!" the cook yells. "Let's get up there and start heaving everything into the shaft to slow them down."

With only a moment's hesitation, Singer leaps up and grabs a rung directly below the one I'm standing on. All four of us climb as fast as we can. As soon as we're high enough, I hear Harold clambering up behind us, the flashlight held between his teeth. When I've reached the third floor, the metal roof of the elevator car below us is ripped open like a beer can torn in two, and light from the lobby floods the lower section of the shaft, revealing a swarm of Grays. With the additional light from the lobby below, it's bright enough that I can see Harold's face looking up at me. He glances down and spots the creatures streaming up through the fresh opening. He and I make eye contact for a split-second. What I see on our cook's face is that same calm, composed expression he wore when he bailed out of the boat. I didn't recognize it that time, but since our heartfelt talk on the roof I can put a word to it now: redemption. I know at that moment exactly what he's going to do, but I'm powerless to stop him.

"Harold, no!" I shout, thrusting out a hand down toward him.

He smiles up at me, winks, then pulls out both of his knives and jumps feet first off of the ladder and into the heart of the attacking Grays.

CHAPTER
TWENTY-EIGHT

I scream long and loud. The cries torn from my throat are more animal than human, rage and despair commingling as one. Singer is directly below me on the ladder and witnessed the entire thing, but we're helpless to do anything about it. I'm locked in a state of shock, my outstretched hand and shaking fingers reaching for nothing. Singer snaps out of it first and quickly climbs up next to me. He grabs my face with his free hand and makes me look at him.

"Scout, we gotta go!" he screams, and begins pulling me up by the arm. I resist for a second, but he's so strong I can't hold on. He drags me up a few rungs before I snap out of my shock and start climbing on my own. I can't see anything but a flurry of activity down there, but whatever is happening, no Grays are coming up after us. I want to take a moment to mourn the sacrifice Harold just made, but we don't have a second to waste. In my head, I say a heartfelt prayer for our friend.

When we finally reach the tenth floor, Red and Stretch hang off to the side so Singer can muscle open the doors. Once he's done that, the two of them collapse onto the tile hallway, pale as ghosts and gasping for air. Singer and I don't wait, but sprint to Juanita's station and each grab a heavy filing cabinet. When we're about to toss them into the shaft, I hesitate and stare down. A few floors below us a Gray is speeding up the ladder, its pale face upturned and glaring. Singer holds his steel filing cabinet out, about to drop it.

"What about Harold?" I yell back at him.

He pauses for a second, his chest heaving. "Harold is gone, Scout. This is what he wanted. Okay? Let's make sure these bastards pay for it."

I clutch harder at his arm, not sure what I intend to do. I know he's right, but the thought of our friend down there is crushing my soul. Like Eve, the rational part of me knows he's already gone, even if my heart still clings to the belief he could be alive. Singer drops the heavy filing cabinet straight down. The advancing creature is sheared off the ladder, and seconds later both hit below with a tremendous boom that shakes the building. He grabs the other one from me and tosses it down the shaft. The cabinet impacts whatever is down there with the force of a two-hundred-pound missile.

"Grab whatever else you can find!" he screams at all of us.

I choke back a sob, and nod in a daze. My eyes

misting over, I stumble after him and run into the examination bed in the room behind Juanita's station.
The two of us carry it back and fling it down the dark
hole, listening as it crashes ten stories down. We do
the same with Juanita's desk, and with as many heavy
chairs from the other rooms we can find. As soon as
Red catches on to what we're doing, he and Stretch
grab what they can and heave down whatever they
can carry. After we've tossed enough into the abyss to
fill a moving truck, Singer holds up a hand and peers
down the darkened shaft.

"I don't hear anything, do you?" he asks softly.

I'm crying so hard it's hard for me to hear much
of anything. My chest is shaking, and my hands are
trembling. I try to get ahold of myself, but I'm having
a hard time coming to grips with what just happened.
I think back to how badly I handled it when we lost
Dog, or when Lord went Gray, and when Simon left
us. I try as hard as I can not to tumble into my familiar
abyss of depression. Red edges close to the open doors
and peers down into the darkness.

"No, nothing. I think that did it. But I don't know
how long that'll hold them."

Red and Stretch are both armed with shotguns
now, although I have no idea where they got them.
They both watch as Singer forces the doors closed.

"If anything starts to come through, you blast the
crap out of it," Red tells Stretch. The tall man feeds
a few shells into the chamber, and sits down across

from the doors, his long legs straight out in front of him. He's still pale as death, but has his wits about him enough to follow orders.

Down the hall, Google is standing by the open door to the room with the broken window. The little genius is completely out of his element and looks as terrified as I've ever seen him. He's pointing into the room, his clothes flapping a little from the frigid breeze coming from inside.

"Scout, you need to see this," he says, his voice pinched and high.

We hurry towards him. As I pass by, I pause long enough to give him a fleeting hug. He holds onto me for a second, his magnified eyes staring up at me.

"Harold?" he asks in a small voice.

I shake my head and give him a tight smile, a false one constructed of little more than sadness. He understands what I'm not able to say out loud, and he hugs me again while his shoulders shake with emotion. I kneel down a little so our eyes are level.

"Keep an eye on Carly and Tiny, okay?" I ask. "We're not out of this yet."

I pull away from him and dash into the freezing cold room, joining Singer and Red at the shattered window. The view from up here is out over the lobby far below us. The road in front of the tower is snaking down towards our little house in the near-distance. Everything is white and silver with ice, like the cheery picture on some corporate Christmas card. That is, until I look down and see what has to be hundreds of Grays staring up at us with Hunter at the head of the pack. With his red hair blowing in the wind, it's a simple matter to pick him out of the crowd. He points up to us.

"Is this the best you got, Scout?" he screams.

I'm not entirely sure what he means, until one of the creatures drags something into view and dumps it on the ground. It's Harold, or what's left of him, just a bloody mass so mangled he's no longer recognizable as a person.

"Gotta give him credit. He fought like hell, and he wasn't even special like us!" Hunter yells, as he kicks at the lump who used to be Harold. "But you're going to have to do better than that. I've got some damn voice in my head that won't shut up, telling me we need to get up there. We're coming, Scout, so buckle up."

Anger flares white hot behind my eyes, and, even though I know I shouldn't get sucked into his taunts, I can't help myself. "Screw you, Hunter!" I scream, my fists clenched at my sides. "This time I'm going to kill you myself!"

I turn and run toward the stairs leading to the roof, Singer hot on my tail. His eyes narrowed into slits, he sprints past me and together we fly up to the roof. Just before we crash through the door, I see all the weapons stacked neatly on the inside landing where Harold put them for safe keeping. Saying thanks under my breath, we each grab one and burst into the bright daylight. I skid to a stop at the low wall and look down.

"What are you going to do?" Singer asks as he steps up next to me, rifle in hand.

"I'm going to kill that son of a bitch," I say.

He nods. "Solid plan. But there are hundreds of those things out there besides him, you know."

I raise the rifle and sight down the barrel, searching. "Then we'd better get started."

He tilts his head. "Okay. Let's do this."

Singer aims down into the mass of creatures and starts firing, his trigger-finger moving so quickly it blurs. Whatever gun he's got is so loud it could be a cannon going off next to my ear. Below us, Grays start twisting and falling as he scores head shot after head shot. The rest of them follow some unheard command and start dashing around, turning themselves into harder targets; Hunter's doing, for sure. The heavy rifle feels completely foreign in my hands, the metal so cold I could swear it's burning me. Even though Singer has given me several lessons on how to use these awful things before, I'm suddenly blanking on what to do with it, like a monkey presented with a complex puzzle box.

"How you doing there, Scout?" Singer yells in my direction.

"I don't know what I'm doing!"

He shoots half a dozen times before answering me. "Just remember what I showed you. Snug the stock against your shoulder, look down the barrel, and gently squeeze the trigger. You've got this."

I take a deep breath and do what he says, sighting down the long barrel. I don't pull the trigger yet, because I'm trying to pick Hunter out of the churning mass below. With his red hair he should be easy to spot, but he's nowhere to be seen.

"Where's Hunter?" I yell over the thunderous noise next to me.

Singer stops to reload. "I don't know!" Searching, he leans out and looks down at the base of the tower. His eyes fly open in disbelief, and he pumps fresh bullets into the chamber of his rifle at a frantic pace. "Scout, look down there! The Grays! They're climbing up!"

My heart racing, I push aside my fear of heights and peer down. Sucking in a breath of arctic air, I see a swarm of the creatures scaling the side of the tower. They're moving from one window ledge to another, shuffling from side to side as they ascend, like free-form rock climbers attacking a sheer cliff. A few have already made it to the windows on the third floor.

"Take out the climbers!" I yell. "We can't let them get to the fifth floor or they'll get in."

Singer is already on it. He squeezes off three shots, and a trio of Grays tumble away and crash unmoving to the ground. I run over to the side of the building on my left, and see just as many coming at us that way. I try to calm down and think about Singer's lessons, and what he told me about the proper technique, and remember something about slowly exhaling while gently pulling the trigger. I do my best, but I jerk and my first shot hits nothing but innocent dirt at the base of the building. I growl under my breath at my own incompetence, and wish I had taken the time to practice more when I had the chance.

"You hanging in there, Scout?" Singer asks from his side of the roof.

"No, not really! I don't know what I'm doing."

He rushes over and takes five shots, connecting with head shots almost every time. Each Gray is blasted off the side, and one by one fall with individual thuds to the frozen ground below. I'm about to ask him why he's so good at that, but I remember he's one of those people who are naturally good at everything. I'm about to warn him to check the other two sides when Red and Stretch burst through the stairwell door, each with a weapon in hand. Both of them are panting in air colder than a deep freeze.

"Figured you could use a hand," Red says.

"They're coming up the sides," Singer warns them, pointing all around us. The two men split up and each take a ledge, and immediately their guns start going off in a near-continuous stream of fire and smoke. I'm pretty sure I hear Red laughing over the din.

"We've got to get Hunter," I yell over the noise. "The one with the red hair. It probably won't stop them completely, but he's the one giving them orders."

The Grays keep coming, more and more of them

ascending with increasing speed as their dim minds figure out the best way to manage the sheer walls. I try my hand at this gun thing again, squeezing off some more shots. The big rifle bucks on my shoulder, and I realize I'm finally getting the hang of it when I pick a few of them off. But as many as I take out, just as many are there to take their places. Leaning so far over and aiming down like this isn't a natural firing position, but I begin to figure out that even if I hit the wall or ledge in front of them, the shards of brick I blow off are almost as effective as hitting them dead on. Either way, I'm holding my own, if just barely.

Singer, meanwhile, is so efficient he has time to help the rest of us out. He scurries from one side of the roof to the other and lends a hand to whoever needs it the most. Okay, most of the time he's helping me, but I'm not proud and I appreciate the assistance. I don't know how many creatures we've knocked off the walls, but after about fifteen minutes of this, with dozens piled up on the ground, their numbers seem to be waning. There are still plenty of living ones scattered around, probably forty or fifty, but they aren't trying to scale the tower. I take what feels like the first breath since this began, and just when I start to feel like we might come out of this okay, Red runs over to me.

"Shorty's still monitoring the sound machines," he says, still puffing from the exertion and excitement.

"Yeah. And?"

"And he says the one at N5 just went red. It's down."

A chill runs up and down my spine. Singer, still blasting away, hears enough to lean toward us. "What'd you say?"

"Another section of the perimeter defense just went down." He points towards the wooded, dry section of land Harold and I were looking at earlier. "Over there. Towards Dayton."

"Could it be a malfunction on the board?" I ask, hopeful.

"Could be, but I doubt it."

Singer squeezes off another half a dozen rounds, then starts to reload. "So, we've got more coming is what you're saying."

"I'm saying we need to be ready. It could be one or it could be a thousand. There's no way to know."

I've got all my fingers and toes crossed that it's just one, but there's no way we'll be that lucky. Singer and I exchange a quick glance as we start reloading again in preparation. Red takes his cue from us and does the same. Stretch yells that he could use a hand, and the handyman dashes over to help him out. Singer motions me close.

"What do you think? You doing okay?"

I give him a tiny nod. "Yeah, I'm okay. We've got plenty of ammo, but not enough bodies up here if there's another assault. It'd be great if I was better at this. I'm not built for this sort of fighting."

"You're doing great, and I'm here if you need backup."

I pat his arm. "Thanks. But Hunter is still out there somewhere. These things would likely still have shown up because of the Abuela and Tiny, but they're not capable of coming up with anything creative on their own. That's all Hunter. We can't let him get away again or he'll never leave us alone."

"Agreed. Got any ideas?"

I think for a moment, trying to concentrate over the sounds of guns going off as Red and Stretch yell in fear and triumph. The number of living Grays below has dwindled down to no more than twenty or so, and hardly any are trying to climb the walls. One that tumbled down early in the assault landed on the roof of the concrete awning over the main entrance, its arms and legs bent in unnatural angles like a smashed bug. An idea comes to me.

"You just thought of something," Singer says. "I can tell."

"Yeah, I did, but you're not going to like it."

He pauses from loading his rifle, his eyes locked on mine. He lifts one eyebrow. "That's no way to sell it, you know. What are you going to do?"

I reach up and give him a fleeting kiss. "Just cover me, okay? And take out Hunter if you get the chance. Promise?"

He grabs the sleeve of my shirt. "Cover you? What are you talking about? Where are you going?"

I pull his hand away and dash for the steps. "Just cover me!" I yell back at him. As I reach the door leading down, I hear Stretch squeal for reinforcements, followed by a barrage of gunfire. I take a quick look behind me and see Singer torn between following me and helping out.

"Scout!" he yells, taking a step toward me.

"Help them, but be ready!" I scream back at him. I fly through the doorway and down the steps, barely touching any of them on my way to the tenth floor. When I burst through into the hallway, I see everyone gathered at the frosty window at the end of the hall, each of them peering down at the action taking place below them. I rush over to Annie.

"Come with me," I order her.

She pulls back. "What? No way. Why?"

"I'm trying to save everyone, that's why. Including the kids. I need your help."

"But why me?"

I think back to what feels like decades ago, when she attacked the Gray right before Dog was killed. She went after that thing like someone possessed, with no regard for her own safety. She did it to save Carly and Tiny, knowing full well that monster should have shredded her on the spot. When it comes to the kids, she's a lot tougher than anyone gives her credit for, which is exactly what I need right now. I may be the only one to see this in her, but, when it comes to protecting the little ones, she's the type who could bring a knife to a gunfight and win.

"Because you're the only one left who can do this. You want to keep the kids safe, right? Then follow me."

She stares at me for a second, and I see a glint of crazy light up her eyes at the thought of something happening to the children. That's the exact kind of lunatic determination I'm going to need. Whatever she sees in my expression must be enough to convince her, because she narrows her eyes, runs her fingers through her thick red hair, and nods at me in a way that silently acknowledges it.

"For the kids," she says. "Let's go."

We run for the stairwell leading downstairs. On the way, I spot Red's power screwdriver and scoop it up and toss it to her. We go through the door and I motion her to stop for a moment while I listen, just in case any Grays have made it through the barricade down below. Hearing nothing, we hurry down. She's behind me puffing with fear and exertion, and I make myself slow down so she can keep up. When we get to the landing on the fifth floor, we're stopped by all the furniture Singer and I piled up earlier. I wish we could get to a lower level, but that's impossible now. I open the door to the fifth floor.

"Come on," I tell her, my voice just above a whisper.

"What are we doing?" she hisses back to me.

Instead of answering, I crack open the door

and peek in. The hallway here is a carbon copy of the tenth floor, complete with a nursing station right across from us, and the evenly spaced doors leading off in either direction. The lights overhead are turned down low, but it's bright enough to see where we're going. I motion her to follow me.

We hurry down the hallway until we're under the room on the tenth floor, the one with the broken window. We step inside and make our way to the window, still reinforced with thick plywood and steel rebar. I hold the rifle out.

"Here. Please tell me you know how to use one of these."

She jumps back a few feet, her hands up like she's being arrested. "Oh, no. Get that thing away from me."

"Damnit, Annie, I can't do this without you. I need your help. Take it."

She shakes her head, her bright red hair flipping side to side. "No, I can't. You don't understand. I just can't."

"Why not?"

Her fists are pressed against her temples like she's in pain. "Yes, okay, my dad taught me how to shoot when I was a kid, and I'm good at it. But one night, after he'd been drinking, he was shoving my mom around," she says, her voice high and tight, almost like a little girl's. "He was getting angrier and angrier. I don't remember why, but he used to get that way all the time. He started to hit her. I grabbed the gun and told him to stop. He just laughed and came at me, and…"

Oh, god. She always talked about how she grew up with just her mom, but I had no idea what happened to her dad. "Annie, I'm sorry about that, I really am, but that's the past. Right now, the kids need you. If we can't stop these things…" My voice trails off, my meaning clear.

She stares at me, and her lips compress into thin lines. She thrusts her trembling hands out and I shove the rifle at her. She takes it and expertly slides the chamber open to make sure it's loaded. She flips it on its side to see if the safety is off, then sights down the barrel.

"That's kind of impressive," I tell her.

She wipes at her eyes. "Yeah. Whatever."

I lay my hand on her shoulder, then turn to the window and start removing the screws holding the plywood in place. When each screw hits the floor, it pings softly, like a tiny bell chiming. Once that's done, I remove enough of the brackets to slide the metal rods out. I lift the plywood square out of the way, wincing a little at the bright outside light streaming into the room. Cold air batters us.

"Are you going to tell me what we're doing?" she asks, her voice a lot steadier than I thought it would be.

"Yeah. I'm going to drop down to the canopy over

the front door. Then I'm going to bait Hunter into showing himself, and Singer is going to finish him once and for all."

She blinks in surprise. "What am I here for?"

"If any Grays make it onto the canopy, I'm counting on you to kill them. I can handle a couple at a time, but if I know Hunter, he'll send a whole platoon of those things up to get me. I can't be fighting them off and baiting Hunter at the same time. Plus, if something happens to me, you need to board this back up to keep them from getting in. Can you do that?"

That crazy glint in her eyes fades for a second as she realizes what I'm asking her to do, but eventually she nods at me, her head bobbing a little manically.

"Annie, can you do that?" I repeat.

"Yeah, I can. But damn, Scout, you might die! Isn't there any other way?"

"No, not that I can think of, but I'm open to suggestions if you have any."

She doesn't, unfortunately. I take a moment to look at her, to really look at her. We've been together through so much, and I realize now how much I don't know about her. To me she's been little more than a babysitter to the kids, and not much else. I think back to when she clinically sewed up Dog's cheek, something I could never have done. And now I find she knows how to handle a weapon? If we ever get out of this alive, I vow to change all that and get to know her for real. I wish I had done that before. I smile at her.

"Thanks, Annie. We never could have made it this far without you. Really."

Her broad face surprises me with a smile, but it's a conflicted one with undertones of sadness and remorse. Perhaps she's thinking the same things about me? That would be nice.

"Same to you, Scout. Now go out there and let's kill that son of a bitch."

I pat her arm again, then slide the window open and climb onto the sill. Looking down at the canopy below me, I see for the first time how high up I really am, and my legs get a little wobbly. Damn if it isn't a lot farther down there than I thought it would be. It's at least twenty or thirty feet. She peers over the edge.

"Sure you can survive that? I know you've got super powers and all that, but it's a long drop."

"One way to find out," I reply with a lot more bravado than I feel, then I jump.

CHAPTER
TWENTY-NINE

I try not to close my eyes as I push off, but I can't help myself. I feel the ledge slide away from under my feet, sense a rush of air blowing my hair back, and in less time than I thought possible, I crash into the concrete canopy. As I hit, I roll a few times to minimize the impact, but even so I feel the shock through my feet and up into my legs. I'm pretty sure my ankles have been rammed up into my thighs. I lay there for a moment, breathing hard, trying to decide how many bones I may have just broken. Like the roof of the tower, the top of the canopy is covered in gravel. The stones digging into my back remind me I'm still alive and kicking.

"Scout, you okay?" Annie shouts from the window on the fifth floor.

I give her half a wave and sit up, flexing my legs. I twist them around a few seconds, until I'm sure there's no permanent damage, then realize just how open and vulnerable I am right now. I scoot back and kneel down near the dead Gray I saw earlier while I catch my breath, doing my best to hide in plain sight. Overhead on the rooftop I see Singer looking down at me, and I give him a wave, too. He's too far away for me to make out details, but I'm sure he's pissed as hell at what he's seeing right now. Assuming I live through this, I'm going to hear about it later,

"Hey, Scout!" I hear from elsewhere above me. It's Google, his little head popping out of the tenth-floor window. "Here, catch!"

I have no idea what he's talking about, but then I see him holding something out, and I realize he's got the steel ax in his two hands. With a small outward toss, he drops it towards me. I rush forward and grab the metal handle before it smashes into the concrete at my feet. I heft the sturdy weapon in my hands and appreciate just how awesome it feels. If I ever needed a confidence builder, this is it. I swing it around a few times to get the weight of it, smiling as the broad head catches the light. Under my breath I apologize to Chuck for being slighted like this, but I'm sure he'll understand.

Just as I'm about to turn around, there's a burst of gunfire above me. Glancing up, I see Annie shooting down as the remaining Grays start to swarm up the walls towards my position. I may have miscounted earlier, because there's suddenly so many coming at me I can't even count them. I was right — Hunter is sending in the reserves. His mental control over these creatures continues to be annoyingly impressive.

Almost before this final assault can really get going, it's clear Annie has matters under control. She's so efficient and accurate, I'm beginning to think I won't have anything to do, and I'm okay with that. But as skilled as she is, she can't get each and every one, which becomes very evident when three creatures clamber over the edge of the canopy and rush at me from different directions. I launch myself at the closest one with the ax held high, connecting with its skeletal head just as it starts to rear up. The force of the weapon in my hands is incredible, and the Gray flies backwards and off the roof in an uncanny imitation of a diver doing a backflip. I spin around and catch the second one just above its stomach, and it soars soundlessly off and lands twenty feet away on the frozen ground, its gut a shredded mess. I'm about to pull it back for a final swing when the last one grabs at the ax with both hands and tries to wrench it away from me. The damn thing is bigger and stronger than me, and just as I feel my grip loosening there's a sudden movement and a thud next to me. I jerk in alarm until I realize it's Susan. She quickly takes one of the Gray's arms in her two hands, flexes, and breaks it in two. With only one hand left on the handle, I'm able to jerk the weapon away and cock it back for a home run swing. But before I can, Susan storms in and lifts the Gray off its feet, tossing it out and over the edge. It lands with a sickening thud on the concrete Trinity

House sign down below, where it lies broken and still. She stares at it, her hands fluttering at her sides.

Breathing a little heavy, I give her a one-armed hug. Her skin is as scalding hot as always, but it actually feels good in the frigid air. "We have got to stop meeting like this," I tell her warmly. "But thanks. You do know how to make an entrance, don't you?"

She stares down at me, and her mouth moves. To my utter surprise, a raspy sound of sandpaper on metal grinds out from between her lips. It's not a word, at least not that I can tell, but any sound at all coming from a Gray is enough to make me take a step back in shock. Ignoring everything going on around us, I lay a hand on her arm.

"My god, you're trying to talk, aren't you?" I ask her.

I want to quiz her more, but suddenly there's another burst of gunfire above us that seems to go longer than a string of fireworks. I duck down low again, and Susan follows my lead. When the roaring finally stops, I look up and see Singer waving at me.

"Scout, you okay?" he yells, and I flash him the okay sign. "I think that's all of them," he says. "But I still don't see Hunter."

I give him a thumbs up. Susan's hands are still twitching at her sides, so even though Singer doesn't see any Grays, some are still in the area. I don't know if it's just Hunter or not, but now that I've got time to catch my breath, I decide it's time to put the real reason I'm down here into action. I walk to the front edge of the canopy and strike what I'm hoping is a defiant pose, feet apart, arms crossed, the ax still in my hand. I look all around me, and in the near distance all I can see are clumps of trees and bushes. Beyond those are the backs of the houses where we stayed. There are way too many places for that son of a bitch to hide, unfortunately. My heart is fluttering in my chest at what I'm about to do, but I clear my throat, determined not to let my voice crack.

"Hey, Hunter, it's over!" I shout into the void. "Guess what? Your Grays are dead, and we're not. You lost!" I wait a few seconds, trying to pierce the darkness in the trees, desperate to detect any movement or sign he's still there. I can't see him, but I know he's here because Hunter's ego would never let him lose to me.

"Come on out, you…you pussy!" I scream, really leaning into it. "A girl just beat you. And not just any girl, it was me! You gonna come out, or are you too scared? You pussy!"

Out of the corner of my eye I see a flash, and before I can even think, I snap into slo-mo. There was no gradual sensation of it coming on this time. No bees buzzing in the back of my neck. One moment it was off, and a microsecond later it was on and dialed to ten, just like it did when Hunter threatened us at Cedar Ridge. As fast as I can move in the thickness, I jerk to the side and sense more than see something hot and deadly whizz past my left ear. Behind me the bullet smacks with a deep rumble into the wall of the tower, flakes of brick expanding outward. I focus on where the first shot came from, and see another dim globe of light swelling like a ball of lava. I quickly shift positions again and the second shot sings past me.

I'll be damned. I really can dodge bullets. Who knew?

Three more flashes erupt from the trees, and three more bullets fly harmlessly past me. I reach down and scoop up a handful of gravel from the roof and fling the rocks toward the trees where Hunter is hiding. Not waiting to see what happens, I grab another bunch and do it again. And a third time for good measure. The deadly fusillades tear into the trees, shattering bark and leaving bright gashes of raw wood where they hit. Shredded bits of leaves begin to float dreamily down to the ground like ash from a bonfire.

I stop then, and wait, keeping my gaze glued on where I think Hunter is, poised and ready to dodge again if necessary. After a minute or so of waiting in slo-mo time, I see a subtle movement and a dark shape begins to fall from a low branch. My slo-mo shuts off as fast as it came on as I watch as Hunter tumble down to the ground. He lands on his back and is still, the rifle clenched in his hands. Even from here I can see multiple bloody wounds across his chest and arms, the deadly aftermath of my makeshift barrage. I find I'm both exhilarated and incredibly sad at the same time. I've never killed anyone that wasn't a Gray before, and even though it's Hunter, I'm shaken at what I've done. He was once part of our group. My hands are trembling, and whatever's in my stomach threatens to make an unscheduled return trip. I slump to my knees with my hands to my face and sniff back a tear, trying to hold them back, although the blurring in my eyes tells me I'm too late.

Then Hunter sits up.

Before I can react, Susan leaps off the canopy and lands on the ground in a full sprint directly at him. He sees her coming and, from a sitting position, lifts the rifle and fires without taking the time to aim. The shot grazes her left arm, but a wound that minor is never going to slow a charging Gray. I'm about to jump off the roof and go after her when he shoots again, this time hitting her somewhere in the midsection. That second one staggers her, but she keeps pounding toward him, her head down and arms pumping. He gets off a third shot a split-second before she arrives, but his shot is wild and misses. She rips the rifle from his shocked hands. With less effort than it would take a normal person to snap a pencil, she breaks the gun in half, the wooden stock shattering in her powerful hands. She stares at the remains of the weapon in her grasp, then flings the pieces to either side of her. As I watch in horror, she stands over Hunter, panting, before she sinks to her knees and topples over.

Hunter scrambles away from her crumpled form,

crab walking madly backwards. I leap off the canopy and land with a lot less grace than Susan did, but when I get my feet under me, I sprint towards him. He's trying to stand when I get there. I grab him by the throat and lift him off the ground, his feet kicking the air like he's at the end of a hangman's noose. I'm so furious at what he's done that my earlier grief is gone, and I'm tempted to squeeze his neck so hard it snaps in two. He gasps for air and tries to smack my arms away, but he's too weak from his injuries and the blows have no effect. As I hold him aloft, he stops squirming and looks like he's trying to concentrate. His body vibrates, and I realize he's about to go into slo-mo. I can't let him do that, not now! Before he can make that happen, I bring the ax up and smack him across the temple as hard as I can. His head snaps to the side, his eyes roll backwards, and he goes limp. I hold him above me long enough to make sure he's not faking it, then I toss him down in a heap and rush over to Susan.

She's still toppled over on her side, but she's already fighting to sit up. The wound on her arm isn't serious at all, just a furrow that looks worse than it is. The one on her stomach is more worrisome, but with her natural healing ability even that one has already stopped bleeding. This is one time I'm thankful that it takes more than a gunshot to the gut to put down a Gray. I wrap my arms around her in a heartfelt hug, not even concerned that her scalding skin feels like it's burning the hair off my arms.

After a few seconds, I help her stand up. She's a little wobbly on her feet, but otherwise seems none the worse for wear. The wound on her shoulder already looks like it's partially healed. I'm trying to figure out my next move when Hunter groans and slowly sits up, a hand to his head. I stalk over to him and hold the ax up high.

"Don't try anything stupid," I warn him. "Or the next time I use this it'll be to take your head off."

He doesn't react, but just sits there looking like he just woke up from anesthesia, his eyes unfocused and staring at nothing. There's a huge bump on the side of his head where I smacked him, but he shares our healing ability and the swelling is already going down. He tries to stand, but I force him to the ground.

"You don't understand," he mumbles, his words slurred like a drunk. A concussion will do that to you, I guess. "I need to get up there. I don't know why, but something is making me. Damnit, Scout, you gotta let me go."

"Yeah, that's not going to happen," I tell him. Staring at him now, as pitiful as he looks, I almost wish I had killed him before, because now I don't know what we're going to do with him. "You're not going anywhere."

He struggles to stand again, but I'm holding him back. He fights me some more, his arms moving with weak conviction, but I've got the upper hand. Not only that, but Susan is hovering behind me with her fists clenched, breathing hard, almost as if she wants to have a go at him herself. I can't blame her. He has that effect on people.

"No, you don't get it," he pleads, and this time his voice catches and I swear he's starting to cry. His eyes are wide and crazy. "I have to get up there. It's in my head and it won't stop! Make it stop!"

I feel my anger leaching away as I stare at his pathetic form at my feet. I shouldn't feel sorry for him, not after everything he's done and all the anguish he's caused, but I can't help it. The Abuela's siren song is stuck in his mind, and there's nothing he can do about it. She can't turn it off, and he can't resist it. As horrible as he is and as much as I despise the son of a bitch, I almost feel sorry for him. I wish I didn't.

I reach down and grab him by the arm. I'm about to pull him to his feet so we can figure out what to do with him, when I hear shouting from high above me. I glance up and see Singer and Red pointing to my left and waving their arms madly, like they're trying to guide a plane in. Movement lower down the tower catches my eye and I see Annie doing the same thing. With my heart suddenly clogging my throat, I look where they're pointing and gasp. My grip on Hunter loosens, and he sits down so hard his teeth clack together. Next to me, Susan's hands start fluttering so badly the tremors travel all the way up her arms. I've never seen one of these things look nervous, but she does, and that makes me even more worried.

"Holy shit," I hiss.

A mass of Grays begins to emerge from the cover of trees a few hundred feet away, but unlike Hunter's group of less than a hundred, this time there are more. Hundreds more. So many I can't begin to count them. And they just keep coming, like a swarm of locusts advancing on a cornfield.

There's got to be a thousand of them, and they're headed right at me.

CHAPTER
THIRTY

Hunter sees them, too, and tries to take off, but I shove him down so hard he grimaces in pain when he smacks into the frozen ground. Next to me, Susan's eyes narrow to slits and her hands twitch like mad, but she makes no move to leave. In fact, she takes a protective step closer, almost shielding me like I would shield Carly. While we watch in fascinated horror, the Grays continue to advance.

"Holy shit," I repeat, so shocked my feet seem to be locked in concrete.

The army of Grays continues to come closer, more than I've ever seen before, all different shapes and sizes of them. They're not aimed at us, not exactly. No, they're heading directly for the base of the tower, and they're all looking up, their soulless eyes fixed on the upper floors. They may not even have noticed the three of us, but that'll likely change soon if we can't find some cover. I grab Susan's arm and drag her into the nearest bunch of trees, slowly, edging cautiously away, as if we're backing up from a surprised rattle-snake on a trail. Hunter follows us, still crawling. I'm desperate to find a place to hide, but we're trapped out here in no-man's land with only the skinny trunks of trees for cover. There's no possible way to get into the tower, and the houses are basically indefensible against an army of this magnitude. We could run, but recent experience has proven these things are faster than me. I don't know what to do.

Through the branches of the trees, I can just pick out Singer and Red on the roof. They've got their guns out and aimed down at the horde, but they've got to feel as sick and overwhelmed as I do right now. It's just the three of them up there, and I honestly don't think there's enough ammo in the world to stop a mass this huge. If these Grays make a concerted effort to attack the building, I don't see how they can stop them.

When the creatures are less than a hundred feet away, a single Gray steps out from the group. The rest of them stop their slow march, and I realize now how deathly quiet it is. I release a breath I didn't know I was holding, and I'm suddenly terrified they heard even that small sound. Behind me, Hunter whimpers in terror, and I have to say I'm pretty damned happy knowing he's just as scared as I am.

The lead Gray keeps moving away from the group and walks closer to the base of the tower. His head is tilted back and to the side, as if there's a song in the air the rest of us can't hear. It doesn't move for a few moments, its head still cocked to the side. My heartbeat is thundering so loudly I can't believe it's going unnoticed. The creature looks down, then its gaze slips over to where we're hiding. I cower behind the trees, making myself as small as possible, when its face contorts into a sort of smile, giving me a two-fingered salute.

"Come out, Scout," he says, not unkindly. His deep voice is grating and harsh, like a rumble of gears breaking free from ancient rust.

My knees almost give way, and in fact I do start to tumble over until Susan steadies me in her strong arms. It's my brother. My god, I never thought I'd see him again, not after our last encounter at the farmhouse. I was sure he would never leave that place, but it looks like I was wrong.

"Lord?" I ask, my own voice a high squeak that's out of my control.

His lips twist into that smile again, as if he's trying his best to comfort me but has no idea how to configure his face correctly. I step out of the cover of the trees, and hear Hunter moan again. Susan doesn't try to stop me, instead moving along in my wake as I clear the shadows and walk into the light. I'm aware of each step as I inch closer, the crunching sounds my shoes make on the frozen grass jarring in the silence. My progress stutters when the massed Grays behind Lord churn around behind him like an angry mob, but he holds out both arms imperiously and the movement stops. I don't know what else to do, so I keep going. Lord sees me edging closer and steps towards me slowly, as if he's intent on not spooking prey.

Now that we've narrowed the distance between us, I can tell it's him for sure. So much of him is the same as before the change, especially in how he carries himself, as full of swagger as ever. His face is thinner than I remember, but his eyes still possess that inherent twinkle of life and intelligence that's absent in other Grays. He's picked up more scars since I last saw him, too, some long ones across his chest and arms that speak of wounds that would have been fatal to a normal person. His white hair is longer now, well past his shoulders. Bits of leaves are stuck in it.

As I ease closer, the army behind him surges toward me. Lord senses this and throws out his arms again, almost as if he's throwing up a wall against their very nature. The throng behind him stutters to a halt, but the creatures remain agitated. Every instinct they have is telling them to attack me, and only Lord's force of will is holding them back. I feel Susan's steamy breath on the side of my neck. Her fluttering hands dance at her side.

"Hunter?" he asks, pointing to the ground behind me.

I nod. "Yes, that's him."

Lord twitches a finger and a pair of creatures dash toward us. They bypass me and Susan and grab Hunter by the arms. He yelps in pain and surprise as they pick him up and drag him into the open area between us. When they drop him, he stays down, his round face pale against his red hair. Lord stares down at him, and Hunter whimpers something and crawls backwards a few feet on the frosty ground.

"I trusted you," Lord growls.

Hunter's gaze shoots left and right, as if he's searching for allies or a way out. I almost feel sorry for him. Almost.

My brother steps toward him. Silently, more than a dozen Grays follow in his wake. They form a ragged circle around Hunter, their soulless eyes boring into him. I reach back and take hold of Susan's hand, terrified at what I think is about to happen, but unable to look away.

Hunter, to his credit, shakes himself and stands up tall. He turns in a full circle, slowly spinning in place and making eye contact with each of the Grays slowly closing in on him. For some reason that look of terror in his eyes is gone. If anything, he appears almost defiant, like he's daring them to come closer. His feet are spread apart, and a look of deep determination is written across his freckled face. His brow furrows in concentration.

"Something's wrong," I whisper to myself, still clutching Susan's hand. "What's he doing?"

Just when the circle of Grays is so close they could touch Hunter, they stutter to a stop, their feet shuffling on the hard ground. I've never seen confusion or hesitation in these things before, but that's exactly what's happening now. As one, they stagger backwards and look at each other, turning away from Hunter. Two of them shudder, then their eyes slide towards Lord. They shake violently again, as if torn between competing primal instincts, then the pair advance on my brother instead. Almost before he can react, they launch themselves at him.

"No!" I scream. I try to run to him, but Susan's got my hand in her vice-like grip, intent on keeping me safe. I watch in horror as the pair soundlessly take Lord down, the three of them tumbling and thrashing on the frozen ground.

"Hunter, stop it!" I yell at him, but he ignores me.

Unlike all other Grays, Lord isn't mute. He howls in surprise and pain, but manages to throw both of his attackers away from him. He leaps to his feet, breathing heavy. As ferocious as these two are, my brother is bigger and stronger than both of them. He braces himself this time, and when the first one charges at him, he heaves it twenty feet away. It lands hard, and takes a few seconds to get up. Lord quickly grabs the second creature in a headlock and twists violently. The Gray convulses once as its neck is broken. Lord throws it to the frozen turf and spins around just as the first one comes at him again. This time my brother latches on to its outstretched arm, lifts the creature over his head, and smashes it to the ground. Before the Gray can recover, he picks it up and heaves it down again. And again. He does these four more times, until what's left is little more than a mangled bag of skin filled with shards of bone. The ground around the two of them is flattened and splattered in blood, the bright red a stark contrast to the surrounding field of white. He tosses the body of the second attacker away almost in disgust, turning towards Hunter.

"No more. You're done," he growls, pointing at him.

Hunter smiles. "No, I don't think so."

Three more Grays detach from the group and throw themselves on Lord, taking him down again. I'm sobbing as I watch the three start to tear and slash at him. My legs grow weak as I stare at the rolling bodies, certain that my brother won't be able to overcome so many attackers. Then one is thrown away, followed by a second. Lord struggles to his feet, lifting the third one high in the air by the neck, his hand squeezing. The dangling Gray is weakly kicking and swinging as its life drains away. My brother is panting, his frozen breath clouding the air in front of his face.

"Well done," Hunter says, smugly. "You always were an impressive son of a bitch. That's one of the reasons I never liked you. Let's see what you do with this." He makes a sweeping motion with his arm, and ten more Grays rush at Lord.

At first, my brother manages to hold them off, but there are too many and their sheer weight is enough to buckle his knees. I can see him slashing at their grasping arms and hands, throwing some of them away, but as strong as he is, he's all alone. More creatures from the main pack join in, until there are so many I can't see my brother under their mountain of ashen flesh.

Hunter, meanwhile, is standing by himself and smiling, his arms crossed in comfortable satisfaction. He's got that look in his eyes that's always terrified me, that chilling expression of heartless joy, like a shark closing in on helpless prey. I finally manage to rip my arm away from Susan and run to him.

"Stop it!" I plead, snatching at the sleeve of his coat. "You're killing him!"

He looks down at me and smiles, those shark eyes void of any humanity. He smacks my hand away roughly.

"That's the point, isn't it, sweetheart?" he asks.

"Hunter, please! Stop it!"

He grins at me again. In a sort of sing-song voice, he says, "Too bad, so sad. I'm afraid he's already dead."

He turns away from me. I stand there, stunned to silence, my gaze locked on the blood-soaked ground where Lord was just moments ago. But I've got no chance to grieve for my brother as two creatures grab me in their scalding hands. Several others march back and go after Susan. She throws herself at them, and she's holding her own until more join in. In seconds she's overwhelmed and they pin her to the ground. She struggles ferociously, but they're too much even for her tremendous strength.

Hunter stares at the army of Grays, and like a choreographed flash mob, hundreds of them rush the tower and start climbing up the sides, scaling all four walls simultaneously, as unstoppable as lava streaming down a volcano. There's no way Singer, Red, and Stretch will be able to stop them. Everyone will die. Singer, Carly, even the Abuela.

The Abuela…

Wait. What did she say to me upstairs? If you ever need help, call on me. Was that it? I didn't understand what she was talking about then, but I think I do now. I close my eyes and reach out to her, calling her name, pleading. I throw open all the doors of my mind, and scream into the void surrounding me. I wait, nearly doubled over in desperation as frozen tears leak out from the corners of my eyes. I reach out for her, begging her to help me.

"Querida. Scout…" comes her voice in my mind, and I feel her now, just outside the open doors of my consciousness. I latch onto the Abuela's words and draw her closer, reeling her in. I sense her warmth, her very being, and I grab hold and embrace it.

"Abuela, you've got to help me. They're coming for you! For all of you!"

I sense a heartfelt sigh. Just like the one in her room during our first meeting, it's filled with sadness and regret. "I've told you before," she says. "I don't know how to control it. I can't turn it off."

"No, no, I don't want you to turn it off. Remember

when we were in the furnace room and we yelled for help? Remember? Together our voices were so loud and strong it was like we were shouting across the entire universe. They were so powerful we even called Susan onto the ice from miles away. Remember?"

There's a pause. "Yes," she replies in my mind, her voice ghostly and thin. "I remember."

"We need to do that again. It's the only way!"

"But I'm so weak, querida. So tired. I don't know if I can…"

I break out of my head long enough to witness the swarm of Grays as they reach the fourth-floor windows. Singer and the rest have started shooting, taking out as many as they can, but they'll never be able to stop them. There are too many, and they'll be overrun in seconds. As I watch, several make it to the fifth floor and smash a window, heedless of the shards of glass shredding their skin as they start to crawl in.

"You have to! We have to!" I shout at her, my inner voice shrill with panic. "It's almost too late!"

Nothing happens for a moment, and a horrible sensation of loss inundates me, coupled by crushing disappointment that Hunter's going to win after all. Then I feel her invisible hand brush against mine, followed by a sudden surge of power within me as our two minds combine into one, just like they did in the furnace room. With all the rage and force I can muster, I concentrate, my eyes screwed shut, and I throw my hands out in front of me. In my head I form a single word and blast it out to the world with everything I can put behind it.

"STOP!"

The effect on the army of Grays is instantaneous. Like an invisible bomb just detonated in the middle of them, every single creature convulses and lifts its white-haired head in shock. The ones nearest to me jerk so hard they nearly topple over. On the tower, the climbers all let go and tumble to the ground, where they scramble to their feet and scurry around in confusion. Hunter's smug grin is ripped away, replaced by a twisted look of confusion and anger. He spins around, his eyes boiling with fury.

"Who did that?" he screams, fists clenched into tight balls at his sides.

I smile and stand as tall as someone my size can. "I did," I tell him.

I'm not sure Hunter believes me, at least not at first. He takes a step in my direction, but I don't back away. I can feel Susan over my shoulder once more, free now and ready to defend me if I ask her to. I place a hand on her arm to hold her back, giving it an affectionate squeeze. Meanwhile, a hundred emotions contort Hunter's face as he decides whether he should charge at me or not. I find I'm enjoying all this more than I should, but that's okay.

"No. I don't believe you!" he yells, stomping his feet to punctuate each word. His complexion runs through the full spectrum of reds as he tries to process what's going on. "You can't! You're just a girl!"

"Yeah, I am. And I'm the girl who's going to kick your ass."

I concentrate again, pointing at Hunter with both hands, and blast out another mental command. Immediately the massed Grays all spin and focus their dull eyes on him. Slowly, they advance, every single one of them, a thousand creatures with only one outcome piercing the fog of their minds.

Hunter closes his eyes and tries to counter my order. I can sense the impressive level of control he's mastered over these things, but, as strong as he is, his power pales compared to what I have at my command. The Grays don't slow down, and quickly encircle him once more. But this time, instead of just a handful, it's the entire army.

It's at that very second Hunter realizes he's outmatched. I'm so short it's hard for me to catch sight of him with so many Grays between the two of us, but I can sense his utter panic. In the past, I've felt pity for him, but no longer. Not now. Not only did he just order the death of my brother, but he's threatened the people I love. Again. I'm done with him.

"Scout! Stop them! Please!" he yells, his tortured voice rising to a wail.

I catch a final glimpse of his face between the churning ashen bodies. His eyes are huge and pleading, his hands extended in front of him to ward off his impending destiny. The only emotion I feel now is one of relief that I'll never have to deal with him again. I give him a two-fingered salute.

"Goodbye, Hunter."

I send out a final command. At the same moment I reach out my open hand and clench it into a tight fist. As a single unit, the army of Grays lunge at him. I hear a mangled scream that cuts off suddenly, and then there's nothing but the wet sounds of the creatures taking him apart.

It's over nearly as quickly as it began. The Grays are still slashing and tearing, but there's nothing left for them to attack. Hunter is gone. I take a deep breath, throw out my arms, and issue the most powerful command yet.

"GO!"

If my earlier order telling them to stop shocked them like an exploding bomb, the result of this one is even more extreme. The entire army leaps up and scatters, sprinting away from me like a shock wave following an atomic blast. There's no rhyme or reason to their retreat, no organization, just an overwhelming need to obey. Several of them are so focused on escaping they dash blindly into the sides of the tower itself, bouncing off the solid brick before recovering and sprinting away again. In minutes, the only living Gray left in the compound is Susan. Her hands twitch once more, then lay still. She's staring down at me, her head canted to one side.

Nearly shaking in relief, I take a few unsteady steps to where I last saw Hunter alive. On the frozen ground in front of me is an irregular stain of deep red that almost glitters in the freezing air. Scraps of flesh and body parts litter the area. A shock of his red hair has been trampled under a thousand feet. What's left of his jacket could be mistaken for a shredded trash bag.

Haltingly, I move toward where my brother was attacked. The ground here is soaked with blood, too. I intentionally don't linger there for more than a second or two, afraid I might see something that I can never unsee. I don't need any other visual proof to know he's gone forever. I'm sure of it. My eyes fill with tears again and my throat clenches. My head dips down so far my chin is touching my chest.

I hear a whooping yell from up high, and I see Singer and the guys hopping up and down and celebrating. They have no idea what really happened down here. All they know is one second they were about to be overrun by those things, and the next their attackers were in full retreat. Annie is hanging out the window where I left her, the gun resting on the ledge. She's smiling at me.

As I'm standing there, in a daze and unsure what to do next, Susan comes up and lays her hand on my shoulder. Shy of saving my life over and over, it's the most human thing she's ever done. I reach up and take her hand in mine.

"Thank you," I tell her fondly. "We couldn't have done this without you."

She hesitates, then does the totally unexpected and gives me a hug. The gesture is awkward, like her arms are made entirely of sticks and right angles, but it still counts. Then I realize I have to retract my previous thought, since this embrace now qualifies as the most human thing she's ever done. It makes me wonder what's really happening to her. She's changing, bit by bit, right in front of me, that much is for sure. I wonder if it's possible for a Gray to ever revert back to normal? I don't know, but I can't wait to find out. Just as she breaks her embrace, I hear my name being called. It's Google, his head framed by the broken window on the tenth floor.

"What?" I yell up at him.

"You'd better get up here!" he replies. "It's the Abuela."

I'm not sure what he means, but it can't be good. I don't know how else to get up there, so I sprint to the lobby and into the open elevator doors, hoping to find a way up. The walls inside the small car are dented and buckled, as if a pair of pissed-off rhinos did battle in there. The ceiling overhead has been shredded, the metal edges jagged and shiny where they were ripped apart. Beyond that the piles of filing cabinets and the rest of the crap we threw down the shaft has completely blocked the way. I won't be getting upstairs through that.

Dashing back outside, I almost run into Susan standing there at the base of the tower. As I watch in desperation, she jumps up and grabs the lower sill on the second-floor window above her. She hangs there briefly, then drops back down. She reaches behind her and pats her own back.

"Wait," I say, blinking rapidly as I figure out what she means. "You want me to hold on to you while you climb up?"

Her only reply is another pat on her back. My fear of heights gives me a full-body shiver as I consider it, but I don't know any other way up.

"Okay, let's do this."

I leap onto her back and wrap my arms around her neck. She leaps up, latching on to the window-sill above her head again. She's so strong my added weight doesn't slow her down in the slightest. She pulls us up and gets her feet under her, only to spring up to the next window. She does this again and again until we reach the fifth floor, although I can't tell how high we are because my eyes are clamped shut. I only crack them open when she forces the window aside and we crawl into the room. I drop off her back and catch my breath, then sprint out of the room and up the stairs to the tenth floor.

I burst into the hallway and see everyone gathered at the far end, by the window where I left them. Google, Carly, Tiny, and Juanita are huddled around the Abuela, and their heads lift as one when they hear me enter. Their eyes are downcast and red from crying. I rush to them, panting.

"What is it?" I ask. "What's happened?"

Everyone but Juanita steps back, and I gasp when I see the Abuela. She's slumped in her wheelchair, her eyes closed. Her naturally dark complexion is pale.

"She's gone," Juanita whispers, wiping a tear away.

I kneel down next to her. My hands are shaking. "But…how? She was fine when I left."

"I don't know," the nurse says, sniffing. "We were watching the fight, and she was okay. Well, we were all terrified, but she was talking. Mainly about you. Then she closed her eyes, and before we knew it, she was gone."

I take hold of the Abuela's jeweled hand. Her delicate skin is cooling already, her fingers loose in mine. I choke back a sob of my own, because I know what happened. She died because she helped me. She must have known the stress would be too much for her, but she did it anyway. She sacrificed herself for all of us.

The door to the roof stairway opens and Singer and the guys hurry into the hallway. He and I make eye contact, and he sees me holding her hand. I shake my head at him. Red figures out what's going on right away, and his eyes shimmer with emotion.

"We're going to need three graves," I tell them.

The next few weeks are crazy busy.

The weather changes just like that, warming into

the mid-70s overnight, and the icy ground thaws quickly as it bakes in the hot sun. It turns out that Red has a tractor that somehow still works, and over the next few days he uses it to dig a mass grave far away from the compound for all the Grays that were killed. Red, Stretch, and Shorty also dig three graves in the grassy area not far from the sound machines where they first found us. That's where we bury the remains of Harold, Lord, and the Abuela. Honoring Hunter with a grave or a service of any kind never even entered my mind. He may have been one of us in the beginning, but that son of a bitch caused all of us unimaginable pain and anguish. The sooner we forget about him, the better.

The simple service for the three is nice, but short, mainly us and some of the residents standing there deep within ourselves. I've already said goodbye to my brother twice before, but that doesn't make it any easier this final time. When we've all said our farewells, the three older men fill the graves while everyone but me trudges away. I stay a while longer. Each person here had a profound impact on my life in one way or another. In the old days, I would have sunk into a deep pit of depression, but I must be getting better at processing losses like this. I'm terribly sad, but not to the point where it cripples me. I'm not sure if that's progress or not.

We work for weeks to bring the Hill back to life, like removing all the plywood from the tower windows, restoring the lobby as well as we can, stuff like that. Google, Carly, and Tiny have really discovered how much they like the TV in the house, and it's all we can do to pry them away from the glowing screen for meals, showers, or just to come up for air. So, basically, they're behaving like kids their age have acted since TV was invented. Tiny, meanwhile, is too young to understand how special he is, but the rest of us grasp his importance. From here on out, everyone on the Hill will make sure he stays safe and sound.

Even with our resident handyman pulling out all the stops, the elevator is a total loss. Singer and I haul everything out of the blocked stairwell so we have access to all the floors once more. Juanita moves her remaining patients and equipment to the lower levels. She hasn't gotten over the death of the Abuela yet. She loved the old lady, even though their relationship was complicated.

A month after the attack, one night after we've both showered and I've spent an inordinate amount of time tending to my teeth with my favorite toothbrush, Singer and I are lying in bed after the others have already called it a night. I run my tongue over my slick teeth and marvel at the minty taste that I will never take for granted. The covers are pulled up tight under our chins. The lamp next to the bed is on and throws a warm glow on the ceiling. I can't believe how quickly we've gotten used to things like electric lights. He stirs next to me.

"I'm bushed," he says, snuggling into the pillows.

I scoot over and rest my head on his shoulder. His long black hair is still damp, and smells of baby shampoo. His skin is warm. We're both tired, but it's a good tired. We've done all we can here, and the Hill is almost back to its pristine condition. Vegetables are growing in the greenhouses, the solar panels are silently doing their jobs and powering the compound, the sound machines are up and running, and everyone seems pretty happy, which is amazing considering what we've been through. I have never worried less about the safety and welfare of our group than I do right now.

"Me, too," I mumble into the crook of his neck.

Neither of us feel the need to say anything else. I'm about to drift off when he moves around next to me. I hear some pages flipping, and crack an eye at him, then prop myself up on an elbow.

"What are you doing?" I ask, mildly irritated and intrigued at the same time.

He holds up the moldy copy of *Hamlet* I found so long ago, the one he read to me in the office building right before Lord went Gray. That was the first time we were alone together, and when I began to fall for him. It seems like a lifetime ago. I reach out a finger and touch the crusty cover.

"Want me to read it to you, just like the good old days?" he asks playfully.

"I'm not sure how good they really were, but yes,

I would love that."

I scooch closer to him. He opens the heavy book to a random page, and starts reading. He even does it in a faint British accent, which I find undeniably sexy for some reason. I'm barely paying attention to the story, more intrigued by the odd references and even stranger language of that long-ago time. I wonder if people reading our literature in five hundred years will find our language just as hard to decipher? I imagine they will, and for the first time in a long while, I feel positive the human race will actually be here five centuries from now. I'm smiling as I drift off.

A few weeks later, Singer and I are having breakfast at the little table in our house. The TV is off and the kids are outside playing for once. The silence between the two of us is comfortable, with neither of us worried about filling the void with conversation. I'm eating some toast with butter on it, an old favorite of mine. Singer is munching peaches out of a can. When he's finished, he rinses out the can and puts it aside. We'll use it for something later on, like planting bean sprouts or something. We recycle and reuse everything now. We've learned how irresponsible and wasteful we used to be as a species, and know we have to do better.

"Penny for your thoughts," he says, wiping his hands off.

"'Penny for your thoughts?'" I ask him, sure I've heard that expression somewhere before. "Where'd you get that? That's such an old man thing to say."

He shrugs, grinning back at me. "Nelson said it. He was teaching me some card game called Cribbage. It was fun, even though he kicked my ass about a dozen times."

"Well, my thoughts are worth much more than a penny," I tell him. "It's going to cost you at least a dollar."

"Okay, a dollar for your thoughts, then."

I dust the crumbs off my hands and the corners of my mouth. I'm not sure if he knows me so well that he's figured this out already, or if he's just making casual conversation. Truth be told, I have been thinking about something lately. For a few weeks now. I just haven't worked up the nerve to talk to him about it. I drum my fingers on the table.

"Do you remember what the Abuela said about Tiny?" I finally ask him. "She said there were others like the two of them, with the power to stop people from changing. She could tell they were out there, but she couldn't find them. She said they were like distant stars in the night sky, or something like that. Remember?"

He nods at me, interested. "Yeah, I do. And?"

I tilt my head, motioning outside where we hear the kids laughing. "I don't ever want to take the kids from here. This is their home now, and will be forever. They'll grow old here, and Tiny will keep everyone from changing as long as he's alive."

"That's exactly what we wanted, right? The Hill has a chance to be mankind's new home. I'm not sure what you're getting at."

"Singer, there are so many other people in the world that need saving. Younger ones like Google and Carly who are living day to day out there, barely getting by. They don't stand a chance. They'll hit 240 months old and they'll change, then they'll go Gray and die. I can't stop thinking about them. I have to do something to help them."

He crosses his arms and stares at me. I can see his mind working behind his brown eyes. He looks down and to the side, thinking. "Okay, I get that," he says slowly. "What do you want to do about it?'

I reach out and extend my hand. He uncrosses his arms and takes mine in his.

"That last command I gave to Lord's army, when I ordered them to leave, will stick with those Grays forever. They'll never come back to this place again. They can't. There may be some new ones that could, but they'll be no big deal. Small groups of two or three, like normal, and the sound machines will keep them away. I'm not worried about the Hill or anybody living here."

He grips my hand harder and peers directly into my eyes. "Scout, are you thinking what I think you're thinking?"

I stare back at him, our eyes locked. "If it's that I want to save as many of those innocent people as

I can, then yes. Singer, I want to save more people. I want to find those distant stars and share them with the world."

He sighs and strokes his chin thoughtfully, but doesn't say no. "You're crazy, you know that? Just when we finally get a chance to settle down, you want to head back out there?"

"Precisely."

He grins at me. "Yeah, I thought so. I've always said I'm with you to the end, even if that means leaving this place. You got any ideas?"

I stand up and give him a big hug. "Yep. I know just where to start."

CHAPTER

THIRTY-TWO

Saying goodbye is never easy, especially when Carly's involved. She doesn't like change of any kind, and me and Singer leaving is almost more that she can handle. I lavish her with hugs and kisses, and promise over and over that we'll be back. She's dubious at best, but lightens up when I promise I'll keep my eyes peeled for art supplies to augment her dwindling stock.

When I approach Tiny and Google, Tiny touches his fist to his chest in what I assume is his way of saying goodbye. When I mirror the gesture back to him, his smile is huge and warm. Google, for what has to be the first time ever, is at a complete loss for words. His eyes shimmer behind those thick glasses, and in the end he gives me the gift of a rare embrace before turning away. Annie tries her hardest to keep it together, but then we both break down, blubbering and sobbing harder than kids heading home after summer camp. Of all the people in our group, she and I have been together the longest. That has to mean something. Tiny is getting older and doesn't like being picked up these days, but he relents and lets Annie do it this time out of a sense of sympathy.

Susan is standing off to the side, quiet as usual. She's got her black and white poncho on again, which is a good look for her, humanizing her to a certain degree. I walk up and put my hands on her broad shoulders, gazing up into her eyes. I'm searching for some sort of twinkle indicating budding intelligence. Is there a spark there? Maybe. I hope so.

"Protect them," I tell her. I don't have to reinforce that order with a mental command. I know she will. I give her a brief hug.

Singer already has the boat packed and ready to go. We're all gathered outside our house, and everyone waves as the two of us cross the grassy field toward the sound machines. When we get there, Red is waiting for us.

"You take care of yourself, Romeo," he says, his normally stoic voice cracking ever so slightly. "It's a crazy world out there."

Singer shakes the older man's hand. The two of them have grown close since we got here, and I know my boyfriend is going to miss the reserved handyman. Red looks over at me with an arched eyebrow.

"Where you going first? Maybe back to that Church Island place you keep talking about?"

I give him a hug. "We will soon, trust me, but there's something else I've got to take care of first."

Red nods, then lifts his walkie talkie and orders Shorty to power down section SW6. He motions us on through, and we pass by the sound machine and down towards the waterline. Behind us we hear him telling Shorty that we're clear.

We kick through the thigh-deep trash to the boat. I hop in as Singer pushes us out into the nasty stuff, then he jumps gracefully in. We paddle through the disgusting debris and junk, and out into open water. I place my compass on the bench in front of me, checking our heading. Our combined strokes are easy and strong, and the two of us can row all day if we have to. We're not exactly in a hurry, but we don't want to waste time, either. There are people out there who need us, and the longer we take, the more of them will change and die.

We continue like that for several days, sleeping in the boat at night. It turns out, when you have a chance to prepare properly and you aren't sharing an over-loaded boat with a zillion people, spending the night on the open water isn't all that bad. The beauty of the night skies and Singer's harmonica playing help, too. "Sophisticated Lady" never sounded so haunting and melancholy.

At one point Singer reaches into his backpack and withdraws a thin paperback. The cover is battered and dog-eared, and the pages are yellowed with age.

"Remember this?" he asks, holding it up.

It takes me a second, but then I do, and my eyes

light up. It's the book I grabbed from the lending library at Church Island before the attack. I smile at him. "Yeah, I do. I forgot all about it."

He flips it over, reading the cover. "*Jonathan Livingston Seagull* by some guy named Richard Bach. Want me to read it to you? We've certainly got time."

It's a short book. We take turns reading it out loud while the other is rowing, and we finish it in a single afternoon. When I gently close the cover, we both sit there in silence.

"That was…interesting," he finally says.

It was. The story itself is simple, but the meaning behind the words is profound. I didn't know what to expect, but its message means more to me than I ever thought possible: we can all be so much more than we think we can, and our destiny is in our own hands. I take the thin paperback from him and tenderly tuck it away in my own backpack. I'll read it again later, to myself next time. I'm so glad I chose that one, or that it chose me. I wonder which one is true.

A few days later, I spot our destination in the distance and we adjust our course to intercept it. When the aluminum hull of the boat scrapes on the gritty asphalt, we hop out and pull it to higher ground. Just as the two of us are walking up the gentle slope of the parking lot, a pack of three Grays concealed behind a rusted-out car jumps up and starts charging in our direction.

"You see those things, right?" Singer asks, reaching for his knife, and wondering why I'm not doing the same.

'I do," I answer him.

His head swivels from me to the advancing Grays, and back to me again. "Don't you think we should, you know, do something?"

I gently push down his hand, the one holding the knife. "It's okay. I got this."

As he watches, I lift my arms and make a sweeping motion. In my mind I mentally issue a command.

"Go!"

The trio of Grays screech to a halt, their arms pinwheeling for balance, then turn and sprint away as if the parking lot is opening up behind them. We watch their backs until they disappear in the distance. Singer turns to me, his eyes round in surprise, until he figures out what just happened. He slowly holsters his blade.

"I didn't know you could still do that," he says, peering at me with amused, half-lidded eyes. "I guess you've still got that mental 'thunderpunch' thing, huh?"

I smile at him, laughing. "'Thunderpunch?' I kinda' like that. To be honest, I wasn't sure I could do it either."

"Sort of a trial by fire, don't you think? I figured you'd lose it when the Abuela died."

"Yeah, I thought I might, too, but I wasn't sure. I don't know if she somehow passed it along to me as she died, or helped unlock something I had inside of me all along."

He stares where the Grays ran off, pursing his lips. "I gotta say, this should make our upcoming adventures out here in the world a little easier, don't you think?"

"I do indeed."

We start walking again, until we reach two massive steel doors built into the face of a cliff. They're over twenty feet tall, studded with rivets the size of quarters. They look strong enough to contain a small nuclear blast, which is exactly what they were designed to do. I lift my fist and knock as hard as I can. The doors reverberate with a deep booming rumble, almost as if the very mountain itself is resonating.

I stare straight ahead at the fading green paint, and wait. A minute or two later, there's a distant humming as the twin doors begin to creak open. We hear footsteps approaching from inside, and in no time Ted's surprised face appears in front of us. He looks the same as ever, like a balding, aging hippie. Today he's sporting a long ponytail. His color is better than the first time I met him, probably the result of an improved diet. His face lights up.

"Scout! I'm so glad to see you. Good lord, what are you doing here?"

I reach out and lay a hand on his arm, squeezing it gently. As I grin up at him, peering into his red-rimmed eyes, I'm more certain than ever he's one of those distant stars the Abuela once saw.

"I've got a question for you," I tell him. "Are you still bored to death here?"

He nods immediately, almost as if he were somehow expecting the question. He puts a shaking hand to his forehead. "Damn, you have no idea. I'm about to lose my mind. I don't know how much longer I can take it."

"I thought that might be the case," I say, smiling warmly and taking his free hand in mine. "Tell me, Ted, how'd you like to help us save the world?"